# MURDER:
## Season by Season

Four seasonal stories about murder

*by*

Cathy Ace

Copyright 2008 by Cathy Ace

Murder: Season by Season
First edition. First published 2008
ISBN: 978-0-557-01972-4

All rights reserved. No part of this publication may be reproduced, stored in a retrieval system or transmitted, by any means, electronic, mechanical, photocopying, recording or otherwise, without the prior permission of the copyright owner.

This book is a work of fiction. All the names, characters and incidents portrayed in it are fictitious, and any resemblance to actual persons, living or dead, events or localities is purely coincidental.

# MURDER: Season by Season

## Contents

Foreword 5

WINTER: The Corpse with Eight Faces 7

SPRING: The Hon. Miss Wilson-Smythe
Hunts for Cousin Harry 81

SUMMER: Out and About in a Boat 129

AUTUMN: The Fall 177

# Foreword

My thanks go to Shirley, John, Sue and Geoffrey for all their love and support; without them, none of this would have been possible!

By the way – as you're reading, please remember that I made this all up! Some places might be real, but I've messed about with them to make them fit with my plans and schemes......none of the people are real, either!

*Cathy Ace*
*October 2008*
cathyace.com

# WINTER

## The Corpse With Eight Faces

### A
#### Cait Morgan Mystery

# I

If I'd known I was about to spend a weekend cooped up in a snowbound hunting lodge twenty kilometres from civilization in the middle of British Columbia with a killer on the loose, I dare say I wouldn't have got onto the minibus. But I didn't. So I did. And there I met the people who were about to share the dubious pleasures of the aforementioned weekend with me.

With hindsight, I suppose I should have seen it coming: I was off to a birthday party for someone I hadn't seen since we'd left school thirty years earlier, and she'd also invited her three – yes *three* – ex-husbands, her just-fired literary agent and her estranged mother. Add her current fiancé, who's temper, it all turned out, had a fuse about two millimetres long, and you get the picture. It was likely to be a very fraught weekend! Just for good measure you can throw in the discovery we all made later that day that she'd been working on her autobiography, *and* her accusations that everyone she'd invited, apparently, had a dark secret somewhere in their past......and I'm guessing you're *way* ahead of me. And that's not fair. So hold your horses, and I'll catch up with you as quick as I can.

Let's get back to the minibus. I'd just got off a flight from Vancouver to Kelowna: it only takes about an hour or so, so you're longer at the airport than in the air, which is pretty annoying. But, anyway, it was better than having to fly all the way to the UK for the party – which was where it was originally supposed to be: back in the Land of My Fathers.....not that I ever had more than one Dad, it's just that that's what we Welsh people call Wales....back in the land of my hostess's Fathers, too, if you catch my drift. You see, Meg Jones and I went to school together in Wales, where we grew up two streets apart and both allegedly poor, but certainly happy. Whilst there's no denying that my position as an Assistant Professor of Criminology at the University of Vancouver means I've certainly fulfilled my parents' hopes and dreams for *me*, it is equally unquestionable that Meg has far surpassed any expectations that *any* of us from Manselton, Swansea, might have had for *her*: she's one of the world's wealthiest authors, with a string of bestsellers to her name and a few movies too. You know her, I'm sure – yes, *that* Meg Jones, romantic novelist par excellence. Anyway – the minibus.

Initially the Big Birthday Bash was going to be at the house she'd bought in Wales, but the renovations weren't finished in time, so, instead, she had 'borrowed' a big old hunting lodge outside Kelowna, BC, close to where she'd just bought herself a vineyard. Yes, I *know* – most of us are happy with buying wine one bottle at a time, or maybe by the case at a push, but Meg never was one to stint – as evidenced by the *three* ex-husbands – so I guess she thought that buying a whole vineyard was the way to go! Given that there aren't that many choices of route to get to Kelowna in December, the Coquihalla

Highway being a slippery mess for most of that month, all her guests were meeting up at Kelowna International Airport, so that we could travel on to 'McKewan's Lodge' together. I'd never thought of Meg as a control freak when we were young, in fact I *know* that *that* role had been reserved for me, and I'd done my best to grow into it and make it my own with the passing years. But I suspected she'd have *'people'* now, who made things run smoothly for her. I knew I'd have *'people'* if I was as rich as she'd become!

I was the last one getting onto the minibus: living by my mother's dictum that you should always go before you left, I'd been going....and they'd nearly left without me. Which, on reflection, might not have been a bad thing – but I do agree that hindsight is always 20/20!

As I stood at the top of the steps, trying to spot a place to sit, I ran my psychologist's eyes over my fellow guests: Meg had told me who would be there in one of her e-mails, which had popped up in my 'inbox' from time to time over the last year or so, since we'd got back in touch after pretty much thirty years of not having so much as spoken to each other on the phone. To cut a long story short, I'd spotted Meg promoting her first movie on one of those late-night chat shows: having overcome my initial disbelief that it was, in fact, the girl who'd been my Best Friend at school, I e-mailed her via her website, and, eventually, she phoned me. That first phone call was very odd: she was in her mid-town condo overlooking the Manhattan skyline, I was in my little old house on Burnaby Mountain in Vancouver, but we could have been back at Llwyn-y-Bryn School, ducking out of gym class and sneaking a smoke behind the bike-sheds. It was *great* to hear her voice, to hear her news and to know she hadn't changed at all, really. She was the same old Meg, and I was the same old Cait – Best Friends Forever.....and we'd been that when that phrase actually *meant* something! But, of course, as Best Friends do, we'd drifted apart as the years passed: inseparable between the ages of five and fifteen, hormones and boys got the better of us, and by sixteen we had both developed other friendships and liaisons, and, by the time we left school at eighteen.....well, we were certainly going in different directions. Like I said – long story, short.

I grunted general 'Hello's' as I pushed along the minibus's little aisle, that was barely wide enough to cope with my ample proportions *and* my winter coat. I thought it would be fun to sit at the back and try to work out who everyone was as we drove to our final destination. Some people said 'Hi' to me as I passed, but a few were looking out of the windows at the surrounding mountains, which were, ominously, missing their summits: it was 3pm and the sky, whilst still holding some promise of maybe another hour of daylight, was thickening with blue-black clouds. On reflection I should have seen them as metaphorical, but at the time I only saw them for what they were – storm clouds gathering, ready to dump a whole bunch of snow on us.

Sitting at the back of the bus (Meg laughed at that later when I told her, because she and I always used to try to get the back seat of any bus that took us on a school outing – as far away from *any* teachers as possible!) I could see the tops of heads, and that was about it. From the sketchy explanations Meg had sent me I was pretty certain that the bald, liver-spotted head belonged to Joe Goldblum, Meg's New York-based ex-literary agent, and I assumed that his wife, Martha, was sitting next to him. He was apparently well into his seventies, and looked to be one of those guys who'll retire when he dies....maybe. His features reminded me of a garden gnome, but without the whiskers or the bonhomie – and there was no red, pointy hat, of course! He wasn't the warm, fuzzy type, to be sure. At least, that's what Meg had said in an e-mail to me when she told me she'd fired him – about a month earlier. I wondered why on earth she'd invited *him*! His wife was swathed in furs and, almost literally, dripping with diamonds. Her small, chubby hands sparkled as she fiddled about her head, trying to ensure that the seat didn't mess up the back of her hair-do: I was amazed she looked so fresh, but found out later that they'd flown in the day before and had spent the night at a local hotel before getting onto the bus.

Across the aisle was a woman, probably in her late sixties, sitting alone: I was surprised that I didn't recognise her, because I was pretty sure it was Meg's Mum, Jean Jones. Of course I'd known her when I was growing up, but I couldn't place the woman at all: I remembered Meg's Mum as short and round with a red face and thick, dark hair. This woman might well have been short, it was difficult to tell given that she was seated, but she was as thin as a rail and had snow-white hair cut in a 'pixie' style. I'd noticed as I'd passed that her face was pinched into a look of disapproval, and that she had a sallow complexion to boot. Sour-faced would just about sum it up. And that wasn't how I remembered Meg's Mum at all. Odd for me, given that I've got this famous 'photographic memory' thing!

Directly in front of me was a man I had no trouble recognising: Luis Lopez, Meg's fiancé, and the world's most famous Latino TV cop – thanks to a weekly show where every conceivable type of crime committed in LA was solved by Luis, pretty much single-handedly, and with a 'suspend your disbelief' reason for him to have to remove his shirt in every episode. Like the rest of the Western world I was glued to the screen every week, as Luis strutted his unquestionably well-worked-out, thirty-something-year-old stuff for all to see. Now here I was, little Caitlin Morgan, sitting within a foot of the man that most women in North America would like to kidnap and make their love-slave. Truth be told, knowing he would be there had meant I'd made up my mind to *definitely* come: of *course* I wanted to see Meg again – but to see Luis Lopez, in the flesh.....well, a girl would fly a lot further than an hour from home to do that. As I sat there considering my fellow travellers I could smell his aftershave wafting back towards me: like him it was dark and exotic. Meg certainly didn't do *anything* by halves! And a toy-boy at that – at least ten years her....OK *our*....junior! You *go* girl!

Alongside Luis was a tall, round, ruddy man with a thatch of unruly, iron-grey hair, a checked suit and a bow tie. Given that I work at a University, it didn't take much of a stretch to cast this man as Dan James, Professor of English at Harvard, and the man Meg had walked out on before she'd set off on her epic journey across the USA. He was the one who'd told her she'd never hold down a job for more than a week because she was too dumb. Oh boy, must he be eating his words right about now!?

In case you haven't been keeping up with your supermarket magazines, that was how Meg came to write her first bestseller – the day after her fortieth birthday, she walked out on husband number three, Dan, took herself off across the USA on a series of buses, and wrote, as she travelled, about a woman hitting forty and finding true love for the first time. Upon her eventual return to New York, she'd *literally* bumped into Martha Goldblum in the hat department at Macy's, they'd struck up a conversation, Martha had then introduced Meg to her agent husband, who'd read Meg's manuscript and the rest, as they always say, was history. Except, of course, that in this case is was *her*story, with Meg's first book being on *all* the reading lists of *all* the TV chat-show hosts that matter – you know who I mean, you don't live under a rock – and it then became a mega-grossing movie. I suspected that Meg didn't need to put pen to paper ever again, she'd probably made so much money from that one book, but, Meg being Meg, she *did* keep putting pen to paper, and each book became yet another 'fastest-selling-ever' volume. Her book launches were Harry Potter-like, but for grown women: of course, they didn't dress up like wizards, but they sure lined up around the block to be the first one to get their hands on the *new* Meg Jones. A signed copy of a first edition could become serious collateral in certain circles!

So, if the fat, ruddy guy dressed like a professor *was* the professor, then the younger guy with what appeared to be a wife must be Peter Webber, Meg's first husband, with his now-wife, Sally. Once again, I felt a bit wrong-footed, because I thought I would have met Peter when we were all growing up in Manselton together: he'd lived in the street behind Meg's. But he looked so....well, *old*, I suppose....I couldn't imagine that he was only my age. I mean, forty eight isn't *old*, is it? Not these days....fifty *is* the new forty, after all! And the sandy haired guy with the sandy haired wife-person next to him looked a *lot* older than me. Or, at least, a lot older than the person I see in the mirror in the morning without my reading specs. Meg had told me that the only reason she'd married Peter was so they'd have enough 'points' to be able to emigrate to Canada in the 1970's: I know that about two weeks after we'd finished our A-level exams in the June of '78, she'd gone and got herself married, and had been out of the country before I'd even left for University in the October. It had floored us all – all those of us who knew the girl for whom hedonism was an art-form, and the idea of being married was something she'd laughed at, almost as hard as she'd laughed at the idea of having children.

But, at eighteen, she was married and gone.....and I'd left Swansea for University at Cardiff, where I met new people to whom I'd reminisce over a few pints about the "Deadly Duo", which was how Megan Jones and Caitlin Morgan – Meg and I - had been referred to since we'd hooked up on our first day at school. I was always sure that Meg would make her own inimitable way in the world...and I'd been right.

So, straight out of school, she'd married Peter, moved to Vancouver where he'd worked as a lighting technician in the booming movie industry...... which Meg and I had agreed in e-mails was ironic, given that that was where I was living now. Then she'd then moved to New York with him, following the movie shoots of the day, divorced him – I had no idea why - and had taken up with, and then married, someone called Adrian. He wasn't mentioned on her website as anything more than a name.....'Adrian, a musician'.....and I guessed he was the wrinkly guy sitting at the front of the bus. Meg had never mentioned him in any of her e-mails to me, so I knew nothing about him. There was something vaguely familiar about him though, but couldn't put my finger on it. Despite the darkening skies, he'd been wearing sunglasses when I got onto the bus, and had a deerstalker pulled down on his head: it takes some nerve to wear one of those things, so I suspected that he was no shrinking violet. We psychologists are good at spotting that sort of thing, you know. But where on *earth* had I seen him before? He was thin, almost to the point of emaciation, haggard, grey-haired and with long, tapering fingers.....I'd noticed them right away. Who *was* 'Adrian', the musician? A famous conductor? Had I seen him raise his baton when I'd been living in London working at an advertising agency in the 1980's, and going to classical concerts at the South Bank as often as my ridiculous working hours allowed? Or maybe he'd been a piano player in one of the many, *many* pubs and bars I'd frequented when I'd being doing my Masters in Criminology at Cambridge during the 1990's? A photographic memory is all well and good – except when it lets you down!

Anyway, then Meg had gone on to divorce this 'Adrian' person after a few years, and married Dan James, who eventually took up a Professorship at Harvard. He'd been offered the post thanks to the phenomenal success of some poems he'd written – which I have read, by way of research, and they are.....well, I suspect that 'puzzling' would be the kindest word, because he seems to like to use a lot of Greek quotations...not allusions, which I could probably cope with, but actual *Greek*: all *very* Ezra Pound. And, as I said before, Meg had left *him* to take to the road, after which she met the Goldblums, acquired great fame and wealth for herself, and she'd just recently announced her engagement to the ravishing Luis Lopez, who'd played the lead in the movie they'd made of her first book. Quite a life for a girl from the brick terraces of Manselton!

But my little distraction from the icy journey away from the city of Kelowna, beyond the subdivisions and into the rolling countryside, was over – everyone was identified, nine of us in all, including myself, and there was no more to be done, except continue to puzzle about the strangely familiar 'Adrian', which was just fine, because that's when we pulled off the road and onto a long, winding driveway.......just as the snow started to fall in big, fat flakes.

# II

Our arrival was pretty chaotic: the huge, log-built 1930's Lodge, named 'McKewan's' for the man who'd built it, rather than for the family which now owned it, had a large covered porch area - which was useful, because it took forever to get all our bags off the little bus. I only had a small wheely-bag, but it looked as though Martha Goldblum had packed for a month! *Finally* over the threshold, and out of the swirling snowflakes, Luis offered to carry our bags to our rooms, and we all looked about for Meg, our hostess, who was nowhere to be seen. I thought at the time that she could have made a bit more of an effort to be there as we arrived, but it turned out she'd been tied up in the kitchen with the caterers, who were just finishing their preparations and keen to get away before the snow really settled in. Just as well, really, or there'd have been four more suspects for me to interview after we'd found the body – but, again, I'm getting ahead of myself!

It took about half an hour, but eventually we'd all worked out which rooms we were in (at least Meg had had the foresight to pin names to doors) and we'd all pulled out of our cases whatever it was that needed pulling out of our cases. The Lodge was pleasant enough: it was old, and there hadn't been many updates made during the last seventy years or so, but it was spotlessly clean. I discovered later that the family that owned it used it as a summer home – and it *felt* very homey, though it had clearly originally been built to accommodate guests, which was handy. Once inside my room I could see that it was small, but adequately and pleasantly furnished, and that it had three doors: the one I'd entered through, from the upstairs landing that ran around the three sides of the house; one that opened onto my own little bathroom, which was very 'country' with bead-board and wainscoting, and a wonderful old claw-footed tub; the third door was locked – I discovered later that it led to another bathroom on the other side of my room…..it seemed that the house had been designed that way – bedroom, bathroom, bedroom, with connecting doors allowing for maximum flexibility. I thought how unusual that must have been in its day, but I liked the arrangement. I made sure that the key in the door between *my* bathroom and the next room along was turned and sitting in the lock in such a way that no-one could get into my bathroom by mistake!

Having checked out my immediate surroundings, I decided I should make my way down to the Great Room, where we'd all agreed we'd meet as soon as we were sorted. Years of living in London made me lock my door, and I made sure that the key to my room was in the pocket of my comfy, stretchy, black cord pants, and started down the big oak-plank staircase that led back down to the entry-way. The Great Room was just that – huge and rather cavernous: it occupied one side of the lodge. It was cheerily, if predictably, decorated: the obligatory stuffed moose, elk and deer-heads stared down at us forlornly from above a great stone fireplace that was the unmistakable focal point of the room, and there was even one of those antler chandeliers, so beloved of Canadiana interior decorators....though I suspected that this one had been an original fixture.  Around the roaring fire was a collection of comfy looking armchairs and sofas, replete with plaid upholstery and Hudson's Bay blanket throws: some were facing the flaming hearth, others offered a 'view' out of the large windows which, if you could have seen through the snow and the darkness, would have been of the rolling valley below and mountains opposite.  I gathered that Meg's vineyard was on the opposite side of the valley, and that we should get a good view of it in the morning.

Meg burst into the Great Room just after we'd all meandered in: a fantastic entrance, if ever there was one.  Joe Goldblum paused his 'working the room' efforts, and the rest of us all stopped making the small-talk we'd been forcing, and turned to see the woman who'd invited us for her birthday weekend.  Meg looked amazing – a closely-fitted amethyst sweater atop a pair of brown slacks doesn't sound like much, but she looked stunning!  Her dark, sleek hair was pulled back in a perfect French twist; brown pearl earrings complimented her deep tan; she was slim, yet curvy; perfectly made-up - to look as though she was wearing no make-up at all, and she was carrying what looked like a gin and tonic in her hand – classy and sassy at the same time.  I immediately felt frumpy, even more overweight than I really am (which is quite an amount anyway) and I *wanted* a G&T!  I loved her and hated her, in equal measure.  There she was: Meg – my Meg – all grown up and looking like a million dollars....which was about a half of one percent of her net worth (see, supermarket magazines *are* useful, after all!)

"My *darlings!*" she exclaimed to the room in general, "Thank you all *so* much for coming to my little party.  How *wonderful* to see you all!"  Her accent was a strange mixture of Welsh inflection and Mid-Atlantic pronunciation.  Then there was a slight pause: I'm sure I wasn't the only one who was wondering who she'd greet first.  It was like the school playground – who would be picked first, who'd be left till last?

"My dear!" exclaimed Luis, and he was on Meg in an instant, kissing her cheek and stroking her arm, as if to signify ownership.  "You are looking *wonderful*, as usual, my darling.  But where have you been?  You were not in your room, I looked."  Until that moment I hadn't really noted Luis's strange way of speaking: he didn't so much speak, as declaim.  And you couldn't help but notice that he was just as gorgeous in the flesh as on the TV....well, *I* couldn't help but notice, anyway.  But he looked smaller than I'd thought he would be: muscular, but quite petite.  In fact, Meg was my height, about five-four, and he was just the same height as her.  TV's a funny thing – they say it puts twenty pounds on you....and I reckon it must put a good ten inches on your height too!

Having been greeted, in the appropriate manner, by her fiancé, Meg turned her attention to me – yes, *me*!

"Cait – darling Cait...you haven't changed a bit," she said, lying.  Even *I* know I've gained at least fifty pounds since I was eighteen, and at forty eight my skin tone isn't what it used to be, nor is my hair colour – which I staunchly refuse to amend with chemicals....but I silently blessed her mendacity and moved to enjoy the hug she was coming towards me to deliver. But, as she came closer to me I could see that there was something in her eyes I'd never seen in the old Meg – a hardness lurked, a chill, a cynicism. As a criminologist specialising in psychology and victimology, I have worked for years to train myself to notice, *and* understand the implications of, all those details about people that most others miss: their body language, their expressions, the minutiae of their clothing, their inter-reactions with surroundings – those unspoken signals that belie their words, and sometimes even their actions. And, despite her glossy shell, I could tell that Meg Jones was an unhappy, bitter woman, with an anger burning her up. I wondered what it could be. I didn't know then that I'd only have to wait a few hours to find out.

These thoughts took but a second, and I was able to respond to her welcome pretty wholeheartedly. We hugged as though we were ten years old.

"Everyone – this is Cait, Caitlin Morgan, my Very Best Friend. We met as we were walked through the school gates by our mothers, on our very first day at school.....so she's someone who knows the *real* Meg Jones....and someone I'm sure you'll all grow to love and admire as much as I do. She's very clever, doesn't suffer fools at all and is a wicked chess player....you have been warned!" People smiled politely. "On top of that," continued Meg, "she's a criminology professor, which is going to be interesting....considering what all of *you* have lurking in your closets!"

Meg was smiling with her mouth, but her eyes were glinting with hate. It was a bizarre welcome, and it stunned everyone in the room. Puzzled looks were exchanged between people who'd only met for the first time on the minibus, and the two couples, the Webbers and the Goldblums, drew closer to their partners. It was as though Meg had thrown down a challenge, and she was waiting to see who'd pick it up.

"Listen to *you*, talking about '*closets*' – what's wrong with calling them '*wardrobes*', like you always used to? *Very* American you've become!" It was Meg's mother, Jean, speaking, and in a biting, disdainful voice which, as soon as she spoke, I remembered from my childhood: she'd always been very nice to me, but I'd heard her talking to Meg like that when she was little, when she'd thought I couldn't hear.

"Hello Jean," said Meg heavily, which I thought was odd, for two reasons: first, I knew that Meg and her mother hadn't been in touch much for the last thirty years, but, nevertheless Meg *had* invited her....but now she sounded as though she wished she hadn't; and I've never been able to come to terms with people calling their parents by their given names – they should be Mum and Dad...or some alternative form of the same. Call me old fashioned – but there it is.

"Hello Meg – no hug for your mother then?" Jean continued in her broad Welsh Valleys accent. I hadn't heard an accent like that since I'd left the UK – and I wasn't missing it.

"Of course," replied Meg, flatly. Everything about her demeanour was screaming 'Keep away from me', but Meg hugged her mother, briefly and weakly, then she turned and announced, "This is Jean, my mother. She's come all the way from Wales, and I'm sure she's *very* tired, hence her snappish comments, which are *so unusual* for her." Meg was clearly mocking her mother. "You too Adrian, I bet you could do with an early night, given that trip all the way from Seville."

"I'll be *fine*," replied the mysteriously familiar 'Adrian', who now, without his hat or sunglasses, looked just like a *much* older version of a rock star I'd doted on, silently, about ten years earlier: you're not really allowed to have crushes when you're in your thirties, so my adoration of Izzy Izzard had always, publicly, been based upon his musicianship, not his rakish good looks, wicked charm and bad boy image.

"You always *could* just keep going, and *going*," was Meg's bitter reply. "Say hello to Adrian Izzard, folks, husband number two, though maybe you know him better by his stage-name Izzy, if you've heard of him *at all*, that is." The Goldblums were looking mystified, but my heart was beating a lot faster than it had been a moment earlier. It *was* Izzy Izzard! No wonder he'd looked familiar....but, *my God*, the life of a rock star had taken its toll on him – he looked about sixty! He'd looked so much more vital ten years ago – what on earth had happened to him? Then I realised that it hadn't been *ten* years ago.....that he'd actually given up music about eight years ago, and that I was thinking of the image of the man about ten years before *that*. And he'd probably been in his thirties then......so, OK, a lot can happen in eighteen years, and he was probably just looking his age! I was still trying to come to terms with the fact that Meg had been married to Izzy Izzard....why the hell hadn't she told me *that*? Had it been such a terrible experience that she couldn't talk about it....or even e-mail about it?

People were nodding politely at my erstwhile heartthrob, who was standing right next to Luis Lopez, one of my current ones....and it was all getting to be a bit much for me. Why wasn't anyone offering me a drink? I could *really* do with one!

"And this is the *Great* Professor Dan James, husband number three," added Meg, still in bitter tones: she made his title sound like an insult as she hissed it at us and flung an arm towards the man in the checked suit. Dan James was big, in every dimension, and seemed to dominate the room: even his smile was big, and his rosy cheeks were the sort that should have been above a Father Christmas beard......in fact, with the right costume he'd have made an excellent Santa, even his voice was perfect – a cross between the man in the famous red suit and the Jolly Green Giant.

"Good evening all," he boomed loud and low. "And thank you, dear Meg, for so graciously inviting me to this wonderful weekend of well-wishing in the wilderness." He seemed pleased about the alliteration. I cringed. Oh dear, a bombast. How sad.

"Oh give it a rest, Dan, there's no-one *here* to impress with your pathetic attempts at witticisms. None of us are impressionable little students, sitting at your feet hoping for a pearl of wisdom to drop from those flaccid

17

lips." Meg certainly wasn't holding back – it didn't sound as though she even *liked* anyone she'd invited.

"And husband number one, everyone: Peter *Webber*." Meg nodded towards the sandy-haired man with the piercing blue eyes. The strange emphasis she'd placed on his surname puzzled me – it wasn't as though it was a particularly fancy name or anything. It was odd. What was also odd was how bitchy Meg was being. Her e-mails had always been upbeat – well, they'd *read* as upbeat anyway: but, then, that's the trouble with e-mails, of course - there's no inflection, no sense of tone.

"Hello folks," said Peter Webber in a quiet voice. Totally American accent, none of the Welsh sing-song left at all. But his eyes......*now* I remembered Peter....he'd been weedy and small when we were young, but with the most electric eyes, which was ironic, considering he'd become an electrician. "This is my wife, Sally," he continued evenly. "I'm sure that Meg will find it in her *somewhere* to be nice to *her* at least – they've never met before, and Sally was hoping to meet the delightful person that Meg seems to be during all her TV interviews." Wow, Peter had a spine! He might look pasty and nerdy, but at least he was standing up to Meg.

"But, of *course*, Peter," cooed Meg, mocking him, "I'm sure I'll be nice to *Sally:* Sally herself looks so *nice*." Meg had insulted the woman before they'd even exchanged a word. I was beginning to feel uncomfortable: where the *hell* was the Meg I'd been corresponding with for the last year, let alone the girl she'd been 'back in the day'?

"I'm very pleased to meet you," said Sally Webber hesitantly. I wondered for a moment if she was going to curtsey. But she didn't: she contented herself with a bob of her head, but I suspected that, if she'd had a forelock, she'd have pulled it for the World Famous Meg Jones.

"The Goldblums – Joe and Martha," said Meg, nodding towards the couple who were standing with their backs to the fireplace. "Joe was my literary agent until recently, and Martha's just along for the ride, as usual." Martha Goldblum opened her mouth as if to speak, but clamped it shut in disgust, pulling her husband closer with her fat little bejewelled hand.

"Uncalled for, Meg," was all Joe Goldblum said, curtly. He spoke for us all. Me included. I wasn't liking *this* Meg at all.

"And that's all folks!" quipped Meg, acidly. "What a funny bunch we are: but, hey, thanks for coming. I guessed Joe would – he wants me back on his books, and Luis hasn't got much choice, have you baby – you *have* to be seen spending time with your *loving* fiancé, don't you? But as for the rest of you – well, I wonder why *you* all came – eh? It's not like any of you *wanted* to see me, is it? So what do you all think you can get out of me? Why *did* you all come? That's the million dollar question, right?"

I felt I had to speak. The tension was almost unbearable. This wasn't how it was supposed to be!

"Oh come on now Meg," I said, as lightly as I could, "I know *I'm* delighted to see you.....you're looking great, and I'm so pleased at all the success you're having......and look, *three* ex-husbands and a fourth-to-be, and there's me with not a one. How lucky can a girl get?"

"Oh dear, *sweet* Cait – you might be bright but you sure can be dumb," was Meg's tired, and rather cutting reply. "If you had *any* idea what these three put me through.....or what *this* one can be like," she gesticulated with her glass towards her ex's and then Luis, "then you wouldn't call me 'lucky' at all! Smarten up, Cait – life's short and then you die....all you can do is make the most of the ride, and mine's been bloody bumpy, to say the least."

This glum philosophy being thrown out into the room didn't help the mood. And it seemed that Luis Lopez was far from happy with the comments Meg had made about *him*.

"You should not speak like this! It is not polite! These people have been important in your life! And I have done nothing to deserve your unkind words!" Luis was declaiming again. Exclamation points included.

"You 'haven't done anything to deserve my unkind words,' Luis?" was Meg's sharp, mocking retort. "You've driven me to *this* stuff for a start," she waved her glass, showering the bearskin hearth-rug with its contents, "and God *knows* what's next!"

Maybe that was it: Meg didn't *look* drunk, but maybe she was drinking so much, on a regular basis, that she was able to control her body, if not her words, or mood. I knew it was possible: I'd seen it before, but that was all a long time ago, and far behind me. Just believe me when I tell you that when you live with an alcoholic you *can* actually make yourself believe that they've stopped drinking: you *want* it to be true, so you tell yourself it *is* true.....until they snap, that is. Until they change before your very eyes and their inner, booze-fuelled demons come screaming out at you. But, yes, they can be very controlled, physically. Up to a point.

"Back on the sauce then, Meg?" It was Izzy Izzard: I told myself I had to think of him as 'Adrian'......he wasn't Izzy anymore. His voice was gravelly, his accent no longer tied to his Boston roots, but floating somewhere in that international place that is 'Rock Star World'. His infamously straight-laced Spanish wife, who had encouraged him to give up his excessive lifestyle, then touring, then recording, and to procreate something approaching a soccer team, ruled his life with a rod of iron – at least, that's what the newspapers said. I wondered if it were true, or whether he was just an average guy with an extraordinary drive and bucket full of talent.

"You never *were* interested in the booze, were you, Adrian – you preferred other forms of mood management, *right?*" Meg was being cruel, and she knew it. "Did Jocasta, or Jacintha.......or whatever that womb on legs you married after me is called......did *she* get you off it all? *All?*"

"It's Jovita, as you well know, Meg. Don't *be* like this. You never were a bitch, Meg," replied Adrian, almost plaintively, "Where's all this coming from? Is it all just gin-talk?" He was echoing my own thoughts.

"Gin-talk? Oh no, Adrian. You'll all be *delighted* to know that I've been seeing a shrink – yeah, a *shrink*. Luis's idea, wasn't it, *darling?* When I bought that big old house in LA, he was the one who got me started with it. And I've stuck with it: three times a week for six months now. *Very* LA – very 'American', Jean, like *closets*," she looked at her mother with a cruel smile on her lips. "And do you know what the freshly-shrunk Meg knows that the un-shrunk Meg didn't?"

I knew I wasn't the only one in the room who wanted to know the answer to that one!

"I have a feeling you're going to tell us, whether we want to know or not," boomed Dan James. "How very theatrical this all is!"

"Ah Dan – *theatrics* would be something you'd know *all* about – acting the part, that's all that matters to you, isn't it? You didn't think I was the right leading lady for you to have on your arm when you got to Harvard's hallowed halls, did you? So you were going to dump me. Eight years of my life, about to be flushed away. I knew it. And I jumped before you could push me. I escaped *that* humiliation, at least. But this isn't theatrics – this is me, Dan, *me*! The 'me' *you've* all created. That's what Meg knows *now*: that she's been made into the person you see today, by the *people* you see today. Are you all *proud*? You should be! I'm wealthy beyond belief, I sell more books than any romance writer, ever, and any screenplay I choose to attach my name to will automatically out-gross even those special effects masterpieces they're all so keen on these days. *You* Dan? You're a pathetic, washed up pseudo-professor, who, if he didn't have tenure, would have been slung out on his ear years ago for fiddling with the sophomores and for not having written anything that's sold more than a thousand copies in over a decade."

Meg was on a roll – we could all feel it, and, like me, everyone was wondering who would be next.

Sally Webber, bless her, came to our rescue.

"I wonder if there's any chance of a drink at all?" She spoke quietly, and lightly. I wondered if she'd been taking anything in – then, noting her rather vacuous expression, it occurred to me that, maybe, she was just as dumb as a stick, and hadn't picked up on the tone of the exchanges. "It was *quite* a journey from LA and I could do with something. A soda, maybe?" She smiled sweetly, and it seemed to have an amazing effect on Meg: her body lost its tension, she relaxed. Meg nodded at Sally, and broke into a smile.

"I'm sorry, Sally – you're right, I should be a better hostess." Meg's voice sounded warm and genuine. Bizarre. "The caterers have set up a sort of bar in the kitchen – why don't we all go through and get ourselves something? There are some little snacks too – though you don't want to spoil your dinner: I'd planned on us eating in an hour – the meal they've prepared will be ready then."

It was as though a switch had flicked in Meg's head somewhere: she was acting like a totally different person, with no carry-over of her previous emotions at all!

Mine wasn't the only puzzled face in the room, then relief swept visibly through the little group....at least, it was visible to *me* in the way that bodily tensions relaxed, eyebrows were lowered to their normal resting places and pallid complexions coloured up, whilst ruddy ones calmed down. Jean Jones even shook her thin little body as though she were a dog coming out of a cold pond. We were all doing the same thing, mentally. Meg was walking ahead of us, leading the way to the kitchen, across the entry hall, seemingly oblivious to the stress she'd caused since her Grand Entrance.

It was going to be tough to try to act as though nothing had happened, but it seemed that the whole group had silently signed some sort of pact to do just that.....and things went quite well, really, until what turned out to be the end of dinner, which was when I messed up in such a way that it might well have led to murder.

# III

Upon reflection, Meg *might* have had something when she said that I am very clever, but that I can be dumb: if ever I was to prove that to be the case, it was that evening. Though, in my own defence, I don't think it was really my *fault* – just my *doing*.

We'd all managed to sort out drinks and a snack, then we turned our attention to getting dinner served. We all pitched in, and soon we were sitting down at the vast oak dining table that was a part of the open plan oak kitchen, that mirrored the Great Room on the other side of the Lodge. We ate a feast of roasted duck – local, with vegetables – local, and a *lot* of wine – not just local, but from Meg's own vineyard. Admittedly the wine had been made before Meg owned the property, but that didn't stop us all complimenting her on each type that we tried. And we tried a *lot*. A *lot*. And so, after about an hour of eating and drinking we were all getting a bit loud: all except Sally, who, it turned out, didn't touch alcohol – she claimed she was allergic to it. *Right*.

Now when I say we were getting loud, let me make it clear that we were getting loud in a nice, friendly way. I was sitting next to Meg – and it was the pleasant, old Meg who sat down at the table that night: we were raking over old times, laughing at past fashion faux-pas, past adventures, past boyfriends, past....everything. And that was the problem – we were talking about the past: I said to Meg that she'd had such an interesting life that she should write a book about it – an autobiography. And she replied that she sort of had already, but that she was keeping it a secret just for now.

And then came one of those moments in life that you'd give anything to change – to go back to, and make it un-happen. Let's call it an accident, or, if you're the type who believes in that sort of thing, the intervention of Fate. Everyone seemed to stop talking at the same time, and the *only thing* you could hear in the room was me whispering loudly to Meg,

"*Really?* You've *really* written your autobiography? Am *I* in it?"

As I looked around the table it was quite clear that everyone was thinking exactly the same thing: were *they* in it? I can recall their faces quite clearly, and *every one of them* was horrified. I swear that some of them had even stopped breathing.

"Oh Meg, what have you *done?*" Peter Webber was distraught.

Meg looked at me as if she could kill me – and all I could do was mouth my apologies to her.

*This* cat was not going back into *that* bag – no way!

The wine that, until then, had warmed the conversations around the table, now fuelled heightened emotions in everyone. Myself included.

As I looked at Meg, I could tell that she'd made a decision. She stood. She was at the head of the table. She swayed a little. She steadied herself. All eyes were on her. *Which* Meg would she be? What would she say?

"I wanted it kept a secret for tonight – but now you know. I was going to tell you tomorrow, on my birthday. Yes, I *have* written my 'autobiography'. I've worked on it with my doctor....my shrink: it's been very.....cathartic. I found out a lot about myself by doing it. And, yes, you're *all* in it. And, yes, I've told the *truth*. That was the whole point of it. And, *yes*, the reason I invited you all here this weekend was that I need to talk to you all, individually, about how you played a part in making me the 'me' I am today. It's an important stage in my therapy. My doctor says it's critical to my future well-being, and I agree with him. There. Now you know." Meg wasn't being bitchy. More than anything she sounded, and looked, resigned. And sad. And almost relieved. She drank down the glass of deep red wine that stood beside her empty plate. I noticed that Adrian did the same. As did Luis and Dan.

I saw a tear trickle down Meg's cheek.

"I don't expect any of you to understand," she added, "but I needed to do it. I have to face up to my past, to be able to face my future." Meg's voice wavered. It sounded to me as though she were reciting some sort of mantra.

"And you don't give a *damn* who you hurt in the process, do you, Meg?" Adrian pushed back his chair and rose to his feet. There was a fire in his eyes. Was it anger – or terror?

"Hurt? *Hurt? You lot?*" Meg's eyes lit up with fury, and her voice was now strong and loud. Clearly we were about to be treated to another glimpse of the Meg we'd met upon our arrival. "Oh yes – I could hurt *all* of you if I wanted to – I know *all* your dirty little secrets, don't I? Every *one* of you has a stain on your conscience – there's quite literally a skeleton in *each* of your *closets*," she looked venomously at her mother. "But that's not what this is all about. Believe it or not, I asked you here so I could ask *your* forgiveness....not to accuse you of what you *know* you've done wrong. Not to point out to you that you've got away with something that could have changed your life – ruined you even! You Sally – I know nothing about *you*.....though I suspect that's because there's little *to* know. Picked a new wife who wouldn't ask too many questions, eh, Peter? Clever boy. But the rest of you........oh, I can't do this *now*. Sod the lot of you! You'll all have to stew on it overnight – I'm off to bed."

And, with that, Meg threw down the napkin she'd been clutching and twisting, and walked out of the room, her head down, tears streaming down her face. She made for the stairs.

The room was silent. Then Sally Webber spoke. "I suppose we'd better clear everything away then?" Every face, including that of her husband, turned towards her in amazement. Once again she seemed to be completely oblivious to the implications of what had just happened. She was clearly a woman who viewed life entirely from her own, blinkered, perspective.

We were all in shock. But we rallied, and dealt with the mundane task of clearing away what had, to be fair, been a very good dinner. As I carried plates and cleared glasses I couldn't help but wonder what Meg had meant about skeletons in closets. For myself, I knew I had none: except I had to admit that the media frenzy that had enveloped me after I'd found my boyfriend, Angus, dead in the bathroom one morning all those years ago, might have made someone think otherwise. No smoke without fire: it's the British way. But that was all behind me. I'd left that in the UK. I was a Canadian now, and had been for years. Why wouldn't that ghost stay where it should be – laid to rest......cremated even! Why would Meg think that Angus's death had anything to do with *me*? The authorities had completely exonerated me – *publicly*, no less, due to the huge interest the tabloids had taken in the case of the initially inexplicable death of the alcoholic, violent boyfriend of a criminology specialist.

It all came flooding back – the photographers following me everywhere, the tutorials I hadn't dared attend, the lectures I hadn't dared to deliver.....the way my life had been raked over, and embellished with all sorts of wicked untruths. It had been a nightmare – a nightmare I always hoped was over. But maybe that sort of thing never goes away. Why would Meg think that anything *she* could say or do regarding that topic could hurt me more than I'd already been hurt by it? And what on earth did she have to apologise to *me* about? We hadn't even spoken for thirty years.......and anything she'd done to me all that time ago had long since healed and been forgotten – not that I could remember any particular hurt in any case.

It was clear that I wasn't the only one going through the process of self examination: everyone was in their own little world as we filled the dishwasher, hand washed and wiped the stemware and finally.....*finally*.....made our way to our rooms, where at least we could be alone with our thoughts, and not have to put on a brave face for the rest of the group.

Eventually I snuggled down under the patchwork comforter on my bed. It had been an emotional day: the excitement of looking forward to seeing an old friend again; the general stress that accompanies a journey on icy roads, which I hate; the anxiety about mixing with a group of people I'd never met, which I'm not good at; and all the emotions stirred up by Meg. I thought I'd never sleep. But I did. Until I received what was, to say the least, a rude awakening.

# IV

"Cait! Cait! Wake up – it's Meg – I'm sure she's dead! She won't answer her door – to her own *mother!*" It was Jean Jones, knocking at my door and screaming for me. I stumbled out of bed, discovered that my bedside lamp wasn't working, stubbed my feet into slippers in the half-light and pulled a robe around myself. The air was chilly. As I opened the door the first thing I noticed was that Jean's lipstick matched her dressing gown exactly – burnt orange.....not a good colour choice with that sallow skin, I thought. True, it was an odd thing to notice, but, there you go, I did.

It was about the only thought I managed before I realised that I had the mother of all hangovers, and that I really should have drunk more water before going to bed the night before.

I also realized that upright wasn't a good position for me, and, as Jean dragged me mercilessly towards Meg's bedroom door I thought my head was going to drop off....mind you, if it *had* dropped off that wouldn't necessarily have been a bad thing - it might have taken my hangover with it. But, as it was, I was stuck with the headache, the quickening waves of nausea and the noise caused by Jean thumping on Meg's door ricocheting around inside my skull. When Jean stopped hammering, momentarily my head stopped banging too - I was grateful for the relief, but she'd proven her point: Meg didn't respond. I figured that, if Meg felt anything like I did, she was probably hiding under the blankets praying her mother would leave her alone - I knew *I* was!

"See!" was all Jean could manage as she flung her arm towards the locked door. She sounded vindicated. I felt resigned to the fact that I'd actually have to do something - but then a light at the end of the tunnel appeared...well, Luis's head and bronzed, bare torso appeared at the end of the corridor, to be more exact.

"What is it, this noise?"

As he spoke I pulled my robe around my ample, yet now sadly unsupported, bosom and surreptitiously checked the corners of my eyes for yukky bits.

"Meg won't answer her door - it's locked - and Jean is worried about her. Can you check your connecting doors and see if she's awake?" I'd mastered all my powers of physical control to make my mouth and furry tongue form that one sentence, and I was spent! As Luis disappeared into his room with a grunt, I tried hard to make spit...but my mouth was as dry as the Valley of the Kings in August, where I haven't actually been, but I'm sure it's *very* dry!

As Luis re-appeared wearing slippers and, sadly, a robe, he was shaking his head - something I seriously doubted I'd ever be able to do again, given my sorry, self-induced state.

"The doors, they are locked," he declaimed with astonishment. Luis then added to the overall atmosphere of a melodramatic soap opera by holding up his hands in a manner which suggested total bewilderment as to why his doting fiancé should want to lock him out of her life at all.

Once again Jean pounced, "See!" she screamed - sounding *doubly* vindicated this time. I winced. Jean was very close, and *very* loud.

"What on earth is going on?" Heads were now, unsurprisingly given Jean's performance, appearing out of doors all around the landing, and the voice seeming to speak on behalf of them all came from Peter; Sally was peering out from behind him in their doorway, like a field-mouse hiding behind a wheat-sheaf.

Once again I tried to clear my throat to speak, but Luis's voice boomed around the huge space of the atrium and landing,

"It is Meg. She is locked in her room. She will not answer her mother. Her mother is worried."

I felt like adding something along the lines of "La plume de ma tante est dans ma valise," as Luis's stilted phrases took me back to years of parrot – like repetition in French language classes. Luis's micro-explanation created little by way of a reaction from anyone, except Jean, who took the ensuing five seconds of puzzled silence as her cue to let rip. Loudly.

"Meg's dead – I know it, I can *feel* it......I'm her mother and I know something's wrong....why won't anybody listen?"

Like we had a choice!!

A murmur of disbelief rippled around the emerging group, and my overwhelming feeling of unreality was compounded as Luis proclaimed,

"I will break down the door!"

Before anyone could protest, he had bounced off the sturdily built cedar door in question with an "Oooofffff!" I was sure that bruising would soon set in beneath the perfect tan, but I suspected that a rather more enduring hit had been taken by the ego of the man who was known world-wide for flinging himself through carefully constructed stunt-doors on a weekly basis.

No-one knew what to say – here was melodrama mixed with embarrassment, and, to top it all, my stomach was beginning to churn: if *I'd* drunk a lot the night before I was pretty sure Meg had drunk more....what if she'd fallen? What if she'd thrown up and.....a gag reaction set in as I stupidly thought of vomit, and I had to work hard to control myself. While I was grappling with a stomach full of stale red wine, supporting myself against the wall as I did so, people began to stumble towards Meg's room.

Soon we were *all* gathered outside Meg's bedroom, trying to calm her mother. No-one seemed to know what to do next, so, being the control-freak I am, I spoke up with a suggestion.

"OK folks, if we're all *sure* she's fine, but want to make *really* sure, the only way to do it is to get into her room. But let's not go wrecking a borrowed house unless we have to. Has anyone got a key for her room?"

Shrugged shoulders all around, and a sad-faced Luis, indicated that no-one had a key to Meg's room. It seemed there was no other option but to break open the door.

"OK then," I croaked resignedly, "Now, if all you....boys..." I chose the word carefully so as to avoid any possible insults, "....just run at the locked side of the door, I'm sure it'll open....after all," I added in deference to my hostess's fiancé, "Luis must have loosened it already."

Luis smiled his warm smile in coy gratitude as the men gathered to rush at the door.

It worked, and the door flung open with a loud crack. Luis fell into the room and Peter flopped on top of him, Adrian grabbed the doorframe to prevent his own angular body from joining the huddle. As I automatically asked if they were alright, I cast my eyes across the room towards Meg's bed. There she was, lying on her side looking peaceful, but ashen.

Jean made to rush into the room, over the two men lying in the doorway, and I tried to grab her back.

"Jean! No!" I exclaimed, every hair on my neck *literally* standing on end. I knew at that moment that Meg was dead and, as my criminology professor's mind went to work, I could see that her body was lying in a very unnatural manner. It didn't look like she'd died in her sleep. Instinctively, I knew that something was wrong with the scene – but, in the shock of the moment, I just couldn't grasp what it was. My 'photographic' memory has helped me tremendously during my professional, academic and even personal life – but that was one unwanted picture I knew would haunt me forever. The detail was burned into my mind's eye. It would never go away. Sometimes I really I hated it my so-called gift.

"She's my *daughter* – she needs me!" Jean screamed as she thrust me aside and with two bounds was across the room pulling Meg's limp body into her arms, clutching her to her bosom and screaming for her dead daughter to wake up. She started shaking Meg, wailing and crying into her daughter's tousled long dark hair. It was phenomenally dramatic. It quite took me by surprise. Jean looked like some tragic Greek heroine – and was wailing like one too.

Everything seemed to be happening at double speed and in slow motion at the same time. People with still-groggy voices crowded at the door; cries of shock and disbelief were on everyone's lips; Jean was screaming; the inside of my head was banging. Someone had to *do* something.

"OK – everybody listen," I called above the hubbub. Everyone fell silent and looked at me as though....well I don't know *what* they expected, and I didn't know what I was going to say, but I just sort of took charge!

"Everyone move back from the door – yes, you too Luis." Meg's fiancé was still flat on his stomach taking in the whole scene from floor level.

"But Meg...is she....she is....?" The question hung in the air. He looked pitifully desolate as he peered up towards me.

"I told you! I told you she was dead!" screamed Jean as she held her daughter's body tightly to her breast. "You wouldn't listen. You didn't believe me. But I knew. I'm her Mum. I'm her Mum!" She sobbed, and wailed, and moaned, all the time rocking and swaying. Then she turned towards our weird little group at the door and, without provocation of any kind, snarled viciously at us,

"You won't take her away from me. I'm not leaving her alone!" Her eyes flashed with hatred. Then, quite suddenly, it seemed as though all the passion disappeared from them and she looked at Meg as if for the first time. Jean took in the sight of all of us huddled and heaped in the doorway, tears welling in her eyes, and said softly,

"Oh my God – Meg's dead. She's dead. What will I do now?"

I have to admit that my heart went out to her: in a split second she'd been transformed from a tigress to a lamb. She let Meg's upper body fall, completely ignoring it as it tumbled from her grip, and she walked towards me repeating the question "What will I do?" over and over, wet-faced and hopeless: a lost soul in a frail body that had just aged ten years in two long, long minutes.

"Come with me, dear, I'll get you a brandy," came an unexpected voice – it was Martha Goldblum, pushing her husband to one side as her own wobbling bulk enveloped Jean within a wing of a pink chiffon negligee.

"Someone call 911," I barked. Luis made a dash from the floor towards his room. Suddenly it seemed that my powers of speech had returned, and my hangover was a thing of the past. I continued to be the only one with any sort of plan of action, so I went for it!

"We need to get out of here and shut the door until the police come." I sounded as though I knew what to do, but I hadn't been involved in a sudden death like this since I'd had my formal training in crime scene management years ago......when a *real* body had turned up at the 'fake' crime scene. This was an even bigger shock than that – I hadn't gone to school with that body, I hadn't played at being Emma Peel in the school yard with that body, I hadn't been quaffing wine and swapping old memories a few hours ago with *that* body. Getting out and leaving it all as untouched as possible, Jean's intervention aside, was all we could do.

"You can't leave her hanging out of bed like that." It was Adrian, speaking sternly, and with surprising authority. We all looked at how Meg's body was balanced on the edge of the bed, where she had fallen from her mother's arms. It *was* a very precarious position.

I hesitated. All my training told me not to touch anything, but this was Meg – she could fall. Of course, I immediately told myself she couldn't get hurt, but if she fell off the bed, then that would be as much of a disturbance of the scene as if she were lifted back *onto* the bed. And I knew in my heart that, for some inexplicable reason, we'd all feel better if Meg was placed 'safely' back on the bed.

I gave in. "OK, I'll lift her up," I almost whispered. I turned to the others, "But only me – you all stay there."

I tip-toed across the room until I reached Meg. Oh Meg. Oh *dear* Meg. I tried to control my emotions.

Reaching under her shoulder I gathered up her right arm and lolling head. She was cold, but not icy. She was certainly still mobile. No rigor. She was surprisingly light. I pulled her right foot back onto the bed and shifted her as little as I needed until she wasn't likely to fall. There. She was safe. Not a body, but an old friend. I had to fight to hold back the tears. I had to be *professional*.

As I re-joined the group at the door I wiped my damp hands on my robe. I thought, "I must wash my hands, *very* soon".

"Well done," said Adrian, in a soft voice, and we closed the door as well as we could, given that it was badly splintered and far from perfect.

There was nothing we could do but await the arrival of the police.

"The power, it is out, and the telephone it will not work – it is dead." Luis's voice echoed around the dim landing. The word "dead" hit us all like a hammer. Only Luis seemed not to notice. "Does anyone have a cellphone? I forgot to charge mine last night," he added.

As he said it I kicked myself that I hadn't been sufficiently well organized to recharge mine before I had gone down to dinner.

"I'll get mine," barked Joe Goldblum.

'Now there's a man who'll never be without his mobile communications devices,' I thought, as the dealmaker returned to his room as fast as his twig-like legs would carry him. 'And thank God for it today,' was my next thought.

Joe reappeared at the top of the stairs and passed me the sleek device with his liver-spotted hand.

"You do it!" he ordered. I suspected that Joe never asked for anything, rather he got what he wanted by instructing people to simply do his bidding.

Obligingly I took the phone, checked the signal, which was weak, and moved around the staircase until I found a spot where the signal was stronger.

"You guys go ahead and get some tea and coffee on the go. Maybe you can rustle up something for breakfast. There's nothing we can do till the police get here," I shouted to the group from my perch at the top of the stairs, and the little group straggled past me, down the staircase towards the kitchen, Sally Webber in the lead, telling her husband she'd noticed croissants in the freezer the night before, and commenting that they'd make a delicious breakfast. 'Odd woman,' I thought.

I was alone by the time the operator finally answered, I briefly explained the situation, gave my name and our location, and then, after a few moments, I found I was speaking to what sounded like a twelve year old girl who informed me that she was the shift supervisor and that she was sorry, but no emergency response could be offered at the present time.

I have to admit that I was speechless – which in my case doesn't mean I actually stopped talking.

"Look," I almost exploded, "about ten minutes ago we discovered the body of Miss Megan Jones, noted author, in her bed. She has no pulse, is cold to the touch, but there's no rigor. We need a doctor, an ambulance and the police. *NOW!*" I was pretty proud of myself – I felt I had acquitted myself very professionally.

"Any sign of foul play?" piped the young voice, brusquely.

I hesitated. "N-no." Something was hovering at the fringe of my conscious mind but refused to come into focus.

"You have suspicions?" she snapped.

"Not exactly….." my voice trailed off.

"Anyone there with medical, paramedic or police experience?" She sounded like the bossy type.

I let my mind skip through the group and was sure of my answer.

"No. At least, not that I'm aware of. I have basic training from my University days in most aspects of crime scene assessment, but that's it. I don't think there's anyone else."

"Who's on the premises?" asked the disembodied voice. I was getting a bit fed up with all these questions, and couldn't help but show it.

"Look, it doesn't really matter who's here, Miss Whoever-You-Are. What we need is an ambulance and some sort of police presence. *Now*, please." I suspect I sounded abrupt – but, hey, she'd started it!

"Well now, there's the problem, you see. We can't send anyone for probably the next twenty-four hours."

I was non-plussed! "What do you mean?" I blustered.

"Have you *seen* the weather, Professor Morgan?"

"Well, it's terrible, that's true," I replied grudgingly as I peered through the high windows ahead of me and saw grey snow swirling furiously, "but surely you can get out to us – we're not *that* far off the main road. We're just about an hour outside Downtown Kelowna for goodness sake! This *is* an emergency after all!"

"I happen to know the property, Professor, and I'm afraid that's the issue. Not only can we not get to the Lodge, but the whole of the area out towards that valley is cut off. It has been since about three this morning. Heaviest dump of snow in recorded weather history fell last night, about a meter in some areas. All our crews are out trying to open roads right now, and all our emergency response vehicles are dealing with a big pile up on the road from the Airport. Also, until these gale-force winds die down, we wouldn't even be able to get a chopper to you."

"So, what do you suggest we do *now*?" I knew I was using my best sarcastic voice, and I could even hear my old Welsh accent appearing more strongly through the cracks that were appearing in my Canadian twang.

"Just what you *are* doing," she replied calmly. "Keep everyone away from the body. Keep the room locked. Try not to disturb anything in as wide a circle around the room in question as possible and keep the room cool. We'll get there as soon as we can."

"Well," I spluttered, "have you any idea how long that might be?"

"Difficult to say at the moment, Professor. The weather forecast isn't good I'm afraid. Says we're in for high winds and snow for at least the next twenty four hours, which is why we can't promise anything. It's pretty bad."

To be fair, she sounded genuinely sorry and her voice had lost some of its gruffness. I began to realise that we could, probably, be a lot worse off than we were. The house wasn't *that* cold, so I assumed we still had heat, and I'd noticed gas rings in the kitchen last night, so we could eat. And Meg wasn't going anywhere. Oh *poor* Meg! If I could keep her room cold enough there wouldn't be a problem with the body for quite a while. We just had to hope that they could get here sooner rather than later. I had lost my sarcasm and ire by the time I responded.

"I understand, Miss……?"

"Supervisor McCarthy," she replied gently.

"OK, Supervisor McCarthy, I'll make sure we keep the scene as it is."

"You called it a 'scene', Professor. That makes me think you suspect foul play, even if you say you don't. Is that the case? I really should alert the Police if you think there's something amiss, even if they can't get there." She now sounded quite concerned.

That question once again. I half-closed my eyes. If I can get to the fuzzy point where everything blurs I can recall the thing I want to visualize much better. In my mind's eye I saw Meg lying on her side in bed, I saw the flowers on the bedside table, the bedclothes……..What was it about Meg, before Jean had gathered her into her arms, that had made me sure it wasn't a natural death? I couldn't put my finger on it, yet I'd been certain at the time. If I wasn't clear in my own mind, what should I say to this girl?

Then she added the questions that changed everything.

"If you're thinking foul play….any idea of who, or how?"

Hearing the actual words, I knew immediately what had been nagging at me: if Meg had died lying on her side, as we had found her, there would have been a lividity stain on her face where it lay on her pillow – but there had been none. She hadn't died lying on her side in her bed – she'd died in a different position, maybe even in a different place, and had been moved after death. I sat down on the stairs. Hard. *Truly* speechless. She'd been moved after death. So she hadn't died in her sleep. So even if she'd found the prospect of facing everyone the next day too daunting, after her performance at dinner, and had killed herself, someone had *still* moved her body……..and who would do that – and why? Or had someone killed Meg? *Murdered* her? Shut her up before she could reveal *their* 'dirty little secret'? That would make more sense. Horrible, frightening sense. But if that *was* the case, then reason dictated that her murderer was downstairs, making breakfast: no-one could have gotten into the Lodge, and safely away again, if we'd been snowed in since the early hours. It had to be one of *us*.

"Professor Morgan – are you OK?" the young voice sounded worried.

I gathered my thoughts. I was immediately on my guard.

"I'm here – sorry, you cut out for a moment there." I had to think fast. I made my voice sound as strong as possible. If anyone was listening to me downstairs, I didn't want them to know that I was rapidly thinking through everything that had happened since I'd got onto the minibus, to work out if anyone had given themselves away as a potential killer. "We'll make sure we keep Meg's body safe," I added, avoiding her questions. "Listen - thank you, Supervisor McCarthy, for your concerns – I'm sure you must be very busy. But, please send someone, *anyone*, as soon as you can?"

"Will do. You'd um...." she was obviously trying to choose her words carefully, "...you'd all better look out for yourselves out there. I'll tell the Chief it's urgent, but maybe you'd better start making some notes or something...how about some photographs....have you got a camera?"

Of *course* I had a camera: I'd brought it intending to take happy photographs of an old friend at her birthday party, not to keep a record of her cold, limp corpse.

"Yes, you're right. I'll do that." I said as non-commitally as possible. I was resigned to some pretty unpleasant duties.

We said our goodbyes, then I was alone in the dim morning light.

I made my way down to join the others in the kitchen-diner. All eyes turned towards me as I entered the room. I looked at the group before me. What was I seeing there? Fear? Hope? Anxiety? All those emotions and more were evident – but the question was, which one of them was fearful because they had Meg's murder on their conscience? If, indeed, the murderer was possessed of a conscience at all!

"So?" Luis's question hung in the air. I swallowed hard and prepared to put on the best act of my life.

"They can't come right now, and they can't say when they *can* come – the snow's a metre deep in places and they're trying to open the roads. There's nothing any of us can do for poor Meg." I tried to sound comforting. "They've asked us to keep her body cool, and off limits. They'll be here as soon as they can be." Sadness and resignation flowed through the group.

"So it's a waiting game?" asked Peter Webber, knowing the answer.

"Sounds like it," replied Joe Goldblum.

I knew there were things I had to do, alone, so I made a suggestion..

"Look folks, I just have to pop back to my room to um...." I thought it best to imply a bathroom break rather than tell them my real plan, "…..but then, how about that breakfast? And maybe someone could light a fire? And what about the power – maybe Peter could work on that?" A general murmuring ensued, as people began to agree to undertake certain tasks.

I was relieved, and got back to my room – fast. I knew what I had to do: pull on some clothes, sneak across the landing and take photographs of my dead friend. I had to try to find any clues about how she might have died, or who might have killed her, *and* not let on to anyone that I knew she'd been murdered in the first place. Dammit!!! More than *anything*, I wanted to sit and cry: to mourn the friend I hadn't seen for nearly thirty years….but I didn't have the time. Before I could mourn Meg, I had to work out who had killed her, and that might not be easy – because, if Meg had been telling the truth the day before, then it sounded like *everyone* had a motive!

# V

It took me about half an hour to do what I needed to do: I began with photographs of everything in Meg's room, which seemed to be exactly the same as my own, except for the pattern on the comforter. The fixtures and fittings were essentially the same, as was their location.

I figured that, since she'd been moved in any case, there was no reason not to examine her body for any signs of what might have killed her. Meg was wearing a nightgown: heavy cream lace edged a deep chocolate silk-satin gown. It was good enough for a red carpet appearance! The first thing I discovered was that she'd died sitting up, leaning back, with her legs straight out in front of her – the indications of the lividity were clear: her lower back, buttocks, the back of her legs and her heels were all purplish. Maybe she'd been sitting up in bed, leaning against a pillow, that was the sort of position she'd have been in, and for at least a couple of hours after death. I'd thought about using a meat thermometer to get her body temperature, and thus allow a calculation of her time of death, but, even if I *could* have come up with a good reason for hunting about for such a thing in the kitchen, the thought of having to push it through her skin and into her liver was just too much for me! Meg had gone to her room around 10pm, and we'd found her at about 8am. That would *have* to do. I'm a criminologist, not a forensic scientist – I'm not *good* with that sort of stuff at all. In *theory*, it's fine….but in *reality* – yuk!

There were no bottles of pills, no potions or powders lying about, no suicide note, no apparent weapons….and not a mark on her body….no pin pricks that I could see, no obvious signs of her having ingested anything corrosive. The lack of patechial haemorrhaging in her eyes suggested she hadn't died from asphyxiation. I hadn't been as thorough as a medical examiner, but I thought I was doing pretty well, given the circumstances. The only 'odd' thing, other than that she was dead, was that Meg's hair was a mess – a real mess. It had been sleek the night before, now it was tangled and matted. And, in parts, damp. I checked out the bathroom: it, like the room, was pretty much the same as mine, but Meg had clearly added her own extensive collection of high-end toiletries and cosmetics. Again, there didn't seem to be anything out of the ordinary there – not if you were a multi-millionaire, in any case.

The bath was dry. The bath-mat was dry. All her towels, except for one hand towel, were dry. Odd. I wondered about that. She'd clearly removed her make-up before retiring – if she'd ever actually got to bed – and it looked like she'd brushed her teeth and applied some frighteningly expensive night cream. So, a normal preparation for a night's sleep…..then what?

All I was getting was a bunch of negatives: nothing, nothing and a big fat nothing! Nothing to signify an intention to kill herself, nothing knocked over in a possible struggle, nothing to suggest how she might have died. I realised that time was pressing on, and that my absence might arouse suspicion – especially in whoever had done this to poor Meg – so I took one last look around the bathroom and the bedroom, allowed myself a final farewell to my old friend, and left Meg's room, pulling the door closed behind me.

I tip-toed back to my room, pretty sure no-one had seen me, then decided I really *did* need some sustenance, and took myself off towards the kitchen.

As I walked in to the kitchen, so did Peter – but it was clear that he'd ventured out into the snowy wasteland beyond the front door. He looked pinched and chilled, though his cheeks were glowing.

"Any luck?" asked Adrian, who was pouring coffee.

Peter shook his head. "The generator's blown – completely. It was old in any case, and something's happened to make it blow several fuses all at once, and there's been some arcing and a burn-out. I won't be able to repair it. But there's an ancillary generator in the shed, too: it's powerful enough for the pump from the well, but that's about it. So, no power for anything else, but we'll have water, at least."

I joined in. "But, I used the loo this morning – it seemed fine," I sounded surprised, because I was.

"Mine too," added Adrian.

It seemed that the tragedy had removed some of the usual 'embarrassment' factors that accompany normal life.

"Every tank would have one flush in it," said Peter, "but without fixing up the back-up generator, that would have been it!"

"Thank goodness we've got an electrician on the premises," I commented, suspecting that we could hold out for a while with no light or heat, but that no water would have made life a complete misery. "Any idea what might have blown the main generator?"

"No idea," replied Peter, "a whole bunch of fuses went – all at once. But, frankly, we're lucky the whole place didn't burn down: it doesn't look like they know what a 'building code' *is* in this place! No GFCI's *anywhere*, old wiring *everywhere* and I swear that *both* those generators are held together with duct-tape! I just hope the little one doesn't give out."

Never very technically minded, I had to ask, "What's a GFCI?"

"One of those special outlets you get where it'll trip before you get a shock. You know, they have the little reset buttons on them?" said Peter, gratefully taking a mug of coffee from Adrian.

I understood what he meant. "Got it," I replied.

"Hey," said Adrian, sounding upbeat, "it could be worse…..we've got water, thanks to Peter here, we've lit a big fire in the Great Room, *and* there's gas for cooking – so we won't starve or freeze. I guess we can wear *all* our clothes to bed if we need to: those little fan heaters won't be much use without any power." Adrian poured another coffee from the old-fashioned pot that sat on the gas ring, and passed it to me.

"*I* haven't got a fan heater in *my* room," I said, wondering why not…..not that it would be of any use now, as Adrian had pointed out.

"There isn't one in our room, either," said Peter.

"Maybe it's just me then," observed Adrian.

"Are you guys *bringing* that coffee? Today would be great!" Joe Goldblum sounded annoyed. I suspected he always sounded that way. His accent was almost music-hall Jewish New Yorker, but with a twang of something else, somewhere in the background.

"Sorry – we kept Adrian talking," replied Peter.

"Hey, Joe, Peter's managed to sort out enough power so we have water – isn't that great?" Adrian sounded delighted.

Joe Goldblum looked underwhelmed, and shuffled back towards the Great Room, where his wife had clearly been a member of the fire-building party.

He shouted across the entry hall. "Martha – the water's back on. Go for it baby!" He cackled.

"Oh Joe – don't talk like that! It's embarrassing!" Martha Goldblum blushed, then she took herself off upstairs as fast as she could go, given her girth and age.

I wandered into the Great Room with Adrian and Peter. A series of 'Well done's' rang out for Peter, whose efforts were much appreciated by everyone, Joe Goldblum aside. Then everyone swooped down on the coffee that Adrian had brought. Luckily, flushing toilets and the advantages of a gas hob were front and centre, so no-one asked me where I'd been or what I'd been doing.

Despite the good news about the water, the mood soon became glum enough: we were all trying to avoid the one subject that was bound to be consuming our thoughts – Meg's death.

Jean Jones was not talking to anyone: she was sitting alone in an armchair, nursing a brandy bowl and staring, red-eyed, into the dancing fire. Peter nodded his head towards Jean and whispered into my ear,

"Taking it badly….poor thing. Anything we can do for her, d'you think?"

I don't know why he asked *me*, but I gave it some thought. "I don't think so, Peter: even though they were estranged, she's still lost a daughter. It's going to be tough for her."

"Do you think she's sick in any case?" he continued. "Her colour's not all that good, is it?"

I looked at Jean once more: this was the first time I'd seen her in proper daylight, and Peter was right, her colour wasn't good. She was slightly jaundiced, I thought, but maybe that was her natural skin-tone: Meg had always tanned well….maybe she'd inherited that sallow, easy tanning gene from her mother.

"You're right, but she has just had one hell of a shock, Peter. Let's give her some peace and quiet for now."

"There's no need to whisper about me behind my back," called Jean across the room in our direction. I was amazed that she'd been able to hear us – we really *had* been whispering.

"Sorry, Jean," called back Peter, "we were just wondering if there was anything we could do for you, that's all."

"Well, you can't bring her back, so no. Bloody stupid question, really Peter Webster. Typical of *you*, that is."

Poor woman – she couldn't even get his name right.

"Sorry, Jean," said Peter again, then he went to join his wife, who was calling to him from a sofa that offered a view across the undulating white valley, and the white hillside beyond.

My heart was heavy: I knew what I had to do, but I didn't want to do it. I had to try to work out, by using my training and skills, who displayed the right psychology to kill. As if she'd been reading my thoughts, Jean Jones called across the room to me, in a voice that everyone could hear.

"So, Cait, are *you* going to work out who killed Meg, then?"

Martha Goldblum had just come back into the room, so we were all present for Jean's little bombshell. You could hear the intakes of breath, waiting for my answer.

I decided to go on the offensive: I saw no other way.

"Yes, Jean – I think I should. Or maybe we can all work it out together." I had to bear in mind the fact that the killer would be unlikely to want me to uncover their identity, and I didn't want to go putting myself in danger. "Let's face it….we're all thinking the same thing, aren't we? That someone here, in this room, killed Meg. And, after yesterday, we're all wondering what it was she knew about us that might have meant that someone decided to stop her from 'telling all' in her autobiography."

"Exactly!" shouted Sally Webber. "I said that to Peter this morning. There's been nothing but funny goings-on since we got here, and I don't like it!"

'Funny goings-on' was the most inappropriate euphemism for murder I could imagine. But, then again, it *was* coming from Sally, of whom I was now beginning to always expect the unexpected.

"How did she die, Cait?' asked Sally, outright. All eyes were on me.

"It's not clear," I replied, honestly enough. "But she didn't kill herself, I can be pretty sure of that."

"Why?" Sally again.

"No note, no obvious signs of a way by which she could have done it…..and her body was moved after her death. Did anyone here do that?" I thought it best to be direct.

Heads were shaken all around the room.

"If someone had moved her, after she'd killed herself….why would they do that? And why would they keep it a secret? And why would they try to make it look like murder?"

"It could have been natural causes," suggested Dan James in his booming voice from beside the fireplace.

"Like I said – she was moved after her death - a couple of hours after her death, actually. So we're back to the same questions – why would someone do that?"

More head shaking all round.

"It makes no sense…." began Adrian Izzard.

Joe Goldblum interrupted. "Oh come off it, Adrian – that's just *dumb*. It makes perfect sense that someone might want to kill Meg: I don't know what she *thought* she had on *me*, because I can't think of a thing, but I don't know the rest of you from Adam….so who knows, it *could* have been one of you……"

"You don't know what Meg had on *you*? Now isn't that *interesting* Joe," it was Dan James again. He looked like a cat licking cream. "I think I might have an idea what it was. I'm surprised *you* don't."

"Oh, and *you're* whiter than white, are you?" snapped Martha Goldblum at the ruddy English professor, rushing to her husband's defence. "Meg and I had long, *long* chats about *you*, Dan James. So you be careful what you say about my Joe *and* my Meg. There's such a thing as libel you know!"

"It would be *slander*, actually, Martha, but thanks anyway." Joe Goldblum's comments were quiet, for him. They seemed designed to quieten his wife, rather than praise her.

"Oh Lord – listen to *that* one, will you!" piped up Jean Jones, who was now sitting on the edge of her seat. "Thought you were like a *mother* to her, didn't you, Martha? Well you *weren't* her mother, *I* was her mother. Not anyone's mother, are you……know what I mean, Martha? Meg and I might not have talked much over the years, but when we did talk, you can be sure she told me all about your 'long chats' – *all* about them. So there! Maybe *you* were the one who didn't want their secrets coming out. But there, I'll say no more on the subject."

It was clear that there was terror in the room: I wondered who'd accuse who next.

"That's enough Jean: your temper and your anger is upsetting Sally," Peter Webber's voice was quiet, yet strangely commanding. "Can't we all just be quiet….and….wait?"

"*You* should know all about keeping quiet, you're good at that – right?" Adrian Izzard surprised me with that one. His eyes were narrow, and he looked nervous, but he pushed on, nonetheless. "Meg told me about you. Does the wife know? I wonder." He left that comment hanging in the air.

Luis Lopez had been sitting quietly on the floor beside the fire while all the barbs had been slung around above his head. Then he joined in, declaiming, as usual. I found it very irritating!

"But Peter is a good man. I cannot believe you would speak against him. If anyone has kept something from his wife, and the world, it is you, Adrian. I am famous, like you once were. I have people who throw themselves at me. I know what this is like. But you, you have a *real* skeleton in your closet – like Meg said. I do not think you will have told anyone about this skeleton."

"Ha!" exclaimed Joe Goldblum. "All this talk of closets is making me thirsty – eh Luis? Come with me to make more coffee."

And the mood was broken.

But I'd made some real progress: in less than ten minutes I'd gleaned that whatever it was that Meg knew about the people in that room, she'd clearly shared the knowledge about each person with someone else. I didn't think that anyone would be lining up to share their *own* dark secret with me….but they might tell me what they knew about another person! It was worth a shot. Now all I had to do was get each person alone, and use any devices possible to get them to come clean about what they knew. It was a start. So I started.

## VI

I decided to begin with Joe Goldblum. He was heading for the kitchen, and Luis hadn't moved, despite Joe's encouragement, so I volunteered to help with the coffee, and hot-footed it after the brusque little man. It sounded like he knew something about Luis Lopez…..or was I imagining it? I had to find out.

"I'll give you hand with the coffee, Joe. I'll be glad to get out of that atmosphere for a while." I'd decided to play 'pathetic' for Joe: I couldn't imagine he'd fold for a strong woman, but he might have to put a dumb one right. "It's all a bit much for me, Joe. I mean, I know I'm a criminology professor and all that, but I don't deal with real crimes, you see…..just the textbook stuff." I was lying, of course, but he had no way of knowing that I'd been working on some *very* real crimes with the Vancouver Police Department for some months.

"I guess that's what all you academics are like – no idea about real life." He sounded bitter.

"Luis doesn't seem as bad as Jean, does he? I mean, he seems to be taking it rather well?" I thought I'd cut straight to the chase.

"Luis – ah yes, Luis. He was pretty good for Meg's profile for a while. They were only too happy to have her on all those chat shows and use the photos of the two of them together. Good for business, was Luis. All those women watching him strip off every week, then reading her books and imagining him as the love interest. Yes, he had his uses." He still sounded bitter. I wondered why.

"So, with Meg's profile being so high, and all, and her dumping you as her agent, I bet you were sorry to lose her?"

Joe Goldblum put down the coffee kettle and stared at me with his little beady black eyes. He sneered. "What the hell would *you* know about it? I've put the last four years of my life into building that woman's career – then she threw it all in my face….and all because of him! That….that….bubkis!"

Calling Luis a 'nothing' meant that Joe had little time for him, other than as a publicity prop, obviously. But I wondered *why* he thought of Luis as nothing.

"Why 'bubkis' Joe – it means, less than nothing, doesn't it?" I was playing dumb, and it seemed to be working.

"Yeah – he's worse than nothing – he's a nothing pretending to be a something. Something he's not!"

"How do you mean?" I felt I was getting close.

Joe Goldblum laughed, and it wasn't a good laugh. "You saw that the doors between them were locked this morning?"

I nodded.

"Well, she wasn't missing out on anything by locking them, that's what I mean."

Joe was not making himself very clear, but I was beginning to get an inkling of what he was alluding to.

"You mean, they didn't sleep together…..ever?"

"No point. All he'd have done *was* sleep. Meg wasn't his *type*."

"But they're engaged," I tried to sound puzzled.

"Engaged! Yeah – that was good for her last book. And I'm sure they could have kept it going for a while. You know he's been 'engaged' twice before? But never married. None of them'll go *that* far. They'll go along with it for a while, then they realise how dumb they'll look when the truth comes out. And out it'll come. You can be sure of that. There's an actual movement now that 'out's' stars….did you know that? And it was *my* job to make sure no-one outed him while he was with Meg. She'd told me she was going to finish it….but not before that little snake got her into all that psycho-babble stuff. I was the one who introduced them….so I guess I only have myself to blame. Brought it all on my own head."

So, Luis Lopez was gay. I was disappointed, yet not surprised. It was certainly something he wouldn't want made public: there was still a big difference between being a pin-up for the gay community, and being a member of it! Whilst being gay might not be the problem in Hollywood it had once been, he probably wouldn't get the roles he wanted if the truth came out. A gay man playing a straight romantic lead, or a gay man playing an action cop is not something that's seen every day. He was on the gravy train right now – the world finding out he was gay might push him off. Luis struck me as a man who liked fame: he wasn't known for ducking the paparazzi….though maybe he'd just been leading them a merry dance?

"So, do you think Luis might have killed Meg to keep his secret safe?"

"You think I know that?" asked Joe. "If I knew that then *I'd* be the professor! You're the one with all those brain cells Meg told us about. You work it out. All I'll say is that he might be earning a lot right now – but he spends it fast too. It costs a lot to keep his men-friends quiet. A lot! But not all of them want money. There was one who just couldn't take the pressure – killed himself, about five years ago, when Luis was 'engaged' to that starlet who's in all those action movies these days....you know, the one who can't seem to keep her clothes on?" I nodded, I knew who he meant.

"So Luis really *does* have a skeleton....in his *closet*?" I couldn't resist: it had to be said! The edit button that's supposed to control the links between my brain and my mouth seemed to have stopped working for a moment.

Joe Goldblum's eyes sparkled wickedly. "Yeah – you could put it like that....." then he smiled in a different way, warmly – at his wife who'd come to see if she could help us in the kitchen.

"Ach – the cavalry – good.....I'm gonna get back to the fire, I'm cold. I'm sure you two women can manage," and Joe waved as he headed back towards the Great Room.

"What can I do?" asked Martha Goldblum. She seemed relieved to have escaped the rest of the group.

"Not much – we just have to wait for the water to boil through," I said, gently. "It was such a shame that Jean was so upset that she had a go at you......but I'm sure she'll feel a bit better soon. But hey, you were a good wife to come to Joe's rescue, when Dan James started to say nasty things about him."

Martha rolled her eyes. "Professor Dan James is not a nice man, Cait, and that's the truth. Meg *did* tell me all about him – oh the things he used to get up to with those girls at the University. I found it hard to believe, I have to be honest." I wondered just *how* sheltered a life Martha Goldblum had really lived – not *that* sheltered, I reckoned. She drew closer to me – I felt a confidential conversation coming on....which was just what I wanted. "I've never told anyone this," she began, promisingly, "but when I first met Meg she was still in a real state about Dan James, and she'd left him four years earlier! She never told me much about the *other* men in her life, but that Dan had stripped her of her dignity, and that's the truth. She told me he as good as killed a man, you know." No, I didn't know, but I wanted to find out.

"No!" I whispered, conspiratorially. I wanted Martha to feel as though we were two girls, having a gossip: it seemed she liked gossip.

"*Yes!*" she replied, clearly believing that I couldn't believe it! "Not as in killing him outright, of course," she sounded a little disappointed about that, "but what he did to him definitely led to his death! It seems that the young man had written some poetry that Dan criticised very cruelly in class. It pushed the boy over the edge and he dropped out of school. He'd worshipped Dan, apparently, and he just couldn't cope with his ridicule. The poor boy ended up living on the streets, eventually took up drugs and died, penniless and alone. And all because of how Dan James treated him. It's was as good as murder. Meg said so, and she worried and worried about the poor boy who died. She'd followed up on his life and tried and tried to make Dan go to him, before he died, and apologise, but Dan said that he had to speak the truth, and that the boy's poems were rubbish. Of course, no-one at the University knew anything about it: they thought the boy just couldn't cope with the workload, and....you know....just dropped out, like they do. But Meg knew, and she never forgave Dan. She said that his pride would be his downfall."

"Do you think he might have killed Meg to stop her from telling the story to anyone else?" I sounded excited.

Martha Goldblum thought for a moment then said, insightfully, "The proud are often not brave. And I think that whoever killed Meg must have been brave........or foolhardy. You say you don't know how she was killed, so I'm assuming you've discounted a lot of the obvious methods. So what's left? I think that if you can work out how she was killed, and work out who Meg had become since you knew her, then you'll understand who would have been capable of doing it and who would have wanted to do it enough that they risked it." Martha Goldblum beamed at me with a very knowing smile. "But I'm sure you *know* all that, dear – to be sure, you're a bright girl. Now – let's get this coffee in to those people: we're both thinking that one of them must be a murderer, but they all need some coffee."

As we worked together to get the coffee from the kitchen to the Great Room I began to amend my first impressions of Martha Goldblum: I'd had her pegged as a vain and grasping woman. Even Meg had characterised her as 'being along for the ride'. But now I suspected that she was, in fact, a very astute woman, hiding her intelligence under a facade of fussing and fine fripperies. She'd been clever enough to both give me a reason why someone other than she or her husband might have wanted Meg dead, as well as implying that she had nothing to do with it. It wasn't just the coffee and extra croissants that were going to be food for thought for me, as we rejoined the group that morning, because I couldn't help wondering what Martha's secret might be.

The atmosphere amongst the group was strained, and it seemed that everyone was trying to avoid making eye contact with everyone else: some were sitting, some standing, but no-one, other than Peter and Sally Webber, were in close proximity to another person. I began to wonder if the Webbers were, in fact, joined at the hip, and could see that I'd have problems trying to get them alone – one apart from the other. But then I reasoned that Sally had never known Meg, nor Meg Sally, so it was most likely that Sally had nothing to do with Meg's death.....but then, what if Sally had been acting to protect her husband? The psychology was right – she treated him almost as a part of herself, which, for a woman who's entire world view seemed to revolve around her own needs, was quite something. If Peter was a part of *her*, she might act on his behalf to protect herself. It was worth considering. I *couldn't* discount her as a suspect.

As for the Goldblums? They'd both been quick to offer up possible killers: Luis and Dan both clearly had at least one reason each why they might not want Meg's autobiography being made public.....and maybe there were others about which the Goldblums knew nothing. I was hoping that Meg had shared her knowledge about all the other people in the room.

"Have we got any more sugar, do you know, Cait? Or butter?" Adrian was the only one in the room with a smile on his face: he was about a quarter of the size of Dan James, but, from the way he was making a meal of hot croissants slathered with butter, you'd have expected him to be as fat as the professor!

"I could look," I replied, trying to be helpful, but still feeling a tug in the pit of my stomach as my old heart-throb used my name.

"I'll come too," he replied, and the two of us headed to the kitchen. I was pretty certain that any extra butter would be in the fridge, and I headed that way, while he started opening cupboard doors, trying to find the sugar.

"So how's the 'investigation' going, Cait?" he asked quite conversationally, his head inside a cupboard, his cigarette-ravaged voice sounding more husky than it had the day before.

I didn't think there was any point in trying to deny that I was, in fact, 'investigating', so I decided to play along. "It's moving along, I guess." It was important that I didn't give anything away.

"I bet the Goldblums couldn't *wait* to tell you about what Meg had told them about other people. They seem the type."

I decided to go for it.

"I'm getting the impression that Meg shared what she knew about each person with at least one other person: that could mean that whoever the killer is they will need to kill again to stop their secret from seeing the light of day."

Adrian thought about that and said, "I get your point. That could be dangerous for whoever it is who knows the killer's secret." His voice was low, but I could catch every syllable,

"Exactly," I replied.

"And it could become dangerous for you, if the killer knows that you've been told their secret too. So why are you risking it, Cait? Why not just wait until the cops come, and let them sort it out?"

He deserved a truthful answer.

"There are nine of us here, Adrian. Now, I know *I* didn't do it..."

"And neither did I," interrupted Adrian, with a smile. "But then, I would say that, wouldn't I?" His eyes twinkled wickedly. *There* was the man who'd held my attention on screen with his suggestive poses and engaging presence. *There* he was.....and my heart skipped a beat. Izzy Izzard lived! Rock on!

I smiled back at him, delighted to be sharing such an intimate moment with the man whose image had been all around me for so many years. "Yes, you would," I agreed. "So let's assume that there are *seven* suspects left. Only one of those is guilty of murder: the other six have something in their past they'd rather forget, and which certainly hasn't come to public attention before now. Do you think it's fair that they should have to allow their secrets out to protect themselves against official suspicion? Don't you think it would be better if we could get this sorted before the police arrive? Then everyone except the murderer will be able to decide about making their secret known – or not."

Adrian nodded. "You've got a point. But I don't have any secrets: when you're as famous as I was, you don't have anything in your life that the press haven't raked over a dozen times – with photographs! Everyone who cares to check me out online can find out about *my* bad habits and dirty little not-so-secrets! My life's been an open book, whether I've wanted it that way or not."

"But not recently," I noted. "You've been out of the spotlight for years now – maybe Meg knew something from your more recent past?"

"I don't see how she could have: first of all, there's nothing *to* know; and, secondly, she'd been out of my life since before I ever hit the spotlight. I mean, we kept in touch for a while after our divorce. It was a tough time for both of us, and, although we realised we couldn't live together anymore, we weren't totally done with each other when we split: so we got together occasionally for a night here, an afternoon there. I even met her once after she'd taken up with that Dan guy. Can't see what she saw in him myself. But she seemed to like spending afternoons in their little Greenwich Village apartment writing poems to each other. And she said he looked after her, and taught her a lot about cultural stuff. You know – art, the opera, classical music. Don't get me wrong – I love all that stuff, but I don't like to be force fed it from an exclusive silver platter. I saw nothing of *that* Meg – the Meg I was married to was one of the most hell-bent party girls I'd ever known. Great fun. Always the centre of attention. We had some good times….and some not so good times too. Maybe she was ready for some namby-pamby poet. But he doesn't seem the type: I can't picture him picnicking in Central Park, reading Greek to Meg….which was what she told me they did."

I *could* picture Dan doing that: I could also picture Dan the bombast treating Meg as some sort of project. It must have massaged his ego to always be with someone who knew less than him. But Meg was a quick study - I knew that from our school days – and I had a feeling that it wouldn't have taken her long to catch up with Dan, whose 'knowledge' was, I suspected, voluminous rather than insightful.

I watched Adrian (I still couldn't help but think of him as Izzy) bend and stretch, opening cupboard after cupboard. I wondered if he knew anything about anyone else.

"So do you know someone else's secret?" I decided it was best to just flat out ask.

He turned and smiled. His green eyes sparkled. "Maybe more than I even knew that I knew," he said, enigmatically. I was hooked! Of *course*. I tried not to appear coquettish as I leaned nonchalantly against one of the big old oak counters.

"What *do* you mean, Mister Izzard?" 'Don't flirt – don't flirt – married with lots of kids….not for you….be good….' flitted through my head. I don't know why!

"There's been something puzzling me since I met the Goldblums," he said. "Have you noticed how….well, 'stock' they seem? It's like they watched a bunch of movies starring Jewish New Yorkers, and they just modelled themselves after the stereotype. Or is it that the stereotype exists *because* it's real? I don't know anyone like them, so I've got no-one 'real' to compare them with. And that woman – if I didn't know better I'd have said she was Irish."

Sometimes my right eyebrow just shoots up on my face and gives away my emotions....I must work harder to control it. Adrian obviously took my wandering eyebrow to mean that I was surprised, which I was. Though I'd had the feeling that there was something about them that was very....theatrical.

"I know," he said, responding to my eyebrow, "I might sound completely dumb....but it's been nagging at me. Some of the things she says, she sounds just like my Mom: and she was born in Cork and moved to Boston when she was ten – never lost the accent or that special way of speaking....in fact, I think it got stronger with the passing years." We both smiled. I'd visited Boston some time ago, and I knew what he meant – there was an Irish 'something' in the air there that it was hard to place, but was almost palpable. And I don't mean all the Irish Pubs!

"But I don't know them, or anything about them: they came into Meg's life long after we'd essentially lost touch. So, no, I'm not going to announce that they are really a Boston Irish couple by the name of Sullivan, who are pretending to be Jewish just so old Joe could get his foot in the door of the world of New York literary agents....though that might not be a bad idea!' he laughed.

"So Meg never told you anything about anyone?" I had to press him.

Adrian was clearly having a conversation with his conscience. I tried to help him along.

"Anything I can find out might help.....a really good reason for someone to want to kill Meg. After all, we know it's happened, and that it must be one of us....so......" I let the thoughts float across the kitchen towards him.

"Peter Webber seems like a real *nice* guy – wouldn't you say?" he began. I nodded. He continued.

"Meg loved him a great deal, you know. She'd never have divorced him, except that he gave her no choice. She'd lived what she told me was a perfect life with Peter: they worked hard, saved their money, bought a little house and he was doing real well in the movies – moving up whatever the ranks are for lighting people. Then there was an accident: he hit a little girl who was riding her bicycle on the road. He drove off. He went to work on a movie being shot in New York. He was supposed to return to Canada after the shoot, but the director liked him so he stayed on for another movie, and then another. Meg moved to New York to be with him. But she couldn't re-make the life they'd had: the dead kid was like a ghost between them, she said. They drifted apart and then got divorced. And Meg ended up alone. She was pretty much in free-fall when I met her. She was working at a bar on Staten Island where I played: we matched each other's wildness, and we clicked. Simple as that. No money, odd hours, but some great parties!"

"So that's Peter's secret, eh?" I asked.

"Yeah. Pretty crappy, I agree. He was telling me last night that he and his wife do a lot of work with young kids through their church: I guess we all compensate in our own ways – all try to make our peace somehow. Maybe we even *over*-compensate."

I wondered how Peter's standing in the community would change if he was found out to be a hit and run driver. Might he have killed Meg to keep his secret? What if Sally knew? Might she?

"But *you* have no dark secrets, Adrian – is that right?"

Once again, the globally famous eyes twinkled at me – and *just* at me.

"That's right Professor Cait Morgan.....not a one."

He produced a pack of sugar and filled the sugar bowl.

"Better get back to the others, so you can try to squeeze a secret or two out of someone else, right?" He grinned, wickedly, and I nodded. "I bet that Dan James could tell you a thing or two: if he was Meg's cultural mentor, she probably spilled her heart out to him. She was a mess when we split – we both were. She'd have been looking for someone to trust....maybe he was the one?"

We wandered back towards the Great Room. Dan James was rushing towards me, a huge coffee stain across his shirt-button-straining stomach.

"Look at the mess!' he exclaimed. "It'll never come out!"

"Have you burned yourself?" It was my first instinct.

"No, I'm fine – it wasn't *that* hot. You and Martha took so long to bring it in to us it was only lukewarm." Dan James clearly couldn't ever resist the temptation to criticise the efforts of another person. I could easily imagine him brow-beating a young student who adored him with a string of scathing criticisms of his writing efforts. I suspected that Dan James would have enjoyed every second of it, and would have used it as a great opportunity to point out to the student how stupid he was, and how much cleverer Dan was than he. I could cast him in *that* role easily enough... but as a *killer*?

"Was it black coffee?" I asked.

"Yes!" Dan James looked puzzled.

"That's good," I said. He didn't look as though it were.

"What do you mean?" he snapped.

"If you get the shirt off right away and bring it to me in the kitchen, I can get the stain out for you. That's a cotton shirt, right?" He nodded. "Right then – so, quick as you can, get the shirt down to me here – I'll get a kettle boiling."

Dan didn't seem to be used to being told what to do, so he trotted off upstairs quite meekly. Well, when I say 'trotted', what I mean is that he hauled his not inconsiderable bulk up the hefty banister, huffing and puffing as he went: I wasn't sure if he was just so out of shape that he couldn't cope with the stairs without panting, of if he was cursing at me, or the coffee, as he went. Either way he returned to me in the kitchen in about five minutes, holding the stained shirt, and wearing another – exactly the same.

"We'll need a big bowl and this boiling water," I announced as he offered me the soiled shirt. "Can you hunt about for the biggest mixing bowl in the place, please?' I thought it best to be polite, and meek, with this man......if I wanted him to tell me anything, that was.

Dan James was tall, so peering into the tops of cupboards was a much easier task for him than it had been for Adrian. I was beginning to wonder if I'd *ever* get out of the kitchen, but then I told myself that at least this way I was able to get people away from the group. The image of a lioness looking for stragglers at the back of the wildebeest herd popped into my head: Dan James didn't look much like a straggling wildebeest.....but that was how I had to think of him.

"It's terribly sad about Meg, isn't it, Dan? I'm sure you must be very upset?" He didn't *look* upset – well, OK he did....but it seemed to be more about his shirt than about Meg. He was distracted when he answered.

"What? Oh yes, a tragedy, a tragedy. A great loss to the world of popular fiction." He was still huffing and puffing.

"Not the *literary* community?" I knew that would rile him.

"Oh *no*," he looked surprised – horrified, even. "I don't think Meg would have envisaged herself as a member of *our* community. She wasn't a literary writer – just a novelist." He obviously made a huge distinction between the two. "Meg wasn't well versed in *literature*: she'd read the basics as a child and had a pretty good schooling, I *suppose*, but she wasn't up to date at all. I taught her everything she knew, such as she had the capacity to retain my education....but you have to have the *background* to be able to use knowledge. My Faculty prides itself on being able to spot and nurture raw talent – but, given that I teach at *Harvard*, we only attract those with the *right* backgrounds in the first place. Not that it works out well for every Faculty, of course. Where is it you teach again?"

"I teach at the University of Vancouver."

"Nice little place?"

I nodded, biting my tongue, and biding my time....we were still waiting for the kettle to boil on the gas hob. "Don't know it myself," he added, in a tone that spoke volumes about *him*, rather than my University.

"We manage," was all I could muster, without embarking upon a pointless diatribe: I needed to find out what it was he knew about our fellow guests, not leap to the defence of my certainly imperfect, but nonetheless wonderful, place of work.

"So do you think that Joe did a good job for Meg?" Dan had exclaimed earlier that he thought he might know what Meg had on Joe, so I thought I'd chance my arm.

"Joe? Joe Goldblum? I suppose he did. They sold a lot of books together, and I suspect he did some very good deals for her when it came to the movies. He's the type, after all."

"What do you mean – 'the type'?" I couldn't let that one pass.

"Oh you know – one of those hard-nosed, hard-hearted agent types who live for the deal and can't see the wood for the trees. His partner was almost the exact opposite: he had a real eye for good work, not just some sort of popular pulp that would rake in the dollars by catering to the lowest common denominator in society."

I was intrigued – this was the first I'd heard about Joe Goldblum having a partner. "I didn't know that Joe *had* a partner," I said.

"Yes," replied Dan James, panting as he crouched to look into one of the lower cupboards, "Weiss & Goldblum – W&G – that's the name of the agency. But Julius Weiss has been gone for a long time now. I think that's what Meg meant about Joe when she said we all had a secret: a disgruntled author came into the agency's offices one day – they'd turned down his manuscript – and he shot Julius Weiss in the back of the head. Then he took himself off and jumped off the Brooklyn Bridge. Joe was at some convention, or book fair, or something, certainly he was out of New York at the time....and after Julius's death he kept the agency name, but continued the business alone. He never took on another partner. The strange thing about it was that it was *Joe* who turned down the murderous author: Julius didn't even know about the manuscript in question – he'd never even seen it! The accepted version within literary circles was that it was *Joe* who was the author's target, not Julius at all: the author shot the wrong man.....though no-one ever knew if he'd known that or not. The author left the manuscript that had been rejected on the desk beside Julius's dead body – covered in blood apparently – and do you know what Joe did?"

I couldn't imagine, but I was looking forward to finding out. I shook my head, which I knew was all the encouragement Dan James would need.

"Joe published the work he'd originally turned down by the author who'd killed his partner....and made a fortune off it! He made *money* off his dead partner! *That's* the sort of man he is. And I know this to be the *absolute* truth because I happened to know one of the writers that Julius had represented before his death: Joe kept his involvement with the publication a secret. I don't think *that* would go down very well amongst his fellow agents, do you?"

I doubted that literary agents would have the same reaction to making a good deal for a dead author's book, that led to the murder of a business partner, in quite the same way that others might......but, then, maybe I was being unfair to agents!

"And this all happened, when?" I asked, trying to work out how Meg might have known about it.

"It was when I was still in my infancy as a writer – so, as I said, about twenty five years ago. And Joe has never looked back since."

"So Meg would have found out about this because....."

"Oh I *told* her, of course! When I found out who she'd hired as her agent I felt I had to warn her. You can't be too careful when you're dealing with that type." We were back to 'types' again: I thought about what Adrian had said earlier, and I decided to try another approach. Dan was, by now, holding his shirt over the giant mixing bowl he'd found, while I prepared to pour boiling water over it. He was, therefore, unable to 'escape'.

"Do you know anything about Joe Goldblum's background? You know, where he came from, and so on?" I began to pour the water across the stain. Dan answered me through the steam.

"Well, he's clearly from New York – that *accent*! *Oy veh!* Who could mistake it?" *Exactly*, I thought, but obviously Dan was going on face value, as I had suspected he would. "He just sort of appeared, apparently, with a pile of money and he bought his way into Julius Weiss's business: Julius was the one who started it, back in the sixties. Joe came along in the early seventies and they worked together after that. I don't know what he'd done before joining forces with Julius. Julius was highly respected: Joe has always been seen as the sharp one. A lot of newer writers avoided W&G after Julius's day: they wanted someone who could help them make great work, not just shift volume. And volume is what Joe is known for."

Dan's insights were interesting. And the stain on his shirt was gradually disappearing too, which was a bonus....for him. As we stood there, heads together over a steaming bowl of laundry I could sense that Dan had more he wanted to say. It didn't seem within his character to be backwards in coming forwards, and forwards he came – at full tilt.

"And his wife – Martha. That's another thing. There was a rumour going about that she and the partner were....you *know*...." He winked at me. I got the picture, and mouthed 'Ah', knowingly. He carried on, gossiping with glee: he was really enjoying himself – I could imagine him at Faculty cocktail parties, full of high-balls and spite. "There *was* some talk at the time of Julius's death that Joe was having Martha watched – you know, by a private detective....all *very* cloak and dagger. And the word on the literary street is that Joe found out what they were up to and that he and Julius were going to break up the business. Then Julius was shot, and all the business stayed with Joe. Quite handy for him, I'd say: I'm not sure how many of their writers would have made the choice to move with Joe. But Julius's death meant they didn't have a decision *to* make."

I wondered how far Dan would go with this train of thought – or gossip. "So was the word on the literary street that Joe had a hand in Julius's death?" I pressed. Did Joe Goldblum have a murderous heart, after all, I wondered?

Dan James looked around, for all the world as though he was afraid of being overheard, then he drew close to me and stage-whispered, "I wouldn't put it past him! It seems very convenient that he was out of town when it happened, and that it looked as though he was the intended victim – *that's* such a good way to put people off the scent, don't you think?"

I knew that that sort of plan had been tried before, sometimes to great effect, but I was still working on whether Joe's attention to detail for deal-making might have been put to use when it came to the attention to detail needed to set up the murder of his partner – and get away with it.

"Martha had a complete breakdown after Julius's death too – which just added fuel to the fire. Went away up to one of those euphemistic 'Rest

Homes', they said. For about *seven months*." Dan James emphasised the time frame and raised his eyebrows in a very unpleasant manner. I felt like I needed a wash after talking to this guy. Yuk!

"What are you two doing here? Your shirt – it is clean?" It was Luis, carrying a tray of empty coffee mugs and pots. I'd obviously missed any chance I might have had of snapping up a second croissant!

I held up the shirt so we could all inspect it. The stain was, essentially, gone – but the shirt needed to be soaked or laundered....and without any power, it was likely to be the former rather than the latter. Dan took the dripping shirt from me and wrung it dry over the kitchen sink.

"I think I'll soak this in my bathroom," he announced. "I don't want anything else being spilled on it. Thank you for your help, Cait – quite wonderful!" He dried his hands and scurried out of the kitchen towards the staircase.

"You did not want more coffee?' asked Luis, beginning to run hot water into the sink – there being no point in loading up the dishwasher.

"No, I'm fine with just the one cup, thanks," I lied. Usually I like to main-line caffeine until about 2pm, then just buzz nicely through the afternoon, coming down just in time for a restorative Bombay and tonic in the evening. But today – I'd have to manage on just the one mug....I had more important things to do.

"How about you wash, and I'll wipe?" I suggested. It seemed like a good way to get some time alone with Luis.

"That is a good idea. Jean and Martha have offered to prepare lunch when I have cleared these things away. I think that Martha is trying to keep Jean busy. Jean is not in good shape." Luis's formal English was charming: it sure was a winner with the ladies, which now seemed very ironic to me.

"How are *you* doing, Luis?" I sounded concerned. I *was* concerned. Was he a cold-blooded killer who'd just despatched his pseudo- fiancé in an attempt to prevent her from not kissing – but telling anyway? Or was he truly sorry to see someone he cared for - in a professional, if platonic, way – gone?

"I am very sad. Meg was a special person. Very understanding." He smiled a half smile and I shot back a look of commiseration. 'Very understanding' was *quite* an understatement in my book! "I do not know what I will do without her. We must make some plans to remember her properly: her fans would want that."

Luis had touched upon something that hadn't occurred to me: there'd be likely to be some sort of outpouring of public grief for Meg's death. I'd been thinking of her in relationship to just the people at the Lodge, and as my old school-friend. But Meg Jones had become so much more than that. I had visions of Luis accompanying a lily-draped casket through some grand Hollywood-style funeral. I suspected he'd play the part of the grieving fiancé with aplomb: it might even turn out to be just the thing to allow him to be able to stop visibly dating women for some time....he could portray 'devastated by the loss of my one true love' for years, if he played it well! I wondered if that thought might have pressed him to murder?

"Who would take charge of such a thing?'" I wondered aloud.

"I have asked Joe to do it. Meg and I were engaged – she and her mother were not close. It would be wrong for her mother to do it. It is my place. Joe knows the people to contact. Joe will do a very good job."

"Joe introduced you and Meg, didn't he?" I asked, sounding quite innocent.

"But yes. He knew we would be good for each other," was Luis's truthful, if misleading, answer.

"Do you know if Meg's business was in order? I mean, who will run the business now that she's gone?"

Luis nodded. "Meg has a good business manager. He will work it all out. He was against Meg firing Joe. I think Joe will once again represent Meg now."

Maybe there was *another* reason for Joe to get rid of Meg? Without her around he'd be put back in charge of her work, and start making a percentage on all the sales that were about to be made posthumously. I was surprised he wasn't already on the phone ordering extra print runs of Meg's books.....then I realised I'd been in the kitchen for so long he could probably have done all that already and I'd be none the wiser!

"Have you formally asked Joe to take the reins again?" I was now *very* curious.

"Joe had already broken the sad news to Meg's business manager, and he is the one who has asked Joe to 'take the reins' again. I have only asked him to make the funeral arrangements."

"There'll have to be an autopsy, you know, Luis. There's no way of knowing when they'll release her body. Then you'll have to get it from Canada to wherever you'll be having the service." I didn't want to sound like a know-it-all, but in this case I did, in fact, know it all.

"We have discussed this already – while you were out of the room. Joe, Jean and I have agreed that Meg's memorial service should be in New York: she spent many years there. It is a more literary place. She has been living in LA just a short time. People will fly to New York for the service, I am sure. She will be cremated here. We will transport the ashes only. Her mother will stay with the Goldblums until it is all over."

It seemed like I'd missed quite a lot! But, then, I'd learned a lot too. And I still wondered what I could learn from Luis. He might have been Meg's 'fiancé', but I was beginning to wonder how close their relationship had been: were they just social acquaintances, with a fake public facade, or had they been real friends?

"You've lost your best friend, I'm sure," I was acting innocent again, and, by now, I was wiping mugs and stacking them on the big draining board to air dry properly.

Luis stopped washing and looked me straight in the eye. "She was a *true* friend, you are right. I will miss our talks....our closeness. I will miss her warmth." I guessed he was speaking figuratively, not literally.

"You don't have any suspicions about who might have done it....do you?" I whispered.

"I can only think it is that Adrian," he spat out, hatefully. "He is a man with blood on his hands already, Meg told me. And I could see last night that he was afraid that Meg might tell about the dead woman and the dead baby in his past. He was frightened. I saw that."

"What dead woman? What dead baby?" I was shocked. Adrian Izzard had a dark secret after all. I was disappointed in him.

"The dead woman? A girl, young, found dead after one of his concerts in his dressing room. He was on drugs. He said he didn't know what had happened. He was *very* famous then, *very* rich, he made her disappear."

Now I was puzzled. What on earth did Luis mean? This slightly stilted use of English could obscure, as well as charm.

"How do you mean – 'disappear'?" I asked.

"I don't know – Meg did not tell me everything. What I know is that the police never knew about her being in Adrian's dressing room. That her body was found by the police *outside* the concert stadium, after the band had gone. Adrian told Meg afterwards – that is how she knew. When they were married she was his inspiration. His famous song 'The Muse You Are' *was* Meg. He wrote that when she left him. It was his first big hit. She left him because of the dead baby."

"Dead baby?"

"Yes, stillborn. His drugs, she said. Then she could not have babies any more. He killed their baby."

Wow! When Adrian had made that comment about people over-compensating to make amends for their past, he might well have been talking about Peter Webber working with kids, having killed one in a hit and run....but he could have been talking about himself! If his drug use had somehow managed to cause the death of the unborn baby that he and Meg were expecting, then having seven children with his current wife could equally deserve the term 'over-compensating'! I mean, everyone knew that Jovita Izzard was her generation's equivalent of Yoko Ono – always portrayed as robbing the music world of a unique talent by stealing Izzy Izzard away for herself. But what if it came out that Izzy/Adrian had no recollection of how a young girl had met her death in her dressing room....what if Jovita herself didn't know about the stillborn child that he and Meg had lost? Could keeping those two facts a secret have driven 'my life's an open book' Adrian to kill his ex-wife? I didn't want to believe it. I couldn't believe it: for all his bad-boy image at the height of his popularity, Adrian seemed to be a genuine, warm person...his body language spoke of openness and acceptance of others. *Could* he have killed Meg? I knew, only too well from my experiences, that *anyone* is capable of murder....given the right motive and an opportunity. Could these two deaths in Adrian's past be the motive he needed to act?

By now Luis and I had cleared all of the dirty dishes, and I wanted to be sure there was nothing else he might be able to tell me before our chance to be alone disappeared.

"I'm very sorry for your loss, Luis. But I don't think that Adrian's the type to have killed Meg."

"Type? What do you know about his type? Rich, famous people do not live like other people. They have their own rules. Adrian is not as well off as people think. If he sold no more music, his family would suffer. We all know he has a very large family. The security at their mansion in Seville is very expensive – it says so in all the papers." It rather amused me to think that Luis Lopez read the same sorts of magazines that I did. I wondered if he believed his own publicity? If he really understood what he could lose if the public turned against him? I suspected that Luis was astute enough for the answer to both questions to be 'yes'.

As I hung up the tea towel to dry, I realised that everyone I had managed to get alone so far had presented me with at least one good reason for another guest wanting to kill Meg, and stop her autobiography from ruining their life. The only people I didn't have anything on were Jean and Sally.

And then I had to admit that, despite Sally not knowing Meg, she was married to Peter – and that she might stop at nothing to protect her own world by protecting her husband.

So there was only Jean. No-one knew anything bad about Jean. I told myself that it was unusual for a parent to kill their own child – *very* unusual – so the chances that Jean had killed Meg were slim. But I felt I had to push on and get a proper understanding of the situation. I wondered who had the dirt on Meg's grieving mother?

# VII

I *finally* managed to get back to the Great Room. It was warm, and the fire was dancing merrily in the hearth. The mood in the room seemed to be more relaxed than when I had left it....which was about two hours earlier! I needed a sit down, and, for some reason, I fancied a Bombay and tonic: the dimness of the room, the firelight, the way that people were just hanging about, almost languidly....it made me feel quite 'festive'. I know that sounds a bit odd, but it felt like the holidays....as though we should all be gathered around a big old Christmas tree singing carols....not fretting about when the police would arrive, and which one amongst us was a murderer.

"How's the sleuthing going?" It was Adrian, at my elbow, and with a warm smile on his face.

I couldn't have looked happy, because I know that right at that moment I wasn't *feeling* happy and I was making no effort to conceal the fact.

"You've had your nose to the grindstone out in that kitchen, Cait....how about a drink," he continued cheerily.

I know my face lit up. I'm easily pleased.

"I could *kill* for a Bombay and tonic," I said. There was another one of those silences as I spoke – it seems I can actually *create* them to order! I couldn't take back my ridiculously inappropriate words, so I just added, "Sorry – you know what I mean," and hoped everyone did. Frankly, given what I'd discovered to date about the nature of the people in the room with me, I was beginning to care less and less what they thought of me. Frankly, *none* of them had any right to judge anyone, about anything!

"Oh, poor Cait," said Adrian. "Stay there – I'll get you one. Heavy on the gin?" I nodded eagerly.

"Anyone else?' called Adrian to the room.

"I wouldn't mind a glass of sherry," replied Dan James, somewhat predictably. "It's not as though any of us will be driving today, what?" Honestly, the way he tried to make himself *sound* English, when all he did was *teach* it, was laughable.

"*I'll* have another brandy," said Jean Jones. All eyes turned in her direction. Sally Webber looked horrified, and Jean noticed her stares. "There's no use looking at me like *that*, young woman," she chided Sally, "I want a medicinal brandy, and I'll have one, thank *you* very much." That seemed to be an end to the matter.

"You're right, Jean, brandy *is* medicinal," agreed Martha Goldblum. "Maybe a small one for me too please Adrian?" Adrian nodded.

"So – a Bombay and tonic, two brandies and a sherry. Anyone else?"

"How do we know you did not poison Meg? And now you will poison us all!" Luis Lopez's voice rang out across the room from the book-corner where he was sitting.

There was what could only be called an 'awkward' silence: for once, I wasn't saying anything when it happened, which made a pleasant change. I wondered how many people were thinking that what Luis had said might be true.

"That's *great*, coming from you!" snapped Adrian. "Here I am, trying to be helpful and lighten things up a bit – and all you and *him* can do," he gesticulated towards Joe Goldblum, "is put your heads together in corners and phone everyone in the world who can help you both cash in on Meg's death! Besides – if Meg had been poisoned, and if there was any reason for it to have been *me*, then Detective Cait wouldn't have been first to ask me to get her a drink – *would* she?"

All eyes now looked at me. I felt myself blush.

"We *all* know what she's up to," continued Adrian, "she's been pumping us for what we know about our fellow guests. You've just about covered all the ground now, right Cait? I've been keeping an eye on you: you've had everyone on their own out in that kitchen.....except Jean and Peter - and Sally, of course. I'm sure you'll get around to them soon....but don't think you've got to hide it from the rest of us: we all know what you're up to. But, like I said, you'd better be careful Cait – if the killer thinks you know their secret, you could be next."

Talk about 'next'! Adrian Izzard would have been 'next' if I'd had my way! If I'd had a knife in my hand I'd have stuck it in him, right there and then! Why on *earth* did he insist upon being so *melodramatic*! I wasn't in any danger! We were all sitting in one room – together: what could happen? Things only 'happen' when groups split up....when two people decide to go to the cellar, or the attic, for no apparent reason....*that's* when things 'happen'! And I wasn't planning on leaving the group *at all*. Then I realised that, at some point, I'd have to go to bed, and that then I'd be alone....and I didn't like that thought. So I stopped thinking about it.

"Maybe Luis is right – but maybe all I'll do is to poison *your* drink, Cait." Adrian was being wicked.

"But there's a flaw in your plan, Adrian," I said. I had everyone's attention again....the group looked like the spectators at a tennis match, their heads bobbing this way and that.

"Go on then – what is it?" Adrian asked, his eyes twinkling. Deliciously.

"You might get rid of *me* because you think *I* know your secret," I said thoughtfully, "but you wouldn't know who'd *told* me....so there'd still be someone, in this room, who'd know. But you wouldn't know *which* one to kill, along with me, to make sure that your secret died with us."

"OK then," rebutted Adrian, quick as a flash ('not just rakishly handsome, and wicked, but clever too', I thought to myself in the same flash) "like Luis said, I'd just kill you all! I'd poison *all* the drinks. How's that?"

"Don't you think it would look a bit suspicious if the police arrived to find you the only survivor of a mass poisoning?" asked Martha Goldblum.

"I guess," acknowledged Adrian. "OK then – I'll let you all live....and I'll face up to *whatever* it is that someone knows about me.....though, frankly, it can't be *much* of a secret."

"You should not be too sure!" called Luis from his comfy armchair – then he looked frightened at what he'd done.

"Oh dear – I think that *someone's* just given himself away!" All eyes turned towards Luis – I was glad to no longer be the centre of attention. Luis looked terrified. Luckily he wasn't sitting directly beneath any of the stuffed animal heads, because the similarities might have been too funny....given the circumstances.

"I do not know what you mean!' Luis rallied.

"Oh, I think you *do*, Luis." Adrian's voice had changed: it had lost its levity. "Meg told you something about *me*, didn't she? Something that maybe only she and I knew about? Did she tell you about the baby we lost? Was that it? The world-famous 'breeder', Izzy Izzard, with a stillborn baby in his background? It *might* be a secret, but that's because it was the way *Meg* wanted it. Only two or three people even knew she was pregnant, she was so small. And the bigger part of the so called 'secret' is probably that Meg blamed *me* for the baby's death. It's what broke us apart. Our relationship couldn't cope with the loss, the fact that Meg would never be able to conceive again, due to the complications of the still birth.....and all the recriminations that followed. She said *I* was to blame: I told her that continuing to drink like a fish and smoke like a train while she was carrying our child was like signing its death warrant. She never forgave me."

It looked like Adrian wasn't going to say anything about the young girl found dead in his dressing room. Interesting.

There was a series of little gasps around the room.

"Oh, that's so sad!" exclaimed Sally Webber.

"She never told *me* she'd been pregnant," said Jean Jones, quite annoyed.

"Me neither," said Martha Goldblum, sounding equally miffed.

"Well you're not her *mother*.... no matter how much you might like to *act* like you are," said Jean Jones tartly. "*You're* not part of our family: and if me saying I'll come and stay with you two in New York until the Service is over is giving you any ideas, then I'll stay in a hotel!"

Martha Goldblum's expression showed that she knew she'd been put in her place – but that she didn't necessarily like where that place was! Jean Jones looked angry.

"Mother your *own* kid," Jean snapped at Martha. "Oh, *no*, I *forgot*....you can't...........'cos you *gave it away*. Well boo-hoo for *you*. *Your* bed, lie in it!"

Martha and Joe Goldblum both nearly fainted. So there *was* a child! Meg must have told her mother during one of their very few mother/daughter chats.

"I'd always *heard* there was a child," it was Dan James, speaking excitedly from his prime position - leaning against the fireplace. Dan obviously decided it was in for a penny, in for a pound.....though maybe now that I was a good Canadian it should have been 'in for a cent, in for a kilo', which I didn't think had quite the same ring to it. In any case, he forged ahead. "One hears so *much* on the literary grapevine of course," he swaggered, "but a good deal of it is complete *tosh*, of course! Was it Joe's, or was it Julius's? I mean – *everyone* knew that Martha's 'breakdown' came after your partner Julius had been killed – he took a bullet meant for *you*, didn't he Joe? I wonder what *else* of yours he took! So do tell Martha – who was the father? I *have* to know!"

With Martha and Joe still reeling from Jean's comments, I wondered how they'd react to Dan's. There were many puzzled faces around me, most people not knowing who 'Julius' was, but I suspected that they were working hard to put two and two together. Some of them would probably come up with five, some three....maybe some would even make four.

"I won't *stand* for this sort of talk!' said Joe. His voice was high, and full of emotion.

"*Whoever's* it was, she couldn't get rid of it 'cos it would have been a 'mortal sin' – that's what Meg said. That's what Meg told her *mother*," crowed Jean.

"That doesn't sound very *kosher*, Martha," observed Adrian, wryly, "and you should believe someone who's married to one of the world's most infamously staunch Roman Catholics, when they tell you they know the meaning of the phrase 'mortal sin'!"

"Oh my God, Joe....what's to become of us?" cried Martha Goldblum. She was beginning to unravel. I've seen it before, and once they start, sometimes you just can't stop them. "If *she* knows," she nodded towards Jean, "and *she* knows," she nodded at me, "and *him*, and him," she nodded towards Dan and Adrian, "then soon *everyone* will know! We'll not have any friends at all Joe – no-one will speak to us! Oh, Joe....I can't go on, I can't....it's all too much for me, help me.....please help me!" Martha was wailing, and weeping. Tears were streaming down her face.

"Now look what you've done – you unfeeling bastards!" Joe Goldblum was incandescent. "Think you're so Goddam *clever*, don't you Dan? You swan around as though you're some sort of literary genius, eh? Well you're *not*. Meg told me about all those poems you wrote........*together*! The ones *you* published without giving *her* any credit. She told me what you said to her when she asked you why her name wasn't on them. Telling her she was just an unschooled barmaid, that she had no place having her name on them with your name was just about the worst thing you could have done to her, Dan. If she *hadn't* waited tables, *and* worked in a bar, you'd never have been able to sit around in Greenwich Village on your fat arse all day, playing about with the words *she'd* written and shoving the odd bit of Greek in amongst *her* thoughts to tart it all up........just so it would pass some phoney 'literary litmus test'! You're a *fake*, Dan James......and if they find out about it at Harvard I don't care how water-tight that Tenure Contract is....I bet they could break it, and you'd be *out*. Fraud is fraud, that's that!"

I was annoyed that my powers of persuasion hadn't wheedled this little nugget out of Joe when I'd had him on his own. I wondered if anyone else had held back anything. I was beginning to suspect that they might have done.

Now it was Dan's turn to start to glow with anger: it suited him better than it had suited Joe – Dan had the right colouring and shape for it. There was a very *real* possibility that he might explode....he was so close to it already, his shirt buttons straining.

"Look to your wife, man," replied Dan James, trying to deflect the barbs thrown at him, "can't you see she's distressed?"

"Distressed?" replied Martha Goldblum, obviously feeling she was now more capable of sticking up for herself. "I'm not *half* as distressed as I will be if this all comes out at Synagogue! Oh Joe......what if they find out *there* that we're a couple of Romans from the first ever housing projects built in South Boston? What'll our lives be like then, Joe? Oh – I can't go on.....I *can't*. You've got to stop them from *telling* anyone." Having spoken her piece, Martha Goldblum dissolved into tears again. Her husband looked at her sympathetically, but didn't move to comfort her physically at all, which I found interesting.

"Dan – and the rest of you....listen up!" Joe's tone had changed: he was about to try to take control, I could see it in every move he made, in every glint of his eyes. "There's a deal to be done here, people. If *our* secret is out, and if it's the *only* one, or one of only a few, then someone.....anyone here......could hold that over us. *I* say that *everyone* should share their secret with the whole group. That way, no one person has the upper hand. Right now some of us are exposed, some aren't. Let's level the playing field. Right Adrian? Right Dan? And what about you, Luis? You know that I know all about *you*.......I don't want to hold that over your head.....are *you* in?"

I couldn't fault Joe Goldblum's logic: nor could I fault him for, inadvertently, assuring my own safety....*that* point was not lost on me at all: if everyone knew everybody else's secrets, then there'd be no point in the murderer targeting *me*! And I felt better knowing that.

"*I'm* in," I said, as brightly as one cup of coffee, no gin and tonic and a growing suspicion that everyone around me was so hateful that they might have *all* have had a go at killing Meg would let me be! My inner being called 'Save Yourself' to me.....and she's usually worth listening to.

"My secret........" I continued, immediately drawing everyone's attention, "is that I didn't, and I emphasize *didn't*, kill my boyfriend, Angus, who I found dead on the bathroom floor one morning about eight years ago. I emphasize *didn't* because the photographs of me being led to a police car which were splattered across the morning newspapers, and the internet, have led quite a number of people to quote the old adage 'no smoke without fire' to my face, *despite* the fact that I was completely exonerated. Of *course* the police hauled me in – why wouldn't they? As a professor of criminology I am only too well aware that most murders are committed by a spouse or partner, ex-spouse, family member or someone they are close to."

I knew that my professional observation would touch everyone in the room: they all fell into one of the categories that I'd just mentioned when it came to their relationship to Meg. I gave my comment a moment to sink in: like they say, or, presumably *used* to say, in vaudeville......'timing is everything, folks'.

Suspicious glances were cast about the room like so many yellow flags at a CFL game. And I was the referee. Maybe I should have worn my back and white striped sweater that day, but I hadn't been planning on overseeing the Grey Cup Final of murder. Or maybe I had?

By the time these thoughts had floated across my tired little brain, enough of two seconds had passed to make me think it was time for me to speak again.

"I thought that, with a few secrets out already, if I added in mine, then it would get the ball rolling. My secret, here in my new life in Canada, not back in the UK, where *everyone* seemed to know about it, is that I was held on suspicion of murder. But, no, I didn't kill Meg. To be honest, I have no idea how Meg *was* killed. I can't think *how* anyone did it. Whoever killed Meg was very clever." As I spoke my last sentence I tried to make sure I cast my eyes over everyone in the room: would anyone give themselves away by looking smug?

"*I* have something to say about how Meg might have died," interrupted Peter Webber. All eyes turned from me to him. "I've been thinking about the power panel, and I reckon somebody *did* something that involved the electricity last night, and *that's* why we blew a bunch of fuses all at once. It might not have been anything to do with Meg....but, just like you've been trying to find out our secrets, Cait, so I've been asking everyone about their power usage last night after dinner. People all did the usual stuff, in fact everyone did just about the same stuff. The only *possible* overload condition was when both Adrian and Jean both had their little room fan-heaters turned on at the same time. They drink power!"

"We haven't got a heater in *our* room," Sally Webber sounded a bit annoyed.

"No, dear, I know," replied Peter to his wife, patiently. "I think that Adrian and Jean have them in *their* rooms because they both have a room that *only* has an aspect to the north, everyone else's room has at least one aspect to the west or east. The rooms facing north only would never get as much light or sun as all the other rooms. That's probably why those rooms have the extra heater. But," he returned his attention to the room in general, "as I said, it seems that we were all able to use as much power as we liked throughout the evening. It seems like Martha was the last one to use the power last night, and to find that it was still working just fine.....unless *you* used anything and it worked after 4am, Cait?" I shook my head – I'd been sound asleep by then.

But it wasn't lost on me that *if* electricity had somehow been involved in Meg's murder, then Peter Webber had just narrowed the time of death to somewhere between 4am and about 7am, or Meg's body wouldn't have been cool to the touch. Everything he'd said had been most helpful.

"So there you are then," continued Peter Webber, "no-one's told me about *anything* that could have caused what I saw in the shed. So I have to assume.......that someone's *lying*."

"Hey! Who knew – we have *two* sleuths in our midst! Way to go Peter!" It was Adrian. He started a round of applause. No-one joined in.

"Well, *that's* not the secret Meg told me about you!" Jean Jones was looking right at me. I could feel my eyebrows rise. Both of them. I thought we'd got past *me* being the centre of attention.

"What do you mean, Jean?" asked Adrian. Maybe *he* was sleuth number three.

"Cait said that *her* secret was about that boyfriend of hers being found dead. That's *not* what Meg told *me*! *She* told me you cheated at school. *That's* what Meg told me. All the time. She said it wasn't fair, but that you always got away with it."

I was flummoxed....which is not something I get the chance to be very often – who does? Frankly – who *wants* to be?

"I don't know what you mean, Jean – nor what Meg meant. I never, *ever* cheated – at school or anywhere else for that matter – not in my whole life! Never!" I was trying to make sure I was being clear. I also sounded hurt, because I *was* hurt.

"You *used* that photographic memory of yours – but you never told anyone you had it. There – *that's* cheating!" Jean's harsh tones were now benefitting from a liberal dose of venom. But at least now I knew what she meant.

"Ah.....I *get* it," I said, light dawning. "Well, OK – yes, I *do* have a photographic memory. Not that such a thing actually exists, but I won't go into the technicalities right now.......suffice to say I do have an unusual ability to recall things I have experienced, especially things I have seen and heard, in a very detailed way, at any time, at will. When I was in school I didn't even know I had it: I honestly thought that everyone was just like me, and I couldn't understand why people just couldn't seem to remember things the way I did. When Meg and I studied together I would recite whole chunks from lessons we'd had weeks earlier. Bless her, she told me I was weird more times than I care to remember. And, to be fair, it was Meg who brought me a book about memory one day that helped me to understand how I was different, and how to begin to train my gift. By the time we hit the Lower Sixth I was even better at using it – and I used it to help both Meg and myself. But that's not *cheating* – that's just *me!* I can't *not* remember things. To be honest, sometimes it's a curse: imagine walking around with all the experiences you've ever had right there in living colour, in your head. In fact, Meg's initial research on my behalf was to find out how to help me *forget*, not remember. Believe me – a person doesn't *want* to remember everything."

It was clear that the people in the room thought that my 'revelations' weren't terribly interesting – or even particularly revelatory. Dan, whose beady little eyes had lit up when I'd said I'd join in, looked especially disappointed.

"Well, it *sounds* like cheating to me," concluded Jean. Frankly, I didn't give even *one* hoot, let alone two, how Jean felt – but it *did* hurt that Meg had mentioned my 'gift' to her mother in such a way. Despite her closeness to me, and her seeming to understand about my memory, had Meg *really* thought that to use it was to cheat? Was that why she'd been trying to help me to *forget?* Meg had always been good at all the creative things at school, like writing essays, and poems, and doing art: I'd been good at all the 'remembering' things. Being gifted creatively and using it to create isn't cheating – why should me using *my* gift be characterised that way? I was still stewing on this when I realised that Adrian was speaking again.

"Well, thanks for those insights, Jean," he was sounding bored, "but how about *you* Peter? How about you stop your electrical sleuthing for a moment and do something really useful, and fess up about *your* past problems? I'll tell you now – *I'm the one Meg confided in about you* – so if *you* don't tell them all, then *I* will...." Adrian's twinkling eyes looked more malevolent than I'd seen them before. "Or doesn't even the little woman know?" he added, pointedly.

"Oh Peter!" Sally Webber choked back tears, and held her husband's arm close to her little body.

"I'm sorry Sally darling," Peter Webber held his wife close, hugging her to himself. He was looking deep into her eyes as he spoke. It was quite touching. "I hate to say it, but Joe's right. It's a good idea if we all tell everything. Then no-one's on their own. None of us will tell, because we all have something to lose. *I* might as well do it. I think Adrian *would* tell them if I don't....and I'd rather them know the *real* story."

Peter turned his attention from his wife to the group. He cleared his throat, as if for a public speaking engagement. "I'm not *proud* of what I did, and I've tried hard to make up for it ever since. But there's no *question* it was wrong. But I have confessed it directly to my Lord, and I am Saved. So it doesn't matter what you *think* of me. But it *does* matter that no-one finds out, because I could be deported from the US to Canada, and probably put in jail for a long time."

"But we're *in* Canada now!" called Jean, "I don't understand what you mean. Will they put you in jail just because you came here for this weekend? Why would you come if they would?"

I supposed they were fair questions – for Jean.

"The Canadian Authorities aren't looking for me. They don't know, or care, who I am. They never found out *who* hit that poor little girl on her bicycle, in the middle of the road, at night. So they don't know it was *me*. I'd only had one beer – I hadn't drunk more than that. But I panicked, and drove off. I wanted to give myself up – but Meg wouldn't *let* me. We were trying to get pregnant. We were so happy! She didn't want it all to change. So I *didn't* go to the police. I sat and watched the parents cry their faces raw on TV. I noted how the story moved from the newspaper's front page, to its inside pages, and then I saw how it disappeared altogether. True, this is the first time I've come to Canada since I left in 1983, but I don't think it'll be a problem. Even if they *knew* it was me....*they'd* be looking for Peter Webster, born January 9th 1960, not Peter Webber, born September 1st 1960. I managed to fiddle around with a few bits of paperwork so that I got my Green Card as a slightly different person and I became a US Citizen as that 'new' person. I've been Webber for so long now, that Webster doesn't usually bring a response from me at all.....though it was tough to start with. Not as tough as it must have been for those parents, losing their little girl, of course. My Lord has forgiven me, now I must try to forgive myself and make amends. That, I believe, is the only secret I have. And now you all know. My fate lies with the people in this room."

Peter Webber had spoken eloquently. I couldn't have been the only one in the room thinking that his secret was one that none of us would have wanted. But, to my mind, one of the things that struck me about Peter's story, was that, once again, it was *Meg's* doing that the matter hadn't come out at the time. Interesting.

"I love you Peter," said Sally Webber, looking at her husband with eyes that radiated joy. "We are *all* Sinners. The Lord *forgives* us all. He sent his only Son to Save us. I am *proud* of you, my darling." She kissed her husband on the cheek. Peter smiled at her, and she at him.

I thought I might throw up.

"Good for you, Peter," called Adrian across the room. "The version varies a little from the one Meg told me – but then I'm guessing that'll be the case for all the things she told us about others. Maybe it's good that we all get a chance to put our side of the stories out there. Meg *did* have a talent for making it seem like nothing was ever *her* fault, didn't she? So.....who's next?"

I admired the way that Adrian was managing the situation – though I did rather wish he'd get back to the idea of bringing me a drink.

"What about you, Dan? An outsider might think that the Goldblums - if that *is* their name....," Adrian raised an eyebrow towards the Goldblums, "....have got it in for you Dan. Joe's accused you of fraud and Martha was hinting at something else this morning. What about it Dan? Are you man enough to confess?"

Dan James seemed to be shrinking as I looked at him. The bombast was deflating, to be replaced by a person with a much smaller ego. The phrase 'taken down a peg or two' wriggled into my conscious mind, and stayed there.

"I can understand why Meg thought she had a hand in creating my best-known works," began Dan James, (*I* was thinking that they were his *only* known works, but that's probably quite bitchy on my part!) ".....and she *did*, in a way. She was a good writer, an intuitive one. But she wasn't a *poet*. We'd sit and talk about themes I was thinking about exploring, and she'd tell me her thoughts, and jot down little notes about a topic: it was like a parlour game for us. But she didn't construct the works – I swear she didn't even understand most of the layers beneath their surface. They *weren't* her work – they *were* mine. But I *never* told her she was an unschooled barmaid, Joe: I would *never* have said that. I *loved* Meg. She'd been on her own for a couple of years since you guys had split up," Dan nodded towards Adrian. "She didn't mention a child to *me*. The first I heard about that was today – which is an odd discovery to make about one's ex-wife....about whom one thought one knew everything. I thought we'd never conceived because we were being careful: we'd both agreed that children weren't for us. She said she was on the Pill. Odd. She was fun, she inspired me, she helped me in so many ways, in little ways.....and I hadn't grown to despise her....not when my poems were published. *That* came later." Dan James was a good speaker. Maybe his lectures would be more interesting than I'd thought they would be. He was holding our attention, and using very sympathetic body language....seemingly unforced.

He looked at Joe Goldblum, his face a picture of reason: he either really meant what he was about to say, or else he was a very good actor. "You're right, Joe, we didn't have much money, and Meg held down whatever job she could, for as long as they'd keep her on. But *that* was the problem: she went through job after job after job. She got fired from them all! Something would go wrong with every place: she'd mess up the cash register once too often; too many customers would complain that she'd brought them the wrong thing; she'd turn up at 1pm for a shift that should have started at 10am, and argue the toss when the roster was right there on the wall! There was always *something*. So, yes, Joe, she *did* get through a lot of jobs, and she *did* work all the worst hours....because she was never anywhere long enough to develop the sort of seniority that allows you to pick the better shifts!" It seemed that the process of recollection was painful for Dan James.

"I worked *too*," he added plaintively, "I wrote articles for PR agencies: pieces of fluff for filthy lucre....but not under my own name, of course! I didn't want the literati to think I'd ever prostituted my talents. But I had no choice. And then I managed to get my poems published, and everything changed. I was the toast of the town – and when 'the town' is New York – well, one might as well be the toast of the *World*! I was overwhelmed by the response. *Truly* overwhelmed. I seemed to offer just what everyone who mattered wanted – at the very moment that they realised they wanted it: it changed my life. It changed *our* lives. But Meg just couldn't *cope*. She didn't like the people I was invited to mix with: she felt she didn't fit in. She still worked because, although the book was well received, it was never going to make me any real money. So, often, I *would* be out 'swanning about' as an outsider might see it, whilst Meg was pulling the late shift at a bar or a diner somewhere. The offer from Harvard was a Godsend. It offered a good, steady income. They wanted me so badly that I was able to negotiate a very good tenure deal, and there was accommodation thrown in. And Meg loved the idea....."

"Hmmm!" grunted Martha Goldblum. She looked as though she didn't believe Dan, and he noticed right away.

"I tell you, Martha, she *loved* the idea! She knew she wouldn't have to do any dreadful jobs anymore, and she said that we could have a real life in a beautiful setting, and that she was looking forward to being a supportive housewife. When we moved there she bought recipe book after recipe book: she threw herself into the life of the campus – for about six months. Then it was as though a light went out in her. I never *knew* what happened, though I had my suspicions. I swear I hadn't done anything to hurt her, or harm her in any way. She just *changed*. I couldn't *reach* her any more. It was the beginning of June 2000, I'll never forget it. It seemed as though, overnight, she turned into a complete bitch! There's no other word for it: nothing I did, or could do, was right; anything I said was deemed a criticism; I was either hanging around the house too much, or never home. I couldn't win! And I didn't *know* why. And I didn't have the courage to face her with my suspicions. Then, in December, just a few weeks before Christmas, she wasn't there anymore. Not a note, not a word – I came home from a lecture and she was gone! Some of her clothes were gone – things that made me, and our friends, think that she'd planned to go. Our friends said she'd probably come back one day – just walk right in as though nothing had happened. And I hoped she would.....for months. Then I got served with divorce papers by a lawyer from Boston: and that was that. No goodbye – nothing. She got back in touch when she rolled into New York four years later and hooked up with you, Martha. But for those four years, when she was on her famous 'road-trip', I didn't hear a word – only from her lawyers."

"Well that's all very *sad*, Dan," said Martha, picking up on the fact that we were all veering towards Dan's picture of himself as the slighted husband, "but what about that poor boy who killed himself because of what you said about his work? What about *that*? That's a bit more of a juicy one, don't you think? How would they take *that* in the Ivy League?"

"I don't know what you mean, Martha," replied Dan, sounding genuinely puzzled. "There was no-one who killed himself because of my critiques. What rubbish was Meg feeding you, exactly?"

I, too, was beginning to wonder about the extent to which Meg had seen the world through a somewhat distorted lens.

"Oh don't be *coy* now, Dan," mocked Martha Goldblum. "A boy – whose name I either never knew, or cannot remember – he was in your class; he looked up to you, worshipped you in fact; you ripped through his creative efforts, and he dropped out; he ended up living on the streets and eventually died of a drug overdose. Maybe it was *that* that turned Meg against you? Didn't *that* happen around the May or June of 2000, towards the end of the school year? That's what Meg told *me*! That was the secret she told me – that your heartless actions led to the death of a poor young man. Cut down by helplessness and depression, because you undermined him completely!" Martha had spoken with emotion – she, too, knew how to hold a room.

Eyes turned from Martha to Dan: we all wanted an answer, and he seemed willing to supply one. It surprised most of the people in the room.

"I think you're talking about an upperclassman called Robert. It must be him. When I said that I didn't *know* why Meg changed, but that I had my suspicions – well, I suspected that *Robert* was the reason she changed, but not in the way you mean it, Martha. I suspected that Meg was having an affair with Robert. It wasn't Meg who made me think that, but Robert. He wasn't a pleasant young man: in fact, he was quite wicked....but not in a playful way. It was a part of my responsibility, of course, to review, critique and grade work submitted by my students: Robert would put something into each of his submissions that *hinted* that I was being cuckolded, or that he was familiar with my bedroom, or with parts of Meg's body that wouldn't normally be on public display. He toyed with me throughout the whole course. But he didn't 'drop out' because of me, Martha: he'd been encouraged by the Resident Dean to seek counselling about his drinking and his drug use: he was quite well known to the Cambridge Police, and there were a number of complaints made against him at his Hall of Residence. No-one was surprised that he didn't return: I got the impression that he'd dumped Meg before he'd left at the end of the year. But she tried to track him down: I found out because she used a private investigator, and paid him with our credit card. She lied about why she'd hired him, but I guessed. I understand that Robert did, indeed, succumb to his hedonistic ways. Though it had nothing to do with me."

There was a stillness in the room: the stillness that comes from no-one knowing quite *what* to say next. So I thought *I'd* better say something. Sometimes, I think that the sound of silence is highly over-rated.

"Every one of us is explaining our 'dirty little secret' so reasonably, aren't we?" I knew I sounded sarcastic – I meant to. "So who's next to paint themselves as having been hard done by by Meg?"

From his corner vantage point, Luis Lopez stood and declaimed to the room, "I am a homosexual. It is nobody's business. I am more than my sexuality. But Meg, she helped me to keep this a secret so that I can continue to work. Joe knew this. He introduced us. Meg and I had a very good relationship. I did not kill her." Then he sat down again, as though he expected everyone to clamp their gaping mouths shut, and carry on as though nothing had happened.

"You're a *gay-boy*?" shouted Jean Jones across the room, seemingly oblivious to the possible impact of the term.

"I am a homosexual," was Luis's blunt response.

"Dear *God* – what's the world coming to?" exclaimed Jean Jones. "So what was Meg doing – saying she was going to *marry* you? What good is a man like *you*, to a *woman*?"

"Meg and I were very good friends. We cared for each other. We both gained from our engagement: she was more popular because she was associated with me."

"Ah....Meg as the beard? Perhaps the Phyllis Gates of her day?" asked Dan James, pointedly.

"This was our business, nobody else's," replied Luis, just as pointedly.

"No *other* skeletons in your *closet*, Luis?" I *had* to ask.....it might turn out to be the only other time in my life I'd get to use that phrase, and have it so heavy with meaning.....or was it just black, twisted humour?

"I do not know what you mean!" Luis was getting angry. He was on his feet and ready to declaim us all to death.

"I think you do......." I said. I decided I had to push him. I wondered how quickly he would snap. As it all turned out, it was pretty quickly.

"I will not stand for this!" he screamed – like a girl!

I felt like saying, 'So sit down then,' but resisted. *Sometimes* the 'inappropriate' message manages to get through just *before* I open my mouth.

"So tell us the truth, then, Luis," said Joe Goldblum. "Tell us about the guy on Sunset."

All heads turned to watch Luis's reaction – and it wasn't good! He pushed over a little table that was placed at the side of his seat. A lamp clattered to the floor, the bulb smashing. Luis's naturally dark colouring flared up with anger. His voice was high pitched as he spat words towards Joe Goldblum. "You will *not* talk about my life this way! We have an agreement. You are as bad as Meg said. You are a *schemer*!"

"And your temper is as bad as Meg *told* me it was: maybe *you're* the one who lost it so much that you killed her," responded Joe Goldblum. "She said you were like a child – unable to cope when you couldn't get exactly what you wanted. Did it all get too much for you, Luis? Was Meg going to 'out' you, so you killed her? Or was it that story about the guy on Sunset coming out that made you do it?"

Luis kicked the broken lamp across the floor and roared – yes, *roared*! The he collapsed back into his chair, and buried his face in his hands.

Finally looking up at us all he said quietly, "I had broken off a relationship with a certain person. It could not develop in the way he wanted. He was hurt by me. I know this. But I did not mean for him to take his own life. I did not believe he would do it. But he did. And it made me very sad. But this was not of my making. I did not kill Meg – because of this, or anything else." Luis seemed very certain about that. We all let it sink in. "People can die around you when you are famous, and it can make your life very difficult. This is true for you as well, I think, Adrian. Meg told me about a girl who died in your dressing room – did *she* kill *herself*, because she *wanted* you but could not *have* you?"

Now all heads swivelled back towards Adrian.

He shook his head. "Oh *man* – so Meg told you about that. Wow – I thought that was long gone. Oh *man* – we had some wild times backstage in those days: I usually didn't know what day it was, what city I was in....or even the lyrics to songs I'd written myself, sometimes. I told Meg about them finding a girl in the band's dressing room one night we were playing in....somewhere.....Ohio I think: none of us even *saw* her. They found her when we were on stage – no-one knew who she was or how she'd got in. And she was dead. OD'd by the look of it. *Man* it was bad......."

As I was listening to Adrian I thought how glad I was that it only seemed to be now, as he recollected his time on the road, that he used the word 'man' as he spoke: it was very annoying, and quite sad really – a guy in his sixties should have developed a sufficiently broad vocabulary to allow for a range of exclamatory remarks – not just keep on repeating the same one!

"So it was nothing to do with *you*?" asked Luis, his voice dripping with sarcastic disbelief.

"No, it wasn't. Honest," said Adrian, bluntly.

Everyone in the room seemed to be completely emotionally drained, myself included.

"If you're still getting that drink, Adrian, I think I might have a fizzy water, please," said Sally. Dear God! That woman was unstoppable!

It was as though we'd all been slapped in the face. We all climbed down from our near-hysteria and took stock. There we were, a strange group of people, huddling around a shrinking fire in a day that was growing dimmer outside the walls of the Lodge. Though the fire was burning down, I felt hot, and claustrophobic. But my mind had been piecing together everything that had been said, and I needed to do something.....and to do it with Peter Webber:

I needed time alone with *him*! I decided that I'd better take the bull by the horns – though I have never been able to understand why anyone would *want* to do anything so foolish....but, then, I suppose that if you're hanging onto them, they can't gore you to death!

"Let's all take five minutes," I suggested. "But listen, before anyone leaves this room, there's something I must say."

Once again I was the centre of attention – whoop de doo!

"You all know that I've been snooping – and we've all decided to come clean with each other about our pasts.....but there's something else I need to do. I *know* we all know that one of us killed Meg. And I think we all want to know who that was...."

"Well, I certainly do," said Martha Goldblum with feeling, "because I'm not going anywhere on my own until it's sorted out. Joe – you do *not* leave my side, you hear?"

"Surely the *only* one who doesn't want the killer to be known is the actual murderer?" said Sally Webber. I suspected it was the most cogent thing I'd heard her say all day.

"And that's my point," I added, keen to get on. "If you all agree, I'd like to look around everyone's room. I don't want you to think I am snooping unnecessarily, though – which is why I'm going to suggest that someone accompanies me: Peter – would you do the honours? If everyone agrees, that is....but I'm sure everyone *will*, because only the murderer wouldn't want me poking about......" I thought I'd made my point quite well. Everyone nodded: some cautiously, some with maybe a little too much enthusiasm. "Thanks," I said, quickly, and Peter and I collected room-keys and made our way upstairs. "We'll be as quick as we can – but it would be better if no-one went to their room before we've finished." I didn't want anyone removing what might be incriminating evidence.

"Drinks anyone?" I could hear Adrian asking as I walked up the stairs. There was a G&T *somewhere* in my future, but not for the next little while, it seemed. I didn't plan on missing lunch – though by now it was going to be more like 'linner' (my personal term for the meal between lunch and dinner – just in case you were wondering!).

While Peter stood at the door, I ducked into Meg's room. I didn't look at her body – I needed her cellphone. I recalled that it was beside her bed. I picked it up and left the room. I looked at the battery reading – good. I'd only use it for one call.....that would be enough. But I'd do it when I was alone....we'd get through the rooms, then I'd go for a quick 'loo break'!

By the time we'd covered the two big double rooms being used by Peter and Sally (he'd insisted we go into their room first) and the Goldblums, then Dan's and Luis's rooms, which were very much the same as my own, Peter had told me that when he and Meg had reconnected, upon her buying a place in LA, they'd never actually got together – rather, as with me, she'd kept in touch by e-mail. Peter had also made it clear to me that he and Meg hadn't really kept in touch after their split, and that, therefore, everyone downstairs was a stranger to him, and Sally, of course.

"But that's not quite true, is it Peter?" I noted, as we went into Jean's room: it was at the back of the Lodge facing, as Peter himself had noted, north. The room was very dark: I clicked on the flashlight we'd brought with us. How on earth they find anything in those TV shows when all they have is a flashlight, I'll never know! Believe me, if I could have turned on the lights, I would have done! But, without power, all I could do was stumble about in the gloom, variously illuminating the floor and bits of furniture that seemed to leap out at me from dark corners. The room's layout was similar to my own, but different enough to cause a few stubbed toes and a little swearing.

In between my un-deleted expletives, Peter leaped to his own defence. "No, you're wrong," he said from the darkness that was the door to the landing, "We really *don't* know anyone down there."

"You know Jean," I reminded him.

"Oh *Jean*," he replied, dismissively. "I couldn't say that I *know* her. She was Meg's Mum, and that was it. I never spent any time at Meg's house when we were young, and, when we got together, and then left the country.....well, that was it: Meg never kept in touch with her Mum at all. I haven't seen her since 1978!"

"But I bet Meg talked about her a lot?" I pressed, as I poked around in the bathroom.

"Well, you're right *there*, I guess," replied Peter, sounding thoughtful. "Meg didn't have a *good* word to say about her, though. I think, in the end, she just wanted to get away from her. We got married about a month after her Dad died. Do you remember Meg's Dad?"

As I stood in Jean Jones's bathroom, peering into a hamper full of wet towels, I saw her dead husband as clearly as if he'd been standing in front of me: he'd been a short, round man, with heavy eyebrows and a broad smile. Whenever I'd seen him at Meg's house he'd always been wearing the same outfit: a long-sleeved undershirt and big wide brown braces, which held up his trousers almost under his armpits. He'd been a happy man: always a quip or a story, and, as often as not, some silly little trick that involved a sixpence. All *that* had been when I was quite young, of course. As I'd become a teenager he'd become more distant, had grown thinner, around his middle and on top of his head, and, finally, I recalled, he'd been a pretty bad tempered man with a local reputation for rolling home from the pub at all hours.

"Yes, I remember him," I replied.

"Well, I think it *was* his death that made Meg want to leave Wales. She blamed Jean for it." Even in the dim light, I could see that Peter was uncomfortable. "I mean......her Mum and Dad had a row one night, which seemed to be the norm for them, but this was a *really* bad one, she said.......and the next morning Meg found him dead at the bottom of the stairs: apparently Jean had insisted he should sleep on the sofa, and he'd fallen while making his way down from their bedroom. His neck was broken. Meg was devastated. In fact, thinking back, it changed her in many ways: when we were together we were happy....but she always used to make me promise that if she ever said or did anything that reminded me of her mother, Jean, that I was to tell her....because she didn't want to become anything like her. I think that Meg really was *afraid* that she'd become like her mother."

"It's not so odd," I said as I finally rejoined Peter at the door, "I mean, Jean's not exactly warm, fluffy material, is she? Who *would* want to be like her?"

"True," replied Peter, still thoughtful.

I nipped into my room, made a quick call on Meg's cellphone, and then came back to meet Peter. As I made my way towards the top of the stairs, Peter called to me, "What about Adrian's room? Don't forget that one!"

"Oops, I almost did," I lied, and I pushed open the door and did my thing again with the flashlight. It was odd, but I didn't get any sort of frisson from looking into drawers that contained Izzy/Adrian's underwear (at least he'd brought some!) and socks. I'd thought there might have been, but there was nothing. Nothing except the mounting excitement I was beginning to feel as the case clicked into place in my head. By the time I had closed the door to Adrian's room, and Peter and I had rejoined the group, I was pretty sure in my mind about who had killed Meg, and why. Now all I had to do was decide what to do about it!

# VIII

When you look into the face of someone you know has killed, and who is lying about it, you can see their lie in so many ways. And when I walked back into the Great Room, I knew I was right: Meg's murderer was giving their identity away in so *many* ways....why hadn't I seen it before? I told myself not to be so *tough* on myself: I'd needed to work out the method *and* check everyone's room before I could have been sure. And even then, it was still hard to believe. But, like I said, there it was – body language, affectation, tone of voice, interactions, relationship to physical surroundings....*everything* was screaming, 'I did it!', followed closely by, 'I don't care!' Which was *almost* as interesting.

Once I'd taken some time to digest everything I'd seen and heard since I'd got onto that minibus the day before, I'd managed to work out who might have possessed the right psychology to be *able* to kill, and who might have *wanted* to kill Meg. I had also, finally, worked out how Meg must have died, and how the person who was guilty might have given themselves away: which was why I'd had to poke around everyone's room. It was only when I put these two parts of the so-called 'investigation' together, that it made sense: if you could call it that!

So now – what to do about my conclusions? I had to remind myself that I *was* just working with a theory.....I didn't *know* that the person who I believed had killed Meg had *actually* done it. But I could see no alternative.

I wished there was someone there with whom I had felt enough of a connection to discuss my theory: someone whose opinion I would value. But there wasn't. True, I liked a couple of the people there......but as for what I had to decide? No, I had to decide alone, then follow through and live with the consequences.

Having suddenly realised that cooking by candlelight might sound all well and good, but that it can get messy, the group had, apparently, moved en masse, to the kitchen when Peter and I had gone upstairs, so when we returned to the Great Room there was a meal of cold cuts, soup, bread, salad and a giant cheesecake on offer. As we all served ourselves, the light of the re-built fire flickering, the candles that had been lit lending a warm glow to the room, I could sense that everyone was feeling worn out by all the emotion of the day. My watch told me that it was 5pm: it felt much later. I was very hungry, so I decided that my decision about what I should do, or say, could wait until I had eaten. But all the food tasted bland: I knew that my body needed me to eat, but my palate wasn't up to it. Even the Bombay and tonic, that had been so *very* long in coming, didn't refresh me. I was beyond refreshing!

By the time we'd all had our fill of savouries, we knew that a difficult moment was approaching. I looked at the cheesecake that was, presumably, to have been Meg's birthday cake. I knew I wasn't alone in wondering about whether eating it was something we should, or shouldn't do.

"I'll cut the cake," said Jean Jones, determinedly, "but I'd just like to say a word or two first." A low murmur spread through the room. No one objected to Jean's suggestions. She stood in front of the blazing fire, holding a cake-knife: it was a dramatic picture - the serrated blade looked especially large in this tiny woman's hand and it reflected the flames that burned behind her. Effectively not much more than a small silhouette, the victim's grieving mother spoke loudly, her thin voice cutting through the roar and crackle of the logs that sparked and shifted in the hearth.

"Meg wasn't a *nice* girl, and it sounds like she didn't grow up to be a *nice* woman......." it wasn't what people had expected from the mother of the deceased, but that was Jean for you! "She made people miserable – that's what you've all been saying all day, isn't it? She made all *you* lot miserable, anyway, and before you lot, she made *me* miserable too. Never applied herself as a girl, and she seems to have come by all her new-found wealth and fame almost by chance. I bet *anyone* who spent four years just swanning around on buses and doing the odd job here or there could write a book. I bet *I* could, anyway. No sense of responsibility, that girl. And not many morals either, by the looks of it!" I could tell by my fellow-guests' faces that they all wondered what was coming next!

"But she's gone, now," continued Jean, still in harsh tones, "and they say you shouldn't speak ill of the dead. So I won't. But I haven't got anything nice to say about her....so let's eat the cake."

And with that, she walked to the little table where the cake was resting, and sliced into it with the knife. She cut piece after piece, and Sally sprang to her side passing plates to everyone around the room.

"Junior's," whispered Joe to Martha, who smiled and ate quickly. But there were no other words spoken. What little conversation there'd been through the earlier course, was now over. Maybe people were having their *own* thoughts about Meg, as they ate the birthday cake she'd never share. Personally, I was still grappling with what to do next and trying not to choke on the cheesecake as I swallowed. It had a good texture, but I couldn't taste a thing. I knew that Joe's comment to Martha had meant that the cake had come from the famous Junior's in New York, and I wished I could have enjoyed it more....but I couldn't. Such a waste of a good cheesecake.....

Eventually we'd all finished and, once again, there was a general movement towards the kitchen – everyone carrying something. Because it was so dark we all agreed that the washing up could wait....which left us all with the dreadful feeling that we just didn't know what to do next. I mean, it wasn't as though someone could suggest board games, or charades, or anything!

We all wandered aimlessly back towards the Great Room: we were like a tide ebbing and flowing across the entry hall. Everything seemed unreal: we were all tired out, but it was way too early to retire to our rooms; we wanted the day to be over, but knew that we probably wouldn't sleep; we didn't want to be there, but there was nowhere else to go. We were all in a strange place, psychologically speaking. 'Limbo' would just about sum it up.

As we all tried to 'settle' into our 'places' – everyone *had* their place, and no-one seemed to want to move about – Adrian, who was sitting closest to me, between myself and the fire, looked around at me and said, "So – whodunit, Cait? Do you know yet? Or do we all have to lock our doors tonight and pray that the murderer is fine with just killing Meg?"

I knew that it had to be done: and I knew that this was my opening. Should I lie and say I didn't know....or should I tell the truth and explain what I understood had happened. Did I have the guts to go through with it? And, if I did...what would happen afterwards? That was my main concern. Would we all agree to lock the person away for the night and wait for the police? Would we all stay huddled in the Great Room and take it in turns to 'watch' the culprit, thereby ensuring our safety? It all seemed very melodramatic....but that was the aspect of the thing that had held most of my attention. The Aftermath. I made my decision.

"Yes, I'm pretty sure I know who did it, how they did it and why they did it," I said pretty flatly. There was certainly no 'Ta-Daaa' about my statement, that's for sure. But the effect couldn't have been more significant if I'd swung naked from the big old antler chandelier that hung uselessly above us and sung it to them. Shock, horror, excitement, fear and palpable relief flooded the room. A quiet chorus of 'Who?', 'Why?' and 'Well done!' rippled through the room. Suddenly the air was charged with anticipation.....from almost everyone. If I'd been in any doubt before, that doubt would have evaporated when I saw the reaction of the person I was *sure* had killed Meg. *That* person said nothing: they pursed their lips into a determined line, and stared into the fire.

"Are you going to tell us then?" pressed Adrian.

"Yes....I'll tell you what I think....but then we'll *all* have some very big decisions to make. You'll understand when I've finished. This is complicated......" I sorted out my thoughts, and began to tell a story. I had to begin the right way: that would be very important.

## IX

"The motive for Meg's murder was love. You have to understand that, to be able to understand anything else." Of course I had everyone's attention, but what held *my* attention was the reaction of one person in the room to my opening words. I was right, it *had* been love. And the removal of that love from them, by Meg. I continued – I knew I'd be talking for a while, so I sipped my Bombay and tonic: it cooled my throat. "But it was love of a strange and warped kind: a love that depended upon ownership. A love that didn't place Meg at the centre of the murderer's world....but which allowed the murderer to blame Meg for not loving them in the way they *thought* they should have been loved. As we all look around this room I think we can all agree that *that* could apply to quite a few people here: Peter, Adrian, Dan – Meg dumped you all, didn't love you the 'right' way; Joe – she dumped you too, and I think your engagement was on the line Luis, right?" I didn't *expect* anyone to react to my rhetorical questions....but you never can tell, so I paused for a moment or two before continuing. Nothing. Move on.

"Martha – she didn't love you like a mother, but, Jean, she didn't love you like a mother either. You each drew me a different picture of Meg – Sally, I know you didn't know her, so, in total, you gave me seven different Meg's to choose from....and I added in my own Meg, of course. The Meg *I* knew was fun, wild, a bit of a dare-devil, had a brilliant creative mind but it flitted about, never resting anywhere for long: she found it hard to buckle down and study, she didn't like to be with people who criticised her or who couldn't keep up with her, and you were right when you said she never took the blame for anything, Adrian.....she didn't, not during her school years and not, according to all of you, at any time after that either. Each of you met a Meg who was an increasingly damaged person: she dealt with the damage in her own way....which seems to have mainly consisted of ignoring it. But you can't ignore damage for *ever*....it'll get to you in the end."

The faces in the firelight were all looking anxious, and thoughtful. I knew they were digesting what I was saying, and, so far, no-one seemed to want to disagree with me. I pushed on. I was trying to get them to *understand*.

"When Meg took off to write her block-buster novel, she did so as a woman who had had to face some tough times: she'd removed herself from everything she'd ever known, and left it behind for a new world; she'd known a brief, idyllic life that was shattered by a tragic death; she delivered a stillborn child, and lost any chance to ever bear any more; she lived though a psychologically challenging time *way* outside any comfort zone she'd ever known; and she'd had a disastrous affair with a young addict, who dumped her, and probably made her feel very foolish, and used. Now – you might say that's she'd brought most of this upon herself, *most* of it.....and you'd be right. But what's interesting about we human beings is not that we *can't* cope with what life throws at us....we can.....what's interesting is *how* we cope. And Meg coped by running away. She ran away from Wales, from Peter, from Adrian, from Dan. She was running away from you Joe, and you Luis. She's always run away: that was Meg's way of coping. Which led me to thinking that maybe, just maybe, Meg had decided she'd run away one more time.....and that she had, in fact, killed herself."

I knew it would draw gasps, and it did. Gasps of disbelief, and gasps of relief.....it was about 50/50. Which, again, was interesting. I waited for people to re-settle themselves. It didn't take long – they wanted to *know*......

"It was quite clear, physiologically, that Meg's body had been moved after her death. She died sitting up, with her legs extended, and stayed that way for a couple of hours after death. Then she was laid in her bed, the way we found her this morning. Luis, did Meg run a bath last night? Her bathroom connected your rooms – you would have heard her, I'm sure."

"She did not. It was odd. She bathed every night. She did not like showers. If she took her bath last night it must have been very late, I think." To be fair, Luis did *seem* to be thinking.

"It *was* very late, Luis – it must have been not long before 4am. I'm surprised you didn't hear her."

"I sleep very well," replied Luis, just a little defensively.

"How do you know Meg took a bath at 4am?" It was Adrian. He sounded genuinely interested.

"Because that's the only way it all works out: Sherlock Holmes famously said something along the lines of....when you've got rid of all the ideas that don't or can't work, then what you're left with is the only explanation....however odd it might seem. And that happened here. Peter helped a lot.....thanks Peter." Peter looked uncertain. He clearly wasn't sure that helping me was a good thing. I decided to keep plugging away.

"Martha said that the power still worked at 4am. That means that Meg wasn't killed until after that, because it was her murder that blew the fuse-panel, Peter, as you so helpfully suggested."

Faces turned towards Peter – they were the faces of people trying to decide if he'd known about the reason for the blown fuses *before* he'd come up with his suggestion that they were linked to Meg's death. It would have been a great way to cover up, after all.

"Meg was killed by electrocution, in her bath," I announced, there were more gasps. "Once Peter told us about the fuses, and I thought about how

Meg's hair had been wet when I held her, I knew there could only be one explanation. But I don't know much about how electricity works: I know it can pass through the body without leaving much of a mark, but I also know that the 'Hollywood' way of just dumping a hairdryer into the bathtub won't kill anyone....because the circuit will trip off before any damage is done. But Peter explained that this house isn't fitted with those newer outlets...which means that whoever did this to Meg either knew *all* about how electricity works, and knew that tossing an electrical appliance into the tub would kill Meg because those safety outlets weren't going to kick in....or they knew *nothing* about it, and just threw something into the bathtub believing it would do the trick! Then there's the question of premeditation: did they plan to kill Meg, and to kill her this way, or was it the act of a moment of anger, with an appliance to hand? I noticed that Meg's bathroom contained no hairdryer. Now, neither does mine....but I brought my own: we women with long hair need to dry our hair, or sit around for hours with it wet. Meg had long hair, and she was hardly the type to not have all the comforts with her, so I had to assume she'd brought a hairdryer with her, but, as I said, there wasn't one. Would she really have gone to bed, or *back* to bed, with wet hair? No. I think that Meg had been having problems sleeping, after going to bed in a bad mood, and had decided to take a bath to calm herself into sleep. She died in that bath, sitting up, with her legs extended. So whoever came into her room, which I think we can safely assume she didn't lock, was someone with whom she felt comfortable naked."

Glances were exchanged around the room. Everyone was trying to think who would be eliminated by this assumption.

"She might allow an ex-husband to see her that way, a current fiancé....especially a gay one....a mother, a confidante, Martha.....but probably not an ex-agent, Joe, or someone she hardly knew, Sally." The field was narrowing, but not by much.

"So," I continued, "an appliance was dropped into the bath, possibly Meg's own hairdryer, Meg suffered a fatal electric shock, and the power went out. What happened then? Well I can tell you that the murderer calmly put their hand into the bathwater with Meg's dead body still in it, and pulled out the plug: her body didn't show any signs of the puckering that would signify she'd been lying in water for hours, but it did show cooling, and that suggested she'd lain exposed to the air. So then, around 6am this morning, the murderer went back to Meg's room, lifted her from the bath, dried her off and put her into the bed. The plank floors don't allow for there to be any visible drag marks, and Meg's body, as I discovered when I lifted her myself, was remarkably light. I reckon anyone here could have done it – getting her out of the bath would have been the toughest part, but the position of the claw-foot tubs in these bathrooms would have allowed for someone to hook their arms under Meg's armpits, and pull. It would have been difficult, and wet, work, but the killer managed it. They also dried off the bath, and replaced all Meg's wet towels with dry ones. Which, by the way, was a mistake." Once again, there were suspicious looks flying around in the firelight. I was almost done.

"The killer would then have put Meg's nightdress on her, tucked her in, and would have presented themselves as a member of the group that discovered the body, carefully concealing their guilt."

"*Peter* wasn't up and about in the night – I'd have known about it," called Sally Webber from her seat against the black window.

"And I know *Sally* wasn't......not that it *could* have been her anyway.....I mean......" added Peter, trailing off into silence.

"And Joe snores like a train – I wake when he stops: I'm afraid he'll stop breathing, so I know *he* didn't do it," interrupted Martha Goldblum.

"*You* were awake at 4am," broke in Luis. "Perhaps *you* are the killer!"

"Be sensible, man," said Joe Goldblum, "why would she *say* she was up and about at the time of the murder if *she* was the murderer? Not even Martha's *that* dumb!"

"Thank you, dear," said Martha Goldblum, then realised what her husband had just said, and looked annoyed.

"Couples might give each other an alibi," I said, pointedly. But I knew I'd have to come clean soon. Not even *I* could cope with this level of tension for much longer. I decided that I should forge ahead. "You all know each other's secrets now – so you all have as good a chance as I do of working out who had a good enough reason to kill Meg....if there *is* such a thing. What I can tell you, as a professional, is that it takes more than a *reason* to kill someone. And it takes more than an *opportunity* – whether that opportunity is created, or naturally occurring. What it also needs is the ability of the killer to believe, deep within them, that they are more important than the victim: that their needs and desires outweigh those of anyone else. Sometimes a death is caused by an outburst – a fit of rage, a lashing out: in those instances the loss of perspective, the loss of judgement, the aspect of putting oneself before *all else*, is temporary – and it is usually gone very quickly: the killer may or may not make an effort to cover up the results of their fatal outburst, or their connection to it, but the feeling of terrible remorse, of a psychological burden they will carry for evermore, poses a real threat to their sanity, and their ability to live anything approaching a normal life thereafter. Was *this* such a killing? Is the murderer now feeling that burden? Or does the murderer still feel they were right to do what they did? That they were justified in removing Meg's ability to maybe expose them and their secrets?"

I couldn't wait any longer. It had to be done. I was sad. I was tired.

"So who here felt that Meg could be wiped out, and with her any chance of their secrets coming out? Who felt so much more important than Meg? Was it about ownership? Was it, as I said, about love? And who here *could* kill? Has anyone here ever killed before? Peter – your hit and run; Adrian - an unexplained dead body; Dan – your wife's lover's work, ridiculed; Joe – *your* wife's lover dead, too; Luis – a suicidal ex. So many deaths. So much guilt. And what about you Jean? What about your *husband*? I remember Mister Jones.....I never did know his name: Meg called him 'Daddy'. How did *he* die? Did he fall....or was he pushed? *Why* was Meg so keen to get away from you after his death? Why was she so *frightened* that she might become like you? Peter – it's time for the truth.....you were lying weren't you? Meg saw something, didn't she, the night her father died?" Horror and apprehension was in the air.

Peter nodded, then said, quietly, "She didn't *see* Jean push him, she was hiding under her covers. She *heard* her do it. Apparently Jean screamed a whole bunch of obscenities, then she literally kicked him down the stairs. That's why Meg had to get out."

"Yes," I replied. "It was the first time that she ran away: that's where that pattern started – you always have to find out where a thing *starts*, you see. So......" we all turned and looked at Jean, "what was it? A fit of temper and a hairdryer that was close to hand.....or was it a thoughtful act, using the little fan heater from your room? By the way, I know the answer, so just tell the truth Jean."

Jean Jones smiled a very unpleasant smile. "Oh you're so *clever*, aren't you Caitlin Morgan? Just be careful you don't get so sharp that you cut yourself, my girl! It's all well and good throwing accusations around.....but there's no proof, is there? Not about Meg, *nor* about Hywel....that was Meg's father's name, by the way – Hywel. So you can *say* what you like. Sticks and stones, girl. I'm not saying anything, and that's that. The police would *never* believe that a mother would kill her own daughter – nor her own husband. And you've got nothing: no fingerprints, no marks, no nothing."

"How do you know, Jean?" Asked Adrian, sharply.

"Well, if everything was wiped down, like Cait said, then it stands to reason, doesn't it?" she gloated.

"I found the hairdryer in your room, Jean," I said, flatly. "Your hair is very short – not the sort of style that calls for a dryer that must have cost hundreds of dollars. And what about the hamper of wet towels in your room, Jean? *Why* so many? You'd have had to have bathed half a dozen times today to use all those towels. And why were *you* the only one *prepared* for the discovery this morning? We all looked like unmade beds when we discovered Meg....you were very well put together....burnt orange lipstick – *before* 8am? Matched to your dressing gown, no less. Lots of attention to the wrong sort of detail there, Jean. And your *constant* referral to Meg as some sort of possession? What of that? You gave birth to her, but she'd stopped being your daughter a long, long time ago – why did you keep reminding us you were her mother?"

"Nothing – like I said, nothing," repeated Jean Jones loudly. Everyone in the room was clearly thinking through what I'd been saying, and it seemed to make sense to them too. "So how did I know she was even having a bath at 4am, then, clever clogs?" added Jean venomously.

"Maybe you got up to use the loo and heard the water running....or maybe you were just going to try to talk to her about your secret.....just a mother and daughter chat....and found her in the bath....you tell me.........."

"I'm not telling you nothing, cos you *know* nothing!" said Jean, vindicated.

"You're the only one here who's actually killed before, Jean — killed when they meant it," said Peter Webber, holding his wife close to him.

"Yes, none of *us* have ever killed *that way* before," said Adrian, "but *you* have. I bet that makes a big difference, right Cait?"

"Oh ask little Miss Smarty Pants, why don't you?" mocked Jean.

"It does, Adrian," I replied. I knew I'd sound like a know-it-all, so I just set about answering him. "If you've come to terms with having taken one life, research suggests you might find it easier to justify planning to, and then taking, another life. The mechanisms for dealing with the remorse are already in place. Also the unknown, the 'impossibility' of killing another human being, is no longer an issue for you.....you *know* you've done it before, so you *know* you can do it again. Isn't that true, Jean?"

"Rubbish — all rubbish! If I'd killed Meg I'd have told you *all*.....don't pretend that any of you *liked* her.....you must have all *hated* her. Look what she did to you all! She was a bad lot was Meg. Just like her father: all fun and laughter when there were other people around, but when you were on your own with her....not much fun then, *was* she? Yes, I can tell by all your faces that you know what I mean. Good with that tongue of hers, *wasn't* she? Boy, oh boy, but she could turn the air blue! Just as well she *didn't* have kids — God knows what *their* mouths would have been like!"

"And where do you think she *got* that mouth, Jean?" It was Peter again. He was clearly angry, but still spoke softly. "She got it from you! *You!* When Meg told us, just last night, that *we* were the ones who had made her what she was....she was *right*. We all chipped in our own little bit of Hell for her....and Cait was right too, Meg *was* damaged, and we all added to that damage.....but where did the damage *start,* Jean? With you! That's where....with *you*. Oh I *know* that these psychologists always say it starts with the mother — that you've got to go back to the womb and all that....but I think Cait's got it right. I think *you* killed Meg. To stop her from writing about you and her father. You're *unbelievable!* She told me how bad you were to her when she was growing up — how you would hit her and undermine her every way you could.....and I thought she was exaggerating! Oh Jean.....how *could* you? Your own *daughter!*"

Jean's fighting spirit was at its height. I could tell there was no way she'd confess. So I thought I'd push her just one more time. I spoke again.

"You know what's ironic about all this Jean — about what you did to Meg, and about what we've all been through here today? I called Meg's shrink this evening: the number was, predictably, programmed into her cell. I asked him about the 'autobiography' they'd been working on together, and do you know what he told me?" I knew everyone wanted to hear this one! "He said that what Meg had been doing was a part of her therapy, that she'd been working through past issues, writing them down, and that she'd invited us all here so she could apologise to *us* for how she had wronged *us*. She wasn't working on an autobiographical *book*, she'd just put together some notes for their sessions, and she realised she'd wronged us all. He knew what she wanted to say to us all: Peter — she wanted to apologise to you for not letting you give yourself up; Adrian – she knew it wasn't your fault that the baby had died, and she was sorry that it had poisoned her against you so much that she spread bad stories about you; Dan, she realised she hadn't supported you in the one way that mattered – with your work - and she wanted to come clean about the affair, which *was* why she left you. Luis – she *was* breaking up with you, but because she liked you and wanted you to be happier than you could be covering up with her, and Joe, she wanted to thank you for all you'd done and apologise for firing you and not trusting you. Martha – she'd broken your trust by telling your secret to her mother – she had to open up about that. To me....she wanted to apologise for taking my boyfriend off me when we were sixteen....a boy who meant nothing to me six months after she stole him from me! And you, Jean, she wanted to apologise to you for not having been there to support you.....as you battled liver cancer. She knew you wouldn't be able to travel for much longer, and she was planning to take you around the world with her."

I allowed time for all of this to filter through to the individuals, and the group. We *were* a group now: we'd always have this to bind us together. Nothing would be the same, for any of us, again. We all knew that. No-one spoke. We were all thinking about ourselves.....and Meg.

Then Jean's harsh voice cut across our thoughts like a knife. "Thinking about Meg, are you? Thinking about your futures? Six months. That's about it for me! So I haven't got long to go, and I'll be with her. It was funny when you said she was killed for love, because she was....for the lack of love she gave *me*! If she was going to tell everyone, then she didn't deserve the love of a good mother."

"A good *mother*? A *good* mother?" Adrian had exploded next to me, he was on his feet. "What would *you* know about that? You *killed* your daughter, because she didn't love you *enough*! Love has to be earned...it's not a right! You gave her life....then you poisoned it for her. You might be sick, Jean, but don't expect *that* to sway my opinion of you. You're a cold-hearted bitch!"

"So will we tell the police about Jean?" Needless to say, it was Sally Webber speaking.

"Of *course* we will! She *killed* Meg, you *stupid* woman! What do you *expect* us to do? Draw straws and get someone *else* to confess to it just so that Jean can live her last six months outside a cell? No way!" Adrian was still angry.

"I don't *know* what we should do, but I know we should *talk* about it." Joe Goldblum could smell a negotiation, and he was going for it! "I mean....would anyone *know* that Meg was murdered? From an autopsy? Could we ask for there not to *be* an autopsy? Would there be *bound* to be an inquiry? Could we say we just found her dead.....and forget all the rest of it? The memory of her for her fans would be much happier that way. I mean, it's not like she was a crime writer.....if a crime writer died like this it could be great publicity....but a romance novelist? It kinda messes with the image – a murderous Mom and all. It might be a kindness to Meg to not involve her mother......"

"You are right," agreed Luis from his dark corner. "It would for Meg's memory if she *had* just died. I will lie for Meg. She lied for m the least I can do."

"That's outrageous!" boomed Dan James....finally having a chance speak....or having something to say, at least. "This woman has murdered innocent person: whatever you might think Meg *was*, she was, *essentially*, a innocent. And she killed her – because of *pride*, and to no effect in any case....because she wasn't going to *publish*! Jean, you're a stupid, ignorant woman who put two and two together and got six....you killed your husband, and you killed your daughter....*why* should we let you get away with *that?*"

It seemed that at least two of Meg's ex-husbands agreed on something: they were both baying for blood. I wondered about Peter: I wondered what *he* would say. Would *he* prove to be the voice of reason? Would he side with the eloquent Joe and supportive Luis?

"What about you, Peter? What do you think?" Martha Goldblum's question startled her husband. He looked at her accusingly.

Peter Webber looked at his wife, and then around the room. Again, as was his habit, he spoke quietly. "I think, at a time like this, we should ask ourselves 'What would Jesus do?'" Mouths fell open. He continued. "But, on this occasion specifically, I think it's better if we ask 'What would Meg do?' She knew about all of us, and it seems that she had worked pretty hard to understand her own flaws. And what was she going to do? Forgive us all. She was going to take her mother on a wonderful trip, not throw her to the mob. I think, for once, we should take our lead from a mortal, rather than the divine....though I think they are both the same on this occasion. I think we should forgive Jean, and all agree to tell just one more lie....a lie that will protect Jean, but that will also protect Meg's memory from some pretty awful revelations. Who knows what might come out in a court of law about this weekend, after all.........."

For all his talk about Jesus, I wondered to what extent Peter Webber was saving himself. Call me cynical, call me anything you like, but that's what I wondered.

Of course, everyone else got to thinking about what Peter had just said: I don't think it had occurred to anyone until then. And I could *feel* the mood change. And I didn't like it!

"Peter's got a point. It might well be what Meg would have wanted," murmured Adrian.

"Hmmm – I suppose you could look at it that way," rumbled Dan James from his fireside spot.

"Martha?" snapped Joe Goldblum.

"I think it would have been what Meg wanted," she replied quietly.

"And I agree with my husband," piped up Sally Webber.

So, once again, all eyes turned towards me. See what I mean about 'Aftermath'! There always *is* one....and it always *stinks*!

# X

I looked at the faces of the people in the room with me. Already these people were my co-conspirators, and I could tell that they wanted me to play along with their request that we lie about Meg's death. Peter's comments had shown everyone what I'd known all along – that, if Meg's death was portrayed as anything but natural, or accidental, then there'd be an investigation that would try to uncover what I'd tried to uncover – who might have wanted her dead....and why. Then there'd be cats out of bags all over the place. Not good. Not good for the people sitting here in the firelight with me. Not good for their families, or their futures. But good for Justice. And good for poor Meg.

I'm one of those annoying people: I don't like to do things that *I* think are wrong. Quite often, however, what *I* think is wrong, and what society in *general* thinks is wrong, are two different things. So, for me, it's all about personal ethics. But murder? Even *I* think that's wrong! Even *I* think that the perpetrator should not be allowed to get away with it: I'm a victimologist, for goodness sakes! Why would I dedicate my life to those who've been wronged, if I *didn't* think that those who had wronged them should be held to their responsibilities? And now, I was being asked to act contrary to all my natural instincts. And I didn't like it. Not one bit.

If I agreed with everyone else, I'd be safe – otherwise, maybe I'd be the next one waking up dead! Yes, if I agreed, we'd all come up with a version of the discovery of Meg that could be seen as presenting a natural death: she could easily have died sitting up in bed. But I wondered about the forensics involved. I decided to play the thing out. For the moment.

"We *could* stick to the whole story about how we found her in bed," I said. "None of us will have to act that....all we'll have to do is tell the truth, which is always for the best. But there might be internal indications of electrocution that I know nothing about. So we'll have to say that someone *originally* found her dead in her bath – that her hairdryer must have fallen in by accident, and that she was pulled out of the bath, dressed and put into bed, for decency's sake. If we decide to do this, I believe that Jean should be the one who says she pulled her daughter to the bed. That would be psychologically believable. We all know that Jean's a good enough actress to carry it off: and she wouldn't want to bring any of us into it – she's the one with everything to lose."

Heads nodded around the room. It seemed like my plan was going to be accepted.

"But there *is* something else, Jean," I added. "I need to ask Joe and Luis something: what happens to the income from Meg's as yet unpublished manuscripts, her future book sales and any movie income, and all that? Do either of you know about her 'estate'?"

Joe and Luis exchanged glances. Luis nodded at Joe to encourage him to speak. Joe spoke.

"As far as we know, she didn't have any plans in place to circumvent everything going to her next of kin....her mother. Neither of us knows what's in her Will....or even if she had one....but I don't think she was the sort of person to plan her business very well. Meg didn't deal well with 'tomorrow'." I suspected that Joe was right.

I spoke again. "So Jean – for the rest of your life, you'll be a wealthy woman. Who knows....you might even be able to buy yourself a new liver......" People were shifting in their chairs. I *wanted* them to be uncomfortable. I *wanted* them to understand the impact of what they were doing. "But I guess that's unlikely. But, if everything goes to you, then *you* die....who gets it all? Have you any relatives?"

Jean shook her head.

"I didn't think so. So here's what you're going to do: you're going to set up a charity that will get everything after your death. It'll bear Meg's name and it'll support....what do we think is *appropriate* guys.....global training for girls who don't want to grow up to be like their mother? Sex, drug and alcohol abuse counselling? Still-birth grief counselling? Support and education in literature for young people? A creative writing programme for teenagers......what?"

There was a general murmuring in the room.

"They're all good ideas, Cait," said Peter. "But if we're going to make sure that such a charity is set up....shouldn't we do it properly? I mean, I know of a large number of very good charities that are out there already....many of them could do with a little help.....couldn't we set up a Foundation, and help out *lots* of programmes?"

This idea drew a louder rumbling of approval.

"How about you and Sally work with Jean, and Joe and Luis, to make that happen then, Peter?" I said. I was hating myself as I said it, though. "This could be something to come from Meg's death that's greater than even *she* could have imagined."

"Oh Peter, you're so clever! Cait's so clever! Can we spend the rest of our lives giving away money to people who need it! Oh, what wonderful work! How kind of Jean to do that with all of Meg's money." Once again Sally had managed to stun me with her words. But, bless her, her heart *did* seem to be in the right place!

"So we're all agreed?" I asked, knowing that everyone was. "Joe, Luis – did either of you mention any suspicious circumstances surrounding Meg's death to anyone you spoke to?"

Both Joe and Luis shook their heads.

I was pretty much on my last legs by now: I wanted my bed! But I still had a few things to say. "I didn't say anything to the police dispatcher.....and, if I hesitated at the time, I can explain that by saying I was mystified that the body had been moved after death. So there we have it – Jean will not be accused of killing her husband and her daughter; we will all lie; Jean will accept her inheritance, graciously, and the four...well, including Martha, five.....of you will work with Jean to ensure the equitable distribution of Meg's current and future wealth. I'm sure that knowing that all your work will have a charitable outcome will redouble your efforts, Joe....maybe to the extent that you even have to drop your other clients and just work for the Meg Jones Foundation. None of us will ever speak about the things we have heard and done here this weekend, because we've all got too much to lose. So there: Jean, you're safe, we're all safe. All we have to do now is work on our consciences so that we don't have sleepless nights about this. And all you have to do, Jean, is come to terms with the fact that you killed your daughter for no reason – no reason at all! Not that your own selfish obsession about your reputation, even after a death you knew you would soon face, could be called a 'reason' to kill your own flesh and blood. You put yourself before Meg – you saw what people might think about you, even when you were dead, as being more important than her life. Maybe you'll manage to forgive yourself for that before the cancer gets you – but I never will."

I stood – there wasn't much more to be done. "I'm going to practice sleeping right now....I'm exhausted. Maybe when we get up in the morning we can all see this in a different light. But I, for one, know I'll be wanting to get away from here as soon as I can: as soon as the police have got here - as soon as they've interviewed us all....which they *will* do.....I'm *off*. Minibus or not – I'm *out* of here. Thank you, and goodnight!"

I pulled myself up the stairs, crying with tiredness and.....what was it? The turmoil inside my soul....that was it. I was coming to terms with the fact that I'm naturally a 'retribution' person, rather than a 'greater good' one. I knew that our decision downstairs *was* for the greater good......but had *justice* been served? I knew I wouldn't sleep much that night, for all my rhetoric: Justice is such a huge concept that, when you start to think about it, it's difficult to stop. And it's *so* complex. Is it 'an eye for an eye'? Or is it about forgiveness and trying to make good come from bad? See....*big* stuff! Murder *always* involves big stuff........

# *SPRING*

## The Hon. Miss Wilson-Smythe Hunts for Cousin Harry

Featuring the personnel of the
**WISE Detective Agency**

# I

Carol Hill unlocked and pushed open the door to the WISE Detective Agency's offices on Thursday morning, and knew immediately that it must have been Annie Parker who had closed up the night before: Annie always imagined that no-one would guess that she'd been leaning out of the office window sneaking a sly smoke, but Carol's nose was hyper-sensitive to the merest hint of nicotine – as her doctor kept reminding her, you couldn't be *too* careful when you were trying to get pregnant.

Carol flung open all the windows, allowing the cool end-of-April air to waft in and carry the offensive odours away with it, then filled the kettle and plugged it in, ready for the demands of a 9am meeting of all four partners in what had become their surely-doomed business venture.

Carol had prepared all the financial statements necessary to prove to her three partners that they had very little time left before their money ran out: when they'd formed their business in February they'd all felt buoyant, invincible even. Brought together by a perplexing series of deaths, Carol Hill, Christine Wilson-Smythe, Mavis MacDonald and Annie Parker had formed themselves into the WISE Detective Agency (their respective heritages being Welsh, Irish, Scottish and English), and had set up shop in offices just off Sloane Square (that they'd never have been able to afford if not for the fact that they were being donated free of charge by Christine's father who, some suggested, did, in fact, have more money than God) and had started 'detecting'.

Actually, they'd only had three paying cases, each of which they'd managed to bring to a successful conclusion, but none of which had feathered their rather pathetic little financial nest. Today was D-Day, as Carol had named it – Decision Day..... *what* were their plans going to be for their immediate collective, and individual, futures? They *had* to decide!

Little did she know that by the end of 'D-Day' the personnel of the WISE Detective Agency would have become embroiled in a vicious and audacious kidnapping, done their best to apprehend a cold-blooded murderer, that the life of one of the four partners would hang in the balance, and the life of another would be changed forever. Blissfully unaware of any of this Carol rehearsed how she'd give Annie what for about smoking in the office....when she finally arrived!

Mavis arrived at 8.45am, her nursing and military background allowing her to plan any journey with precision. Annie rushed in at a minute before nine

– complaining bitterly about the bus service to Sloane Square - and the three sat waiting impatiently for Christine's arrival, with coffee and tea, but no biscuits: Carol felt they couldn't run to biscuits. Conversation was strained, especially following Carol's telling off of Annie, with no-one wanting to start The Big Discussion without all four partners being present. By ten past nine Annie Parker had had enough.

"This is bleedin' annoyin'," she exclaimed, expressing the emotion filling the room. "I know 'er Dad's money's keeping us 'ere, so to speak, but why can't Chrissie ever be on time for anything?" Annie's broad London accent always seemed to shine most when she was annoyed, or whispering, or in danger.

Mavis MacDonald's rolling Scottish brogue didn't need an excuse – it was front and centre whenever she opened her mouth, but pleasant to listen to for all that.

"Och, I know dear," she replied soothingly. "But she's one of those girls for whom the world has always waited – so what can we expect?"

"True," agreed Carol, resignedly.

Annie hadn't expected such an easy-going comment from the ever-punctual Mavis, nor the agreement from Carol, who was reliability personified.

"Jeez girls, if it was *me* late you'd be bangin' on about it for ages – why's Chrissie whiter than white all of a sudden?" Annie sounded annoyed.

"I love it when you call us 'girls'," chuckled Carol.

"Well, you know what I mean," sulked Annie.

It was true that none of them had been girls for some time: Mavis had retired from her post as Matron at the Battersea Barracks the previous December as she had passed her sixty-third birthday; Carol was fast approaching thirty four and had gone so far as to give up her well-paid job as an administrative manager in The City so that she could de-stress and, hopefully, conceive the child she and her husband David longer for; Annie was looking fifty-four squarely in the face, and not enjoying the hot flashes she got as she did so. The redundancy package she'd been given upon being "chucked out by those Swiss bastards who bought the company", as she so daintily put it whenever asked about why she wasn't still one of the best-known Lloyds' Brokers' receptionists, was almost gone. They all needed to do something with their time, but Annie, most of all, needed to generate an income. Soon.

The telephone rang. Carol jumped, regained her composure, and picked up the receiver.

Annie rolled her eyes towards Mavis and said, "Bet that's 'er! Some bleedin' excuse or other."

Carol was listening intently and said nothing but, "We're on our way," before she hung up.

"So? Little Honourable Miss Hoity-Toit was it?" Annie loved to make fun of Christine's high birth, but deep down felt an enormous respect for the girl who, coming from money and not needing to, held down a tough job as a Lloyds' Broker, played the piano, bridge and field hockey very well, could speak five languages fluently and was on more charity committees than you could shake the proverbial stick at! And she was only twenty eight. And she was pretty. And she was very, very smart. Mensa smart in fact. None of which annoyed Annie at all – she just liked to make sure Christine was kept 'in her place'.

Carol seemed lost for words. But this was not an affliction from which Annie ever found herself suffering, so she pressed gentle, happily well-organised, happily married, happily overweight, but unhappily un-pregnant, Carol a bit further.

"Come on Car, what's up?"

Carol looked directly at Annie through narrowed eyes and, very uncharacteristically, let go with both barrels.

"I'm not a bloody 'car', Annie, I am a person – I am *CAROL! Don't* use that name for me, you *know* I hate it! And put your coffee down, *now*! You too Mavis!"

Mavis's eyebrows silently remarked to the room that it was unheard of for Carol to raise her voice to Mavis.

"You're both coming with me," continued the overwrought Carol. "Christine's in a mess – her cousin's gone missing and her Aunt Agatha wants us over at her house to help track him down. I said we were on our way."

Annie and Mavis exchanged knowing looks.

"Time of the month Car? Sorry, *Carol?*" enquired Annie, sarcastically.

Carol burst into tears, and blubbed, "Yes it *is* almost that time of the month, and I'm feeling so wretched I'm sure I'm not pregnant…..but there's no need to be so cruel about it!"

Annie immediately felt awash with guilt and held her face in horror. She really hadn't realised the implications of her snide comment. She got up and hugged Carol.

"Oh I'm so sorry darlin', I didn't mean nothin'. Honest. I never thought………well, that's me all over innit? Silly old mare, that's me. Just ignore me Car, love. And wipe them eyes while I nip outside and find us a cab….I'm assumin' we can afford a cab between us? Where are we goin' anyway?"

"Wraysbury Square," replied Carol as she wiped at her eyes. "In fact, Lord Wraysbury's own house – you know, the really, *really* big white one they always show on documentaries about the landed gentry? Turns out, Christine's Dad's sister is Lady Agatha Wraysbury. Who knew? I mean, when they say money goes to money they mean it, don't they? In London landowning there's Grosvenor, then Cadogan, then Wraysbury – they have to be worth billions!"

Both Annie and Mavis could tell that Carol wasn't back to her usual self yet: Carol never commented on social status, coming, as she did, from the delicately balanced class known as The Home Counties Set…..in other words, the families, like hers, that had a long lineage, rural roots, quite a bit of land, but often not a lot of cash. And they often turned out girls like Carol – homey and a bit homely, large, loving and warm, not ambitious except on behalf of their own family members, and never happier than when they were messing about with horses, or dogs, or their own brood of rosy-cheeked offspring.

Eventually Annie managed to hail a cab, having walked to Sloane Square to find one, and all three "girls" finally stood at the door of the largest mansion on Wraysbury Square. It didn't even have a number, it just said "Magna" above the door. For some reason Carol seemed to know that this was a reference to the fact that Lord Wraysbury's estate, near Windsor, included the little island where the Magna Carta was signed in 1215, which had, apparently, only been signed by King John at all thanks to the noted intervention of Lord Wraysbury's ancestors, many of whom had continued to shape British, and by extrapolation, much of the world's, law. She shared this mini-history lesson with Annie and Mavis as they waited for the door to be opened to them, which it was, not by the 'Aged Faithful Retainer' Annie had expected, but by a handsome, strapping young man of no more than twenty five years, and no less than six feet and four inches – a delightful combination, as far as Annie was concerned.

"We're here at the request of Christine Wilson-Smythe," announced Mavis MacDonald briskly, the power of speech seeming, momentarily, to have left both Carol and Annie.

"Come in, won't you." The smiling young man's strong Irish accent made it sound like an invitation to dance. "I'll let Her Ladyship know you've arrived. Would you wait here in the library, please. I shall return presently."

As he waved them into a vaulted room that was stuffed to the rafters with sets of law-books that were measured by the yard, rather than by the volume, Annie blew out her cheeks in appreciation of their greeter's visible attributes, behind his back. Carol managed a coy smile. Annie was glad of that at least: she hadn't meant to hurt the girl she'd all but mothered since they'd met at a secretarial college more than a decade earlier.

"Down, girls," admonished Mavis with a twinkle, ever the schoolmarm when it came to Annie and Carol.

But the strapping young man, sadly, didn't return at all – instead it was Christine who rushed breathlessly into the grand room.

"Oh thank you for coming," she gushed, "I don't know *what* I'd do without you – Aunt Agatha's in *such* a state I've had to sit her down with a brandy. It's Harry, he's not been seen since yesterday morning and she's sure something's happened to him, though of course maybe he's just gone off on another bender............and the police said that last time was the last time he'd get away with it, if you see what I mean.........and Aunt Aggie is so beside herself she's like two people..........and we have to find him before the police do because it could mean prison you know, depending on what he's done this time........ which is why Aunt Aggie doesn't want them called in yet….." Christine finally drew a breath. "You *will* help won't you? Aunt Aggie said money's no object, and I know WISE is as skint as the proverbial whotsit, and it *is* a real case and all that.........and she really is *very* rich. I've agreed four thousand a day plus expenses *and* a ten grand bonus when we find him. Will that do?"

Three astonished faces were turned towards Christine. Mavis spoke first. Years of dealing with nursing emergencies allowed her both to keep her cool and act calmly in the face of adversity....or a wonderful piece of news, like a much-needed injection of cash.

"I think that's a fair fee," she responded coolly, " especially when considering the level of delicacy involved – but we won't do anything illegal, Christine." Mavis was very firm.

"Oh, *of course* not," replied Christine sweetly, "I didn't mean to imply any sort of impropriety – just that if we can find him before we need to call in the police, we can bring him home, and away from any....bad influences....or whatever."

"Well, just so long as we're clear on that one, Miss Wilson-Smythe," replied Mavis formally.

"Oh come off it Mavis, it's *me*, Christine – don't Wilson-Smythe me, *please*! Anyway, it was Aunt Aggie who wanted a fee agreed before she'd even let me call you – she's very business-like you know, in fact, she might even give *you* a run for your money Mavis!"

Mavis's eyebrows suggested that she thought this hardly likely, but she turned to Annie and Carol, purposefully hooking her short, neat grey hair behind her ears as she did so. All three of her colleagues knew her mannerisms well enough to know this signified she meant business. Serious business. Mavis spoke gravely.

"Well, what do you say girls? It's four times more than anyone else has ever paid us, and if we find him quickly we could have the money in the bank by the end of the week – then there'd be no worries for another few months, I'd say."

Annie managed a "Duh! Go for it!" and Carol nodded vigorously.

"Right then!" Mavis, again characteristically, turned militarily on her heel to face Christine once more. "I'm assuming you're for it?" Christine nodded. "Of course, we'll need to get *all* the facts as they are known," continued Mavis addressing Christine, "and we'll need the family to be *honest* with us – no hiding things they don't want us to know....we need *real* insight and information to be able to do our best, *you* know that Christine – can you make sure that the family understands that and co-operates?"

"But of *course* dahlings," gushed Christine. "I told Aunt Aggie all that this morning, before I called. By the way – we can have that nasty meeting about money some other time can't we? Much better to be making it, than talking about it, eh?"

Christine was surprisingly light-hearted in her manner as she introduced her three colleagues to her Aunt in the upstairs Drawing Room. Lady Agatha Wraysbury wasn't what any of them had expected: red-headed, freckled, small, compact and hard-bodied, she sat curled in a large armchair that was upholstered in a jovial floral print, featuring pink cabbage roses, sipping amber liquid from a huge brandy bowl. She wore faded jeans that moulded themselves to her slim body, and a white shirt with a stripe that exactly matched her new-penny hair-colour. Carol thought she looked about forty five, Annie guessed fifty and Mavis put her at fifty five. Mavis turned out to be on the button. Her feet were bare. As she rose to greet her guests, it was clear she was just about five feet tall: so almost a head above the diminutive Mavis, but both Carol and Annie felt as though they were towering over her as they shook her hand. She was a gracious hostess: tea, coffee and home-made biscuits were already spread on a silver tray, and she allowed Christine to take the lead in what she referred to as their Briefing Meeting.

"Now stop me if I get any of this wrong, Aunt Aggie," Lady Agatha Wraysbury nodded as Christine began, "Harry left here at about eleven yesterday morning saying he was off to meet a friend he plays rugger with. You don't know the name of the friend or where they were meeting, but he set off in his black VW Golf from the mews behind the house by about eleven fifteen – and we know this because your chauffeur saw him leave. Alone. Right?"

Lady Agatha nodded. Christine continued, her clipped tones seeming at home amongst the dainty antique furnishings of the delightfully bright and flower festooned room in which the little group was huddled.

"I've tried and tried his phone, but it's going directly to voicemail. Now – to be honest, none of this might be very unusual except that Harry's playing in a Fives tournament out at the Westway sports centre near Ladbroke Grove this week – he's good, plays for the Old Etonians' Under 25's and he's particularly good at Fiddles...."

Annie could contain herself no longer.

"Chrissie darlin'," Annie bobbed her head and smiled nervously in the direction of Lady Agatha, as though begging her pardon for an unfortunate break in etiquette, but continued nonetheless, "what's Fives, and is any of this relevant?"

Carol glared at Annie and Annie glared back, twice as hard.

Christine, ignoring the looks that were replacing whole conversations between Carol and Annie, simply looked puzzled and answered quite snappily, "Fives is a handball game, and *of course* it's relevant, or I wouldn't be telling you, would I!? It was invented at Eton, where a small, hard ball was played against the walls of the chapel there, between the buttresses, and it's now played all over the world.....well, they play it in some parts of Europe and, apparently, they're nuts about it in Nigeria. Anyway, Harry's always been very good at it. He played right through school and University, and now he plays in a league mainly made up of other Old Etonians, Old Harrovians and suchlike. It's always played as a doubles game, but Fiddles is when just two people play. Harry's very competitive and he's gone through a lot of partners – they don't seem to be able to keep up with him....that's why he likes to catch a Fiddle game whenever he can."

Annie was almost squirming with questions, but she kept quiet for a moment longer. Christine continued, staring at Annie in a very meaningful way. "Harry was due to play Fives with a new partner yesterday at 2.00pm – *that's* why it's relevant, Annie," she announced, vindicated, "but Aunt Agatha only knows that the new partner was someone Harry plays rugger with at the pub, and who, presumably, went to the sort of school where Fives is played. We don't have a name."

"The pub. Do we know *which* pub?" asked Mavis politely.

"It's Harry's second home," answered Lady Agatha, jumping into the conversation, "The Prince of Wales on the King's Road. It's the first place I thought of. He's such a fixture there they all know him."

"Do we know if he made it to the pub yesterday – or the sports' centre?" asked Annie. It was the obvious question, and the one Mavis had been about to ask.

"Hang on a minute everyone," piped up Christine, "I've done my homework, so just let me finish....."

Annie sighed. Patience was not her strong suit. Christine gave her another meaningful look, and Annie tried to calm herself. Christine referred to a small notebook. Carol sipped her sweet tea and nibbled a chocolate biscuit, it was very good. Christine composed herself and spoke seriously.

"I have not yet traced anyone who has seen Harry since he left here yesterday morning. I have spoken to three people, all friends or friends of friends, who were at the Prince of Wales pub at various times yesterday and no-one saw Harry there at all – a phenomenon that was commented upon by the landlord of the pub, no less! Harry also never arrived at the sports' centre, which annoyed the organiser of the Fives' league, who also happens to be a friend of a friend, and with whom I have already spoken twice this morning, establishing that not only did *Harry* not arrive for his match, but that his new partner, a Rob Walsh of Lisson Grove, was also a no-show. Harry's car is not at the sports' centre, nor at the pub. Aunt Agatha doesn't want to report the car as missing or stolen, because it might be that Harry's off somewhere driving it about...blissfully unaware that we are in any way concerned about him."

Once again, Annie felt compelled to speak. So she did. She just couldn't help it.

"And why *are* we concerned, exactly?" she was more than curious. She could think of any number of reasons why Harry might not be where he had been expected to be – all of which revolved around large quantities of alcohol and girls, but she was unsure how blunt she could be in the presence of the boy's mother, who also happened to be the poshest, and richest, person she'd ever met in the flesh.

"Harry's a *good* boy," answered Lady Agatha, pensively. Maybe she caught the muscles in Mavis's eyebrows twitching, or maybe she was aware of how others might see her son's behaviour, and her own. In any case she pulled herself upright in her chair, put down the glass she had been nursing, and looked earnestly at all four of the women grouped around her. She smiled sadly as she spoke.

"I know you'll think I'm a mother blind to her son's imperfections, but I don't believe I am. It's not easy growing up with money and a position in a society that's obsessed with both. Or being the second-born son. It's so easy to get side-tracked, or just coast along for years without doing anything at all. I have seen it a dozen times in other boys. But Harry's doing well – he's not like his older brother, of course, who's taken to the law so wonderfully well.......Harry does rather drink beer as though it's going out of fashion, and he's made more than one rash decision when it comes to girls and the balance between socialising and getting his head around University life, or a job. But, *finally*, at twenty four, he knows what he wants to do, and he's beginning to do it. He's going to be a chef – and I think he'll be a good one. He's just spent a year working his socks off in the kitchens of a chateau we used to stay at when he was a small boy in the Dordogne. The owner's a lovely man, a friend of a friend, and he was delighted with him: it seems that Harry is possessed of an excellent palate and has developed some impressive culinary skills during his time there. And he didn't get into even one tiny little bit of trouble. He's a changed boy – he's found his path." Lady Agatha's expression suggested that she was as surprised at these discoveries as she was proud of them. Her eyes were less sad as she continued.

"Harry's grandmother and I have become so very proud of him: you see, his grandfather would have loved to have been a chef, and had a lifelong love affair with food. But, of course, the family 'business' was law, so he had no choice, nor did Harry's father, really....but nowadays, I think it's more acceptable to be....different. Though I'm not sure that my husband sees it that way. But Harry's grandmother is having a new lease of life through his interest in food it seems – we've noticed how excited and involved she's become recently, and Harry spends a good deal of time with her these days. She has a suite on the top floor here, which she moved into when Harry's grandfather died......it's always been known as the Dowager Suite. I expect I'll end up living there one day myself, when William, Harry's older brother takes the title." Lady Agatha Wraysbury looked wistful as she continued. "Anyway, I haven't mentioned anything to her yet – I don't want her worried. Her health hasn't been all it could since she turned eighty last year, though, as I say, she's been very encouraging about Harry's newly discovered talents. Anyway, as Christine will tell you, if Harry's not at the Prince of Wales, or playing some sort of frantic sport, he's at Squares – that place off Soho Square with the head chef who swears a lot on television?" She looked quizzically at the group, and all four acknowledged they knew the place she meant. Who didn't?

She continued. "Last night Harry was due to be interviewed for a job in the kitchen there. We haven't told his father yet. But he was so excited. He said it would be his dream job. He wouldn't have missed *that* for the world." Suddenly Lady Agatha Wraysbury looked tired. She continued in a quieter voice. "I'm not a stupid woman, ladies. I am a woman who knows her son. Something is wrong. I *know* it. But I cannot tell you more than that. Harry's a good sport – he wouldn't have let down a competing team at Fives, and he would *certainly* not have missed an interview for a job under Chef Baz Keegan. He's a *good* boy. Nothing like his older brother, of course, but a *good* boy, nonetheless."

Mavis, characteristically, summed up the dread hanging in the air as she asked, quite calmly,

"So would I be right in thinking, Lady Agatha, that you believe something happened to your son between 11.15am and 2.00pm yesterday that would have prevented him from fulfilling his commitments?"

Lady Agatha dropped her head and nodded. The strain she was feeling could be sensed by everyone in the room. When she looked up again her eyes were full of tears and pain.

"I think something bad has happened to him," she sobbed. "Maybe he's lying hurt somewhere. Maybe he doesn't know who he is for some reason, or can't speak......" her voice trailed off into gentle sobs.

Christine moved to her Aunt and hugged her shoulders. She looked at her friends, her expression grim, her voice grave.

"I've checked all the London hospitals, and there's nothing. No admissions in Harry's name, nor matching his physical description. Aunt Agatha doesn't want us to contact the police, yet, because she hopes that Harry's just got himself caught up in something that's a bit.......well.......you know? So I've said that obviously we can do some digging, and maybe find out something about this 'Rob Walsh' he was supposed to meet up with yesterday, and see where we go from there. I'm sure we can help." She was gently rubbing her Aunt's back as she spoke.

"Well, we can certainly do our best," replied Mavis evenly. "But, Lady Agatha, I'm afraid I don't believe your story.....there's something you're not telling us. And on that basis we cannot accept the case." Annie looked shocked. Carol looked horrified. Christine rolled her eyes heavenwards, and squeezed her Aunt's shoulders.

"You promised, Aunt Agatha," she whispered to the now sheepish-looking redhead.

Lady Agatha nodded and wiped her tears away.

"You're right, there *is* another reason for my not wanting to contact the police," she conceded. Mavis looked vindicated, Annie and Carol were impressed by her perspicacity. Lady Agatha's tears welled once more, and her voice faltered as she spoke.

"My husband has said that if Harry gets into trouble with the police once more, he'll stop supporting him altogether....and this is such a critical point in Harry's life. I know I said he's a good boy, and he *is*......but sometimes......oh dear......there comes a point in a person's life when it could, frankly, go badly wrong. Harry's reached that point. Some of his so-called friends have already been in and out of rehab on more than one occasion – oh, their parents say they're off at some fancy Spa on Lake Como, or whatever, and it's never discussed around the dinner table or in public, but we all know what's going on. Harry's come close, I'll admit that: he's even been charged with drinking and driving in the countryside down near Wraysbury Manor. His father was livid, of course, and said they should throw the book at him. But they let him off with points and a fine, and that was that. Well...." she looked guiltily about the room, "....his grandmother paid the fine, and he hasn't done anything like it since. But now it seems that they rather pick on him down there, stopping him and giving him breath-tests quite often, which I suppose is why he doesn't go as often as he used, though I can't say I'm sorry he's away from that crowd....." Lady Agatha seemed to be looking far off into the distance, then regained her focus and continued, her voice stronger and carrying more conviction.

"So.....it's important that we give Harry the benefit of the doubt. If we call in the police, his father will probably cut him off without further ado, and I don't want that. This is Harry's Big Chance.....I know that he can make a good life for himself as a chef. I won't let this.....whatever it is......jeopardise his future. That's why Christine suggested that you might help – and I'm all for it. *Please* help me.....*please* help find Harry?"

The mood in the room was still tense, but by the time Lady Agatha left the WISE team to prepare herself for a committee meeting she said she couldn't possibly be seen to be missing, she was completely in control of her emotions and wishing them luck, whilst begging them to work quickly.

When they were alone, all eyes turned to Christine.

"So," asked Annie, "what's the *real* story? What's Harry *really* like?"

Christine didn't hesitate, she spoke rapidly as she passed around a photo of Harry, which showed a mop-haired smiling youth in a rugby shirt who favoured his mother's colouring and had a wicked glint in his blue eyes.

"Aunt Agatha is pretty accurate in her description of him – he really is a 'good boy' at the core, but he's been a bit wild – and getting away with it, too. He's good looking in an ordinary, slightly florid sort of way, as you can see from that photo – it was taken a couple of months ago by the way - and he charms more than his fair share of the girls; from what I can gather, he drinks like a fish, plays sports like a fiend and, apparently, has an extraordinary palate, as Aunt Aggie said, which might, in fact, be the making of him. And I agree with her that there would've had to have been one hell of a good reason for him not to meet with that Chef last night – he's Harry's hero – I know that Harry'd been beside himself about that interview for weeks – he'd even had his precious hair cut short to show he was serious about working in a kitchen."

"So, what do *you* think?" Mavis's question hung in the air.

"I think something *has* happened to him," replied Christine grimly. "I don't think he'd have gone on a bender *yesterday*, of all days." She looked worried.

Mavis nodded. She trusted Christine's judgement.

"Right then girls," Mavis's 'Matron's Voice' called them to order, "let's get a plan of action sorted, and get moving," and they set to, agreeing who would do what to try to locate Christine's cousin Harry.

# II

Harry Wraysbury peeled open his heavy eyelids, and sneezed. Around him was darkness, and the smell of damp. He couldn't move: his hands were tied behind his back and his ankles were bound. He was lying down, curled up in the foetal position. He tried to extend his body, but both his feet and his head hit walls. Wriggling around didn't help: there were four walls very close about him. He tried to sit upright, but there wasn't enough head room.

A disconcerting term, 'Little-Ease', drifted into his consciousness from a history lesson somewhere in his dim and distant past.

Gathering his thoughts and limbs about himself he managed, finally, to bring his feet through his arms so that his hands were in front of his body. He silently, and wryly, acknowledged that his years of athleticism were paying off in the most unlikely manner. It was too dark for him to see the hands he now held up in front of him, and the cords binding his wrists were so tight that he could barely feel his fingertips. He wriggled his fingers, trying to bring some life back to them, and did the same with his toes.

Harry had no idea where he was, or why he was there, but he was pretty certain that whoever had brought him to this predicament had meant him to remain within it.

Finally able to rub his itchy nose, Harry then felt around his wrist-bonds with his tongue. He managed to make out narrow, flat leather cords, possibly leather boot laces, that had been wound around and around his wrists and tied with many knots in several places. He started to pick at a knot with his teeth, tasting the bitterness of the wet leather, even smelling it in the mouldering atmosphere. Then a slight movement in the air brushed his cheek. He turned his face towards the direction of the faint breeze and sniffed.....he could smell bacon. Someone was frying bacon. Not very close by - he couldn't hear the sizzle - but somewhere, not too far off.

The smell set off his saliva glands, which ached as they watered. Harry realised he was very hungry. He wondered when he had last eaten, then what day it was, whether it was day or night, and how long he had been......here, wherever here was. And he wondered why whoever had put him in this place hadn't bothered to do anything to prevent him from shouting out. His instincts told him not to take advantage of this seeming oversight, but to try to get his hands free, or at least to try to get his eyes to focus on something – anything – to allow him some sense of place. He was feeling totally disorientated, and, truth be told, more than a little frightened. What the hell was going on?

As he nibbled at the leather on his wrists he thought back to the last thing he could remember.......it had been a Wednesday morning and he'd been due to collect Rob outside the main gate at Lord's cricket ground, so they could go to play Fives out at the Westway. He'd met Rob and they'd stopped for a quick drink before setting off.....and that was about it......what had happened to bring him to this place........*and* ..........where was Rob?

# III

"Turn the gas down – you'll burn it!" shouted Gary to Natasha.

"Shut you're bleedin' face, or cook it yourself!" Natasha shouted back.

"Please yourself. But I in't eating no sandwiches with no burned bacon in 'em," shouted Gary towards the kitchen.

"All the more for me then," came the reply, just carrying over the loud sizzling.

Gary Gilchrist thought about his girlfriend's response, and decided to take action. He hoisted himself out of his armchair. As he peered into the grimy kitchen he saw Natasha Moon slathering margarine onto slices of packaged bread. She looked up at him, defiantly, through clouds of greasy blue smoke, and poked her tongue out at him.

"Tash! You're bleedin' burnin' it you silly cow! Turn the gas down!" shouted Gary, but the singer on the radio wailed ever louder as Natasha pushed hard on the volume button, and Gary's protests were drowned out. He walked away, grumbling to himself. If it wasn't for the fact that she was pretty accommodating between the sheets she'd have been out long ago....but she served her purpose, he supposed. But he wondered if she had it in her to stick with him and keep her mouth shut, with what he had planned. She might be a good old party girl, but she'd already kicked up a fuss about trying to feed the kid he had so carefully tied up and locked in the coal cellar. She knew too much to let her out of his sight now, he knew that at least. Maybe when he'd picked up the money she'd have to have a little 'accident'....after all, he'd be able to afford a much better class of bird when he was a millionaire.

He'd dropped off the ransom note last night. If they followed the instructions they'd be ringing soon.

Gary looked at the clock on the mantelpiece – almost twelve. He'd better turn the boy's phone back on again. Not long now, he thought, and he snapped open a can of beer. It fizzed onto his hand, and, as he licked it dry, he noticed there was some blood under his thumbnail.

Stupid bugger, fighting like that, he thought. Why hadn't the big feller just gone quietly like the one downstairs? Obviously he should have put more of the stuff in his beer, but how was he to know he'd have the constitution of an ox? If only he'd passed out, like Ginger downstairs, he wouldn't have had to have knocked him out and cut him. And when he'd cut him, he'd bled like a stuck pig, of course. It was all over the inside of van: he'd probably never get it off. Not that it mattered, of course, 'cos after he'd picked up the three million quid they were going to give him, he'd never need to go near no van ever again.

As he thought about the money, he wondered if he should have asked for more. The kid's grandmother had more money than she knew what to do with, so of course she'd pay up. More likely to than his father, who'd probably go all Scotland Yard on them and refuse to pay. No, Granny wouldn't want anything to happen to 'The Spare', so she'd put The Yard lot in their place and pay up. Of course, Gary didn't expect her to phone him herself, some servant or other would do that. There hadn't been anything on the telly, so he was pretty sure she'd have kept the coppers out of it, like he'd said she had to in the note.

Yes, by this time tomorrow he'd be three million quid better off, and set for life. He'd be able to get out of this dump and travel the world in fine style. All he had to do was pick up the money and he'd be on Easy Street. He stabbed at the remote control changing channel, blindly, then he saw something that caught his eye and he stopped.

"Hey – come at look at this Tash – they've got some bloke on the news dressed up to look like him downstairs...makin' out he's diggin' a well in Africa or sumpfink. Cor, 'e looks like him.....Tash.......*Tash* !"

"Bleedin' 'ell Gary, do you want these sarnies or what? I can't be doin' two things at once, can I love? Wha's up?"

Gary and Natasha stood in front of the television laughing and eating their bacon sandwiches. Then the tiny silver mobile phone Gary had set upon the mantelpiece sprang to life. It was just two minutes past noon.

"That'll be Granny I reckon," said Gary with a cocky wink.

"You don't think she'd ring herself, do ya?" asked Natasha, wide eyed, through a mouthful of bacon and brown sauce.

"Nah – some 'underling' I reckon. And I bet they'll be trying to trace the call or sumpfink, so turn the telly down and let's be quick about it."

Natasha adjusted the volume on the monstrous machine in the corner of the room and giggled a little.

Gary pushed the button and said, "Hello," in the deepest, roughest voice he could manage.

"Harry? Is that you?" The voice was posh, a woman. Gary's stomach flipped. Was it *her*?

"Nah, 's'not 'Arry," Gary was purposely brusque.

"To whom am I speaking?" The voice was high, clipped, very precise.

Gary kept his cool, as best he could.

"That's for me to know," he replied, cockily.

"And for me to find out I suppose." The woman was playing with him. Snotty bitch. But he'd have the last laugh.

"I want three million, like the note said, or 'e's dead. Right." Gary tried to make sure it didn't sound like a question.

"Note? What note?" the woman sounded puzzled. She was playing for time. He wouldn't let her get away with it.

"Don't mess with me – you wouldn't 'ave rung if it weren't for the note. Three million like it said, where it said, when it said."

"But I've lost the note...." came the woman's plaintive cry.

Gary knew she was messing with him, and pushed the button to end the conversation. "Tit!" he shouted at the phone.

"What did they say – *what*???" screamed Natasha at him, her eyes wide and wild.

95

"They're trying to trace the call, that's what....she was talkin' rubbish....ramblin' on..........said she'd lost the note...."

"'Ow can she 'ave lost the note?" squealed Natasha. "You *stapled* it to that bloke's ear before you dumped 'im out the van, for Chris'sakes!"

"Exactly!" replied Gary, agreeing. "You can't exactly loose sumpfink stapled to a person's ear like that, can yer?"

"Yeah," replied Natasha emphatically, then added an equally forceful "Nah," for good measure.

They both jumped as the young man's telephone rang again.

"What?" shouted Gary when he answered.

"I'm sorry, I shouldn't have upset you," said the woman's voice. That was more like it. At least she knew who was in charge. "I just wanted to clarify your instructions." She sounded frightened.

"Look," shouted Gary, just about holding onto the very edge of his temper, "like I said in the note to Granny, put three million quid in unmarked notes into a sports bag in the bin by the third bench along from the statue of the Frog Prince in Battersea Park. There *are* only three benches along there and each one has a bin by it – put it in the end bin by the end bench. Noon tomorrow. That's it." He turned off the telephone altogether and nodded emphatically at Natasha. "And then all we've got to do is pick up the money and get out of here! You won't mind helpin' me with that little job, will ya Tash?"

Natasha looked doubtful.

"I'm not sure about that Gar...I mean, they might have police everywhere...."

"You don't think I'm that stupid, do ya? That bin by that bench is surrounded by trees – they won't see us till we've gone, and then it'll be too late. All you've got to do is dress up in them old overalls, act like you're emptying the bin, bring the bag to the van and we'll be off."

When Gary explained it like that, it didn't sound too difficult after all, thought Natasha.

They smiled at each other and shared a brown sauce flavoured kiss.

As his hands wandered over Tash's body, Gary's mind wandered back through the conversation with the Posh Bitch. Lost the note! What did they take him for? An idiot?! They'd pay up alright – and nothing on the news meant they hadn't called in the police. Though what that thing in Africa was all about, he had no idea. Now all he had to do was wait, collect the money and ride off into the sunset. He'd put Tash in the firing line, just in case, 'cos, essentially, she was disposable. But he'd hang onto her, while she had her uses.

# IV

Christine Wilson-Smythe, this time choosing to use her entire name, plus the Honourable prefix, had elicited a promise from the landlord of the Prince of Wales pub that he would get the captain of the pub rugby team to call her with Rob Walsh's exact address in Lisson Grove. Christine and Annie set off for the general area in a black cab, in the hope that the rugby team captain would call them quickly. Mavis and Carol had made their way back to the WISE Detective Agency's office to allow Mavis to begin the laborious task of calling all the hospitals outside London's North-Circular/South-Circular ring-road, working outwards from the city: her nursing career had taught her that there was an unofficial route you could take to find out who had come through Emergency Admitting, if you knew who to ask. She did, and was about to. For several hours, if necessary. Meanwhile, Carol had been tasked with setting up the files and charge-sheets for the Case, and was to be the information gatherer and disseminator for the team, and was calling all the towing companies in the area to find out if any of them had picked up Harry's car.

Annie swore liberally at the traffic as the cab she and Christine had eventually managed to find battled its way along Park Lane, then became embedded amongst others of its ilk on Gloucester Place. "If this is the congestion zone, it's bloody well named," Annie Parker commented acidly at one point. She became particularly irate at pedestrians who loitered on street crossings, but all the time she watched the little screen on her mobile phone, willing the rugby team captain to call her. Beside her Christine continued her abortive attempt to reach Harry on his telephone. Eventually Annie could tell she'd made a breakthrough, but couldn't make any sense of Christine's side of the conversation.

"That was quite extraordinary!" exclaimed Christine to Annie as she stared at the device in her hand. "Some chap just answered Harry's phone and as good as threatened to kill Harry if I didn't follow instructions in some ransom note he thinks he's delivered."

Annie was taken aback. "What ransom note? Your Aunt never mentioned a ransom note!"

"Indeed she didn't – and I'm sure she'd have mentioned it if she'd received one.....but he said he'd sent it to 'granny', which is very odd because Great Aunt Bess is just the Dowager....it's Harry father who's got all the money, not her.....I mean, I'm sure she's not short....but....you know......" Both Annie and Christine looked worried, and puzzled. The cab driver, who'd overheard some key words of their conversation, also began to peer into his rear-view mirror with a look of concern.

"Did you hang up?" asked Annie.

"No, he hung up on me," replied Christine.

"Well......," Annie smiled nervously, "I think you should call him back, Chrissie, and find out what he thinks he put in his so-called ransom note."

Christine reflected for a moment, then agreed. She redialled Harry's number. Annie waited with baited breath, trying to read the notes Christine was scribbling on the pad balanced on her knee. Finally Christine pushed the redial button again, but looked at Annie darkly as she said, "He's turned the phone off completely. It's going to voicemail again. The man sounded serious. There was something in his voice. Something I didn't like. I think he was trying to *sound* serious, you know, sort of gruff and rough, but.......underneath it all.......I think he really *was* serious." Despite what she *said*, Annie knew what she *meant*.

"Bum!" remarked Annie, succinctly. "What does he want?"

The cab driver slowed long before he really needed to at a set of amber lights and fiddled with the volume control on his radio. His passengers were in no doubt that he was straining to hear what they were saying, so Christine whispered.

"Three million in unmarked notes, here..... then......" Christine pointed to the notes on her pad. She didn't want the cab driver to know what was going on.

Annie was aghast. "You think they've kidnapped 'Arry?" She'd never been very good at whispering, especially 'h's', but tried her best. But neither of them were quiet enough to escape the practised ear of the cabbie.

"If some bloke wants three mill in notes, he'd better have a bloody big bag for it, and be a weight lifter.......or take it in hundred pound notes.....and no bugger takes *them* these days, not even us cabbies. Too many fakes around."

"We're having a private conversation, if you don't mind," called Christine, annoyed.

"Sort of conversation you should be having with a copper, if you ask me," retorted the cabbie.

"Look darlin'," responded Annie, her hackles up, "number one, we're not askin' you, and number two, we're private detectives and quite capable of sorting this for ourselves, ta very much, so keep your bleedin' nose where it should be – in other words, pointin' straight ahead and out of our business!"

She pushed shut the privacy glass with a bump and the back of the cabbie's head could be seen to be disagreeing with her outburst, but he pushed on towards their destination.

"Oh Chrissie – he might be right you know.....I mean, we 'aven't really dealt with anything like this before." For Annie to show any reluctance to get involved with a case was unusual – for her to suggest contacting the police, especially when it was against the client's wishes, was very serious indeed. Christine knew that, and was deep in thought for a moment or two, not sure how to respond.

The mobile phone in Annie's hand trilled into life. She answered it, still in shock. She grabbed the pad from Christine's knee and scribbled an address.

"Yes," and "Ta love," were the only words she'd uttered, then she pulled open the glass that divided the passenger seats from the driver and shouted, "Siddons Crescent, Lisson Grove. Know it?"

The cabbie's grumpy "'Course I do," floated back towards her.

"Quick as you can then, darlin' – as you *know*, we're in a rush!" and she snapped the glass partition back into the closed position.

"Right," Annie continued, "we've got about ten minutes, looking at this traffic. First things first – do you think this is just some chancer who's found Harry's phone and is playin' with us?"

Christine considered this very rational question for a moment, but her instincts told her that the man on the phone wasn't just playing around.

"I think he's really got him," she replied grimly. "*And* I think he might ….hurt him. There was something in his voice….."

Annie could tell that the telephone conversations had really touched a nerve with Christine.

"Right then," Annie replied, " you call Auntie Ag's and find out if her mother-in-law got a ransom note for her precious grandson, and I'll call Car and pass on all this info…they need to know about this back at the office…..agreed?"

Christine nodded. There was no question about it – she was worried. She understood why her Aunt had wanted to keep the police out of it, but now she could see Annie's point: maybe more resources and experience than the WISE Detective Agency possessed were needed – maybe she *should* talk her Aunt into calling in the police…after all, Harry was clearly in real trouble, that was none of his making, so his father couldn't *really* get annoyed……..

As Annie called the office to bring their colleagues up to speed, Christine called her Aunt, knowing she had to be careful what she said. She didn't want to cause too much upset, but she needed, somehow, to find out if a ransom note had been delivered to Harry's grandmother. It was going to be tough.

"Aunt Aggie?" she opened, trying to keep her voice bright, "It's me, Christine, look, we haven't got any news exactly, but…..have you spoken with Great Aunt Bess about this yet?"

Her Aunt's voice betrayed the fact that she had been crying.

"Yes dear," she replied, thickly, "I'm with her now. She's sure he'll be fine, and I am too….but of course we're both very worried, as she said, he'd never have missed that interview he was due to have last night."

"Could I have a word with her do you think? I mean, is she up to it?" asked Christine, gently.

"I'll ask her now, just a mo." Christine could hear her Aunt passing on her request then she replied, "Here she is now, Christine dear, don't forget to speak up," and the telephone was noisily passed to the octogenarian Dowager who, as a result of her poor hearing, habitually shouted, blasting Chrstine's eardrum.

"Christine! That you? Found the little bugger yet?"

"No Aunt Bess, not yet, but we're off to meet the chap he was going to play Fives with."

"Ties what dear?"

"Fives, FIVES!"

"Yes, he was going to play Fives. He'd never let another boy down. Never have missed that interview either. Where d'you think he is then?"

"We don't know yet Aunt Bess – but listen – are you sure you haven't heard from him – no-one delivered a note from him, or maybe for him did they?" It seemed to be the best way of asking if the woman had received a ransom note.

"Note? No-one sent any note! Did anyone take a note for me?" the aging voice screamed at her daughter-in-law.

Christine could hear her Aunt's answer, "No mother – no-one brought or sent a note to you here yesterday or today."

"No notes – not today or yesterday. Why d'you ask? Eh?"

Christine had to think fast.

"Well I thought that maybe Harry might have sent you a note telling you where he was going – you two are so close – or maybe a friend of his might have sent you a note about where they were going." Christine thought it sounded feeble as she said it. Annie was beginning to glare at Christine, she was shouting so loudly. The cabbie was beginning to peer into his rear-view mirror with interest again.

"Stupid idea dear....are you sure you girls are up to finding him?" came the acid reply, then the handset was clearly back in Agatha Wraysbury's possession and she spoke softly to her niece.

"Christine darling, why are you asking about a note? Do you think Harry or someone sent a note to his grandmother?" she sounded concerned, and puzzled.

"It was just a thought Aunt Aggie," replied Christine, delighted to not have to scream into her telephone any more.

"Well no-one has brought a note of any sort to the house, darling, I would have mentioned that.....like I would have mentioned something like a ransom note.....that's what you mean isn't it!?" Agatha was clearly moving as she spoke, Christine could hear a door being closed somewhere on Wraysbury Square. "Christine – what's happened – what have you found out?" her voice had raised an octave and a decibel or two. Christine grimaced at Annie and set about bringing her Aunt up to date. When she had finished her Aunt was speechless for a moment, then with a trembling voice said, "I need to speak to Harry's father. This is serious. I'll call you back. But in the meantime try to find that boy Harry was supposed to play Fives with – maybe he can shed some light on what happened yesterday...oh dear Christine ......this is awful...." and she was gone.

Annie's face was full of anticipation. "Well?"

Christine sounded resigned. "She's going to talk to Uncle Richard. I suspect he'll call us off and get the police involved. So I suggest we find out what we can from this Rob chap and then at least we'll have done all we can. Did the other two have any news?"

"No," replied Annie softly, "Mave hasn't had any luck with the hospitals and Car's just....well, you know, organising stuff." Annie would have been quite happy to play at detecting without a business manager, but she recognised that Carol was the only one who was able to manage their, albeit meagre, financial resources so that at least she'd have something with which to pay the mortgage at the end of the month. "And we're there...." she added, as the grumbling cabbie announced that they owed him fourteen pounds and eighty pence.

They alighted and Christine shoved a twenty into his hand. "Thanks for keeping your nose *out* of our business," she smiled. He looked at the note in his hand and rolled his eyes.

"Your business, mebbe, but should be police business......there's some right there if you needs 'em," he nodded towards a police car just pulling away from a second entrance to the mansion block outside which they were standing.

Annie pulled at Christine's arm and shouted "Ta love," towards the cab driver as they walked away. The cabbie made no attempt to give them any change, but did a quick U-turn and shot back towards the Lord's end of the road.

"Wonder what they wanted," commented Annie, referring to the departing police.

"Who knows....but I certainly don't think we want to be talking to them quite yet," replied Christine firmly. "What number is it?"

"106," replied Annie, looking at the numbers above the arched entryway that surrounded and protected the large glazed doors before them.

"Well, if this entrance is for 121-240, then I suspect that the other door will take us to 1-120....so we need the entrance that the police were coming out of," responded Christine blackly. The women shared a look of dread and set off along the car-lined street.

Entering the second set of doors they could tell that flat number 106 would be on the fifth floor. A rickety-looking metal-cage lift was on the right hand side of the entrance. Christine pushed the button. The lift clanked to a stop and she hauled open the gate. Their ascent seemed to be at a pace just above immobile, and they crawled up, passed on the way by a young man carrying three bags of groceries who bounded up the wide marble stairs two at a time. Finally they shuddered to a halt, and they emerged warily from the cage. Annie pointed along the corridor in front of them.

"There," she nodded. Christine pushed the doorbell, which bong-ed inside the flat. A slim young woman wearing a giant towelling bathrobe and rubbing her long wet brown hair with a towel pulled open the door and shouted,

"What *now*?! I'm getting ready as fast as I can!" Upon seeing Christine and Annie in the hallway she looked surprised and confused. "I'm sorry – I thought you were the police again! Who are *you*? It's *not* a good time!"

"I'm sorry to bother you," muttered Christine, now dreading what she was about to do and what she might discover, "We're looking for Rob Walsh. Is he at home?"

"Is he at home? Is he at home? No, he's not at home! The silly bugger's lying in St Martha's with his head split open and his ear nearly torn off…that's where he is. And I want to get to see him as quick as I can. Why do you want him?"

Both Annie and Christine felt the impact of this news. It wasn't good. Not good at all.

"What 'appened to 'im?" asked Annie, sharply.

The girl's eyes narrowed.

"What's it to you?" She looked from Annie to Christine, sizing them up. Annie was also carefully considering the girl in the doorway. Girlfriend, probably. In the shower when the police called. Just been told her boyfriend's been hurt. Declined a ride to the hospital. Trying to get out of the flat to see him. Annie decided to take the direct route.

"Look, I'm sorry about your boyfriend…..but we're trying to track down someone who was supposed to be meeting him yesterday – and we can't find them. So it's important that we talk to Rob. He might be able to help us. But, in the meantime, it might help us if we know how he was hurt."

The girl thought about this for a moment, as she carried on rubbing at her hair. Then she lay the towel across her arm and nodded.

"Well, it can't hurt I suppose…..the police just told me that Rob was found on the road outside Buck House last night, covered in blood. They think he'd been thrown from a moving vehicle. Something had been stapled to his ear. *Stapled!* I don't know what they mean exactly. Anyway, he's got a fractured skull and he's lost a lot of blood. He'd been drugged too." Tears welled in her eyes. It was clear that repeating the news she'd received had, just that moment, made it real for her. "Oh my God – poor Rob. I mean he's a big bugger and all that, but he wouldn't hurt a fly. Why would anyone pick on him?" She leaned heavily against the door-jamb, and both Annie and Christine automatically moved forward to catch her if she fell.

"You need a cuppa," prescribed Annie. The girl looked dazed.

"Maybe I do……" her voice was dreamy, "but I want to get to my Rob," she wailed.

Annie and Christine looked at each other and a tacit agreement was made telepathically.

"Right-o then – what's your name?" Annie's voice was businesslike but quite tender.

"Oh….I'm Janet," the girl replied, quietly.

"Well I'm Annie and this is Chrissie, and we'll get you inside and make you a cup of tea while you get ready and tell us all about Rob – alright?" As she spoke, Annie was steering the girl inside her flat and looking around for the kitchen, which, given the size of the accommodation, didn't take much doing. The girl put up no resistance and was clearly happy to be mothered, just a little.

Annie rolled her eyes and said to Christine, "Where's Mave when you need her?"

"At the office – calling all hospitals," responded Christine conspiratorially. "I'll give her a ring and ask her if she can get us any inside info on Rob Walsh at St Martha's." Annie nodded and set about filling the kettle.

"You get yourself dried and dressed, Janet, and I'll get a nice cuppa going – hot and sweet. Then we'll get you into a taxi and you'll be with Rob before you know it. Alright?"

"Thanks!" called the voice from the bathroom.

"Mavis will get right on it," announced Christine to Annie. "She knows a Ward-Sister there, who was once one of her 'girls'....so we might get something. But what do you think? If Rob was with Harry and he ended up being dumped out of a car outside Buckingham Palace....I mean.....what does it mean?"

"Gawd knows, darlin'," was Annie's honest reply. "I 'aven't got a clue....but maybe Janet here'll know more than she thinks. Look, the tea's steepin', let me have a word with her while she's gettin' dressed?" Christine nodded her agreement.

The noise of the hairdryer inside the bathroom had stopped, and a slightly more alert Janet dashed from the bathroom to the bedroom in her underwear. "I'll be two minutes!" she shouted to the two strangers in her living room.

"Alright love," called back Annie, approaching the closed bedroom door as she did so. She shouted through the door. "Did you see Rob before he went out yesterday at all Janet?"

"Ummmm....yes," a muffled voice called over the slamming of doors and drawers. "He was off to Lord's to meet someone, then he was going out to play Fives, then he was going onto The Prince of Wales, then to some restaurant or other and I didn't expect him to be home till late....if at all. He said he might be out overnight....which is why I didn't miss him....though, he usually phones to say when he'll be home.....Oh God," Annie could hear her crying anew, "I should have known something was wrong....."

"Now, now," called Annie, as comfortingly as one can shout through a door, "It wasn't your fault. If he'd said he'd be out all night then you couldn't be expected to know anything was wrong.... you're blaming yourself for nothing Janet....."

Janet appeared at the bedroom door wearing an oversized England rugby shirt and jeans. Her face was wet with tears. Her eyes were pools of misery and worry. Her hair hung limply, and still somewhat damp, on her shoulders. She pushed it behind her ears and gulped.

"I love him, you know, but I've never told him. I love him so much – he's just a lovely man. Big and cuddly and fun. What if he doesn't make it?" the question hung in the air, to be joined by the trilling of Christine's mobile phone.

"It's the office," she announced. "Maybe there's some news from Mavis."

As Christine listened carefully and took notes, Annie watched over Janet as she sipped at her tea, still crying.

She noticed photographs of Janet with a smiling young man – a very large smiling young man. She picked one up and showed it to the weeping, sipping girl.

"Is this Rob with you?" Annie asked.

Janet's face softened from worry to love.

"Yes, we were in France visiting a friend of Rob's when that was taken. It was last summer – it was a lovely trip. We were staying at some chateau where a friend of his was working. Harry. Posh, but nice."

"Would that be Harry Wraysbury?" asked Annie, pretty sure of the answer.

"That's right," answered Janet quite brightly. "Are you friends of Harry's?" Clearly she was having trouble connecting Christine, but more especially Annie, with Harry.

"He's Chrissie's cousin," replied Annie.

"Ah," this seemed to explain a great deal to Janet. "I think it was Harry he was going to meet yesterday. I know they don't usually play Fives together, but Rob's partner's got a sprained ankle, and I think Harry was nagging him to play. There's a big tournament out at the Westway this week."

"Yes, I know," replied Annie, trying to encourage Janet into thinking she knew what on earth was going on.

"Well.....," Janet was now in thoughtful mode, "if it was Harry that Rob was meeting, where's *he* then? I mean, I know he's trouble and all that, Rob's always talking about all the scrapes he gets into, but what could he have done that would end up with Rob being in the hospital?"

"I don't know darlin'," was all Annie could offer, but it turned out that Christine was able to be more helpful.

"Listen," Christine announced, "I've just spoken to Mavis and she tells me that she's spoken to one of the nurses who's tending to Rob, and he's going to be just fine."

A look of hope lit up Janet's little face.

"Really?" her expression showed that she hardly dared believe it.

"Really," comforted Christine. "The ear injury is superficial, though, you're right, he did lose quite a lot of blood because of a neck injury. The skull fracture is minor, the nurse has seen much worse get fully mended....and there's no brain damage of any kind." Christine beamed at Janet, but Janet looked horror-struck.

"I never even *thought* of brain damage!" she cried, "Oh poor Rob!" she started to sob again.

Annie comforted the girl and pushed her tea towards her once more.

"Come on, drink up, it'll do you good. And now you know he'll be alright, it won't be such a bad journey to the hospital." Janet took the tea, shakily, and sipped, then gulped, nodding.

"Anything else?" asked Annie, warily.

"Not that would interest Janet," replied Christine cagily. "How about we find her a cab and let her get on her way?" she suggested, nodding towards the front door and indicating that they, too, should be on their way.

"Good idea," responded Annie jovially, snatching the cup from Janet's hands and ushering her towards the door. "Got all your bits and pieces?" asked Annie, not making any excuses for the lack of ceremony with which she was hurrying along the young girl.

"Do you think I should stop and buy some pyjamas for Rob on the way," Janet was asking as they began to rush down the stairs.

"Oh, I'm sure they'll have put him in something suitable there, Janet, love – why don't you just go and see 'im and ask 'im what 'e needs, eh?" Annie's mothering had stopped but she managed to keep the concern in her voice. "Look, there's a cab now!" Annie jumped out into the path of a taxi, that screeched to a halt just feet in front of her. She dragged Janet towards the passenger door, pushed her inside and shouted "St Martha's Accident and Emergency – fast!" as she slammed the door on the still-confused Janet. "Give Rob our love!" she shouted at the disappearing cab, then she grabbed Christine by the arm and shouted, "So?"

"OK, don't pull," replied Christine testily. "We need to get ourselves to The Cricketers, just up the road there – fast." She pulled Annie's hand off her arm and led the way.

"What *other* news did Mave get?" asked Annie breathlessly as they hurried along the narrow pavement.

"Mavis's nurse contact overheard more than I wanted Janet to hear, of course. Apparently it was Rob Walsh's overdeveloped neck muscles that saved him. His assailant missed his carotid by millimetres, otherwise he'd have bled to death before they got to him. But, as it is, he'll be fine, in time. She also heard the statement that Rob Walsh gave to the police. He said he met Harry at Lord's, as planned, and that they'd stopped in at The Cricketers' for a drink, but that Harry was taken ill there. Some chap they'd never met before offered to drive them to the hospital in his van – he said it would be quicker than calling an ambulance, so Rob helped him get Harry into the back of a white transit van. Then the guy must have hit Rob over the head. The next thing Rob knew he was lying on the road looking up at Buckingham Palace and surrounded by police."

"Oh bugger!" remarked Annie. It was sounding serious.

"And that's not all – this nurse gathered from the police conversations going on outside Rob Walsh's room that they couldn't see a number plate on any of the CCTV pictures of the van and that they weren't having much luck tracing its whereabouts because, after dumping him at the Victoria Memorial, it had driven into the underground car park on Park Lane and didn't seem to have come out again – but they can't find it in there!" Christine and Annie were both looking excited, but worried.

"So we're going to The Cricketers to try to find out who the guy with the van is?" asked Annie, knowing the answer.

"Yes," replied Christine, "but I'm assuming that the police will have been there before us, so I'm not sure what we can find out that they haven't found out."

"But we can try...." added Annie helpfully.

"Yes, we can try....for Harry we can try......" replied Christine as they rushed across St John's Wood Road and off towards their quarry. Annie wondered if they might have time for a bite or two of lunch soon, since they were going to a pub, but didn't like to mention it to Chrissie, in case she didn't think of her tummy as often as Annie did. Well, thought Annie, you only had to take one look at her to know she didn't, but logic dictated that even Chrissie had to eat, sometimes!

As the landlord of The Cricketers looked up over his ale pumps, he saw an odd couple enter his establishment: one was a lankly, gangly woman, with straggly brown hair, a flushed face and a sweaty brow – she was panting; the other was looking as cool as a cucumber, and obviously came from money. With a pub so close to Lord's he was used to dealing with posh, and the greasy pole climbers too. The gangly one wasn't posh, the rich one was. He wondered what on earth they'd have in common with each other. It wasn't fashion sense, that much was clear.

"G and T please darlin', large one," Annie gasped as she reached the bar. Christine showed surprise, she hadn't planned on them stopping for a drink. Annie carried on, "And my friend here will not only be payin', but she'll also be havin' the same as me – ta love!" Having spoken, Annie repaired to a bench seat where she collapsed and undid the buttons and belt on her well-worn mackintosh.

Christine waited at the bar for the drinks, paid the barman, and brought the glasses to the little table in front of Annie. "Won't be a mo," she whispered, nodding her head towards the 'Ladies' sign. Annie nodded and gulped her drink as though it were a draught from the Fountain of Youth.

The pub was quiet. Very quiet for a lunchtime, thought Annie. She wondered why, then realised that maybe a visit from the law had had an impact. Refreshed by her drink, she picked it up and wandered over to the bar again, ostensibly to look for a menu.

She looked around, spotted the pile of menu's at the end of the bar, picked one out and sauntered nonchalantly back towards the man behind the bar, who was now pulling a pint of frothing brown ale with gusto. Peering at the menu, which was a fruitless task, given that she didn't have her glasses on, Annie observed to the barman,

"Quiet for a lunchtime, innit?"

The man nodded. "They mainly come in between half twelve and two, from the offices round and about," he nodded to the large buildings opposite, "but we had a little visit from the law around twelve so a lot of them must have seen the police cars and decided to give it a miss. Not a lot of people want to be bothered with coppers."

"True," agreed Annie, still squinting at the laminated folder in her hand. "So what did the Old Bill want then? Two old girls are safe 'aving a drink 'ere on their own, are they?" She added her best cheeky grin and a wink.

The landlord smiled warmly. "I reckon....." he decided to chance it, this one seemed friendly enough, "....but what you two girls are doing together I don't know. Bit like chalk and cheese I'd say."

"You'd think wouldn't ya?" replied Annie conspiratorially, bending her head across the bar, "But we're workin' on summat together....can't say too much, you know?" She tapped her nose, and winked again. It was at this point that Christine emerged from the washroom, but, seeing Annie in full swing, she decided it was best to sit with her drink, rather than interrupt a professional at work.

"Anything to do with why that lot was here this morning?" the landlord asked, his curiosity getting the better of him.

"Might be," answered Annie, non-commitally. "Depends why they was 'ere, I s'pose." She raised what she hoped was an inviting eyebrow.

"Well....," the man behind the bar hesitated, "....I'm not sure I should say, see......it might be something they're still working on. You wouldn't be from a newspaper would you? Not one of them that pays for stories and such like?"

'Chancer', thought Annie, and 'Gotcha' was her next thought.

"Well, like you, I can't say too much...." she led him on, "and, as you can imagine, it's 'er over there what 'olds the purse strings, so to speak...." Annie could see the man lapping it up, so she went in for the kill....subtly. "But if you were just to tell a member of the public what it was that Plod was doing here this morning, as they spent the taxpayers' money, and how you were able to help them with their enquiries, not only might you receive an order for a large number of G & T's, which, of course, we probably wouldn't have time to consume, but for which you would receive full payment, but you'd also probably be hailed as a hero for helping out an innocent victim of crime....and that couldn't be bad for business, now could it?"

Polishing a glass took the man's full attention – for about thirty seconds, then it seemed he had made a decision.

"You'd be ordering about twenty of those drinks then, would you, at about a fiver a piece?" he asked, innocently.

Annie knew she'd better play it up, so whispered, "Let me check," and moved to Christine. Bowed heads, whispering and the passing of a small wad of cash ensued, before Annie returned to the bar.

"Twenty G & T's is it, please, mine host," she whispered, and passed the money across the bar.

The man gave it a cursory glance. His expression told Annie he wished he'd asked for more. She hoped he wouldn't hold anything back – paying for information was a dangerous game.

"Couple of blokes come in yesterday – one of them I know by sight, nice chap, lives local. Comes in with his girlfriend sometimes. Not big drinkers. Like I say, nice enough chap. Big bear kind, name of Rob. Anyway, he's got this carrot-top with him yesterday – obviously mates. They're in for a quick one, larking about a bit, chatting away, when the red-headed one says he feels a bit queer and sits down, heavy-like. The big feller starts fussing around him and keeps saying how he'll get in trouble because he's responsible for the little guy. Then a chap sitting further along the bar comes over and offers them a lift to the hospital. I had to agree with him it would be quicker than waiting for an ambulance, but Rob didn't seem to keen. Seemed all for calling an ambulance, or even the police. Anyway – I had to serve someone and by the time I turned back again, the chap from the end of the bar and Rob were carrying the red-headed chap out of the door towards the guy's white transit. Rob didn't look any too bonny by that time either, but, after they'd gone, we got busy, and I never gave it another thought." He seemed to be happy with his recounting.

Annie leaned in, "So I suppose the coppers asked if you knew the chap at the bar who was so helpful?"

"They did indeed, Miss," he replied chirpily.

"Oh no," thought Annie, "he's going to hold out on me," she hoped she was wrong. Out loud she said, "And what did you tell them?"

"Same as I'll tell you – yes, I've seen him in here quite a few times; no, he's not a regular; no, I don't know a name; no, none of my regulars mix with him. He's just one of those guys – here maybe a couple of times a month. Not too local I'd say – usually in late morning as I recall. Strikes me as the sort that slopes off from work for a sly one, or two. Maybe it's his work van he had with him – again, strikes me he'd be self-employed. Scruffy, jobbing type. Didn't look too employable to me. But that's just me – I like my staff clean cut, like him," the landlord nodded towards the young barman who was obviously just starting his shift.

"'Scuse me a sec, Miss," he whispered to Annie, then he called to the new arrival, "Hey, Plod wants to talk to you about a chap you were serving when you were on earlies yesterday – scruffy looking type, sat there nursing a pint of John Smiths then helped that red-headed boy out when he felt bad." The fresh-faced youth wrinkled his forehead, then it cleared.

"I know the guy – Gary. Gary Gilchrist. Plumber. Comes in sometimes when he's got a job in the area. Why do they want to talk to me about him?" The young man seemed genuinely curious, his boss would clearly have been only too happy to show how well-informed he was, if he had been, but his next comment showed Annie that the police hadn't told him about what had happened to Rob.

"Never mind *why*," he snapped back, "just give them a ring – I put the number on the side there. But don't forget who pays your wages around here.....I need three barrels changing and we're low on tonics and bitter lemons....so sort that out, *then* you can call them....right! I can't think it's *that* urgent." He rolled his eyes towards Annie, "These young ones – want it all on a plate, eh?"

Annie nodded sympathetically. She couldn't lose this chance! Looking at the young barman she said aloud, "Oh come on, he's just a lad....he probably doesn't know anything anyway."

Keen not to appear stupid in front of his boss the young man replied swiftly, and with vigour, "Well maybe I do, see! I know he lives in one of those big old houses out on St Martha's Terrace, right under the Westway there. He got really pissed....sorry, I mean drunk........," he nodded at Annie, apologising for his language, ".....in here one night and I couldn't shut him up! That's when he told me his name, all about the house his mother had left him when she'd died and how it was the noisiest house on earth. And he kept shoving some pretty lurid photos of his girlfriend at me......she clearly didn't mind showing her all to the camera, but then she'd have to be a bit of a......certain type, you know........to go for him. He's a nasty bit of work, if you ask me. And I might tell the police as much. Can't imagine him helping out someone for nothing. Might do it if there was a few quid in it for him, I suppose."

Annie put her hand in her pocket and pulled out a ten pound note. "Here," she called to the young man, "have a drink on me." She looked at the landlord and said, "Thanks," then turned and grabbed at Christine, who was quite enjoying seeing Annie in full flight.

"We're off," said Annie, as she dragged Christine out of the door, "and if we're quick we might just get in ahead of the police."

Christine was swift to react, and even managed to finish her drink before Annie dragged her away. "Where are we going?" she asked, as Annie once again leaped into the oncoming traffic to stop a cab.

"St Martha's Terrace, Paddington Green," she shouted at the cabbie, answering Christine's question at the same time.

Once they were sitting Annie flipped open her phone and called the office. Her voice was excited, Christine was agog.

Carol answered the phone. She used her best telephone voice.

"Car, it's Annie – we need an address for a Gary Gilchrist, St Martha's Terrace, Paddington Green. It might not be his name or initial though, it might be another initial – the house used to be his mother's. Try the phone book....."

"I'm not *stupid*, you know," was Carol's sharp retort. "I'm pulling it out as you're wittering on. Hang on a minute, I need both hands....."

"Said the actress to the bishop," quipped Annie to Christine, who, sitting beside her in the cab had no idea what Carol had said, so didn't know why Annie was quipping at all.

"Eighteen," said Carol clearly, then added, "G-a, Gilchrist-a, one-a, eight-a, Saint-a Martha's-a Terrace."

Annie couldn't help but smile. "You sound just like Eric Sykes!" she giggled.

"Thanks a bunch, you old crone," replied Carol. "You need to know I found Harry's car, by the way. It was towed by Great West Towing at 5.02pm yesterday from a 'Residents' Only' parking bay on St John's Wood Road. But enough of that, Harry's more important than his car....why do you want the address – and who's Gary Gilchrist, when he's at home?"

"Pop me onto speaker phone and I'll fill you in as we go," replied Annie. Mavis and Carol asked all the questions that Annie expected, then Mavis asked an extra one, which worried her.

"Och – well done so far girls........but what are you going to do when you *get* there?" She sounded concerned. "Do you not think it might be wiser to let the police take it from here, since their involvement is clearly out of our hands now?"

All that Christine could tell was that Annie was worried again – she could see it in her eyes as she held the handset to her ear.

"Mavis?" mouthed Christine. Annie nodded. Christine had guessed as much – Mavis was the most practical of the four of them, and she'd probably asked what they planned to do when they got to Gary Gilchrist's house.

"Tell her not to tell *anyone* where we're going, that we'll keep in touch, and hang up," mouthed Christine, and Annie did as she was told.

"So – do we *have* a plan?" asked Annie, knowing the answer.

"What do you think?" replied Christine.

"Knock at the door and play it by ear?" suggested Annie.

"Unless you've got a better idea," was Christine's glum response.

"Well, we've got about another ten minutes before we get there – maybe we can come up with something...." mused Annie.

"Hmmm," was all Christine could manage.

"Come on girl," urged Annie, "put that Mensa brain to work....we need every little grey cell working for us...I know you can do it!"

Christine didn't look convinced.

# V

Harry was getting sick of the taste of leather. He'd managed to nibble through one knot, but had then realised that that was a dumb idea, and that he'd be much better off trying to nibble through the flat strands that bound his wrists.

The smell of bacon had long since gone, but now his stomach was aching, he was so hungry; he'd already passed the point where relieving himself whilst fully dressed and curled up in a black, brick box was something to worry about, but the results were less than pleasant.

Harry still had no recollection of how he'd ended up in this place, but, with every passing moment, he was becoming more angry, more frustrated and more determined to get out. He had worked out that his eye teeth were the best to nibble with, but his gums and jaw were starting to ache with the effort. Then finally, a cord snapped, and he was able to begin to try to unwind the leather loops – no use pulling at them....they only got tighter.

A few minutes later and Harry's hands were free. He rubbed his wrists, trying to get the circulation going. As he patted his body he checked for his mobile phone. Of course, it had gone. So he felt around his surroundings. Initially, he discovered nothing new. He was in a brick box – brick walls and a brick floor, but now he could reach his arms above him, where he felt something different – a wooden door. It moved; creaked. He didn't want to make a noise, so decided to try to free his ankles before feeling about any more.

This was more difficult than he had hoped. He could feel the same leather ties on his ankles as he had bitten through on his wrists, and he found several knots, but he had no idea how to release these bonds: he certainly couldn't chew through them!

If he couldn't free his feet, he thought, what about trying to open the lid of the 'box' and find out what was outside? It seemed to be his only option. He wasn't sure if he'd be able to move as slowly and smoothly as he wanted, but got himself onto his haunches and worked out that only one edge of the lid would move. As he lifted it a little, no discernable light came into his tiny world. In fact, nothing happened at all. He risked pushing it a little more, and then more. He had to raise it quite a bit to be able to peer through the gap, where he saw.......nothing, just more blackness.

Encouraged that there was no-one outside the box waiting to hurt him, Harry pushed the lid as far open as it would go and slowly, and very painfully, straightened up to a standing position. Everything hurt. It was excruciating. He didn't know how long he'd been curled up for, but it was long enough to allow his muscles to forget what it was to be straight and weight supporting. He rubbed his legs, his arms, his face and his head. Even his hair ached. But at least he was out.....well, in a manner of speaking. "Rob....you there?" he ventured. There was no response. Somehow, he'd known he was alone.

Harry tried to make out what was around him. True, everything was still dark, but this darkness was less intense and he could gradually make out shadowy outlines of various types of junk, piled to the roof of what was, he assumed, some sort of basement or cellar. There were no windows, but, directly above his head, he could make out some little dots of light. They were arranged in a circle. Harry puzzled over what it could be. Then he got it!

Harry was familiar with the iron coal-cellar covers that dotted some old London streets: they'd allowed coal deliveries to be made from the roadside directly into the cellars below – there was usually a chute that ran from the cover in the street into the coal-hole below. They had one at home in Wraysbury Square. He must have been shut in the coal hole in a cellar, and there, out of reach above his head, and surely opening onto the street, was the metal cover. Not big enough for him to fit through, he knew that, but big enough so he could at least be seen by someone passing by. Now, if only he could get up to it!

But first, thought Harry, he'd have to free his feet. His spirits buoyed by his discovery, he decided to hunt about – carefully and quietly – for something that might have a sharp enough edge to cut leather. He placed his hands carefully on the edges of the coal-hole, and pulled his feet up. Swinging his legs out of the box was a painful job, and then he took a couple of moments to get his balance. He suspected that the only way he'd get across the floor, other than hopping, which might be dangerous and even noisy, was to kneel down and use his arms to pull himself about, which he did. The floor was filthy and there were sharp little things that stuck into his palms, but he propelled himself towards a smallish pile of junk and tried to make out what was there. The faint light from above showed him what had been cutting into his palms – there was a broken old window frame with some smashed glass in it – he couldn't believe his luck. All he had to do was get hold of a piece of the glass and he could use it as a cutting tool. He pulled his no-doubt filthy old pub rugby shirt over his head and wrapped it around his hand for protection........

# VI

Gary Gilchrist rolled onto his stomach and stubbed out his cigarette in the remnants of the bacon sandwich that was perched on the bedside table. He looked across at Natasha as she lay on her back, blowing smoke rings towards the ceiling. He could do worse. But not much.

Natasha Moon stubbed out her own cigarette and looked over at her boyfriend. She was worried about his plans, and the part he wanted her to play in them. She'd never met anyone posh, but knew how rich the boy in the cellar must be and, after all, it wasn't like his family would miss the money.....they had so *much*! But she was nervous about the police. She had found it hard to believe Gary when he'd come home with the two unconscious men in the back of the van yesterday – she'd never known that he was so clever, or so brave.

"Gary....." she sounded dreamy, and twisted her hair coquettishly, "tell me about how you got them again – you were so clever...."

Gary sighed. Ah well, string her along a bit more. Let her bathe in his glory a bit longer. She really was a stupid, gullible little bitch.

"Like I said," he began, sounding important, "I'd stopped off to pick up some stuff from Bloko in Notting Hill, just the usual –a bit of weed, a few tabs and so forth, and he asked me to take some roofies to another bloke in Maida Vale for 'im...so I stopped for a pint at a pub up on St John's Wood Road. Well, I'm in there, mindin' me own business like, when the two of 'em come in. It's not like they're tryin' to hide, or anythin'. I mean the big one's sort of lookin' after the red-headed one and he calls 'Harry' to 'im across the bar.....and they're chattin' away about blackguards and squares, which I'm thinkin' now is some sort of code for the secret police who looks after 'im. Well, of course, I recognised little Harry straight off. I mean, there's enough pictures of 'im in those magazines you're always buyin'. And there 'e is, large as life.....freckles, short red hair, posh accent an' ev'ryfink. Besides, they're both wearing them red rugby shirts with the three feathers on them with a crown and 'Team Wales' printed on their backs, as big as you like........like we wouldn't all spot 'im a mile off anyway! So I 'ad the idea right there and then. I managed to drop a couple of the roofies into their beers and they carries on chattin' like, till Harry-boy starts to feel the effects. So I goes over and offers 'em a lift to the 'ospital, all friendly like. The big one, the bodyguard, is feelin' it a bit too, but 'e 'elps me get the kid into the van....but then he won't play dead, so I thumped 'im with a pipe and down 'e goes too. I shut the doors and brought 'em back 'ere. Luckily, with that stuff, the bodyguard won't remember 'e 'elped me carry the boy downstairs. 'E won't remember a thing. And no-one knows me at that pub. Only been there a few times before....one night I got a bit the worse there, but nothing to make me stick out, like. So off I went.....and the rest you knows."

"Why did you make *me* write the note?" Natasha's sounded hurt.

"'Cos you've got nicer writin' than me pet, that's why." He thought she'd buy it.

"Oh, really," was her only response. It wasn't a question. "And tell me again why you want *me* to pick up the money?"

"Because you'll look more natural in that cleaner's outfit in the park. And no-one's going to see you anyway, so you'll be fine....don't worry about it." She was beginning to get on Gary's nerves.

"I still think we should have fed him, Gary. I mean, he's got to be used to eating well, what with living in palaces and all."

Gary snapped. He sat up and pushed down on Natasha's arm, heavily.

"Look Tash – *I'll* say what we will and will not do. And he can miss a few meals. Jeez, Tash, he's a friggin' Prince – second in line to the bloody throne......his grandmother's the bloody Queen for Chris'sakes....you're not gonna make friends with '*im*, are you? You're just some old slag from nowhere, and 'e's friggin' Prince Harry," he placed a heavy emphasis on the 'aitch'. "We don't want 'im *seein'* us, anyway, do we?"

"But he's seen you already, Gary. *And* the other one did. Do you *really* think you killed him when you pushed him out the van, or will he have talked to the police already?"

Gary gave Natasha's arm a painful squeeze before he leaped out of bed and pulled on his underpants.

"Shut up, you silly bitch. They don't know me, and they won't be able to finger me. If the bodyguard wasn't dead when they found 'im, then I've lost me touch. I knows just where to cut 'em to make 'em bleed, see....and there's been nuthin' on the news, so, no, I don't think he's talkin' to the Old Bill. I think 'e's dead. And I think Granny'll pay up and they'll keep it all hush, hush.

They're good at that. Besides.....when we get away with the money we can look like whatever we want......"

Gary Gilchrist headed for the bathroom and some peace and quiet. He might have to shut her up sooner than he'd thought. She was starting to drive him bonkers. Same as all women, his mother included. *She'd* nagged at him for years and years.....till he'd had enough. Still, she wasn't saying much now, was she? Not under them bricks in the cellar. He wondered how the Little Prince would feel if he knew he was locked up just feet away from the bones of a stupid old bitch who'd nagged her loving son just once too often. He smiled as he looked at himself in the bathroom mirror. Women....can't live with' em, but you can kill 'em, he thought wryly.

Natasha was still worried, but now in a different way. What did Gary mean about cutting that other one? And how would he know how to do it, anyway? She'd always felt quite safe with Gary – sure, he was a bit rough, and he'd given her a few slaps in the months they'd been together. But only when she'd deserved it, like he'd said. Which seemed to be more and more these days. But, surely, he couldn't really be anything like they said he was at the Frog on Gloucester Road....surely he couldn't be a 'psycho'! He could be quite thoughtful at times, quite nice....of course, that was usually when he wanted something.....

Natasha slapped her own hand when she realised she was nibbling at her nails....she'd almost managed to stop that, Gary said only babies bit their nails...she'd get up and make a cup of tea for them both - strong, like Gary liked it........

# VII

Annie and Christine jumped out of the cab at the end of St Martha's Terrace, and wandered along until they could tell where number eighteen was. It was an unkempt house in a row of up-and-coming counterparts: with the standard Georgian three stories up, one storey down, these houses were obviously being bought up and renovated. But not the Gilchrist house: it was clear that whoever lived there cared nothing for the potential of the home nor owned either a paintbrush or a window chamois.

"So?" asked Annie, pointedly. "Come on Chrissie – you're the brainy one! We need something to get us in the door – something that'll give us a good reason to go through the house. I mean, we're assuming that Cousin Harry is there, right? I mean, actually in the house?" Christine nodded. "So what can we do that'll get us past a kidnapper with a 'kidnappee' on the premises? How can we make him let us in? Come on Chrissie.......suggestions, please!"

"Hmmmm," replied Christine, still challenging her brain to come up with a good idea. She looked worried. "We could be from the Council....that might get us in and give us a chance to look around? A complaint about rats......something like that?"

"I don't think he's the sort who'd welcome a visit from the Council," replied Annie glumly, "and I don't think we look like we're rat-catchers, either. Besides, the last thing I want to do is go hunting around an old house that looks like it's probably actually got more than it's fair share of vermin!"

Christine bit her lip – which Annie knew was a sign that she was deep in thought.

"I've got it!" exclaimed Christine. "We could be Estate Agents........with a client who wants to pay him lots of money for the house!"

Annie thought about it for a moment. "Good one Chrissie – it might work." She sounded enthusiastic. "Clearly he's a greedy bugger.....we could play on that. But shouldn't we have a card or something with an Estate Agent's name on it?"

"You're right," agreed Christine. She gave it some thought. "Wait a minute.......we just passed an Estate Agent down the road, around the corner....come on, come with me......let's go in, pick up some details and get a couple of cards for good measure....it doesn't matter what they say, so long as they're women's names, then we can come back and be them!"

"Good thinking, Batman!" Annie slapped her colleague on the back.

"Thanks, Dobbin," replied Christine, her spirits high.

"That's 'Robin' to you," retorted Annie.

They each had a smile on their face as they rushed towards the Estate Agents' offices that Christine had spied.

# VIII

Harry Wraysbury had managed to free his feet. He'd taken off his trainers, rubbed his toes back to some semblance of life, and had re-tied his laces. He was as ready as he would ever be to attempt to get out of the cellar. But, before he even contemplated trying to somehow get up to the tempting plate in the ceiling above him, he decided to try to find the easier way out – the door to the basement: the servants used to live in the basements of these old houses, and they would have needed direct access to the coal to be able to carry it through the house to the fireplaces on each floor, this he knew from the layout of his own home. So the question was.....where was the door from the cellar to the basement?

Harry seemed to be completely hemmed in by piles of junk that loomed up at him in the darkness, but logic told him that he had got in there somehow, so there must be a path out........somewhere.

He was still quite wobbly, and moved very slowly, trying to push his feet forward without knocking into anything. He held his hands out in front of him to help keep his balance. His feet found the edge of one long pile of junk, then he edged along in a different direction, then another. He couldn't determine angles, but he took his bearings from the little holes in the plate above: the plate was in the pavement, with the coal-hole part of the cellar extending out beyond the apron of the house, under the pavement. If this house followed the same general pattern as his own home, the door to the basement would be directly opposite the hole to the street – but that way seemed blocked.

Harry stopped for a moment. He was feeling dizzy. No food, no water, that he was aware of, no real circulation in his extremities and all this darkness had him dazed and confused. He felt so frustrated with his inability to master his surroundings he felt he might cry. He could feel tears welling, and he felt very small and alone. Quite hopeless. *Why* was he here? Where *was* here? What had happened to Rob? What had happened to *him*? Harry felt that if only he could remember something, he'd be better able to come to terms with his predicament......but, other than having a drink with Rob at The Cricketers, his memory was a fuzzy, infuriating, blank!

He sat down, hard, held his head in his hands, and wept. Silently. He didn't want anyone to hear him. All he wanted was to be safe: to be at home in the glorious daylight, with his mother and father, his lovely old grandmother, and even his clever-dick brother.....who wasn't so bad really – he couldn't help being brainy, after all......oh, to be at home...........

Suddenly, in the crashing silence, something caught Harry's ear. It sounded like a front door bell – the old-fashioned type that rings out loud into the servants' basement quarters. Maybe help was coming.............

# IX

"Don't answer it Tash!" shouted Gary roughly as Natasha moved towards the front door.

"Why not?" she asked, surprised.

"Don't be so bloody stupid......think, woman!" he spat back at her. "I'm not expectin' no-one, and you certainly in't......so it can't be anyone we wants to see. Besides....think about downstairs........." he nodded in the direction of the back stairs that led down to the basement and cellar.

"Oh, yeah," replied Natasha, but not really understanding Gary's anger. But then, she never did. "But it *might* be someone we want to see....." she added feebly, hoping it was a friend who might relieve the strained atmosphere that had surrounded her since Gary had come up with this plan of his. "Who is it?" she called through the door, before Gary could stop her.

A woman's voice replied. It was muffled by the heavy door, but sounded friendly enough.

"My name's Annabel Dixon, and I'm from Freed and Henry the Estate Agents around the corner. I wondered if I could speak with the owner."

Natasha turned to Gary and raised her eyebrows in query. Gary pulled her roughly from the door and stood close to it himself.

"I'm the owner," he shouted. "What d'ya want?"

"Well, I think this might be easier if you would open the door, Sir!" came the reply.

Gary thought about it, then opened the front door a crack.

They certainly weren't coppers: two women. One was a bit of a mess, probably somewhere in her fifties - gangly and sweaty, having a hot flash he'd guess...from the experience he'd had of them with his mother; the other one was tall, slim, not a bad pair on her, nice enough face, not that *that* was essential, and looked posh...pearls and a fancy haircut, you could always tell. They *looked* like Estate Agents. They each held out a business card. Gary took them both and read them, then looked at the women – the posh one was Annabel – that suited her that did, and the older one was called Eustelle St Honore....fancy name for a not very fancy woman.

"So?" he asked gruffly.

Annie answered, in character as Eustelle.....who was actually a very large woman of St Lucian origin who was currently sitting at her desk at Freed and Henry, eating a Pot Noodle, not five minutes from Gary Gilchrist's front door. Annie was using her best posh accent. "Might I enquire if you are the homeowner, Sir?"

Gary smiled wryly – he knew common trying not to sound it!

"Yes darlin' I am, and there's no need to Sir me, ta very much. Where you from, darlin'? Plaistow?"

Annie had counted on him spotting her roots, and played on it.

She looked at her feet coyly, then at Christine.

"Sorry Annabel, darlin'," she said brightly to Christine, in her broadest accent, "The cat's well an' truly out the bag, eh?" Then, to Gary, she smiled a cheeky grin and said, "No pullin' the wool over your eyes, eh darlin'? Got a good ear on you. Plaistow it is...know it?"

"A bit," conceded Gary guardedly.

"Look," said Annie, lowering her voice and glancing about her furtively, "me name's not reely Eustelle St Honore – I'm Annie, Annie Parker."

Christine wasn't acting when she looked at Annie in horror. What on earth was she playing at?

"Anyway," continued Annie, ignoring Christine's expression, "they've just taken me on at the Estate Agents round the corner, and this is my boss, Miss Dixon. They thought they'd give me a fancy name for all the fancy clients they're gettin' these days, but I can tell a real Londoner when I meet one....so here I am, plain old Annie Parker from Plaistow...and, my Gawd, have I got a sniff for you!"

Annie was laying it on thick, and Christine could see a glint in the man's eyes. She knew Annie was good....but this was brilliant! She decided to play along in her role as Miss Annabel Dixon – boss.

"Miss St Honore....I mean Miss Parker," she interrupted. "This is not the way we do things at Freed and Henry – and I think we've put this gentleman to enough trouble already. He's clearly not interested in what we have to say." She let the words hang in the air as she made to pull Annie away from the door. Christine hoped she hadn't gone too far.

"Oh come on Annabel, sorry, Miss Dixon," retorted Annie, still in character, "I can tell you're not used to dealing with people who have something that someone else wants – but don't know it yet. Let me tell 'im at least....before you kick me out on my ear that is!"

"Tell me *what*," interrupted an impatient Gary.

"See," said 'Annie' triumphantly, "I knew he'd know he was onto a good thing....."

"Look, will you two sort this out back at the office and just tell me what the 'ell you're on about – you darlin' - you spit it out!" shouted Gary at Annie.

Gary looked vehemently at Annie and she 'capitulated'. Drawing even closer to Gary Gilchrist, something she'd not normally have chosen to do, Annie repeated her act of looking around, as if to make sure she wasn't being overheard then whispered, in her best non-whisper, "We've got a bit of posh who's interested in buying your house. She's got more money than sense and she thinks she's spotted the 'next big thing' out here. We could be talking a mill or more." Annie finished with a conspiratorial wink, and nodded, all but poking out her tongue at Christine/Annabel.

Gary took in this statement for a few seconds then countered with, "How do you know she's serious?" The idea of selling this dump for a million quid seemed like nonsense to him - who the hell would pay that much for it? But a million quid was a million quid. It wasn't three million, of course, which was what he'd have in his hands tomorrow, all being well.....but if anything went wrong with the deal it mightn't be a bad thing to have something to fall back on....and you could have a very soft landing on a million nicker. In fact, if everything went according to plan tomorrow he'd walk away with three million and, since no-one knew who he was, he might even stick around for a quick sale on the old place.

Annie was ready for his question.

"Well Mister......?" she paused, waiting for Gary to fill in the blank.

"Gilchrist."

"Well Mister Gilchrist – what a nice name – the lady in question is so serious that she's asked us to get particulars of the house – numbers of rooms, layout, dimensions, that sort of thing. You see, she's an interior designer and her husband is an architect – so they reckon they can do the whole place up on the cheap, by keeping it in the family so to speak, and make a killing on the resale. Now I know she's got lots of money, 'cos I know where she lives now.....and let me just say this...."

"Miss Parker – remember our promise to retain client anonymity!" interrupted Christine, right on cue.

"Of course, Miss Dixon,' replied 'Annie', brusquely, "all I was going to say was that she lives in a very expensive house and she's just sold another one in Italy – so she'd be a cash buyer for anything under a million two....which might interest Sir."

"It interests Sir very much," replied Gary, feeling his mouth moisten at the thought of over a million for a quick, painless sale. "But I can't have anyone runnin' around the place today......it's not.....very tidy," he spluttered, not being as quick on his toes as the ladies of the WISE Detective Agency.

Christine's phone rang and she looked at Annie, indicating she should carry on with the conversation as she excused herself to take the call. It was Carol.

"Can you talk?" asked Carol, sensibly.

"We're with the gentleman now," was Christine's reply – she pointed at the phone and mouthed "the office" at Gary.

"Right then, so just listen," added Carol.

"I understand," was Christine's safe reply.

"Aunt Agatha just called the office – the police have been there. Don't worry, I *haven't* told anyone where you are....*or* what you're doing – especially *that*, because *I* don't know......anyway.....they've told her what Rob Walsh told them about Harry's passing out yesterday, and she, and Lord Wraysbury, are now fully involving the police in the search for Harry. They are gravely concerned – it's clear that....whoever has Harry, you know.....means business. Get it? *Business!* The *ransom note* was what was stapled to Rob's ear by the way.....and it was addressed to 'Harry's Granny'. The police are puzzled as to why the Dowager Duchess should have been referred to in that way, and why Rob was dumped at the Victoria Memorial. And they don't seem to have the Gilchrist name yet – obviously that boy at the pub hasn't phoned them yet, or else the information hasn't got through to the right person, or they'd be there already, I should have thought."

"Oh my God!" exclaimed Christine loudly – she couldn't help herself....she'd just put two and two together. She needed to be able to talk to Carol without Gary overhearing her. She looked at Annie and Gary as if in a fit of embarrassment.

"Just hold on a moment, Carol, would you dear – I have to talk to Mr Gilchrist for a moment."

Annie was concerned when she heard Chrissie's comment, she'd been doing quite well explaining how it was important that they made up a floor plan of the house today, or else they might lose the sale, and that it would only take five minutes of his time in any case – and that they could be a very profitable five minutes!

"Excuse me for exclaiming aloud like that, Mr Gilchrist, not very ladylike, I'm sure you'll agree," Christine, too, could lay it on with a trowel when she wanted. "But it's our client, you see, well, our potential client – she's called the office to say she's found an alternative property – and it's something that's already represented by someone else....I'll just have to have a detailed word with Carol back in the office to brief her on what to say to the *client*.....maybe you can help Mr Gilchrist understand why it's *even more important now* that we do this quickly Annie?" Christine prayed Annie would pick up on her meaning. Annie did, and went to work as best she could.

Clearly Gary had relented, because Annie called over her shoulder as she crossed the threshold to number eighteen St Martha's Terrace, "Follow me in when you can, Miss Dixon." Could Christine hear panic in Annie's voice? Surely not, she thought. But whatever Annie was trying to tell her, she *had* to talk to Carol. She kept her eyes trained on the half-open front door as she spoke to rapidly.

"Look Carol darling I've got to be quick, speakerphone please?"

"Mavis isn't here," answered Carol. "As soon as you two said you were planning on going into the house she grabbed the first aid kit and ran out to get a cab over to St Martha's Terrace. She thought you might need her there."

"Good thinking," said Christine. "Now listen......Annie's in already – she's good, but I need to be there too. And I think I've just worked out this whole stupid mess....this idiot Gilchrist doesn't know he's got Harry *Wraysbury*, my cousin, hidden away somewhere....he thinks he's got *Prince* Harry!"

"Why on earth would he think that?" asked Carol, blankly. "Your Harry doesn't look anything like......well, I suppose he's a redhead, but he's got such a mop....oh no, he got it cut......but he doesn't *really* look like him....I mean....does he?" Carol seemed non-plussed, then added, "But, of course! *Your* Harry looks enough like the other one for some small-brained, mean-spirited, opportunistic idiot to think he's the *real thing*. And obviously this Gary Gilchrist is just such a person. That's why he dumped the poor boy Rob outside Buckingham Palace! 'Granny's' the Queen!! The cheek of it! Mind you – what's really worrying is that he's got away with this much! I suppose the 'Powers that Be' knew that the *real* Harry was off at some village in Africa working with a youth labour group – it was on the news today. But even *so*. I mean, young men being bounced off the tarmac at the Victoria Memorial should send up a few danger flares....and that they couldn't *catch* him....I mean Rob Walsh might have been a *bomb*...if you see what I mean. I most *definitely* think we should tell the police what's going on," she added firmly.

Christine was torn. "If the police show up mob-handed while Annie and I are inside...and *she's* inside already remember – it won't matter if Harry's there or not....*we'll* be the ones in danger. And if Harry *is* there," added Christine desperately, "maybe Annie and I can get him out without it all turning into some sort of hostage nightmare with SWAT teams and goodness knows what involved."

There was a silence in the office off Sloane Square.

"Here's what I suggest," said Carol, in her best 'organising' voice, "I'll telephone the police in ten minutes and tell them what's happening at the Gilchrist house, what our opinions are about the Gilchrist man himself, and why we believe he's done what he's done so far. During that ten minutes you get yourself and Annie out of the Gilchrist house – with some sort of opinion about whether you think Harry's on the premises or not. The police can be on the spot in five minutes after that, I should think, and by then we'll all have a good idea of who's where. Agreed?"

Christine agreed, still not sure that they were taking the right course of action – her instincts were to charge in and save cousin Harry herself.

As Christine walked up the steps towards Gary Gilchrist's front door, Carol put her watch on the desk in front of her.....willing the next ten minutes to pass.....without anything bad happening....to anyone....she wondered about how she could make the time pass faster.

At that very moment, Harry Wraysbury's fingers found a metal latch on a wooden door that he was immediately sure would lead him out of the cellar. He clicked it, gently. He cracked the door open and heard a woman's voice call out, not far away.

"Mister Gilchrist – it's Annabel Dixon here – the front door's still open.......I'm coming in now....are you all upstairs?"

Harry didn't know anyone called Annabel Dixon, but he knew that voice! If only he could place it. It reminded him of the river....of Henley; of the box at Ascot and picnics beneath the Anne Boleyn Oak on their country estate.....damn....who the hell was it??? He didn't dare call out, but the voice made him feel safe, and gave him the courage to open the door further.

And then everything went horribly pear-shaped.

# X

As Christine walked through the front door of number eighteen, St Martha's Terrace, she looked up the staircase ahead of her and saw Annie beginning to descend.

"You've got a lovely place 'ere," Annie was saying in a chatty voice, smiling at Gary Gilchrist who was just behind her. Hearing Christine enter below Annie called down to her.

"Oh, Miss Dixon – I think this is just what our lady is after – all the right rooms in all the right places....but Mister Gilchrist says we can't see the *basement* or the *cellar*," Annie placed particular emphasis on the words, hoping Christine would understand what she was trying to imply, "because they're full of junk. I said we could just estimate their sizes and maybe come back another day to measure them up....."

Standing just inside the front door, Christine was quick to catch on. "Ah, so there's a *basement* and a *cellar*....." she repeated, and transferred her gaze from Annie at the top of the stairs towards the door straight ahead of her, along the ground floor hallway, that clearly led to the back of the house. The door was open and, as she looked, she was taken aback to see a filthy, bloodied head, followed by a filthy, bloodied torso, creeping slowly up the back staircase. Christine couldn't help herself,

"Harry!" she cried.

Harry was astonished. Cousin Christine! Of course, that was *her* voice he'd heard.

"Christine!" he shouted back – delighted to see a face he knew, though completely puzzled about why the cousin he hardly ever saw these days should be.....here.....given that he still had no idea where 'here' was!

Gary Gilchrist looked horrified. He didn't know exactly what was going on, but his instincts took over and he did what came naturally – he pulled a Stanley knife out of his pocket and pushed out the small, but deadly, blade to its fullest extent. Annie was on the stair below him. He had her head in a vice-like grip in the blink of an eye. He held the triangular blade to her throat. Annie stopped squirming and gripped the banister the instant she felt the blade touch the skin of her throat.

Gilchrist's voice was rough, angry and cold.

"Don't move, bitch," he shouted into Annie's ear. She wasn't moving a muscle. "And you – you stay where you are, or I'll cut this one," he shouted to Christine, who was also frozen to the spot.

"Christine!" Harry called again, not knowing or, frankly, much caring about what was going on at the top of the stairs. He ran towards her, flinging his arms around her neck and trying to drag her through the open front door. "Let's get out of here," he cried, but Christine remained rooted to the spot.

Without taking her eyes off Gilchrist and Annie for a second, as though her gaze could keep Annie safe, Christine said to Harry, "Get out of here – now! Run out onto the street, and look for a very short woman with short grey hair....she'll help you. She's a nurse....a good one. Her name is Mavis. We work together. And tell her the police will be on their way very soon...."

"They're almost here - and I'm here already," came Mavis's voice from just outside the front door.

Christine felt an enormous sense of relief.

"Your cousin is right Harry," said Mavis to the frightened, and very confused young man, "the best place for you is out here – come away with you now, and let me see if you've been hurt. Christine," she added firmly, "the police are coming, they'll be here any moment, I can hear the sirens," Mavis wanted the Gilchrist man to know, as well as Annie and Christine.

"You bitches," hissed Gary. "I don't know who you are, but you won't get away with this! This one stays with me 'till I'm out of here safe," he added stonily.

Natasha Moon appeared behind Gary and Annie at the top of the stairs: she looked horrified and panic-stricken. "What's going on Gary?" she wailed. "Oh my God Gary, you're not going to hurt her are you? She's been so nice to us......" she said in disbelief.

"Shut your face, you stupid bitch," he spat back towards her. "This is nothing to do with you – I'm gettin' out of here now – you can stay or go as you please....just stay out of my way!" Then to Annie he shouted, "Move!" and he began to try to push her down the stairs.

Annie held her ground, grabbing onto the banister even tighter.

"Move... or I'll cut ya – and don't think I won't – I've done it before and I can do it again!" he pushed the point of the knife into Annie's neck. She could feel the warmth of blood trickling down onto her chest.

Every fibre of Annie knew that she was terrified, and yet she also felt strangely calm, despite being able to hear her own heart thumping faster than she'd ever felt it thump before. Part of her brain knew that she needed to play for time – time that would allow for the arrival of the police, while another part of it was telling her to risk the knife, pull away from this madman and run down the stairs. With a knife at your throat there's no safe choice between fight or flight.....you have to come up with a third option.

"Yes, you cut that poor Rob Walsh, didn't you?" she dared to answer back, her voice sounding strange even to her own ears. At this comment, Harry, who'd been focussing on Mavis on the front doorstep and the half a dozen police cars that were converging on the house, turned to face the tableau at the top of the stairs, horrified by what he heard. Rob......*what* had happened to Rob? Was Rob hurt?

Annie was still talking – Gary couldn't believe it.....and neither, frankly, could Annie herself!

"But luckily, for him," Annie's voice echoed in the eerie stillness that had befallen the group, "he survived, and he was able to tell the police everything, Gary. He knows your face Gary, and now so does Harry, and so do I, and so does Harry's cousin, Christine......"

Gary seemed puzzled, "Harry's cousin, what the 'ell you talkin' about you dozy bint?"

"Oh come off it Gary," shouted Christine, realising that Annie might not have the full picture, and not wanting them to lose the upper hand....if you could call it 'the upper hand' given that Annie's life was being threatened by a vicious kidnapper. "We know you thought you had *Prince* Harry locked up in your cellar, but what you've got is a poor kid by the name of Harry Wraysbury – my cousin Harry - it's just his misfortune, and yours, that his name's Harry and that he looks a bit like the Prince – but he's not.....so, whichever way you look at it....you're stuffed! You injured a perfectly innocent friend of this young man's, you sent a ransom note to the *Queen*, and I suspect you'll pay the price."

Given that she had a knife at her throat Annie was still able to manage a change in her expression that showed Christine that several pennies were dropping at that very moment, and that Annie was piecing together the strange puzzle they'd spent their day trying to work out.

"What do *you* know about it!?" shouted Gary, sounding just a little panicked. "You don't know nufink, you don't, you silly cow – nufink – just like all the rest of 'em in't ya! Fink's ya knows ev'ryfink, when you knows nufink – well I'll show *you* – I can *always* show a woman 'er place – even my stupid old mum thought she could boss me around, well I showed her who was boss, when I cut 'er..... and I can show *you* lot too!"

"What do you mean, you cut your mother? You told me your Mum died and left you this house," shouted Natasha.

"Well there ya go," snarled Gary, "I always said you'd believe any old rubbish I told ya!"

Natasha's chin started to quiver. She was close to tears. She'd had enough. *More* than enough. She didn't *need* this! She didn't *want* this. Gary was a horrible man – she had to stop him!

"You and me is over, Gary Gilchrist, you hear! And I won't let you go hurtin' anyone else!" As she shouted, Natasha grabbed at Gary's greasy, lank hair.

Annie didn't feel the knife slice into her flesh, but she felt it scrape across her collar bone as Gary turned, responding to Natasha's attack. As the pain shot through her whole body, Annie screamed.

Spinning around, Gary slashed out with the knife towards Natasha's throat.

"Shut up Tash, you silly bitch," he shouted, and Natasha did – grabbing at her slit throat and falling to the ground, gurgling.

Annie took her chance....even as the unfortunate Natasha was falling, she grabbed Gary's left arm, the one without a knife at the end of it, pulled it and spun him around. He lost his balance.....teetered for a second, with a surprised look on his face, then tumbled, headlong, down the stairs, thumping down the steep flight one tread at a time.

Annie grabbed onto the banister, to support herself, but she, too, was reeling. Then Christine felt Harry push past her, saw him leap over Gary's crumpled form, that now lay at her feet, and sprint up towards Annie, two stairs at a time.

The police constable who was first through the front door had never seen anything quite like it – a staircase strewn with bodies, walls covered in blood and a young man who he would have sworn was a shirtless Prince Harry screaming at him to fetch a doctor. Luckily, a level-headed superior was right behind him, so he didn't have to decide what to do next!

# XI

Christine was pacing along the hospital corridor. She had been for four hours. What were they *doing* in there?

"Come and sit down," whispered Mavis, but Christine felt that moving about was the only way to make everything alright for Annie.

Carol was sitting in an incredibly uncomfortable plastic bucket-chair next to Lady Agatha, who was holding onto her son's hand as though she'd never let go of it again.

A nurse bustled out of the operating room area.

"What's happening – will she be alright?" asked Christine – all faces turned towards the harried nurse.

"The doctor'll be out in a minute," she answered, then rushed off through a set of swinging double doors.

The 'minute' seemed like an age to the little group that had been waiting, tense and tired, for news about Annie's injuries. The paramedics had done what they could for her on the scene, but it had been clear that Annie had lost a lot of blood, and no-one had told them *anything* since she'd been whisked into an operating room on arrival at the mercifully close-at-hand St Martha's Hospital.

Harry had been cleaned up and had been pronounced fit to leave, when he wanted; the police had interviewed Christine, Mavis and Carol, as well as Lady Agatha and Harry himself; Harry had spent some time with Rob Walsh, who was in another wing of the same hospital, and now all they could do was wait. And wait.

Finally a doctor came. He looked as tired as they all felt. It was close to midnight. Christine felt as though a cold hand was gripping her heart. Carol could tell by looking at her that Christine felt the responsibility of Annie's condition very personally. They dreaded what the doctor might say, but they all needed to know..........

"Miss Parker is in a stable condition...."

"Does that mean she's going to be alright?" was Christine's panicked query.

"With time, and a good deal of rest, she'll make a full recovery. Though she'll have some significant scars from the attack. We might need to do some follow-up cosmetic work, but that can wait for now." The doctor couldn't have been more succinct, nor his words more comforting to all those present.

Christine, Carol and Mavis all looked at each other with wide grins. Mavis stood and reached forward to shake the doctor by the hand. Carol promptly burst into tears and hugged Lady Agatha, who hugged back. Harry pumped the air with a bandaged fist and Christine finally sat herself down and held her face in her hands, not crying, but laughing.

"When will we be able to see the patient," asked the outwardly calm Mavis.

"Well, so long as you don't stay too long, you could see her in a few moments....they're just taking her up to the private room that Lady Wraysbury has arranged for her. Ward A – Room 1....the best suite in the house," he smiled, and winked at Mavis as he walked away.

"Come along then," said Mavis, gathering the group together in her most efficient manner, "if we're going to see her let's do it and get it over with so she can get some sleep – then the rest of us can get to our beds and do the same."

Annie looked very small in the large room: she was propped up on pillows, her neck and shoulder area heavily bandaged, her hair covered by a green paper cap and with tubes coming out of her 'good' arm. She looked pale, but her eyes were open, and she was smiling.

"Oh Annie!" cried Christine as she pushed into the room ahead of the rest, "it's so good to see you looking so...."

"Crappy?" offered Annie.

"Well.....you have looked better," conceded Christine.

"It's alright Chrissie darlin'," replied Annie with a feeble wink, "I haven't got to worry about what I look like in here, and they wouldn't give me a mirror anyway. Besides, they tell me that all the scars will be under my clothes....when I'm wearin' 'em anyway!"

Christine, very uncharacteristically, burst into tears. Her Aunt comforted her. Mavis picked up the chart that hung at the foot of Annie's bed and cast an experienced eye across its pages.

"You've been a lucky girl," she pronounced, re-hanging the chart and smiling, "and I don't think we've got long before you're fast asleep in that bed there, young lady. They've given you some very nice sedatives that should keep you resting for a while, whether you want to or not!"

"Oh Mave – I *want* to – believe me, I *want* to," replied Annie, "I ain't half tired, you know."

Then she added, looking at Carol, "And *you* don't look none too bonnie, neither. What time is it? Does your David know where you are, Car? It must be very late, love" she concluded, looking out through the picture window at the lights of London in the darkness beyond.

"Yes," replied Carol, smiling wanly, not minding one bit that Annie always made fun of how she had to let her husband know where she was and when she'd be home. "I phoned him hours ago, before I left the office to come here.....he sends his love, Annie, and said he'll come with me to visit as soon as he can."

"Ta love," replied Annie, "and send my love back to him. Say I'm sorry I kept you out so late.....but tell him to be grateful that at least I'm sending you home sober this time..."

The tension was easing in the room. They could all see that Annie was still Annie – all be it a sliced up and stitched back together version.

"By the way," added Christine, "let me introduce you to my cousin Harry: Harry, Annie; Annie this is my elusive cousin Harry."

"Thanks for coming to rescue me," said Harry, meekly.

"They told me in the ambulance that you stopped me from falling down the stairs – so thanks for that Harry – I'll come and watch you play that Fives thing one day, maybe."

"That would be great," replied Harry. "But with Rob all cut about too, I don't know where I'd find myself another partner!"

A chuckle rippled around the room. It stopped abruptly when Annie asked, "How's that little Tash – is she alright?"

Mavis answered: no-one else seemed to be able to.

"Natasha Moon and Gary Gilchrist are both dead I'm afraid, dear."

"Did I......did I *kill* him?" asked Annie, horrified. The thought hadn't crossed her mind until then. Everyone could see that she was shaken by the idea. Christine moved towards her and put her hand on Annie's.

"What could you do, but what you did, darling?" asked Christine quietly. "It was self defence....I mean, look at what he did to you! And that poor girl – he just slit her throat wide open......oh Annie – she was dead when she hit the floor...."

"Trying to save me....."added Annie bleakly. "Oh God, this is terrible......"

Harry stepped forward. He struck a formal pose that Mavis thought looked somewhat foolish, but which melted his mother's heart – he looked just like his father when *he* made speeches at the House of Lords.

"Look, Annie," he said, his voice sounding different....strong and manly, not at all like the frightened boy he had been when he had run, pell mell, from the cellar that afternoon. "I know we don't know each other, and I know that mother and cousin Christine both feel awful about what's happened to you, because of what happened to me.....but the man was an animal! Lord knows what he'd have done to me, or indeed, to his girlfriend, given time. The police are already searching the house for his mother's remains: he'd told the neighbours he'd put her in a home for her own good, but now they're pretty sure he killed he so he could get the house. Miss Parker, the man was a lunatic! And you came to save me! Whoever he *thought* I was, I'm pretty sure he meant me no good....look at what he did to Rob! He really meant to kill him, you know!" He stopped and drew breath, then carried on, looking towards Lady Agatha Wraysbury, then back towards Annie herself, "My mother knows that I haven't been a model....well, anything really........just ask father, he'll tell you straight! But knowing that perfect strangers were willing to risk everything for me....well, it makes a chap think. And I had lots of time to do that while the nurses were stitching me up downstairs earlier. And you need to know that you've caused a *change* in me. I know I told mother that I wanted to do the chef thing, but I think I was half doing it to shut her up....and get father off my back too. But now – you've given me a new lease on life, and I'm going to make the most of it. I'm going to be the best damn chef in London, you see if I'm not –

just give me a bit of time, and you'll eat free at my world-famous restaurants for life!"

Smiles filled the room once again, some of love and desperate hope, some of happiness at the positivity of youth.

"Well darlin', you'd best 'urry up, 'cos I in't gonna be cooking up much for some time with this arm," quipped Annie.

"Oh....and I've got some news too.....look!" shouted Carol, and, out of the blue she shoved a little plastic stick towards Annie. Annie peered at it, but couldn't make out what she was looking at.

"Look! *Look!!!*" exclaimed Carol, waggling the stick at Annie, "I did it while I was waiting to call the police this afternoon....to make the time go faster.....I did three of them....and they're all the same....I'm preggers!" She was beaming. "No wonder I felt so bad.....I've *caught*!"

"Oh Jeez," said Annie tiredly, "there's me all banged up and you up the spout....what's to become of the WISE Detective Agency now then girls?"

"Don't go worrying your head about that, young lady," admonished Mavis, wagging her finger at Annie. "I'll put money on it that a few months from now we'll all be back at it....somehow...."

"And, until then," interrupted Lady Agatha confidently, "you can rest assured that there'll be a large lump-sum in your company bank account by the weekend; that my brother, Christine's father, will be continuing in his support of you by providing your offices free of charge; that Annie's private room and medical bills will all be taken care of by Harry's father; and that the Wraysbury family will do everything in its power to ensure that the WISE Detective Agency does more than survive this....that, when it is able, it will *thrive* because of it. You saved my son, in more ways than one, and for that I will be ever in your debt. I have many influential, and wealthy, friends, and friends of friends, and many of them have need of people who can do what you women, collectively, can do. Be assured, I shall be your loudest and most supportive advocate!"

"So I suppose we're going to have to get used to dealing with the Hoity Toity set....." said Annie as she began to drift to sleep, with a wry grin on her face.

"To the Hoity Toities!" said Christine, by way of a mock-toast, but Annie was fast asleep, Carol was already planning the nursery and Mavis was wondering whether she could catch the doctor before she left...just to check on a few of the medical details of Annie's recuperation. Christine smiled at her Aunt and her cousin...dear cousin Harry....she really hoped he had it in him to make a go of it...he really was a good boy at heart..........

# SUMMER

## Out and About in a Boat

# I

"It'll be *boring*, Dad," whined Zach. Dave didn't think that everything had seemed boring to *him* when *he* was fifteen.

"Can we have a campfire?" asked Becky in an excited voice. At thirteen she possessed more confidence and maturity than her brother, but could still delight Dave with her childish enthusiasm.

"That depends on the weather, and what the fire alert level is posted at around the lake," replied Dave, keen that his ex-wife should see that he was going to take this camping trip seriously.

"And you're *sure* this cabin's OK?" Debbie sounded doubtful. She and Dave had been separated for two years, but she still remembered his ability to screw up.

"Mike at work has had it for years," replied Dave, trying hard to not snap at his ex- in front of the kids. They'd promised each other they would never do that, and it usually worked. "Look," continued Dave, eager to get a weekend away with his children in the wilderness – away from Game Boys and X-Boxes and Wii's, "Mike takes his kids there all the time. He's going to run us up there in his boat and there's a little row-boat for us to muck about in when we're there...." he saw Debbie open her mouth to protest, so added quickly "......with life-vests that we'll *all* wear at *all* times."

Debbie still looked uncertain. Dave pushed on.

"There aren't many weekends we can do this: Zach's got hockey from September until May; Becky's skating doesn't wind up till June....and this is the only weekend in July that we can have it to ourselves – come August Mike and his family will be there every weekend. School's just out – let's have a little R&R? A little time just for me and the kids?"

Debbie bit her tongue. She could see the excitement on Becky's face and, inwardly, she agreed with Dave that a weekend away from everything that they seemed to plug themselves into these days might not be a bad idea. She'd be worried sick until they got back safely, of course, but it *would* mean she'd have a weekend when she could do....well, whatever she wanted.

"It's just *Pitt Lake*," emphasised Dave, trying to defuse Debbie's obvious misgivings. "It's one of BC's most beautiful, unspoiled lakes, and we all know that *that* means it's one of *Canada's* most beautiful lakes....because it *is*

'Beautiful British Columbia' after all, eh?" Dave didn't get so much as a smile from anyone for that little quip, so he just kept going. "And it's just ten minutes up the road, for heaven's sake, right on our doorstep – it's not like I'd be taking them to the other side of the world! We'll be in the cabin within an hour of leaving the house, then Mike will come back to pick us up the next day. We'll be out of here at 8am on Saturday, and we can have dinner together on Sunday and tell Mom all about it. Come on kids – it'll be fun….." Dave wasn't going to beg, but he'd get as close as he could.

"*Why* can't I take my PSP?" asked Zach, still whining.

"Because we'll be too busy hiking and fishing and bird watching and cooking up a storm for you to want it," replied Dave, trying to make the alternative forms of entertainment he'd planned sound just as exciting as some multi-level war between androids and aliens in a parallel universe.

Zach didn't look convinced.

"I could make Smores," said Becky sweetly to Zach, "you *like* Smores."

Zach grunted, which both Debbie and Dave took to mean he was going to go along with the plan.

"I'll organise the food and drink," volunteered Debbie, suspecting that Dave would pack fifteen cans of beans and no opener.

"But we'll be *fishing*," was Dave's bright reply.

"Well…just in case you don't catch anything," said Debbie with a sigh. He was so totally impractical!

In reality Dave was delighted: he didn't want to bother with all that. He was thinking about fishing lines and trail maps and compasses, he'd bring along his old guitar and they could play board games, which Mike had told him were always left at the cabin. Dave could picture it now: just him and the children; the magnificence of nature all around them; freshly caught fish grilling on an open fire……wonderful…….idyllic.

"So I'll be here at seven thirty on Saturday morning," said Dave to Debbie as he left the family house in Pitt Meadows to return to his apartment in Coquitlam.

"Don't be late….don't let them down, Dave," called Debbie, hoping he wouldn't.

"I don't know *why* you say that. You're *always* saying that," snapped Dave, sure that the children were out of earshot. "I *can* manage to look after my own children for one night, you know." He hated it that Debbie had no confidence in him. "I'll be here on time, and we'll have *great* fun!" he said with feeling, as he hoisted himself into his clunky old gas-guzzling pick-up truck and pulled at the ill-fitting door. "They'll have a weekend they'll *never* forget," he shouted cheerily as he drove away. And, as it turned out, he was right…..but Dave was thinking more of wieners toasting on twigs above the glowing embers of a campfire……..rather than the rotting corpse and danger that they were about to encounter. 'Fun' was hardly the word……….

# II

It was 7.53am on Saturday morning when Dave's truck screeched to a halt outside the family house. Debbie was peering through the window, and she, Zach and Becky were out of the front door before he could even unbuckle his seatbelt.

"I *knew* you'd be late," said Debbie accusingly under her breath as she started to load cooler boxes into the back of the pick-up. "They thought you'd forgotten! Becky was almost in tears. Why the *hell* didn't you phone?" Debbie was quite clearly angry with Dave.

Dave was angry with Dave, too: he thought he'd gotten out of bed in time to get everything done – but the minutes had flown by, and then he'd run out of the apartment without his phone, so he'd had to go back for it, but then he'd realised he hadn't charged it overnight so he couldn't call Debbie on the way. And then the traffic was awful. And he'd had to stop for gas on the way because he was totally out. It had been one thing on top of another – all conspiring to make him late.

As Dave apologised to the children, Debbie kept loading boxes. And more boxes. And backpacks.

"We *are* only going for one night," was Dave's exasperated observation when the back of the pick-up was half full.

"And that means you'll need bedding, a couple of changes of clothes, swimsuits, sandals, blankets, towels, food, water *and* a full medical kit. I don't suppose you thought of *that*, did you?" Debbie was still hissing angrily at Dave.

"Oh, I'll just spit on a bit of old tee-shirt and they'll clean up fine, right kids?" responded Dave happily.

"Don't even *joke* about it!" snapped Debbie.

Dave hadn't been joking.

"I've packed sun-screen, anti-histamine cream *and* spray, and anti-biotic cream *and* spray, and bug spray, and bandages *and* a sling. There's all sorts in there – everything you could *possibly* need – right?"

"Sure," answered Dave, sighing.

"And I've checked the batteries in the flashlights – all three of them, *and* I've put in spare batteries, right?"

"Sure."

"And the toilet paper is in with the bedding."

Toilet paper hadn't even occurred to Dave!

It had occurred to Debbie at about 2am: she hadn't slept at all – she'd just kept running through lists of things that might go wrong, and lists of things she could pack so they could put them right.

"I've put Zach's blue sandals with his blue shorts, and his brown sandals with his brown shorts."

"Why does he need two pairs of sandals?" asked Dave, mystified.

"Because he's like his Dad used to be – fussy about his clothes."

Dave looked puzzled. "I was *never* fussy about my clothes," he said, sounding quite hurt.

"This from the man who took longer to pick out his Grad tux than I did my Grad dress," said Debbie, rolling her eyes.

Dave could remember no such thing. But then, Debbie was good at remembering things – especially when they were arguing.

"And listen," Debbie pulled Dave close, "Becky has packed a small stuffed bunny in with her bedding. It's George, her favourite. If you see it, don't mention it. It doesn't exist – *right?*"

"Sure," said Dave sighing again, and added a tired, "Whatever," which he knew immediately was a *big* mistake.

"Don't '*whatever*' me!" Debbie was whispering very loudly by now, but she made sure the children couldn't see her angry, exhausted face. "Listen Dave, you're responsible for these children for a *whole two days*, and I know how difficult it is for you to act responsibly when it's just *you* looking after *you*....."

'Oh God,' thought Dave, 'here we go again........'

".......so buck up and be a *Father*, Dave, not just a big kid! *You're* the adult – act like one!"

Dave waved with relief as they finally pulled out of the drive. It was ten past eight, and they were supposed to meet Mike in five minutes. Once they got around the corner, out of Debbie's sight, Dave floored it, which Zach loved, but which drew 'tut's' from his daughter. They finally arrived at the boat launch at the south end of Pitt Lake ten minutes late. 'Not bad,' thought Dave, congratulating himself on a *very* fast trip.

"Sorry, Mike," said Dave smiling, as he jumped out of the truck. "Debbie wasn't quite ready, and then we had to pack *this* lot!" Dave rolled his eyes toward the back of the truck.

"They're all the same," replied Mike: he was smiling, but suspecting it was Dave who hadn't been ready. They'd worked together for five years, and Dave was known for being habitually late. In fact, you could rely on Dave to be totally unreliable, which was helpful, in a way: at least you knew what to expect.

It took thirty minutes to pack everything and everyone into the boat and get going. Zach was smiling and chatting to Mike at the wheel. Dave hadn't seen him so animated in months: if Zach managed a five word sentence in Dave's company it was usually because he was complaining about something. Becky, on the other hand, who usually never *stopped* talking, was the one who was silent: she was holding onto the sides of her seat with both hands, and smiling nervously. Dave suspected she was being very brave as they pushed through the deep waters of Pitt Lake at high speed, heading towards its secluded northern reaches. It took about twenty minutes of bumpy motoring to reach the farthest extremities of the Lake, then about ten minutes of slow meandering to finally get to the cabin, which was situated in what seemed to be a narrow finger of water that was almost completely cut off from the rest of the Lake by a large sandbank.

Mike tied the boat to the end of the wooden pier he'd constructed during previous summers whilst Dave walked with Becky to dry land. She didn't offer to help unload the boat, but went away to sit quietly on the rocky shoreline whilst the boys did their work. Dave thought she looked pale, but she didn't complain....*or* throw up, for which Dave was grateful.

"I'm fine, Dad," she said weakly. Dave ruffled her hair and left her to sit for a moment.

Mike opened up the cabin for them. Dave was somewhat dismayed: he'd expected something more 'cabin-like', but the place where they were overnighting was more like a shack. A new-looking green metal roof sat awkwardly atop a rickety cedar plank structure, which had weathered to silvery grey with the passing years. The heavily padlocked door opened into one large room, which was obviously the only living space. One small window allowed a little light to filter in: it glinted with the freshly disturbed dust. A collection of mismatched kitchen and dining chairs, a big old cabinet, an old kitchen table, a rather deteriorated small orangey-tan 'pleather' sofa and a number of cots stacked against the wall were almost all that was there. Mike pulled a rusty grill from a corner of the room, and set it up, with the new propane canister he'd brought, outside the cabin next to a log-built picnic table and benches.

"Where's the bathroom?" asked Becky of Mike. Dave was worried that she was feeling ill, but she told him not to fuss, and she smiled. Her colour was coming back at least.

"Round the back," replied Mike, and walked her around to the outhouse. When she returned, Dave could tell by her face that the realisation of what 'roughing it' meant was beginning to dawn upon his thirteen year old daughter. She wasn't impressed!

Zach laughed at his sister's face-pulling and called her a 'baby'! Becky pointed out that Zach had to use the outhouse too and that it smelled, but that he probably wouldn't notice because *he* was so smelly. Dave tried to keep the peace, at least until Mike had gone.

The two men went back to the boat to check that they'd unloaded everything.

"The trail map to the tree-house is on the pin-board in the cabin," Mike reminded Dave, "and, here, don't forget the gun-case," he added, as he handed a long, slim metal box to Dave. "Here's the key."

"Gun-case?" Dave looked surprised.

"Look Dave," said Mike, beginning to wonder if Dave was up to looking after two kids in a wilderness with which he was clearly unfamiliar, "there are cougars and bears up here, and they're not used to humans being on their patch. You never know, you might need it. You know how to use a gun, right?"

"Of *course*," lied Dave, taking the surprisingly heavy box from his work colleague. He'd never held a gun-case, let alone a gun, before.

"The row-boat's inside the cabin, behind the front door – don't forget to tie it up properly, right?"

"Sure."

"And the fire alert is orange, so you can have a small campfire, but make sure you douse any embers – right?"

"Sure." Dave thought that Mike was beginning to sound like Debbie.

"And don't forget – the kids don't leave that cabin alone after dark – you go with them, right?"

"Sure," replied Dave wearily, wondering why they couldn't go to the outhouse without him.

"*They* won't know what a bear in the bush sounds like....you will....right?" said Mike, as if replying to Dave's inner question, but raising another in Dave's mind at the same time.

"*Sure.*" Dave had no idea what a bear would sound like....in or out of the bush! "You go, Mike – we'll be *fine*, honest." Dave tried to sound convincing. Good grief, they were only going to be there for, what, thirty hours....what could happen in thirty hours?

Dave waved goodbye to Mike and turned to face the cabin.

"Da-ad – Zach pushed me over and I've cut my leg," cried Becky sitting on the hard, dry ground that surrounded the cabin, covered in dust, and sobbing.

"No I didn't," retorted Zach.

"Yes you *did* – you did it purposely," cried Becky.

"Well *you* started it......calling me '*smelly*'," responded Zach, kicking dust towards his sister.

"Stop it you two," shouted Dave as he carried the gun-case along the little wooden pier. "I don't care *who* started it, or what '*it*' is....Becky – wash that cut in the lake and I'll find the medical box." Dave was beginning to suspect that thirty hours might turn out to be a lot longer than he'd thought.

# III

It took Dave quite a while to sort out the cabin - to get everything unpacked that needed unpacking, to set up the cots and the bedding *and* get the kids changed into their swim-suits. He and Zach had had to wait outside the cabin so that Becky could have some privacy, and she'd taken *forever* to change her clothes. Now she was waiting outside the cabin while the boys changed. Dave reckoned it would take *them* about thirty seconds, but he hadn't factored in the time it took Zach to pull his bizarrely long board-shorts down on his theoretical hips, then up again, then down again, making almost imperceptible adjustments, until the shorts were at what, apparently, was *exactly* the right level. Dave had pointed out several times that it was just him and his sister who'd see Zach, but Zach replied that it didn't matter – they had to be *right*.

"Da-ad," Becky shouted through the half-open door, "I know it's July an'all, but that water sure felt cold when I washed my leg – I don't think I want to go swimming."

"It'll be *fine*," replied Dave, donning his own faded swimming shorts in an instant and emerging from the cabin triumphant. "Help me with the boat?"

"OK," said Becky, brightening.

"Can I jump off the pier, Dad?" shouted Zach as he ran along the creaking wooden structure.

"No – you don't know how deep it is there," his father replied sharply.

"Yes I do! It's four metres at the end of the pier – Mike's boat has a depth-finder *and* a fish-finder, and it showed four metres there."

Dave was amazed at his son's powers of observation – they certainly weren't something he'd noticed before.

"Go on then – but be careful!" Dave had barely finished speaking when he heard a tremendous splash and a joyful whoop! He suspected that the carefully positioned board-shorts wouldn't remain in 'the perfect place' for long.

He and Becky pulled the boat to the shore. It was a funny little thing – bright yellow fibreglass and shaped like a frog's body, with leg-like extensions that Mike had told him gave it great stability. Dave wasn't familiar with the style of boat: truth be told, he hadn't even been *in* a row-boat since his teens, when he and his dad had gone fishing together, and then no more than a handful of times. But he knew how to row, that was the important thing.

"Life vests?" asked Becky, her little arms folded just like her mother's, as she stood over the frog-like boat that still sat safely on the rocky shoreline.

"Of *course*," replied Dave, pointedly, "you can fetch them from the cabin - and bring one for Zach too."

Zach had swum to shore and was shaking himself off. "Dad, when are we gonna *eat?*" he asked, plaintively.

"Didn't your mother give you breakfast?" asked Dave, surprised.

"Yeah – but that was *hours* ago," replied Zach sulkily. "I'm *starving!*"

Dave looked at his watch – it was only 10.30am.

"We'll eat in a couple of hours," he said, meaning lunch.

"Here – Mom packed these for you!" shouted Becky as she threw a bunch of trail-mix bars at Zach.

Zach ripped them open and ate greedily. Dave wondered when Zach's appetite had kicked in: when he'd moved out of the family home it was all you could do to get him to eat anything, he'd been so picky about his food. But that was a couple of years ago, Dave reminded himself, and boys could change a lot between thirteen and fifteen. Tough times.

"OK now?" asked Dave, as Zach handed him the empty wrappers.

Zach grunted. Dave added, "And what do you expect *me* to do with *these?*" He was referring to the wrappers.

"I dunno," replied Zach, clearly not caring.

"Put them in the cabin, then let's go for a row about," said Dave, sternly.

Zach grunted again and made his way towards the cabin.

"Will it be OK to leave it all open like that?" asked Becky, referring to the cabin. "I've got *stuff* in there, you know."

Dave smiled at his teenaged daughter, thinking how she was so much like her Mom – careful, and pretty. He and Debbie had known each other since fifth grade: sometimes something that Becky said, or how she moved, or flicked her shoulder-length brown hair, reminded him of Debbie at that age. But that Debbie was gone – she'd been replaced by a nagging, list-making, penny pinching woman who always put the kids first and never seemed to have time for Dave, not since they'd been born. He missed the old Debbie – she'd been his best friend. Now she was like *his* Mom. For years before the separation she'd treated him as though he were a third child, and he didn't need another Mom – he'd wanted a wife!

"It'll be *fine*," was Dave's far-away reply to his daughter's question. "No-one comes up here – it's like a little secret cove. You saw how careful Mike had to be to get here – all that twisting and winding around the little islands and that big sand-bank? And you can only get here by boat – so we'd see anyone coming. Your stuff will be just *fine*." He winked at her, and she smiled back.

"Da-ad?" Zach called from the cabin.

"Yes, Zach."

"Shall I bring some water?"

"Yes, Zach."

"OK."

Zach finally returned with three bottles of water.

"Let's get going," said Dave, impatient to get out onto the glassy lake. He settled the children into one end of the boat, with strict instructions that there was to be no messing about, and pushed it out into the surprisingly icy waters.

A few fumbles with the oars and he was rowing: maybe he wasn't all that efficient, but they were moving away from the shore quite satisfactorily. About five minutes later they'd moved from the shade of the tree-covered hillside that ascended behind the cabin, and were out in the hot sun of the late morning.

"I should have worn sunscreen," said Becky in a concerned voice. "And so should you, Zach. You know how you burn." Dave could have kicked himself – Zach only had to *see* the sun to burn – he knew that! Why hadn't he thought of sunscreen for his boy?

"We won't be out in it for long, don't worry, it'll be *fine*," said Dave, hoping it would be. "Look, isn't it beautiful?" he nodded his head towards the shore they'd just left and the surrounding mountains: the cabin was on a rocky beach and set back into a low-lying area of brush. Above it soared magnificent cedar covered mountains – there were trees as far as the eye could see, in every direction. 'And they say we're going to run out of logs,' sneered Dave inwardly.

"It's *boring*," said Zach, "there's *nothing here*."

Ahead of him, Dave could see the buoy that Mike had told him about earlier. Apparently it was a safe place to swim.

"We'll tie up in a minute and you can both jump in," said Dave, trying to be cheerful.

"It's too cold," said Becky, dangling her hand in the water.

"Can I take this off?" asked Zach, pulling at his life-vest.

"No, keep it on out here," said Dave, keen to fulfil his fatherly duties.

"Oh Da-ad," whined his son.

"No arguments, Zach!  I know you're a good swimmer, but you can't be too careful."

"But I can't dive with this on...."

"Zach!"

Zach grunted.

"Look Dad, there's a hat in the water," said Becky, pointing to a ball cap that was floating close to the buoy.

"I bet there's a head in it!" said Zach, mocking his little sister.

"Shut up!" snapped Becky.

"Shut up yourself," said Zach, splashing Becky with the chilly water.

"Stop it you two," shouted Dave, trying desperately to tie the boat to the bobbing buoy.

"Get the hat, Dad, see if there's a head in it!" shouted Zach joyfully.

"You can't do that – you don't know where it's been," replied Becky, chiding her brother.

"It's been in the *lake*, stupid," retorted Zach.

"I've told you two already – stop it, or it's straight back to the cabin NOW!" said Dave, already exasperated. "And leave that cap where it is, Zach, your sister's right: you don't know where it's been."

Becky, vindicated, poked out her tongue at her brother, who had already lost interest in the cap and was pointing to something else that was floating nearby.

"Look, Dad, there's a glove too," said Zach, pointing at what seemed to be a large white rubber glove.

Dave peered at it. A big white glove floating in the lake: he wondered where it could have come from. As it floated closer he got a better look at it. He felt his stomach tighten: he could see fingernails. Gloves didn't have fingernails: hands had fingernails.

He was still grappling with that idea when Zach shouted, "Get the glove, Dad – maybe there's a *hand* in it!" He waggled his own wet hand in his sister's face, making her squirm and squeal.

"Right, that's it," snapped Dave, loosening the boat's rope. "We're going back to the cabin now, and we're not coming back out in this boat again!"

He started to row away from what he was now quite convinced was a floating hand as quickly as he could. He was pretty sure that the kids hadn't seen the fingernails – pretty sure they didn't know what they'd *really* seen, and he was working hard to convince himself that he hadn't seen it either. It *couldn't* be a real hand....he'd get them back to shore and everything would be *fine*.

They got back to shore alright, with lots of moans and groans from the children, then Becky busied herself helping her Dad prepare an early lunch, while Zach complained about his Dad not letting him jump off the pier anymore. Dave couldn't tell him it was because he was afraid there was a human hand floating around out there, so he said it was because the water was too cold. The food shut Zach up – eventually. Then they all cleared everything away, which Becky assured them would deter bears.

Slathering the children with sunscreen to protect them from the hot July sun that was now directly overhead, Dave proudly announced they were going to have a beachcombing challenge: he'd typed up some lists of things they had to find and bring to him in buckets that he'd also provided – the winner would get a candy bar. He'd even remembered to print out two of the lists, though the fact that, because they'd be scrabbling around on the shore, both children would likely have wet hands when they were carrying the lists with them had escaped him. Dave watched as Becky carefully read the list, then began to scurry about. Zach trudged away, kicking stones and muttering.

"Don't go off the beach into the brush – stay where I can see you," called Dave to Zach as he wandered off.

"So how am I going to find a pinecone on the *beach*?" asked Zach, as if his father were a complete idiot.

"*I've* found one," was Becky's smug reply, and she held a large pinecone aloft.

"There'll be lots of them, Zach," replied Dave. "Use your eyes – don't just wander along kicking the stones."

"This is *so boring*," muttered Zach, loudly enough so that Dave could hear him.

"Well your sister's doing better than you, so if you want that candy bar you'd better start paying attention," was Dave's tart response. Clearly bribery was the only thing that was going to work.

The day wasn't going quite as well as he'd hoped – but at least he'd managed to convince himself that the 'hand' he'd seen was a left-over from one of the movies or TV shows they filmed in the area....probably just part of a dummy they'd left lying around....like those 'Jaws' sharks they'd lost out at sea when they were making that movie: he'd learned about that when they'd all visited Universal Studios a few years back.

And it was such a lovely day – the kids would enjoy all the fresh air. He planned an expedition to the tree-house after the beachcombing challenge – he'd brought binoculars so they could climb up and watch the bald eagles soar above them. They'd like that.

Then he heard it. It was the most dreadful sound Dave had heard in his life. It was the sound of his usually grunting, constantly bored, fifteen year old son screaming in abject terror. And it froze Dave. Even Becky instinctively seemed to know that her brother wasn't messing about, and her little face showed her own silent fright.

"Stay there, don't move," was all Dave could manage to say to Becky as he ran towards his son.....who was in turn running towards his father, his stick-thin arms and legs flailing, his treasure-bucket and his beachcombing list flying behind him.

"Zach – Zach....what is it?"

Zach was as white as a sheet and he looked as terrified as he sounded.

"Dad – there's a.....I think it's a dead body......." Dave didn't have to ask if his son was kidding around, he could tell that the boy wasn't. Despite the fact that they were almost the same height as each other, he reached out and hugged him as though he were an infant. And Zach let him.

"It's OK, it's OK," he whispered into his son's ear, rocking him gently. "I'll go and look....you go and see if your little sister's alright – OK?" He looked into his son's frightened eyes: the poor boy was shaking. "Go on now – it'll be fine......" and he watched as the brother and sister ran towards each other.

Dave walked over to where Zach had been when he screamed. There, hidden behind a boulder, was what Zach had seen, and it wasn't a pretty sight. Dave looked at what was left of a man: the face had gone – a blasted, bloody mess was all that remained. And there were no hands, or feet. And he was naked. And bloated. It was horrific. Poor Zach – he shouldn't have had to have seen something like that – not at his age. Never!

Dave was rooted to the spot. Horrific though the sight before him was, he couldn't seem to take his eyes off it! For a moment he thought that this, like the hand, might be some sort of dummy left over from a movie shoot – they made some very convincing models these days. But, as the flies that had been disturbed by his arrival began to settle again on the damaged remains, Dave knew in his heart that it was real. This had been a person. Oh, poor Zach!

Dave finally managed to make his body listen to his brain, and he turned to look at his children: they were standing together, their arms around each other, Becky looking tiny next to her tall, thin brother, but seeming to be the one doing the comforting. Dave had to *do* something.....but he didn't know *what*. Here he'd been planning a bonding weekend in the stunning wilderness....now his son would probably be psychologically scarred for life. He wondered what Debbie would say, then he realised that, *somehow*, this would turn out to be *his* fault! What if she never let him see the kids again? What if...........

"Dad – is it really a dead body?" called Becky, obviously not sure if her brother knew what he was talking about.

Dave was panicking – he could lie....he could give them a story about movie dummies and tell them not to mess with it......but Debbie was always telling him that he was a terrible liar – that he could never keep his made-up 'facts' straight....so would he be able to get away with it?

"Yes, it's a dead body, baby," replied Dave, deciding it was best to tell the truth. He took one last look at the thing....and walked towards his children.

"I think we should just leave it where it is, and try to forget about it.....we'll sort it out when Mike comes back tomorrow.....it'll be *fine*, kids, honest....."

"Well, it won't be fine for the person who's dead," replied Becky, in a very grown-up tone. "Do you think he was murdered?"

Dave was stunned.

"'Course he was murdered – I told you – they've blown his face away and cut off his hands and feet – you can't do that to *yourself!* Duh!" Zach was obviously feeling OK! Dave was amazed that he'd pulled himself together so quickly. Zach seemed to have overcome his initial horror, but Dave hadn't!

"So whoever did it has tried to hide his identity," replied Becky, quite calmly.

Dave was beginning to wonder if he'd slipped into a different dimension. Why were his kids so calm? Why were they acting as though it was the most natural thing in the world to find a dead body – and a mutilated one at that – when you were camping in the wilderness?

"You both seem to be taking this very......well," muttered Dave, not sure what else to say. Of course he was glad they hadn't gone to pieces.....but this reaction was puzzling.

Both Becky and Zach looked surprised.

"Dad, we're not little *kids*, you know," replied Becky. "I helped cut up a frog in science last year, and Zach's seen a dead body before – haven't you?" For once, Becky seemed quite impressed with her brother.

"Yeah," said Zach, with quite a swagger, "Pete at school – his Gran died, and I got to touch her face and her hand at the wake at his house. She smelled a bit funny, but it was OK."

Were these *his* children? Dave found it hard to believe.

"So you're both OK – you're not....upset?" said Dave quietly, now by their side: he *was* the adult – he had to be *sure*.

"Yeah! *Sure*!" They answered him as if he'd been mad to ask! Becky even 'tutted' at him, as though *he* were the one to be pitied.

"Good.......I mean, I'm glad you're OK," Dave was relieved, but still concerned about their attitude.

"Dad, you know that glove in the lake, and the ball-cap?" asked Becky, evenly.

"Yes," replied Dave, worrying about what might come next.

"Well, they might belong to him," Becky pointed towards the hidden body.

"They might," conceded Dave.

"So, they could be evidence – I think we should collect them....they could float away and never be found, and that might compromise the investigation into this man's death."

Dave was now totally convinced that his daughter Becky had been taken away and replaced by an alien!

"Where on earth did you learn to speak....and *think*......like that?" asked Dave, blown away by his daughter's calm maturity.

"She's always watching cop shows with Mom," replied Zach on behalf of his sister. "I think they're pretty crappy – but some of them have good dead bodies in them – I like the ones with lots of autopsies when the bodies are all wide open – they're the best ones."

Dave didn't watch much TV – he preferred a cold one after work with his buddies, and then, by the time he got home, he'd usually hit the sack, because getting up at 5am to get a ride to his construction job took it out of a guy. But even so......he couldn't imagine that just watching TV could change his daughter so much!

"Come on Dad – it might be important," said Becky, sounding quite excited. "This could be my big chance – Miss Gilmore at school says I'm good at science – I could make a career of it. This could get me noticed."

Dave was nonplussed: here he'd been worried that his kids would be traumatised for life by the dead body, and all his little girl could think of, at thirteen years of age no less, was a career plan!

"I don't think we should go messing around with any of it, and that's that," said Dave, with all the authority his voice could muster.

"She's right, Dad," piped up Zach, "the hat and the glove could be important."

"You can tell that whoever killed him wanted to hide his identity," repeated Becky, keen to make her point, "Zach said the body had no hands or feet and the face was gone – that way there'd be no fingerprints or dental remnants, so the police might never know who he is....maybe there's a clue in the hat, or the glove, hey Dad....what if there was a *hand* inside the glove! *Then* there'd be fingerprints – it could break the case wide open!" Becky's face lit up as she thought of this grisly possibility. Dave wondered about telling them that the 'glove' had fingernails, but then he imagined he'd have to go out and retrieve the damned thing, and he wasn't doing that. No way!

"Listen, kids, I think we need to forget about the body," said Dave in his most 'fatherly' voice. Both of his children looked at him as though he were the dumbest person on the face of the planet.

"What do you mean – forget about it? It's right *there*," shouted Zach, pointing to where the body lay.

"Yes, Dad," added Becky, "that's just not possible. We can stay away from it, sure, if that makes *you* feel better, but we *should* look around for clues to help the police when they get here. You *are* going to call them, aren't you?"

Dave was astonished that he hadn't thought of that himself.

"Of course I'm going to call the police," was his somewhat terse reply. "In fact, I'm going to do that right now."

"You can't," said Zach in a very adult voice.

"Why not?" asked Dave, still snapping.

"Because there's no signal out here – I tried already," replied Zach.

"You've tried calling the police already?" Dave sounded annoyed with his son.

"No," Zach sounded bored, "I tried calling a couple of the guys from school, and there's no signal here."

"Why would you want to call anyone from school?" Dave was mystified.

"Dad, I just found a dead body – with no face – it's so cool.......I just wanted to tell them....I bet they wish they were here!"

Dave shook his head in disbelief, not at the possible lack of a signal – he'd suspected that – but that Zach could be so cold-blooded about the whole matter. It seemed like all he wanted to do was show off, while his little sister wanted to act like someone on a TV crime show. Dave supposed he should be grateful that they weren't both crying and screaming about the whole mess, but he was still concerned that the horror of the circumstances would suddenly dawn on them. They were on *him*: a dead body, no telephones and no way to get out of the place until Mike came back for them the next day.

Not wanting to appear as though he were a complete idiot he checked his phone – but his son was right, there was no signal. Dave wandered around a bit, hoping that the little bars would appear on the phone's screen, but to no avail.

"There might be a chance of a signal out on the lake," suggested Becky. "You'd be further away from the sheer mountain face out there. Shall we try?"

Dave thought about his daughter's suggestion for a moment – she had a point, but then they'd be closer to the floating hand.....he didn't like that idea.

"We've both got lots of sunscreen on now, Dad, so we won't burn, and we could pick up that hat and that glove – just to keep them safe." Dave thought about how much of her Mom's persistence Becky displayed, but couldn't think of a good reason to not try to get a signal out on the lake.

"Well, we'll all go together, wearing life-vests, with *no* diving, and we'll try to grab the 'clues'.....if we can still see them." Dave sounded hesitant, and his kids picked up on it right away, so they didn't give him a chance to change his mind. Becky ran to get the little fishing net she'd spotted inside the cabin, to better help retrieve the 'evidence', and Zach pulled the boat back to the shore, ready for the off.

"Can you bring something to eat, Becky?" called Zach to his sister.

"Sure," his sister called back, as though it would be a terrible chore.

Finally, Dave once again pushed off, pointing the little frog-boat towards the widest part of the water. He rowed carefully, trying not to splash too much.

"Dad, Da-ad, look, there's the hat," shouted Becky gleefully as she reached out with the net and successfully captured the floating ball-cap. "Now everyone look out for the glove," she instructed her father and brother, in what sounded just like her Mom's voice.

"You keep checking for a signal on one of those phones," said Dave to Zach, who was peering from beneath his own ball-cap in the hot afternoon sun.

"Nothing. Not even *one* bar," said Zach, glumly. "Why don't we try a bit farther out?"

Dave didn't want to venture too far from the cabin, but he saw the sense of trying to get a signal.

"Let's go as far as those rocks," suggested Dave, nodding towards a knobbly little island that was poking its head out of the deep lake. It wasn't more than twenty feet long, and was home to a couple of cedars and some moss-covered outcrops of rock.

The kids seemed to be excited by the prospect of getting to the island, so Dave rowed on, sweating in the heat of the early afternoon. He fancied a beer – but he hadn't dared bring any adult beverages on the trip, in case Debbie had spotted them! Finally, out of breath and completely soaked with sweat, Dave felt the boat bump against the rocks, and he pulled in the oars. Looking around, it was clear that there was nowhere to tie up the boat, so he tried to grab onto a bit of fern that seemed to be growing directly out of a boulder.

"Still no signal," announced Zach, as if to say 'I told you so' to his sister.

"Well at least we tried," retorted Becky, rolling her eyes at her brother. "If you've tried your best, you can't blame yourself," she pointed out, quoting their Mom.

"OK you two," snapped Dave, exhausted and wishing he didn't now have to row all the way back to the cabin again. "Just keep quiet and enjoy the scenery." Becky looked at the sights around her, smiling, whilst Zach fiddled with his ball-cap and life vest, grumbling under his breath that there was nothing to look at and he was hungry. Dave felt exasperated – when had Zach become such a pain in the butt? He used to be a great kid – always running and playing and jumping and full of energy; now he just seemed to want to sit, eat and moan about everything, even out there in the stunning wilderness.

"I can see the glove, Dad," shouted Becky, excitedly. "See – it's just there, between us and the buoy....come on Dad, let's get it."

Dave had to say something......he had to explain about the glove.

"Becky, I think we should just leave it to float around – it's not going anywhere...." Dave didn't sound convincing, and Becky wasn't taken in.

"Dad, it could be *evidence*," she said with emphasis.

"Is it a hand, Dad, not a glove?" asked Zach. Dave was surprised at his insight, and decided to come clean.

"I think I saw fingernails on it – I think it might be a hand, yes, so I think we should leave it alone. I don't want you two having nightmares about floating hands."

"Oh Da-ad....." Becky 'tutted' at him, "now we'll *have* to get it, because what you just *said* is what could give us nightmares, because it's the *unknown* – if we collect the actual hand it won't be half as bad as our imaginations could make it, so we won't have nightmares about it. It's basic psychology." Once

145

again, Dave wondered what had happened to his *real* little girl, and where this person had come from. He gave in, let go of the fern and pushed away from the islet, rowing with as little effort as he could manage: he'd splashed himself with the cool water of the lake, but he was still terribly hot.

Becky once again completed a successful retrieval – this time with more difficulty, but she finally hauled in what was, indeed, a human hand. Dave was horrified that his children paid such close attention to it, noting the way that the flesh had started to fall from the cut around the wrist area, and commenting, very coolly he thought, on how the fish had started to nibble at it. All he could do was try to look away, whilst steering generally towards the cabin.

"We'll put in into a Ziploc and a cooler box when we get back," announced Becky, "it should keep fresh that way." Her brother, for once, agreed with her. Dave was shaking his head as he rowed. God, they were weird!

Back at shore, Becky secured the ball-cap and hand in a manner she felt appropriate for a forensic scientist, whilst Zach planned the next meal. Dave had given up on the idea of them being able to reach anyone by telephone, and resigned himself to spending a night in a mouldy old shack with his children, in close proximity to a dead body, and with a decomposing human hand in a cooler box beside his cot. Not *quite* what he'd imagined!

But the children didn't seem to have missed a beat: Becky was sorting through supplies to work out what they could eat – the idea of fishing now not appealing to Dave at all, considering what any fish they might catch may have been nibbling at - and Zach was trying to work out the directions to the tree-house that were shown on the map.

"Dad, it's real hot – can we go into the forest and find the tree-house: it would be shady there, wouldn't it?" asked Zach, applying some surprising common sense.

Dave couldn't think of a good reason not to go: at least it would get them away from the dead stuff. So they set off into the woods: Zach had the map and led the way, Becky had a small backpack with some snacks and water, and Dave brought up the rear with the compass, though he wasn't really sure why he'd brought it, because Zach seemed to be doing just fine without any direction from him.

It turned out that the tree-house wasn't as far up the hill and into the trees as the map seemed to suggest, but it was a magnificent structure, nonetheless. Zach was first to climb the metal ladder that stood against the tree, then Becky followed, and finally Dave hoisted himself up. It wasn't really a tree-house, more of a tree-platform, with a brown tarp tented over it. Dave knocked off a lot of detritus and Becky kicked bits of twigs, needles and leaves off the platform itself. Then they all looked out: there was only one real direction for viewing, and it was back towards the lake – due south, Dave's compass told him. They'd climbed a good way up the hillside, and then they'd climbed the ladder, so now they were about a hundred feet above the lake, and the view was spectacular. Dave loved it, and he sensed that the children did too. Even Zach grunted what Dave took to be his appreciation. Becky 'wowed' a lot and Dave was just grateful for the moment, and the distance between him and the dead body. Of course, he should have known it wouldn't last!

"Look at the bald eagles," whispered Becky, pointing in wonder to half a dozen birds wheeling above the lake.

"They can't hear you, stupid, why are you whispering?" mocked Zach.

"Zach!" warned Dave, suspecting that their peace had been shattered once and for all. "Let's enjoy this moment – they're beautiful aren't they?"

Zach grunted.

"I like bald eagles, Dad," said Becky, still speaking quietly. "Can we go to Squamish in the New Year when they gather there? They reckon about 5% of all the world's bald eagles spend the winter there – they count them. There's an art gallery in Brackendale where all the counters gather – I saw it on TV. In 1994 they counted a record of nearly 4000, but the recent counts have been way down. Maybe we could volunteer to help them count, eh?" Becky sounded proud that she knew so much, and Dave was suitably impressed. Dave smiled warmly at his daughter: he loved it when she suggested they should do something together.

"Sure," he replied, "so how do you count eagles?"

"Well, I don't *know*, but I'm sure we could help. I know that they're easier to count the worse the weather is, 'cos they stay closer to the ground and the rivers there." Becky still sounded upbeat, but Dave was beginning to have some misgivings about the whole thing. 'Great,' thought Dave, 'I get to sit around in freezing rain while my daughter counts eagles,' but he didn't say anything except, "Sure": they'd sort something out.

"Who d'ya think he was, Dad?" asked Zach, out of the blue.

"Who was who?" asked Dave, still thinking about bald eagles.

"The *dead* guy," replied Zach, as though his father were a complete idiot.

Dave sighed. Of course, the dead guy.

"I have no idea," replied Dave. "And there's no point even thinking about it, because there's no way of us knowing. Come on kids, let's try and enjoy all this," he waved his arm towards the vista, "rather than *that*."

"But it's a *mystery*," said Zach, stating the obvious.

"We could examine the body," suggested Becky, "and see if there are any clues."

"I told you he was *naked*," said Zach, "there won't *be* any clues, duh!"

"There might be – he might have birthmarks, or tattoos," said Becky, sharply.

"I don't care what he might or might not have," interrupted Dave, "you're not 'examining the body' and that's that! Forget it, you two. We'll leave him where he is and call the police when we get back tomorrow."

"I think it'll be the RCMP actually, Dad," Becky pointed out, in her Mom's voice.

"OK, the RCMP, then," replied Dave, feeling like he'd been scolded. The mood was broken for him, and he started to wonder how to entertain the kids for the rest of the day. Obviously they were going to go on and on about the body. He knew he shouldn't have been surprised, but he'd so hoped they could just get back to the way he'd wanted things to be.

"When are we going to cook on the grill?" asked Zach, and Dave was grateful that at least he'd changed the subject.

"We could make our way back to the cabin now and do it right away, if you like," he said more happily.

Both kids agreed, and they clambered down the ladder and followed the trail back to the shore.

Half an hour later, Dave felt they were back on track: they were feasting on wieners, some rather black, some not more than warm, but all perfectly edible, and then they had cookies, all washed down with some cans of soda. Zach went for a swim – Dave deeming it acceptable since the floating hand was now safely out of the water and stored inside the cabin – and Becky cleared their dinner away. She pulled Dave's old guitar out of the cabin and encouraged him to play, which Dave was delighted to do, but he found it difficult to make his fingers form the shapes he'd learned in his youth, so he just strummed tunelessly for a while, before Becky lost interest and started asking if he could play some 'real songs'. Dave did his best, but he'd never been very good at tuning the instrument, so even *he* had to admit that he wasn't as good as he'd hoped. Zach had towelled off after his swim, changed into dry clothes, and then they began to gather some wood to make a proper camp fire....setting off in the direction that led them away from the body.

Although the sun was still in the sky, it had dipped below the mountains and the cabin was in the shade. Dave could tell it was going to be a clear night, and he suspected they might feel the cold. He and Becky set the wood up ready for a good fire, and they all pulled on some extra clothes and dragged some blankets out to sit around the little fire they were going to light, where Becky had laid out the supplies needed to make Smores. Dave's watch told him it was 7pm – and he imagined the firelight dancing in the gloaming, his children's faces happy and tired.....it would be magic.

Then, before they could even light the fire, Dave heard something in the distance – it was a boat engine. Oh no – why was Mike coming back early? Despite the dead body, he'd wanted this night with his kids! Why wouldn't anything go *right*?

If only Dave had known how wrong everything was about to go, he might not have felt so sorry for himself!

# IV

"It must be Mike," said Dave, without enthusiasm.

"No, it's a different engine. This boat's much bigger than Mike's," replied Zach with authority.

"How do you know?" asked Dave, before he realised that he'd just shown himself up in front of his son.

"Mike's has quite a different tone – can't you *hear* it?" Zach wasn't even trying to be patient with his imbecile father.

"Yes. Right," said Dave, as though he could spot the difference.

"It sounds like they're coming right up here," said Becky. Though it was clear that the boat was still some way off, they could hear that the engines had been pulled back and that the boat was beginning to work its way through the shallow channels they themselves had negotiated earlier in the day. "I wonder who they are......"

Before anyone could answer Becky, Dave heard a sound that made his heart miss a beat. He didn't know how he knew what it was, he'd never heard the sound before, but he was certain that it was a gunshot. Then there was another, then another, then a loud 'whoo-hoo'.

Dave had no idea what happened to him next: it was as though something had taken over his whole being. All he was aware of was that, somehow, he knew his children were in danger. It was like a switch flipping in his head. He stood up and immediately kicked all the wood they'd gathered for their campfire away from the neat little pile Becky had made.

"Dad! What are you doing?" asked Becky, leaping to her own feet in disgust: she'd spent ages making the pile and she wasn't impressed with her father at all.

Dave looked serious: she'd never seen her father look that way before. Even Zach felt the change, and tensed.

"Becky, Zach, I need you to listen to me very carefully and do exactly as I say – right?" If Dave's face had made them take notice, his tone made sure they were listening. "Becky – go to the cabin: get our backpacks and put some portable food and water into them; put some warm clothes on, then come back here and pack away these blankets into the backpacks too – we might need them. Zach – help me put the boat and the grill back into the cabin, then go get some warm clothes on. Becky – we'll need flashlights and the medical kit as well. *GO!*"

Neither child asked a question. Neither moaned, nor kicked up a fuss: they both did exactly as they were told. Finally certain that everything had been cleared away, and that they had sufficient supplies, Dave locked up the cabin and put a protective arm around each child.

"We're going to the tree-house. Zach, you have the map, right?" Zach nodded, "We know where we're going and we'll stay there as long as we need to. I'm going to be honest with you, kids: I don't know who's on that boat, but

I don't want to find out. Understand?" Both children nodded. Neither was so dumb that they didn't understand what was in their father's mind: they all felt that maybe the people in the boat had something to do with the dead body, and they all realised that they wanted nothing to do with them.

Zach led the way, with Dave following behind Becky. This time, the trip to the tree-house took longer: it was dark beneath the trees, the flashlights didn't illuminate much at all, and they were all carrying heavy backpacks. Dave had also brought along the gun-case, though he wasn't sure why – he didn't know how to use the damned thing!

As they trudged up the hill towards the tree-house, Becky stumbled a couple of times, and Dave picked her up, brushed her down, and looked into her eyes to check that she was OK: she was obviously apprehensive, but was keeping it together quite well. Meanwhile, Zach was grinding up the hill ahead of them – he was acting like a Sherpa, and doing a great job of it. Dave was proud of his children.

Finally they reached the ladder to the tree-house. They were all out of breath and glowing with sweat. Zach went up first, and Dave passed the backpacks to him, one at a time. Then he made sure Becky got up the ladder safely.

"Stay there – I'll be right back," whispered Dave loudly to Becky and Zach who were peering over the edge of the platform, "I just want to throw a few branches across the trail – two minutes!"

He was as good as his word, then clambered up the ladder himself.

"Give me a hand, Zach," he whispered, and he and his son hoisted the ladder up onto the platform, and out of sight from below. "Now, both of you, start pulling as many branches around the tent as you can," he said quietly, and soon they had made themselves almost invisible - half way up a tree in the forest. Finally, Dave felt they were as safe as they could be.

"Good job!" he whispered, as he hugged his children to him. He looked around: Becky and Zach had laid out the blankets while he'd been hiding the trail. Their backpacks could act as pillows, and they could roll themselves up in the blankets if it got cold, but, in the meantime, they were fine. They had water, snack bars and cookies, medical supplies and, if they needed it, a gun. Looking at the metal box, Dave lost some of the confidence he'd felt earlier. If he needed to use it, he'd work out how to do that, he told himself. In the meantime, there was no reason to suspect that whoever was on the boat meant them any harm: this was just a precaution. They were probably just a bunch of guys letting off some summer steam. That's what he told the kids. That's what he told himself.

"I think we should bed down here, kids: we don't want to draw any attention to ourselves, let's just try to get some sleep, right?"

"But it's still light, Dad," was Zach's accurate observation: the tree-house had been built in such a way that it offered a great view of the lake below, but that meant it was also catching the sun, because it was above the canopy on the hillside below it. Dave realised that his son had a point.

"You're right," he said, "but the main thing is – even if we can't get to sleep yet – we must keep still and quiet. Frankly, kids, I don't want those guys guessing that we're here: they shouldn't notice anything amiss at the cabin, not unless they break into it, and I'm pretty sure they won't know about this tree-house or the trail, but there's no point giving away our location, right?"

Both children nodded.

"We should have brought the hand with us, Dad," said Becky quietly. "What if they find it?"

"Let's not worry about that now, baby, there's nothing we can do about it. Let's just try to make ourselves comfortable – we could be here some time." Dave tried not to sound tired, but he was. The strain was beginning to get to him.

Dave noticed that Becky was edging closer to him on the platform, so he reached out to her, and pulled her into his arms. He could see that she was holding onto something: he suspected it was her stuffed bunny, but he didn't mention it.

"Dad, they won't....hurt us.....will they," she asked, looking up at her dad's with fearful eyes. She might have been born thirteen years earlier, but she could have been a six-year-old at that moment. Dave's heart skipped a beat.

"Everything will be *fine*," he whispered, and Becky relaxed a little, but Zach still looked anxious: in just the same way that his sister had suddenly become a little girl, rather than a little woman, so Zach had become a boy again.

"Dad – do you think these are the guys who killed that other guy?" said Zach. It was the question on all their minds, and Dave supposed someone had had to say the words out loud.

"I don't know, Zach. I hope not, because I'm sure that whoever could bring themselves to do that to another human being isn't going to be a very nice person. But I think we've done the right thing, clearing out of the way of whoever is on that boat."

"Yeah," said Zach sounding nervous. "It sounded like they had guns. We've got a gun, haven't we, Dad?"

"We have, Zach – but don't worry, everything will be *fine*. We won't have to use it," said Dave, hoping they wouldn't.

Below them, down at the shore, they could hear that the boat had stopped its engines and they could all imagine the people tying up the boat at the pier. It was clear to Dave that there were at least three men: they weren't exactly shouting to each other, but the peace was so total that their voices rang out clear and loud, and he was straining to hear every word in any case.

"Keep your ears open for names and anything that might tell us who they are," instructed Becky, suddenly becoming a teenaged sleuth again.

"And keep your voices down," added Dave. Both children settled their bodies into more comfortable positions, and their dad finally patted his daughter and let her pull free from him. She seemed to be rallying.

It was difficult to catch the whole of the conversation amongst the three men who were obviously down near the cabin. Dave thought he heard the name Steve....but it could have been one of them talking about Stave Lake, for all he knew. The voices floated about on the cooling night air. One thing was certain: there were so many references to 'him' that there was now no doubt in Dave's mind that these men had come to either retrieve, or bury, the dead body. He had to suppose that these *were* the guys who'd killed the man, shot his face away and cut off his hands and feet.

"It sounds like they're going to bury him," said Becky, astutely.

"I wonder why they didn't do that in the first place," said Zach, quite conversationally – which was, in itself, unusual for Zach.

"Maybe they didn't have shovels with them when they killed him," replied Dave, immediately regretting his words. Luckily all he got was a pair of, 'yeah's', rather than two horrified children.

"I reckon up there's best," said a man's light tenor voice - it sounded so close that it made Dave jump. Becky reached out for her father's hand, and squeezed it.

"Nah, it's too dark. Jeez, you'll kill yourself – it's a hell of a hill, eh?"

"But it's too rocky to dig down here," came the first voice again.

"Stop arguing!" It was the third man's voice – deeper than the other two, more assertive. Dave reckoned it was whoever was in charge. "We've got to get him away from the shore, so he doesn't float out into the lake, and we've got to get him away from this cabin. Let's find a place along the shore and up into the trees a bit – but not under the big trees, 'cos there'll be roots in the way." Dave could hear that this man at least had some common sense, and he agreed with his logic.

"Look, there's a sort of clearing here," came the first voice again.

"That's not a *clearing*, it's a trail! Jeez, can't you tell the difference?" said the second voice, mocking the first speaker. This man's accent wasn't local. It sounded to Dave like a Maritimes accent: he worked with some guys from there, and that was how *they* talked.

"You're right," said the 'Boss', his deep voice booming in the darkness below them. 'French,' thought Dave, 'he's definitely French Canadian.'

As Dave looked out from the platform, with his ears still straining for every word, a part of him noticed the stunning sunset that was now staining the sky with smudges of yellow, gold, red and brown, the night sky darkening above it, with tiny points of light beginning to peep through the deepening blues.

"Beautiful sunset," he whispered to his children who, surprisingly, looked up at the black silhouettes of the cedars stark against the painted sky and both nodded and smiled appreciatively. He prayed that they would remember the beauty of this trip, not the horror and fear of it. But he, too, was apprehensive: what if the men decided to follow the trail to dig the man's grave? What if they happened upon the tree-house? Dave told himself there was no point in worrying: he had to save all his energies for dealing with what was actually happening, not 'what-if's'.

"I'm a bit cold now, Dad," said Becky quietly, "I'm going to pull the blanket around me. Do you want to share?" she asked her brother, uncharacteristically.

"Yeah," replied Zach, equally out of character.

Dave smiled inwardly – kids! It took something like this to get them to huddle together in a blanket, amazing!

"Come on, let's try up here!" came a loud voice. It was the 'Boss', and it sounded as though he was pushing through the brush directly towards the tree-house. Dave, Becky and Zach all seemed to hold their breath. The crashing and cracking of branches, the cursing as one man or another fell over a root or a branch, seemed to be getting very close. None of them could see the gleam of a flashlight anywhere though, so Dave didn't have a real fix on the men. The noises seemed to get nearer and nearer, then, after what seemed like an age, the voices grew more muffled and, as far as Dave could make out, they'd gone away to their right.

Zach started pointing silently in the same direction, and Dave nodded. There was no doubt about it, they seemed to have picked a spot to stop, and then Dave could recognise the sound of shovels being pushed into the soil.

Dave was embarrassed that his kids could hear the disgusting jokes the men were telling each other as they dug, and he could have killed them for the language they were using. But he knew his kids would survive all that: in fact, he suspected they probably heard much the same at their school every day, kids being what kids had always been!

By the time the men stopped digging, the darkness was total. There was a slim sliver of moon hanging low in the black sky, but it cast very little light.

"Let's get back down and get some beers," the 'Boss' said, and the other two men agreed with him.

As Dave and the children watched the darkness where they thought the men had been digging they finally caught sight of a light, wobbling about down at ground level. The men crashed their way back towards the shore. Dave wondered how they expected to get the body all the way back to where they had been digging – he didn't think *he* could have found a spot in the dark that way. But he told himself that wasn't his problem: *his* problem was keeping his children safe, and, now, as the night chilled off, warm and in some sort of comfort. He was hoping that the burial wouldn't take too long, but, when the men got back to the shore it was clear they were in no hurry.

Dave peered at his watch: the luminous hands showed that the men had been drinking beer for at least half an hour. He wondered if they'd ever get on with their gruesome job.

"Can I get some cookies?" was Zach's quiet request.

"Can you reach the bag with the food?" asked Dave of Becky.

"Sure," she whispered, and pulled one of the three bags towards them. It rattled across the platform, the cookie-tin inside it sounding like a drum in the night. Becky stopped, dead. The three of them held their breath, expecting the men at the shore to have heard the noise.

Somewhere close by a bird flew up into the black sky and cried aloud. Then there was a shot from below them. Becky grabbed her dad's arm. She looked terrified, a little girl again.

"Stop messing about!" shouted the 'Boss' voice.

One of the other men whooped and shouted, then it became clear that they were, indeed, finally setting about their task.

Dave worked out from the conversation they were having that the three men had brought a tarp upon which they had placed the body. It seemed that the 'Boss' was leading the way, with the two other men dragging the tarp behind them. The noise was tremendous as they dragged their charge through the undergrowth. Once again there were stumbles and cursings along the way, but, somehow, they seemed to find their way back to the spot where they'd been digging.

"Toss the bastard in," shouted the 'Boss', and there was a sickening thud. Becky's eyes were wide with fear as she looked up at her dad. He winked at her, and she smiled, weakly. They were all getting used to the dark by now, and the light from the rising moon, even though it was just a slim silver hook in the sky, was bright enough for them to at least see each other.

As Dave looked across the platform at his children he could see two worried little faces poking out from a big, heavy blanket. They looked so small, huddled together; so scared. And *he* had brought them to this. Would he *ever* forgive himself? He doubted it. He wondered if *they'd* ever forgive him: he could live with not forgiving himself.....but if *they* blamed him for this.....what would that mean for their relationship? It had been tough enough to get them to come with him in the first place: now there was....all *this*. Dave's stomach churned: what if they never wanted to be alone with him ever again? What if they never wanted to *go* anywhere with him again? He was back to the 'what-if's', and he told himself not to worry......but he did. He didn't think things would ever be 'fine' again. Not really.

They all listened as more shovelling took place, and then the 'Boss' finally agreed that a good enough job had been done to deter the wild animals from digging up the corpse. Once again the men crashed their way back towards the shore. Maybe *now* they would leave, thought Dave. But he was wrong.

It seemed that more beer needed to be consumed to celebrate a 'job well done' as the 'Boss' had put it, and the men seemed to sit around talking and laughing for ages. Dave wondered at their callousness, then told himself that he shouldn't be surprised, not after what they'd done to the man in the lake.

Dave's watch told him it was 11pm when they finally started up the boat once again. He felt exhausted. The relief of their departure washed over him and, when they all heard the boat pick up speed and head off into the main part of Pitt Lake, they had a group hug and all cheered – but still at the whispering level. It had been the longest four hours of Dave's life. But the night was still young.

Daring a slightly louder whisper Dave said to his children, "Look, I know they've gone, but I still think we should stay here."

"But Da-ad, it's really *uncomfortable* up here," whined Zach, "and I'm *starving*." Dave was delighted that his son seemed to be back to his usual self.

"Have a few of these," said Becky, offering her brother a handful of trail-mix bars.

"I've had *loads* of those today – I'll have the most painful crap of my life when they all come out," said Zach glumly.

"Hey – enough of that sort of talk!" chided Dave. "I know we've been treated to some pretty bad language tonight guys, but I don't expect that sort of thing from you. Got it!" Zach sensed his father's seriousness, and grunted.

"I won't tell Mom about the language," said Becky, meaning to be helpful, but reminding Dave that, somehow, he'd have to explain all this to Debbie when they got home.

"Good girl," replied Dave, grateful for that, at least.

"*Why* can't we go back to the cabin, Dad?" asked Zach, unprepared to give up on the idea of wieners and Smores.

"Because it's pitch dark down there and I covered the trail with branches: it's too dangerous to risk it in the dark. It's better if we stay here till it's light, then we can go back to the cabin."

"Dad," said Becky, hesitantly, and whispering close to her dad's ear, "I've got to go....now. I've been holding it for ages, but I can't wait any longer. Can I just go down the ladder and ....you know.....go pee in the bushes?"

Dave could have kicked himself: of course, they'd probably *all* have to have a pee before settling down for the night. Indeed, now that Becky had mentioned it, he realised his own need. He'd better do something about it.

"OK – we'll put the ladder in place, and we won't stray very far. Zach – you hang on up here while I go with your sister, then, when we come back, you and I can go together while Becky holds the fort up on the platform, eh?"

Two 'OK's' met this suggestion, so Dave and Zach lowered the ladder, carefully, and Dave made sure it was firmly grounded. He climbed down first, and had to admit he was glad to be back on solid ground. It was very dark down there: no moonlight was making it through the canopy of trees. He guided Becky to the ground, and he watched her carefully as she tried to find herself some privacy in the undergrowth. She returned, smiling and looking pleased with herself.

"That's better," she said.

"OK, now you go up and send your brother down, we'll only be a couple of minutes, OK?"

"I'll be *fine*, Dad," she replied, almost mocking him. She was quite the little lady again.

Zach and his dad were back at the bottom of the ladder, their own missions accomplished, when Dave heard something that he didn't like. He was beginning to hate the wilderness – it seemed to be full of things designed to ambush his spirits, just as they were rising. There was no question about it: something was crashing through the trees down the hill, and heading straight for them – he was sure of it.

Zach's face was a picture of terror.

"Up the ladder, quick, Zach," said Dave in his normal voice, which sounded loud in the stillness of the night, and Zach leaped onto the ladder. His foot slipped and he fell, with a crunch. He let out a yelp, which was followed by a growl from the darkness. Zach was immediately on his feet and up the ladder in a matter of seconds. Dave followed him, and, together, they pulled up the ladder behind them.

Becky was shaking again. Zach was as white as the moon. Dave could see blood oozing through Zack's sock. There seemed to be a lot of it. Dave sucked in a deep breath, and took control.

"Becky, break out the medical kit. Zach, sit down and let me get your sandal and your sock off you. Stop wriggling."

"I'll be fine, Dad," said Zach, in a voice that told Dave he'd be anything but.

"Here it is," said Becky, putting the little medical bag next to Dave, and shining a flashlight onto her brother's leg so Dave could see what he was doing.

"Oh dear," was all Dave could manage.

"That's naaaasty!" exclaimed Becky, looking at the four inch shard of wood sticking out of Zach's leg.

"Open up the kit – let's see what your Mom packed for us, Becky," instructed Dave. He searched for something with which he could grip the splintered shard, uncertain that pulling it out of his son's leg was the right thing to do, but knowing that his son couldn't sit on a platform half way up a tree all night with it the way it was.

"Does it hurt much, son?" he asked Zach.

"Not really," was Zach's pained reply. Dave suspected that pride was stopping him from crying like a baby, but that it might not last for long.

Beneath them there was a long, low growl. Something was very close. Dave hoped it wasn't a cougar. If it was......well, he suspected they were pretty good at climbing trees, but he had a more immediate problem to deal with.

"Look, son," he said directly. "It's going to hurt like hell, but I have to pull out the wood. Then we can clean up the wound and put a bandage on it. Tomorrow we'll get you to the hospital and they can check for slivers – eh?"

Zach didn't reply, but nodded, his mouth set in a thin, determined line.

"Use the blanket to pull it out, Dad," suggested Becky, "you don't want to go getting a sliver yourself." Dave knew she was right, and protected his hand with the blanket.

"Ready?" he asked his brave son.

Once again Zach nodded. The growling was now directly beneath them. Dave didn't hang about – he pulled the wood out of his son's leg. Zach didn't make a sound, but Dave could see a tear trickle down his grubby face.

"Well done, son," said Dave, and hugged Zach, allowing his boy to wipe his tears on his dad's shoulder, without his sister ever seeing them.

"You're real brave, Bro," said Becky, smiling at her brother, but looking worried. "Dad – the growling thing......it's right on the tree, down there," she said, looking almost as pale as her brother.

"Give me the flashlight," said Dave in a commanding voice. Becky handed the shaking flashlight to her dad.

Dave shone the light over the platform and saw a pair of eyes looking up at him. It was a bear. A big one, by the looks of it. And it was starting to try to climb the tree. The eyes blinked in the bright light.

'Black bears – make a noise....brown bears – play dead,' floated into Dave's consciousness from.....somewhere. He prayed the bear was black – though he couldn't tell in the dark.

"Make a noise, kids – as much as you can!" shouted Dave, and, with no further encouragement needed they both let rip – screaming and shouting, and banging on the platform.

The bear didn't look afraid. What if it was a brown bear after all? But, after a couple of minutes of sustained shouting, the bear wandered off into the bush. It took its own sweet time, but it went.

Dave turned his attention to his son once again, shining the flashlight onto his cut leg. The cut was deep, no question, but the bleeding was slowing. Dave suspected his son had been lucky. He sprayed the cut with the anti-bacterial that Debbie had packed, and thanked her silently for her foresight. Waiting several minutes, until the bleeding had pretty much stopped, he carefully placed a gauze pad on the cut, and wound a long bandage around Zach's leg, securing it with some of the surgical tape from the pack. He didn't think there was much more he could do. But he wasn't happy. They couldn't go down, that was obvious, but it was clear that his son was in for a painful and uncomfortable night. There were still several hours before the sun would be up, and he felt completely helpless. Once again his mind went to the place where his kids would never forgive him for putting them in harm's way – and where his ex-wife would probably forbid him from ever seeing them again.

He tried to snuggle Zach into the blankets, and Becky along with him, but it was difficult, because Zach had to keep his leg straight out – it hurt less that way. If Dave had thought that the last four hours had been long, they were almost as nothing compared with the next four. He didn't sleep: he was exhausted, yet wide awake. He had to protect his children – from murderers, from bears, from whatever else might smell blood on the air and decide to check it out. He'd never felt so alone, so small or so pathetically useless in his whole life. He wished that Debbie had been with them: nothing ever went wrong when Debbie was around – she made everything alright. How he missed her. Now more than ever, but he admitted to himself that night, high above the trees, with the moon crossing the sky and the nocturnal creatures stirring all around him, that he missed her every day, in every way. She'd never have let them get into this mess: she'd have made it right. Somehow.

With the first light, Dave felt some relief. The kids had slept a little: Becky was curled into a ball, cuddling her bunny and looking like she had done when she was three years old; Zach had laid out flat on his back and had snored fitfully for a few hours. Dave had loved every snuffle and grunt his son had made – whereas he'd constantly checked on Becky to make sure she was breathing, she was so very fast asleep! The dawn chorus was almost deafening, and it woke Zach, who claimed not to have slept a wink. He pulled himself up to a seated position, and assured his dad that his leg was fine, but Dave could tell he wasn't right – he was quiet and withdrawn, but not in the usual way.

When Becky woke it was almost fully daylight: she yawned and stretched, and even asked after her brother.

"Any more bears, Dad?" she asked, smiling nervously.

"No, but I think we should give it a little longer before we venture down," said Dave, remembering from somewhere that bears don't go to sleep until later in the day....but not sure if it were true or not.

"I....um....need to pee, Dad," said Becky, quietly.

"Can you wait?" asked Dave, hoping she could, "Maybe half an hour?"

"I don't know that I can," she replied.

"Me too," said Zach.

"OK – we'll do the same as last night then," said Dave, "but I don't think you're up to going up and down the ladder a lot, Zach, so, when you come down, we'll make our way back to the cabin. We'll take our time, so your leg will be OK. Right?"

Both children nodded. Dave let down the ladder and, when he was on the ground, Becky followed him. Once again she scampered off into the bush, this time, in daylight, a little further than the night before, then she returned and Zach made his way, carefully, down the ladder. Becky held her breath as she watched her brother descend.

"We should check your dressing before we leave," she said, sounding like her Mom.

"Yeah – OK, but let me pee first," said Zach impatiently, then he hobbled off to relieve himself.

As Becky stood waiting for her brother and her dad, she looked up at the tree trunk and she could see the scars made by the bear's claws the night before. She shuddered. The bear had gotten a long way up the tree....or maybe it was just that big: the marks were way above her head.

"Alright?" asked her dad as he came back to the tree.

Becky nodded.

"I'll go back up," said Dave, "pack everything together and throw the packs down – if anything breaks, it doesn't matter – don't try to catch them – just let them fall as they will. We'll sort it all out later – OK?"

Becky nodded again, watched her father clamber up the ladder, and began to look around for her brother.

"Zach – where are you?" she called, wondering what on earth had happened to her brother.

"I'm over here," shouted Zach, from some way off in the bush.

"Where?" shouted Becky.

"Over *here*," replied Zach, loudly, "I'm going to mark where they buried the body."

Dave shouted down from the platform, "Get back here *now* Zach. That leg of yours isn't right, and I don't want you getting lost. Come right back – *right now*!"

There couldn't have been any doubt in either child's mind that Dave was angry. What the *hell* was that boy playing at?

"OK," shouted Zach, obviously not happy that his father wouldn't let him be more adventurous. He was back at the tree within moments, by which time Dave had thrown down all the backpacks, and they only had to get them on their backs to be able to head back towards the shore and the relative sanctuary of the cabin. It might only have been a shack, but it would seem like a palace after the night they'd had.

Dave could see that Zach's leg hadn't bled during the night, so he suggested they left the dressing alone until they were at the lakeside, with better light and some fresh water to help clean it up. The hike back to the cabin seemed to be a shorter trip than the day before, though it took longer due to Zach's leg. But, finally, they got there. It was a wonderful sight. They'd all had quite enough of the forest – they were glad to see the lake once more, and to be on the level shore.

Dave looked at his watch: he thought that time was beginning to lose all meaning, because, somehow, it had become 8.30am. He didn't know where the last couple of hours had gone – but gone they had, and they were two hours closer to Mike's arrival – which couldn't come soon enough for Dave.

Dave opened up the cabin: whoever those guys had been last night, they hadn't been interested in the cabin. Everything was where they had left it. Dave was glad that they'd cleared up so well the evening before, but now he encouraged Becky to collect together all the sticks he'd kicked about – he thought that a campfire and something hot for breakfast would lift all their spirits.

While Becky gathered the wood and built a pyramid for the fire, he examined Zach's leg, despite Zach's protests. He could see that the wound was pretty clean, at least, it looked that way to Dave, but, nonetheless, he applied more antibacterial spray and re-dressed the wound with fresh gauze. Then he gave Becky a hand, and, within the hour, they were sitting around a fire, toasting wieners, then Smores, and singing songs that Dave knew he had no ability to play on his guitar, but he gave it a go anyway.

They were all tired, and grubby, and might never be quite the same again – but it was a happy threesome who rose from their haunches to greet Mike when he tied up the boat at the end of the pier at 1pm.

Dave was so pleased to see Mike that he almost ran along the pier to give him a hug – but he restrained himself, and focussed on beginning to bring all the stuff they'd taken with them back to the boat. Mike ambled along the pier, ready and willing to give a hand with loading, then he spotted the bandage on Zach's leg.

"What happened there?" he asked, concerned. Zach beamed.

"I got a huge piece of wood stuck in there when I fell off the tree-house ladder last night, in the dark," he said, sounding quite proud. Mike looked at Dave askance.

"What were you doing on the tree-house ladder after dark – you weren't alone, were you?" Mike suspected that Dave had let the kids run riot.

"A bear was coming for us – we had to climb up real fast," replied Zach, excitedly, "we'd all gone down for a quick pee after the killers left, but then we had to spend the night up there 'cos of the bear." Zach seemed quite content with his explanation. Mike was anything but.

"What killers? What are you talking about?" he snapped, suspecting that the boy was kidding around. Where *was* Dave? What *was* he up to in the cabin there?

"The guys who killed the other guy we found on the shore: they cut off his hands and feet, but we found one of his hands....and his ball-cap," shouted Becky, feeling that she should fill in some of the details.

Mike was astounded. "You found a *body*? A *dead* body?" They had to be making it up. "Hey, Dave," called Mike, nervously towards the cabin, "what's this your kids are telling me about a dead body?"

As Dave emerged from the shack, laden with bags and blankets, towels and clothes, none of them packed, all just heaped across his arms, he smiled.

"Oh yes," he tried to sound casual, "we found a corpse, collected what evidence we could, but we had to get out of here when the murderers came back to bury the body last night. I thought it best that we spent the night up in the tree-house, then we came down to the cabin this morning for breakfast." Dave thoroughly enjoyed the look on Mike's face. This story could work out quite well for him at the construction site, after all. With him as the hero, of course. Mike scratched his head in disbelief. Maybe they were all in it together.

Mike let the subject drop as they filled his boat with everything that needed to be shipped back to Pitt Meadows. Content that everything was secured, Mike looked back at the cabin suspiciously: he found it hard to believe that they'd found a body there – they all seemed so calm!

"Don't forget the hand, Dad," called Becky as she ran along the pier with a cooler box. Dave helped her into the boat.

"The hand?" scoffed Mike.

"Yeah, the hand," replied Dave, opening the cooler box for Mike to see.

"Jesus – it really *is* a hand – where the *hell* did you find that?" Mike looked aghast.

"I got it with the fishing net, when we were out in the frog-boat," said Becky, quite calmly.

Dave nodded in silent reply to Mike's enquiring looks. Dave was so *proud* of his kids.

Mike was beginning to think that their story was real, after all. "We'd better get it to the police – soon as we get back," he said, trying to take charge.

"We think it'll be the RCMP out here," commented Becky, evenly, "but we agree. We couldn't get a signal to call them yesterday."

Mike nodded. "There isn't one up here – but we'll be able to call them when we get down the Lake a ways," he said, still shaken by what he'd seen in the cooler. "We'd better get going," he added, and they all agreed.

Mike pulled out from the pier, and Dave, Becky and Zach looked back at the cabin, the shore and the trees on the mountainside with memories they could never have imagined would be theirs. Dave wasn't sorry to be heading back to civilisation – but he *was* trying to work out what to tell Debbie. Even so, he managed to pay some attention to their surroundings.

"Look, eagles," shouted Becky above the engine's noise – they were taking it slow through the shallows, but the engine was still thumping quite loudly.

"We'll see a lot more when we go up to Squamish to help with the count," replied Dave, hugging his daughter to him. She was quite happily standing in the boat, not sitting and clinging to the seat the way she had the day before. 'What a difference a day makes,' thought Dave, relieved that at least his daughter seemed pleased at the idea of spending time with him again one day.

## V

"I wonder who that is," shouted Mike, nodding towards an approaching boat. It was just slowing to begin to negotiate the shallows that led from the main body of the Lake. "They're supposed to give way to us," shouted Mike, "but it looks like they're coming ahead. Silly idiots!" He started to gesticulate towards the other boat, signalling that they should stop where they were and let him get out of the narrow channel.

"Dad," Zach called to his father, "that's the same sort of boat that was here last night!"

Dave stomach flipped. He didn't even bother asking Zach if he was sure – he knew his son was right. It might not be the same guys, but if his son said it was the same type of boat, then it was the same type of boat.

"Mike!" called Dave, "Get us out of here as fast as you can – *NOW!*"

Mike looked back at his work colleague in surprise: he'd never heard Dave use that tone before, nor had he seen that look on his face.

"I can't go any faster – it's too dangerous just here," replied Mike, snapping, and wondering what the *hell* was going on. Nothing was ever *simple* when Dave was involved - it was that way at work, too: ask Dave to do something and it immediately became complicated. He should have known better than to offer him the cabin. Never again!

Dave moved closer to Mike, instructed the children to sit down and hold on tight, then shouted into Mike's ear.

"That's the type of boat that brought the guys here last night who buried the body we found. This is serious Mike – they might have come back! After all, who else would be coming up to this part of the Lake – you're the only one with a cabin there.....my gut's telling me it's *them*. Maybe they left something behind – something that could tie them to the murder, or the burial – maybe they left a spade behind....I don't know, and I have no intention of finding out. Just get us out of here – they're dangerous, Mike."

Mike looked at Dave as though he was seeing him for the first time, and he knew his friend was serious. Deadly serious. But there was little he could do.

"I've got to take it easy here, Dave," he replied, now sounding really worried, "but if we can get past them before they get to this narrow part, they won't be able to turn for quite a while, and we can get into the Lake and get going.....though my boat hasn't got the speed theirs has. But I'll do my best."

"Thanks, Mike," said Dave quietly, and patted his colleague on the back.

"You been up to the cabin there?" called a voice from the approaching boat. It was the passenger calling out, over the high pitched rhythms of the engines.

"Just looking around," shouted Mike, waving. Dave was glad he'd thought through the implications of his words.

"Nice cabin, eh?"

"Bit small if you ask me," replied Mike.

The boats were drawing closer together - they were no more than twenty metres apart. Dave could see two men on the boat. There'd definitely been three the night before – maybe these were just two other guys out for a boat ride, in the same sort of boat. That's what he told himself. He looked back from the front of the boat towards his children – they were both as rigid as boards, both looking terrified.

"You guys just out for a wander about?" asked Dave, waving cheerily.

"Yeah, just wandering," replied the guy controlling the other boat. Dave was in no doubt – he'd heard that voice before - it was the 'Boss' from the previous night. He felt his insides tighten.

"Lots of eagles about," Dave called, still trying to sound cheery, and pointing to the sky. The passenger in the other boat looked up.

"Yeah, for sure, eh?" he said. Maritimes accent. No doubt it was them.

The boats were almost level.

"You come through," called Mike.

"Your right of way, isn't it?" shouted the 'Boss'.

"Hey – I'm not the police," replied Mike, nervously, "it's easier if you come forward, then I'll push around you....it's wider here than there."

The 'Boss' was tall – he had long blonde hair tied back beneath a bandana, sunglasses, a red tee-shirt and his arms and neck were entirely covered in tattoos. His passenger was also standing, but he was shorter, bald and also covered in tattoos. Becky stared hard at them, and Zach showed more than a passing interest, turning his head to look at them as they passed.

"Looks like the little guy's taken a knock," said the 'Boss' as they passed right by Mike's boat. He was looking at Zach's leg.

"Stupid kid fell out of a tree being chased by a bear last night," replied Mike, laughing.

"I thought you'd just been up here for a look-see," said the 'Boss', a different tone in his voice.

The boats were moving apart, and Mike was trying to work out just when he could start to pick up some speed. He wasn't really thinking about what he was saying, but Dave caught the inflection in the 'Boss's' voice. He had to do something.

"Yeah, just a look-see....he can't lay around at home all day just 'cos he's got a little cut on his leg.....I don't want him to think he can't get out and about with any little old injury. And we do *get* bears in Pitt Meadows, you know!" Dave thought that should take care of it.

The 'Boss' had cut his speed to almost a standstill, and had turned around to look at Mike's boat. He seemed to be deep in thought.

"You're right," he replied, "get all sorts there, you do."

"We're off, hang onto something," shouted Mike, and Dave did as he was told, which was just as well, because Mike gave it all he could! Mike's boat shot forward, the front gradually rising out of the water. Dave staggered back and sat down with a thump.

"You OK, kids?" he asked. They were both staring back at the other boat.

"They're watching us, Dad," shouted Becky above the roar of the engines.

"I can see that, baby, but we'll be *fine* – Mike's a great boatman, and they'll have to go all the way to the far end of the shallows before they can turn around, and even then they'll have to come back slowly, like we did. So don't worry, Becky, it'll all be alright – we'll get to the South shore long before they do, and we can get the police.....or the RCMP!" he smiled and winked at his daughter, and she smiled weakly back at him. He wondered when it would all end....they couldn't take much more of this.....*he* couldn't take much more of it himself!

"Shall I watch the phones for a signal?" asked Zach. Dave was impressed by his son's cool head.

"You do that – pass one to me and I'll look too," shouted Dave.

Zach managed to pass a telephone to his father without dropping it, despite the ferocious bobbing of the boat. Both he and his father watched for a signal.

"Dad! Dad! I've got bars on my phone," shouted Zach after about five minutes.

"Pass it to me, son," shouted Dave, and Zach passed his phone to his dad. Dave knew exactly what to do. He called Debbie.

"Hello, Zach – is everything OK?" Debbie's voice sounded worried.

"It's me, Debbie, I'm using Zach's phone – he's fine – listen to me, I need you to do something," shouted Dave.

"Where are you? What's that noise?" asked Debbie, sounding really concerned.

"We're on Mike's boat, coming back to the boat launch at the South end of Pitt Lake – don't ask questions, just call 911 and get the police there – NOW! I'm not going to lie to you Debs, this is serious – but just do this for me? And get there yourself – your children need you."

"Oh my God Dave – what's happened?" Dave was beginning to think that maybe this wasn't such a good idea after all, but he'd wanted Debbie there when the kids got to shore.

"Debbie – calm down! We're all fine, and we're all safe. Now just hang up the phone and call 911 – *now!*" He punched the 'end' button. He knew she'd act, and act swiftly. Debbie had never heard Dave sound so masterful before, and she dialled 911 as she grabbed her purse and ran to the minivan. If Dave thought her children needed her, then they certainly would.

"Dad – Dad! They're coming!" screamed Becky.

As Dave turned around he could just about see the other boat exiting the shallows area behind them and beginning to head into the Lake proper. He could see the shore ahead of them, but they were still miles from safety - and even then, without a police presence, he wondered what sort of safety they were really going to get.....they couldn't just leap out of the boat and jump into their truck and drive away.....they'd have to get off, tie it up....all *sorts* of things. What if those guys caught up with them on the water? What if they could even overtake them? What if they had guns with them? They had done last night! Dave decided he didn't like 'what-if's' at all, but also decided to pull the gun-case towards himself with his foot, just to be on the safe side.

"They're just getting up to full speed, Mike – do you think we can stay ahead of them?" shouted Dave.

Mike didn't look around, he called back over his shoulder, "This is as fast as she goes, and I'm not sure how fast their top speed is....but I'll keep her flat out till I have to pull up – I'll do my best, Dave!"

"OK – I'm going to get the gun out, just in case we need it," Dave shouted back, sounding much more confident than he felt.

"What the *hell* will you need the gun for, Dave? You can't go shooting at *people*!" Mike sounded panicked.

"Mike, they killed someone up at that cabin, and they wouldn't be chasing us if they didn't think we knew something about it. They had guns last night, we could hear them shooting.....if they've got a gun today, I'm gonna be ready for them!"

Mike could tell that Dave was serious. He couldn't *believe* the mess they were in. Those guys in that boat – they'd seen his boat's name – they knew he'd seen their faces.....he was in this up to his neck – as much as Dave and the kids, and he was flat out scared! They'd looked tough, and rough, those guys – they were trouble, and they were chasing him. Mike wished he could go faster, but he'd been telling the truth – the boat wasn't capable of more. He prayed they could make it to shore in time. If only he'd known it, all four of them were reciting much the same prayer, Becky going so far as to promise God she'd go to church every week for a year if only he'd get them home safe and let everything be OK.

Dave fiddled with the gun-case – it wasn't easy getting the key into the lock, let alone anything else.

"Can you manage, Dave?" shouted Mike.

"I can't unlock this damn case!"

"Come here, Dave – I'll show you what to do to drive.......here – just keep her straight and flat out – there's not much to it really.....just hang on tight. Give me the case and I'll do it – I'm more familiar with the lock."

Dave gratefully accepted Mike's offer, and they carefully swapped places. Dave felt immediately at home at the helm, and Mike managed to open the lock in an instant. He pulled out the gun, much to Zach's glee, and Becky's horror, and loaded the weapon. He wedged himself into the seat and made sure the gun wasn't pointing anywhere dangerous – which only left one direction - and that was straight up.

Behind them, the other boat was gaining: it was touch and go if they'd make it to shore before the other boat caught them. As Mike peered back he could see that the blonde guy was still at the helm, but that the passenger, the bald one, was standing at his side, also with a gun pointing into the air.

Mike's stomach churned.

Dave called back to him, "We're getting close to shore – I don't know what to do – you'll have to take over again, Mike!"

The men changed places, but this time Dave remained standing, the gun on his hip, his eyes not leaving the boat that was getting nearer and nearer. He wanted Mike to keep the speed up, but he knew that they'd have to slow, to get into the pier. He glanced towards the designated landing area. He could see Debbie. *Boy*, but she'd got there fast!

But he couldn't see any police – nor an RCMP vehicle – or anything resembling a figure of authority. Where *were* they? If Debbie'd made it there in the minivan, surely they could have got a response vehicle there just as quickly?

Debbie was horrified by what she saw on the Lake: her husband was holding a gun, her two children were hanging onto their seats in the bouncing boat for dear life, and another boat was in hot pursuit of her family, with a man holding a gun in that one too! What the *hell* was going on? What had Dave done *now*?

Behind her sirens wailed, and a cloud of dust signalled the arrival of two vehicles – both RCMP. Suddenly Dave felt more confident that it would all work out alright – then he saw the effect that his weapon was having upon the officers, who were already out of their vehicle and peering at the scene on the Lake through binoculars.

Dave could see Debbie run towards one of the uniformed men. She was waving her arms in the air. Dave guessed she was explaining that her children were being pursued by men with guns, and were being watched over by their father who was also waving a gun himself.

At the sight of the RCMP vehicles, the boat being driven by the 'Boss' slowed and turned, then he gunned the engines and began to speed back up the Lake. Mike's boat came to a halt, Dave gave him the gun, which he unloaded, and then, finally, Dave was able to get to his children. The boat was still bobbing on the water as he held them to his chest. They were safe. At last.

"We're *fine*," he said quietly, "just *fine*.....your Mom's here – see? You guys'll be glad to let her get you home safe, eh?"

He looked at his children: Becky had her colour back and was smiling up at him, Zach's leg wasn't bleeding at all and he was glowing.

"Da-ad," said Zach, pushing his father away, "I'm fine. Look, there's Andy from school – wait till I tell him what's happened!"

"Hey – you'll talk to the police before you talk to anyone else, Zach, and you'll only tell people what they say you can tell them. *And* we've got to get that leg checked out before you can go talking to any of your mates, eh? This isn't over, Zach – those guys are heading back up the Lake – they could get off that boat anywhere and literally get away with murder. We have a *duty*, son."

"Yes, Dad, you're right," said Zach. "But you'll come to the hospital with me, won't you?"

"Sure," said Dave, and gave his son another hug.

"You'll tell them how *I* said we should collect the evidence, won't you Dad?" asked Becky, eagerly.

"No *I* won't," said Dave, smiling proudly at his daughter, "*you* can tell them yourself. You were grown-up enough to think of it, and to do it, so you *should* tell them yourself."

"Thanks, Dad," said Becky, beaming.

Debbie had heard all this as she hovered on the shore, and couldn't quite believe her ears: she didn't know what had happened, but her children were different – and her ex-husband was changed somehow too. And the interaction between them was on a whole different level. But she decided she could work that out later – at that moment all she wanted to do was throw her arms around her offspring and reassure herself that they were alright.

Finally they were all off the boat, and Debbie was able to hold her children. Dave explained all that had happened to the most senior officer there, who, in turn, relayed all the information to someone on the radio.

"My daughter has something for you," said Dave proudly, as Becky handed the cooler box to the officer. He looked inside.

"You're a very brave girl," said the officer, "very intelligent too – if the corpse had no face, hands or feet, we might never have identified it, even if we *can* find it and dig it up, but this hand will have fingerprints, so if he's anywhere in the system, we can at least identify him."

"The 'Boss' had a tattoo of a flaming torch on his neck," said Zach, not wanting to miss out on the limelight, "and the bald guy had one too. I reckon they're in a gang and that's their insignia," he added, with an air of authority. "And I marked the place where they buried the dead guy – I put my red hockey team cap there." He sounded very pleased with himself.

"I wondered why you weren't wearing a hat," said Debbie, glaring at Dave, though, frankly, she thought that was the least of their worries, having heard the grisly and terrifying tale that Dave and her children had related to the officer.

"Can I get my son away to be checked at the hospital now?" asked Debbie concerned about Zach's leg.

The officer allowed them all to leave, took the cooler box – which Debbie said they could keep when they were done with it, thank you very much – and Dave thanked Mike. *Profusely.* And apologised for having dragged him into this mess. *Profusely.*

The officer had said that he thought that the suspects would likely try to dump their boat somewhere further up the Lake's shore and flee the area, aware that they could be described by everyone in Mike's boat. Even so, Mike said that he and his wife were going to take a couple of nights away at a local hotel – maybe they'd even stay away until he knew they'd got the guys, because they knew the name of his boat and he thought they might be able to find him that way. Dave could understand why he was scared. He didn't like the idea that the killers had seen him and the kids, he was just grateful that there was no way they could know who *they* were, or where to find *them*.

It was over. Well, it was nearly over: they'd take Zach to the emergency room at Ridge Meadows Hospital, and Dave was sure they'd say he was fine, then they could go home, knowing that tomorrow the RCMP would take their formal statements and they could get back to normal. But first it was off to the hospital: Dave followed the minivan carrying Debbie and the kids in his old pick-up, and they got in to see a doctor within the hour. A clean bill of health for Zach, with some precautionary anti-biotics and a tetanus shot, meant he could spend his time on the trip home on his cell phone calling friends and telling them about his 'great adventure'.

Debbie said that Dave could stay for dinner, and the kids were bubbling over with their gruesome story right through their meal. Debbie suspected that it would be tough to settle the children for the night, and she wasn't wrong: once she'd managed to drag them both away from phoning and texting people, she still had to listen to the details of their night up a tree, for the tenth time. She was just grateful that they were safe, and finally tucked up in bed. She'd even given in to their request to let their dad stay for the night: in fact, Debbie was amazed at how they'd praised their father for his quick thinking in getting them out of the cabin and away to safety. She wondered that Dave could have acted so sensibly, given his track record.

And so, with Zach and Becky safe in their rooms, and with Dave in the spare room, Debbie eventually turned out her bedside light after what had become a very long weekend indeed.

# VI

Debbie hadn't thought that she'd get off to sleep, but she must have done, because the next thing she knew, she was waking from a deep slumber to the noise of something loud, roaring outside the house. For a moment, she didn't know what was happening, then Dave rushed into her room and shouted something that made no sense,

"Get the kids into the basement – round the back....the 'Boss' is outside in a Hummer and I think he's got a gun!"

Debbie tried to get her head around what her ex- was saying.

"Don't turn on any lights!" he added. "I'm on the phone to the cops right now!"

Debbie grabbed a robe and rushed into Becky's room. Her daughter was as fast asleep as she had been herself just moments ago, and she had a tough time rousing her.

"Becky – wake up darling. We have to get down to the basement – here, put this on, and let me find your slippers....here! Don't panic – everything will be fine – I'm just going to wake Zach – come on now, get up!" Debbie tried to sound calm, but she wasn't.

Zach was also completely sound asleep – the panic running through the house not having touched him yet.

Finally Debbie managed to get both children down the stairs and into the basement: their house sat on a ravine, so, although it looked like a single level house from the street, the back had an extra floor that allowed you to walk out onto the bank of a gully that ran right along the street. The children were still half asleep, but they were frightened, she could tell that. She held Becky close. Zach didn't want to be hugged.

Dave ran down the back stairs to the basement. Debbie looked up at him, searching his face for an explanation.

"Listen," said Dave, in a tone Debbie had never heard before, "I know you're all frightened, but we have to act quickly. The police are on their way, but, somehow, the 'Boss' has found out where we live, and he's outside and threatening us."

It all seemed too much for Becky. She started to cry.

"How did he find us.....why won't he leave us alone? I'm tired of this Dad.....I want it all to stop now....can't you make him go away?"

"I don't know *how* he found us darling, and I don't think I can make him go away....but I *can* get us away from him. If he tries to come into the house he'll set off the alarm. I think we'll be safe here, because there's no way to the back of the house from the street. So let's just wait for the police to arrive and they can sort him out – eh?" Dave sounded calm, controlled. Debbie was impressed, if terrified.

"I don't get it Dad – how could he find us?" was Zach's plaintive question.

"I don't know that either, son, but he's here and we have to deal with it, right?"

Zach nodded. Debbie still couldn't get over what was happening. She'd worked out who was outside her house, the kids had explained about their nickname for the man with the long hair who'd been chasing them earlier in the day, and she was in no doubt that he was dangerous. Everything inside her made her want to go outside and rip his head off – how dare he threaten her children! But the knowledge that he was no stranger to guns, and Dave's comment that he thought he'd seen one that night, made her realise that her instincts were wrong on this occasion, and that hiding out until the police arrived was the best thing to do.

Suddenly a loud crash rang out in the night. All four of them jumped.

"Was that a window?" asked Becky, terrified.

"I think it was the window next to the front door," replied Dave. Another crash and a popping noise came next. Becky buried her face in her mother's bosom, crying aloud. Debbie looked pale in the moonlight that came streaming through the basement window. Dave hugged his son, his ex-wife and his daughter. He looked Debbie straight in the eyes and spoke quietly.

"If that alarm starts to ring, then he's opened the door through the side window. He's already shooting at the house. I'm not going to let him hurt any of us – the second that alarm starts, we're out the back door and we're going to make our way along the ravine towards the top of the road....right!"

Debbie nodded. She didn't want to have to drag her children along a dangerous riverbank at night, in their slippers, but she knew that Dave was right: if that man got *into* the house, they'd have to get *out* of it.

"Why are the police taking so long?" she asked, her eyes pleading with Dave for everything to be alright.

"I don't know darling, but they'll be here soon, I'm sure of that....." Dave's quiet, assured reply was suddenly overwhelmed by the noise of their alarm. It screamed out into the night. They all jumped.

"Right – let's go!" ordered Dave. He pulled open the back door and he ushered his family out into the night air. It wasn't cold, but everything that had been still and quiet was now echoing to the sound of their alarm. Across the ravine he could see lights coming on in his neighbours' windows. Soon the whole street would be awake, but that wouldn't help *them*. They had to fend for themselves until the police arrived, and that meant getting away from the house.

"Here, watch your step," Dave said to Zach, "we can't use flashlights – it he gets out the back door I don't want him knowing which way we've gone. Let's get up to the Wilson place, then we can hide under their back deck – right?" Everyone nodded – Debbie understood Dave's plan: the Wilsons lived five doors up and had a big deck that extended out over the ravine. It would be dark and dry, and hopefully safe under there. But they had to get there first! It was slow going. All around them there were lights in bedroom windows, blinds being opened and dogs barking. Their alarm was very loud, Debbie had no idea it would cause such a general awakening, and she hoped that they could make it to safety before the 'Boss' could work out where they had gone. A shot rang out in the night. Even Debbie, who'd never heard a gun before, knew that sound, and it chilled her despite the warm July–night air. Just a little more – a few more metres and they'd be able to hide under the deck.

At last they were 'safe'. Debbie was near to tears, but, by now, Becky seemed to have regained control of her emotions. They were all grubby, their clothes wet with dew and their knees green with the stains of vegetation they'd crushed as they'd made their way along the steep bank of the ravine.

"Everyone OK?" asked Dave – breathless and sweating.

Three nodding heads were all he got.

"Right....now let's just sit it out....but keep your ears open, we might be able to make out if he's following us."

Debbie tensed even more at that thought; already she could hear her heart pounding above the wailing alarm and barking of the dogs. Then she heard a sound she'd never thought she could love so much – the sirens of police cars. Thank God!

"Dad?" said Zach, pulling at his father's arm.

"Yes, son, what is it?" asked Dave, not feeling at all secure despite the approaching sirens.

"I'm sorry Dad – it's my fault....it's all *my* fault," Zach was crying. Dave hadn't seen his son cry for years. It touched his heart.

"It's not *your* fault, Zach – none of this is *anyone's* fault – it's all down to the creeps who killed that poor guy in the first place. It wasn't *your* fault that we found the body, Zach....never think that." Dave's voice was full of compassion for his son, who looked like a little boy again.

"No, I mean about them finding us – it's *my* fault," replied Zach, very upset.

"What do you mean, son?" asked Dave, still trying to hear if there was anyone crashing along the riverbank towards them, but not wanting his son to be ignored in his time of need.

"My hat – I left my hat where they buried the body – and that hat's got my name in it."

"What?" Dave snapped more than he had meant to. "What hat? What name?"

"I left my hat to mark the grave – when I went back there this morning, and Mom wrote my name in it because we've all got the same hats on the hockey team. He must have gone back to the grave and found my hat. We're easy to find – we're the only Schwimmers in the phone book around here. My hat said 'Zach Schwimmer'......that's how he found us."

Dave's heart sank. The 'Boss' knew who they were: anyone connected with the killing knew who they were, *and* where to find them. What if the 'Boss' *was* a gang member? He'd certainly looked like one. Though Dave had to admit that he didn't really know much about 'gangs', he was sure there were a lot of them around....they were always being mentioned on the news: lots of them ran BC Bud to the States and returned with cocaine or guns. Maybe the 'Boss' was one of those! There'd be *loads* of them coming after his family now.....this thing was far from over: it might *never* be over. The whole scenario played out in Dave's head in two seconds flat: if the police got the 'Boss' they'd all have to testify to what they'd seen, they'd be open to all sorts of intimidation, threats, and real danger......Dave wondered if Canada had a Witness Protection Programme like he'd seen in the movies....or was that only in the States? Would his family ever be safe again?

As he looked across his cowering children at Debbie's face, he could see that she was thinking the same as him. Her eyes were wide with terror as the horror of their situation dawned on her too: they weren't just in danger right now – they might be in danger for *ever*.

"Oh Zach," Dave said, gently, stroking his son's thatch of sandy hair, "it's not *your* fault....none of this is your fault. We've got caught up in something that's much bigger than anything we could have imagined....but, you know what, we'll be *fine*....just *fine*. We'll do the right thing: we'll follow through with this, and we'll make sure that the authorities do right by us. Now don't worry about it, let's just keep our ears open and try to work out what's going on up there. Listen – the sirens have stopped...."

Sure enough, the police sirens had stopped, their house alarm had stopped and even the dogs had stopped barking. The silence was eerie, to say the least. Somewhere close by a slight rustling made all four of the Schwimmers draw closer together, but it was clearly just a small creature, disturbed by unexpected guests.

Gunshots rang out. It all sounded so far away that Debbie and Dave could hardly believe that their own house was involved. There were a lot more shots, then everything went quiet. Dave poked his head out from under the deck. He couldn't see anything out of the ordinary – not that he knew what was 'ordinary', under the circumstances.

"You all stay here – I'm going up onto the street to see what's happening." Dave's voice was quiet and calm.

"No, stay here with us, Dave," said Debbie, sharply. She didn't want him getting hurt. Her children needed their father. And *she* needed him too – she knew it in that instant – she knew she'd work hard to make sure he stayed in her life from now on: all the screw-ups, all the irresponsibility – it all melted away. She and Dave would stick together. They *were* only separated, after all: they hadn't gone through with the final divorce yet....maybe they could make it. Maybe. She had to speak her mind. "I don't want you getting hurt, Dave – I need you to be safe. I....*need* you.......we *need* you." She was trying to tell him so much, in so few words. Would he understand?

Dave raised himself to his full height, and reached around his children, circling them with his arms. Then he reached forward and kissed Debbie – not a peck on the cheek, but a proper kiss, on the lips, like they had kissed when they were young and in love. And Debbie kissed back. They felt each other's warmth, they felt their connection, and they both *knew*. It was going to be tough.....all of it....but they'd face it together.

"Eeewww!' said Zach as he looked at his parents. Becky cleared her throat and looked away, containing a giggle.

"Stop 'eeewww-ing' like that," said Dave to Zach, smiling at his wife, his eyes alive with an emotion he hadn't felt in years. Debbie looked so young, so fresh. Maybe it was the dirt on her face, maybe it was her tousled hair and glowing cheeks, Dave didn't know why, but she looked much as she had done when she was a teenager......a pretty girl with dark hair, dark eyes and a cute little button nose.

Debbie was thinking how grown up Dave looked: his sandy hair was catching the moonlight, his freckles were almost invisible....and his expression....oh, she hadn't seen his face look like that in so many, many years. His eyes had always been beautiful, but tonight they looked commanding, compassionate, and full of understanding. Tonight she was meeting David Schwimmer, adult, for the first time, and she liked what she saw.

"I've got to find out if it's safe for us to go home," said Dave, sensibly, "so I'll work my way up the side of the house and see what I can see, eh? No-one will even know....just you guys stay here, where you're safe."

Dave made his way up the steep bank that led to the street, praying that there he would find something that would make him feel that normality was returning, but the sight that met his eyes was anything but normal: four police cars, doors wide open, were all abandoned at the end of their cul-de-sac, close to their house, their flashing lights illuminating the chaotic scene; flak-jacketed officers, with their weapons held high, were running about and, in the distance, Dave could hear more sirens wailing towards them. As he ventured out he could see what seemed to be two bodies on the ground. One officer was kicking something away from the body that lay nearest his house. Dave dared to go further.

"Stay were you are – down on the ground!" called a voice behind Dave.

Dave's arms shot up into the air and he turned to face an officer who was pointing his weapon at him. "That's my house," said Dave, "I was the one who called you – they were after me and my family!"

The officer looked him up and down. He saw a man in shorts, a mud-covered tee-shirt and running shoes. Sure he wasn't armed, the officer motioned for Dave to drop his arms.

"Are we safe.....are they dead?" asked Dave.

"Where's your family?' asked the officer. "Is there anyone inside the house?"

"No, we got out. We hid under our neighbour's deck. Can I get my wife and kids now?" asked Dave, still wanting to know if they were safe.

"Let me check that we've cleared the area," said the officer, and he spoke into the radio that was hooked to his flak-jacket.

"There's an ambulance on the way – any of you guys hurt?" he asked.

"No, we're fine," said Dave, "but I'd like to get them out from under that deck – do you have a flashlight?"

The officer nodded, and he and Dave went back down the gully to help Debbie, Zach and Becky up to the street. People were beginning to dare to open their front doors. As the Schwimmers walked out onto the street, Steve Wilson, under whose deck they'd taken refuge, came out of his house.

"Dave – is everything alright?" he asked – the answer being obvious to all.

"We've had a spot of trouble, Steve, but the Mounties seem to have it all under control."

"Was that gunfire I heard?" asked Steve, surprised both by Dave's presence and his demeanour, which seemed bizarrely calm.

"Yep. There were a couple of guys gunning for us, but they've taken them down. We're going to be fine now – but we sure were grateful for your deck out there. I hope you don't mind – we hid under it for a while." Dave was hugging his daughter to him as he spoke. Steve Wilson couldn't help but notice how proud the girl was looking as she stared up at her father.

"No worries," replied Steve, completely bewildered by what was going on in their quiet little street in the middle of the night. "But what do you mean there were some guys gunning for you – what's going on, Dave?"

Dave sighed. "It's a long story, Steve, and we're all too tired for it just now. I just want to get my kids home to get some clothes together, then I'm going to drive them all over to Debbie's Mom's house to spend the night. I'll come back and see to boarding up whatever needs boarding up – so the house will be secure, but maybe you could just keep an eye on things while I drive them up to Maple Ridge – I'll only be about twenty minutes?"

Steve Wilson felt he could do nothing but agree. "Sure – give me a shout when you're ready to go," he replied, still confused.

"What's going on Steve?" it was Cherie Wilson, peering around her husband, whose large body almost filled the front door.

"Debbie!" she exclaimed, seeing her neighbour in the middle of the street. "What the hell's going on? Are you guys OK?" She sounded concerned, then she saw Dave. "Oh, *hello* Dave," Cherie Wilson's voice took on an acid edge. "I suppose this is all something to do with *you*, eh?"

Debbie was suddenly sorry that she'd spent so many hours over coffee moaning about Dave to Cherie. Cherie was a good woman, and she was only reacting to all the things that Debbie had told her over the past months and years: when Debbie had told Dave he had to leave two years ago she'd turned to Cherie for a sympathetic ear, and she'd gotten one. But now........?

"It's not Dave's fault, Cherie, *really* it's not. All he wanted to do was give the kids some time on their own with their Dad, enjoying all that nature has to offer. It wasn't *his* fault that some moron had killed a guy and left his mutilated body for them to stumble upon; it wasn't *his* fault that the killers came back to the place where they'd left the corpse, or that they tracked us down to our home. I know I've spent hours and hours telling you about all his shortcomings....sorry Dave," Debbie said to her husband, "but you must have known that I would need a shoulder to cry on, and Cherie was that shoulder," then she looked at her friend again and said, loud and proud, "but this wasn't down to Dave. His actions saved us all from God knows what tonight. I'm so *proud* of the way that he looked after us all. I'm seeing him with fresh eyes, and I know that we're in for a tough time ahead, but I think that Dave and I stand a better chance of making it right for our children if we try to make it right *together*. Eh, kids?"

Zach and Becky beamed. Cherie looked taken aback. Dave was glowing with pride and Debbie smiled at him, with warmth and love.

"So would you all like to come inside and continue this 'love-fest' in the warmth and safety of our house, till you can get back into yours?" asked Cherie, still sounding doubtful.

"You guys go on in – I'm going to speak to the police and see what's happening," said Dave, and he kissed Debbie on the cheek as she and the children made their way, happily, into the Wilson house.

"You'll be OK?" asked Steve Wilson.

"I'll be *fine*," replied Dave, and he made his way towards his house.

He was passed by an ambulance, which screeched to a halt almost at his front door. There, surrounded by glass and blood, was the body of the 'Boss'.

"Do you know who he is?" Dave asked of the officer he'd seen earlier.

"Yep – we know him pretty well: Cy Marchand, from Quebec originally. Moved here a couple of years ago and tried to get something going with the local Hell's Angels, but they never took to him – too untrustworthy even for *them*, it seems. We've been looking at him for arms trafficking, but couldn't come up with anything that would stick. He's got two known sidekicks – one of them is over there," the officer motioned to a body bag that was being hoisted into the ambulance, "and the other one is being taken into custody right now."

"If these guys were after us, should we be worried about anyone taking up where they've left off?" Dave asked, terrified about what the answer to his question might be.

"Why do you think they were 'after you', Sir?" asked the officer, curiously. He was having a problem trying to connect Dave with the guys who lay dead on his street. Dave recounted the past couple of days, briefly. The officer nodded slowly.

"You've had a hell of a weekend, Sir," was his pithy comment.

"You're not kidding!" replied Dave. "And I guess what I'm trying to work out is......is it over? Are these three guys the *only* ones we should be worried about....or are there more 'associates' of this Marchand guy, somewhere?" Dave knew that the future safety of his family depended upon the officer's answer.

"I think you'll be OK. Marchand wasn't known to mix with any other groups. In fact, the locals will be glad to see him gone. I can't imagine who the dead guy was, but if he turns out to be connected to some local outfit, then the story you've just told me, which clearly marks Marchand and his cronies as the murderers, will probably have *you* cast as the hero in all this. There could be some very interesting people wanting to shake you by the hand. But I'd decline those offers, if I were you, Sir."

Dave smiled wryly. He was beginning to feel as though, maybe, *please God*, it really *would* all be over.....very soon.

"Any idea when I might be able to get into my house?" Dave was beginning to feel a bit more settled – though he wondered why he'd referred to it as 'his' house – he'd been thrown out two years ago, now all he did was pay the mortgage.

"It's gonna be a while yet, Sir. Is there anywhere you can stay?"

"I thought I'd take my wife and children to my mother-in-law's house for the night: she's just up in Maple Ridge. I could take them there, get them settled, and then come back. If *you're* all going to be here, I don't mind the house being open."

The officer nodded. "I'll tell my boss. Do you need to get your keys? I could go get them if you tell me where they are." Dave thanked the officer, who introduced himself as Corporal Carr, Ridge Meadows detachment. Then Dave met his boss, and then his boss's boss, and finally got the keys for the minivan – his pick-up wouldn't take all four of them.

Bundling Debbie and the kids into the van, he waved his thanks to the Wilsons and they drove off, leaving the flashing lights and the emergency vehicles behind: Debbie's mom was expecting them, and he wasn't looking forward to a warm welcome at her house, but Debbie said it would be OK – she'd explained everything to her, and how *none* of it was Dave's fault.

"So is it really *over*, Dad? Really, *really* over?" asked Becky as they drove through the delightfully normal suburban streets, past darkened houses and parked trucks and pretty-by-moonlight gardens.

"Yes, it's over," said Dave, with conviction. "The 'Boss' didn't have anyone but the two guys we heard him with – one of them is dead and the other is in custody. No-one will ever come after us; no-one will ever try to harm us."

"So we won't have to move house, or school, or change our names, or have plastic surgery?" asked Becky, almost sounding disappointed.

"No, we won't have to do any of those things," said Dave.

"Good, 'cos, I'm gonna move up to the top line next season," said Zach, as though hockey was all that mattered in his life, "and I'm not starting with another team all over again!"

Debbie laughed out loud. "Darling, darling Zach – you and Becky are going to be just fine. We'll have a couple of days with Gran while Dad gets the house fixed up, and then we can *all* go home. *Together*. Right?"

"You mean Dad too?" asked Becky, her face happy.

"I mean Dad too, don't I Dave?"

"Yes, she means Dad too, guys – if that's OK with you......."

"Sure is," said both his children.

"Just one thing, Mom," added Zach.

"Yes?" replied Debbie, wondering what might come next.

"Do you think Gran will give us something to eat when we get there – I'm *starving*!"

"I'm sure she'll be only too happy to give us all something – but then it's off to bed. You might not have school, but tomorrow's going to be quite a day....." replied Debbie, feeling the warmth of her family around her.

"But nothing like that last couple of days, eh?" said Dave.

"I hope not!" replied Debbie. "No more wilderness trips for us for a while, eh?"

"It was actually quite exhilarating," said Zach, surprising everyone in the minivan.

"That's a very grown-up thing for *you* to say," observed Becky.

Zach grunted at his sister, realising he'd crossed a line. "Yeah, well, I guess it wasn't *too* boring," he muttered.

And all was right with the world.

# AUTUMN

## The Fall

### A Case for DI Glover

# I

Detective Inspector Evan Glover burrowed his fingers through his admittedly thinning, but still, satisfyingly at fifty-three, almost entirely black hair as his telephone rang for what felt like the millionth time that day. His heart sank as the extension number display showed it was his boss's boss, Detective Superintendant Williams. Again! It was only three o'clock on Monday afternoon and already Glover was feeling the strain of his boss being on holiday for a week. *All* the Detective Inspectors were supposed to pick up some of the slack when their Detective Chief Inspector was away: Glover was convinced that he was the only one getting lumbered! He missed the buffer between him and the Superintendant – who seemed intent upon making Glover's life a misery.

"Yes, Sir, how can I help?" was his measured reply, though what he wanted to do was scream – 'How do you expect me to do *any* bloody work if you insist upon telephoning me every ten minutes!?' But, then, Glover was known for his ability to keep a cool head under pressure.

"Glover, we've got a dead body," said Detective Superintendent Michael Williams bluntly, "and I'm giving this one to you. Doc Bird just called me from Three Cliffs Bay and I want you to get there ASAP!"

"Suspicious death?" asked Glover, his spirits, oddly, rising as he saw an escape from behind his desk in the immediate future.

"Man's body found on the rocks about noon today. Some surfers spotted it and called the Coastguard – they called it in and Bird took it himself. *He* called it in to me, requesting you." The Super's manner was odd – Glover thought he was holding something back. And *not* something good.

"Why me?" Glover asked. No point beating about the bush.

"You'll understand when you get there," was the Super's terse and irritatingly cryptic reply.

Glover weighed his next response carefully: known as an insightful detective, rather than a slave to procedure, Glover nevertheless recognised that the hierarchical structure within the South Wales police force, and especially where he was based at Swansea HQ, required that he was polite to this man – whatever he might think of him. In Glover's view, Williams was an officious administrator who saw it as his job to make life as difficult as possible for the people who did the actual detecting around the place: indeed, he found it hard to believe that, ten short years ago, the man had held the same position as he did now.

"So we don't know yet, then, Sir," was Glover's somewhat sarcastic response – he knew that Williams would never pick up on his tone.

"Early days, Glover. See Bird about that. I promised him I'd get you down there as soon as possible. Off you go now!"

Glover replaced the receiver, silently cursing at Williams' patronising tones. *God,* that man was annoying. But at least this new case might offer some respite from the spate of break-ins he'd been working on for the past week!

"Stanley!" he shouted into the corridor, knowing that his DS's bat-like hearing would pick up on his name being called.

As Glover sorted out his jacket, peppermints, communications devices and keys, Detective Sergeant Peter Stanley stuck his head into his boss's office.

"Sir?"

Glover looked up and smiled. He liked Stanley. He was a good, steady sort. He could never get over how young Stanley looked: despite being in his thirties, his blonde hair, pale blue eyes and generally boyish looks meant he could have been taken for much younger. He also always had to stop himself from laughing at Stanley's accent: his Bristolian burr always made it sound as though the word 'Sir' was spelled 'Srrrrrr'. He had to admit that he liked it. It was a pleasant rarity amongst the sometimes harsh local accents.

"Stanley, we've got to head out to Three Cliffs Bay: body found on the rocks there, and the Super, in his wisdom, has given it to us. Bring the car round, and I'll meet you downstairs in five, right?"

"Right, Sir," was Stanley's reply as he shot out of Glover's office and off to the car pool, via his own little cubicle.

Stanley had learned soon after his arrival in Wales from England five years ago that the Welsh loved to end their sentences with something that sounded like a question, 'right?' and 'is it?' or 'isn't it?' seeming to be their favourites. But they weren't questions at all. It was how they made a statement with which they expected the listener to agree, unquestioningly. He'd made a complete fool of himself several times by trying to answer the non-questions before he'd learned the lesson, though. But, once learned, never forgotten, was Stanley's motto – amongst others – and he never talked back to Glover in any case: the man was close to being a genius in Stanley's eyes.....intuitive, persistent, saw the detail *and* the big picture....everything a detective should be. Stanley tried to emulate Glover, but suspected he was more the plodding type – he never seemed to see the connections that Glover did. But, if he could just keep working with the man......maybe, one day.......

"Right-o, put your foot down, Stanley," said Glover as he jumped into the car that his DS had driven to the High Street entrance of the almost fanciful red-brick early Victorian structure that rather inadequately housed Swansea's twenty-first century police force, "blues and twos for this ride – the Super said we're to get there 'ASAP', so I think we can make some noise!"

Stanley smiled. He might never answer back, but he did sometimes dare a wry comment.

"You love this stuff, don't you Sir?" he ventured.

"Damn right, Stanley," was Glover's satisfied response, "there are very few perks to this job – but screaming through the traffic at rush hour, lights flashing, sirens blaring, is one of them. Off you go man!" And he beamed as they made their way noisily through the busy City centre traffic jams.

Glover's mind wandered as they wailed through the traffic: you couldn't really talk when the sirens were going, nor make phone calls, but he knew he'd have to call Betty as soon as he could to warn her that he might be late that night. It was with some relief that Stanley reverted to flashing lights only when they had cleared the main roads and began to wind along the hedge-bounded country lanes that were characteristic of the Gower Peninsular – the picturesque area where Three Cliffs Bay was located. Glover had to admit that it wasn't a bad place to have to visit on what was a surprisingly warm, sunny day for the last week of September – but, then, they were due some good weather – they'd all grown webbed feet during the second wettest August in history!

Glover flicked open his mobile phone. This might be his only chance to phone home. He could picture the telephone ringing out in his neat little house.

"Hello?" came a breathless voice. He'd obviously caught Betty busying herself with something.

"It's me, Wife," he announced, smiling.

"Hello, Husband – alright love?" Betty's voice always sounded worried when she asked him that question, which she invariably did.

"Fine....but I might be a bit late tonight. I've got to run out to Three Cliffs – body been found – got to check it out."

"Ah, that's a shame love.....I mean the body *and* you being late." Betty's voice was comforting. "It's that special veg soup tonight, so I'll keep it hot: don't worry," she added.

Evan Glover grimaced inwardly: he knew that Betty was only feeding him this stuff for his own good - he needed to drop a few pounds before they went away on their long overdue holiday: a week on Saturday they'd be off to Scotland, where he'd be able to happily over-indulge in a region where deep-fried haggis *had* to be served with chips, preferably followed by a deep-fried Mars bar, and where dozens of whiskeys would be begging to be tasted – but, in the meantime, there was the soup to contend with, and, he had to admit, he didn't care for it. He *liked* his food. Sometimes he never knew when he'd get his next proper meal....so when he *had* one he wanted it to be just that – a *proper* meal, not some excuse for one, with no fat and ten calories a serving! But there was no denying he'd filled out a bit over the summer: his shirts *were* pulling at their buttons just a bit, and his trousers could have been a little looser. The days when he could eat whatever he wanted because he'd be running it off at rugby practice, or playing it off on the rugby field at the weekend, were long gone, and his small frame, ideal for his beloved position of fly-half, was now beginning to feel the strain of carrying what were, if only he'd admit it, about twenty extra pounds. So he sighed, and resigned himself to vile, watery, vegetable soup for a couple of weeks – it was a small price to pay, he supposed.

Betty Glover knew that she wasn't pleasing her husband's palate these days. And she hated it. She always wished there was more she could do for him than just make sure he was well fed, had a comfortable home to return to at the end of what could often be a gruelling day, and was well turned out when he left it the next morning. Evan Glover constantly reminded her that she did so much more for him than this, but, to Betty, listening to him talk through his cases, keeping house and volunteering at the Citizens' Advice Bureau didn't seem to be so very much. As a graduate in psychology with a counselling background, she wanted to be by his side every minute – encouraging him, supporting him. But she knew that that was unrealistic. All the same, they didn't spend enough time together. Work always came first – it had to: nature of the job. But soon – oh Betty Glover was looking forward to their holiday so much!

"Just under two weeks now," she added brightly, knowing that her husband would understand what she was talking about, given that he himself was the one crossing off the days on the kitchen calendar.

"I know, Wife, not long now. And I *might* not be too late tonight. Might be a jumper, might not. Might be an accident – we'll see. In any case, it'll be dark by about seven, so we can't be there too long!"

"Alright Husband – say 'Hello' to Peter. Tell him to keep you safe....and don't go too close to the edge – you know what you're like with heights!"

"Yeah, yeah.....bye Wife," signed off Glover, sighing, but smiling. Betty was right, of course, he wasn't good with heights, and he hoped this investigation didn't mean he'd have to go peering over cliffs.

"Betty says 'Hello'," said Glover to Stanley, pocketing his phone.

"And did she tell me to look after you, too, Sir?" asked Stanley, risking a wry smile at his superior's expense.

"As per usual," conceded Glover.

Three Cliffs Bay was still about ten minutes away, so, with no information about the case to discuss, Stanley ventured a personal observation.

"I expect Mrs Glover will be looking forward to your holidays, Sir?"

Glover and Stanley didn't often have 'personal' conversations – the job meant they had little time for that, and they kept their 'off the job' socialising to a minimum: Glover didn't think it was fair to impose himself on Stanley in his spare time. He knew he'd never liked it when *his* superiors insisted upon inviting him to their homes or social gatherings, so why should he make Stanley suffer?

"She certainly is," replied Glover, but he decided to deflect the conversation a little, "but you're off before us – what are you planning for next week?"

"Ah......" replied Stanley, clearly regretting that he'd opened the topic for discussion. "I'm off to camp, Sir. Scoutmaster Camp, to be precise, Sir."

Glover's mind raced. Was he missing something?

"What's a 'Scoutmasters' Camp' when it's at home?" queried Glover, truly puzzled.

"Well, Sir – you know that Scouts, Boy Scouts, go off to camp, Sir?"

"Yes….." replied Glover warily.

"Well, when all the kids go back to school, so all the camps are over, the Scoutmasters, the Scout *Leaders*, get to go to camp and compare notes. We have presentations about new things coming through the Movement and so forth and….well…..we let off a bit of steam, Sir."  Stanley was clearly uncomfortable.

"So you're a *Scout* Leader?" asked Glover in amazement.

"Scout*master*, Sir. Yes, Sir, sixteen years now, Sir…..and I was a Venture Scout before that, though they've gone now of course, and before that I was a Scout and a Cub Scout too….there weren't any Beavers in those days – I've been involved since I was eight, Sir. Nearly thirty years now." Stanley was doing something Glover had never seen him do before – he was glowing with pride. Glover took a sideways look at his Sergeant. He imagined his youthful head above a Scoutmaster's garb, and decided it would suit Stanley. He could imagine how positive, encouraging and supportive of young boys Stanley would be, and how, frankly, he'd be an exemplary role model for any child.

"Just *blokes* at this Scoutmasters' Camp, is it?" asked Glover pointedly.

Stanley flushed pink.

"There are a *few* women, Sir – we have mixed Explorer Scout Units these days so they need women leaders, and then there are the Scout Network leaders – a few of them are women too."

"So where does this week of canvas-covered debauchery take place?" asked Glover, smiling.

"It's not *that* at all, Sir!" Stanley was quick to point out, somewhat seriously. "There's a lot we can learn from each other, when we all get together like that…."

"Oh, I *bet* there is Stanley….I *bet* there is…." Glover was playing with Stanley, gently, and they both knew it. Stanley took it like a Scoutmaster. He just kept going!

"We're off to a place in North Devon….it's got a good Camp Lodge and a great big field for tents. The chap who runs it is a good sort, and there are at least four pubs within walking distance…so we never get on any of the landlords' nerves too much! But the best thing about it…."

"Don't tell me….it's the toilets? Right? It's actually *got* some?" Glover laughed.

"How d'you know, Sir?" asked Stanley, quite taken aback.

"Third Swansea, 1973-1976, Wolf Patrol," answered Glover, giving the Scouts' three-fingered salute to his companion. "I remember digging 'lat pits' at camp. Filthy job. And it always seemed to be me who got to do it!"

"Same here!" exclaimed Stanley – delighted to have something in common with his boss.  "And this place has really good ones – all tiles, hot running water, closed shower cubicles, the *lot*!"

"Ah, the joys of roughing it….." smiled Glover.

"Ah, the joys of *not* roughing it so much…." replied Stanley, laughing.

"So," ventured Glover, "any attractive Akela's on the horizon?"

"Not many Akela's tend to come…." replied Stanley warily.

"But are those that do of the 'plain face and sensible shoes' variety…or are there any who could warm a young Scoutmaster's cockles?" Glover was being wicked. He rarely got the chance to tease anyone except Betty, and he was enjoying every moment of it!

Stanley sighed. "Honestly, Sir," he said, quite plaintively, "there's no-one. Not there – not *anywhere*. I mean, what with the job, and Scouting, I don't really have that much time to socialise. And being a Bristolian in a Welsh City does mean I stick out a bit like a sore thumb….a lot of girls I meet are just too put off by the combination: an English copper's just too much for them! But with the Scouting group – well, yes, we're from all over, and we've already got something in common, so you can promise Mrs Glover that I'm always keeping my eye open Sir, but nothing yet!"

"Pity – Betty reckons a good woman would be the making of you Stanley," concluded Glover, becoming more serious as they approached their destination.

"As you've mentioned before, Sir," was Stanley's sighing observation.

"Next on the left Stanley," interrupted Glover. "It's just before Penmaen Church, on the left, a tiny turning….there!"

The car swung awkwardly into the turning. Stanley had to concentrate hard to avoid the hedges that were now threatening the squad car's paint job. They pushed along the lane as far as possible. Then their way was barred by a straggling group of other official vehicles.

"Try and squeeze it into that corner there," said Glover indicating a slight widening in the lane, and he leaped from the still-moving car.

"Sir," was Stanley's formal reply, all thoughts of personal conversations now gone.

"Anybody here seen Bert Bird?" cried Detective Inspector Glover as he approached an ambulance and a police car at the end of the lane.

"He's just coming up now, Sir," came the reply from a suddenly very erect uniformed Constable who, until that moment, had been leaning nonchalantly against his car, laughing at the orderlies who were literally soaked to the skin and struggling to manoeuvre a heavily-laden stretcher along the narrow, winding path that led up, steeply, from the beach below.

Walking forward, Glover could see Bird not too far off, and decided to wait where he was for the man. The tide seemed to be right up in the bay below – he didn't wonder that the orderlies were soaked. He had visions of them battling to get the body away from the sea as the tide raced in – Three Cliffs was known for a fast tide that could rip and swell dangerously on occasions.

By the time Dr Albert Bird reached Glover he was smiling warmly. His cheeks were rosy and he almost seemed to be having a good time: he might have been on a seaside hike for all you could gather from his expression. The men enjoyed an excellent working relationship and were friends as well as colleagues: in the past ten years they'd shared many a Post Mortem and many more pints!

"Lovely day for it!" was Bird's first observation, followed rapidly by, "Unless you're this poor chap, of course!"

Glover looked around at their setting: but for the emergency response vehicles, and the sad reason for their being there, it was, as Bird had noted, a lovely day for it – the sun was still some way above the horizon, the sky was a pale and fresh blue, and the sea glinted invitingly below them, surrounded by the craggy forms of the Three Cliffs themselves and the green grass of the hill-tops. It was stunning.

Then Glover saw the body bag. To business.

"Do we know what happened?"

"Ah, I suppose you mean can I tell you 'did he fall, or was he pushed'?" Dr Albert Bird, Director of Forensic Pathology for South West Wales, and HM's Coroner for the same District, seemed pleased with himself at being able to use the well-worn phrase.

Glover smiled. His friend might be pushing sixty but he was still a kid at heart: maybe those surprisingly young children he had, and that no-less surprisingly young wife, were what did it. Or maybe it was the man's unstinting dedication to what Glover saw as excessive exercise....he never seemed to be still for a minute, and all his pastimes were, to Glover's mind, incredibly energetic. Either way, what Glover admired in the man was his enthusiasm for everything he did, and the incredible knowledge-base upon which his enthusiasm rested.

"*Can* you say?" asked Glover, hopefully. Maybe there'd be some resolution to the Super's caginess earlier on.

"Not yet, Evan," was Bird's quiet response. "If he wasn't dead when he went over, the fall would most likely have killed him: his injuries are extensive, especially around the head and neck – I suspect spinal shock – a broken neck to the layman, but I'll have to have a better look at him back at the 'ranch'. I can tell you that I can't see any obvious signs of attack – but, to be frank, even that's pushing it, given the state of the body."

"Bad?" Glover suspected he could guess the answer.

"Bad," replied Bird seriously. "He's bounced down a couple of hundred feet of jagged cliff-face. Not pretty."

"Any chance of an ID?" was Glover's next, obvious question.

"Yes, I'm afraid so, Evan. And you're not going to like it," Glover looked puzzled, and somewhat worried, but Bird continued sadly, and in a low voice. "The reason why I mentioned your name to the Super, was because of this," he handed a wallet enclosed in a plastic evidence bag to Glover. Glover pulled on gloves and opened the wallet.

Glover caught his breath. *No. It couldn't* be! Peering out at Glover, from a blurred drivers' licence photograph, was the unmistakable face of the

Great One, the One and Only GGR Davies – the best fly-half who ever earned a Welsh Rugby Cap, and Glover's sporting hero of thirty years' standing. He couldn't believe it.

"*This* is the man you found? The body is *GGR*?" asked Glover – his eyes begging Bird to deny it.

"I'm so sorry, Evan," said Bird gently. He reached out to his friend and touched Glover gently on the arm. "I know what GGR meant to you – and I have to admit that I can't be a hundred percent sure because of the damage to the face....but all the other physical attributes are consistent with this being the man we found. The Great One is no more. It's a sad day for you, I know, and a sad day indeed for Welsh rugby."

Glover couldn't have agreed more. The huge party thrown by the Fire Dragon Brewery from which GGR had retired as a 'super-salesman' just a week ago had been headline news across the whole of the Principality. He could imagine the next set of headlines right now: 'GGR Dead'; 'The Great One - Gone'. Not many people in the world could be recognised merely by their first three initials, but GGR Davies was one of them. Suddenly the 'Did he fall, or was he pushed?' question took on a whole new meaning for Glover. He knew that, if the identity of the body was confirmed as GGR, he wouldn't have a moment's peace until the manner of the man's death had been fully explained – no peace in his own mind, no peace from the press!

But for now, on a personal level, he was still trying to come to terms with the loss of the sporting hero he'd watched through the Glory Days of Welsh Rugby, stuffing it to the English, and anyone else who'd dared to allow the man to get his hands on the ball. Four Triple Crowns in a row, three Grand Slams – the 1970's, those were the days! And GGR had been there every time – he'd been magic! He was more famous than all the other players of his generation put together. He'd inspired a thousand Welsh schoolboys to get out onto the field and run towards the try-line like a train! Including Glover. Could it really be *his* remains inside that pathetic bag that was being hauled up from the beach? Surely GGR Davies was immortal?

"When will you know for sure?" was Glover's glum question to Bird.

Bird gave it some thought.

"Well, it's going to be an unpleasant identification for any family member," he replied, grimly, "so I'll start with dental records."

Glover pulled himself together. Focus on the job, focus on the job.

"Right-o, Bert, not a word about this possibly being GGR to anyone, until we know for sure. Get him back to your place and put a rush on identification, quick as you can – right?"

Bird nodded. "This one's mine, I'll handle it myself," he confirmed, signifying that he'd carry out the investigation into identity and the post-mortem examination himself, rather than passing it to one of his team of forensic pathologists.

"Meanwhile, I'll hang onto this," Glover nodded at the wallet, "and we'll do some digging around about GGR's supposed whereabouts. This might *not* be him. He might be going about his business completely unaware that someone has his wallet in their pocket." Glover suspected he was clutching at straws. "But before you go, can you point out to me where the body was found – maybe we can work out where he might have….." he hesitated, "….fallen from?"

"Absolutely," replied Bird, "I'll walk you over now – we found him pretty much directly below where the RSPCA lot found the dog."

"RSPCA? Dog?" asked Glover.

"Wheaten Scottish terrier, found dragging a shooting stick tied to its lead, over on the cliff-top there. The RSPCA have taken the dog; your chaps have got the stick. I noted the telephone number printed on the dog's collar. Dog's named 'Arthur', by the way. Here it is."

Bird handed Glover a scrap of paper with a mobile phone number scribbled on it.

"Damn!" responded Glover, his sunny disposition now completely clouded over. "GGR had a dog just like that – I saw it with him in the photos on the front page of the 'Evening Post' last week. Oh Bert, I'd give anything for it to *not* be him!"

Bert Bird could feel Glover's sadness, and shared it: maybe not to the same depth as his friend and colleague, but to some extent.

"Anyway – the phone number's a start – let's give it a go," Glover added, knowing he had to begin somewhere. Pulling out his mobile phone, he dialled the number Bird had handed him. He got the ringing tone, and quickly realised that he could also hear a musical tune ringing out from inside the approaching body-bag. He pushed the button to disconnect. The music stopped. He redialled. Once again the unmistakable strains of 'Bread of Heaven' could be heard coming from the stretcher that was now right beside Glover. Then the music stopped again and Glover heard a familiar voice: a voice that had given triumphant interviews throughout the 'seventies; a voice that had given opinions about Internationals for the following decades; a voice that was unmistakably GGR Davies.

"Sorry I missed you – leave a message and I'll ring you back – Diolch yn fawr".

Glover looked resigned. It wasn't a formal identification, but for a body to be found near another man's dog, *and* carrying another man's wallet *and* his mobile phone….well, it was pushing 'coincidence' a bit too far. GGR's whereabouts were no longer in question.

"Looks like we've got a few pretty strong reasons to believe it's him then," admitted Glover, unenthusiastically. Bird sadly nodded his agreement.

"Better take a look at him, I suppose, and I'd better get that phone too….it could help us out. Amazing it stills works, frankly!" was Glover's next unhappy statement.

The orderly unzipped the bag slowly, with respect.

The injuries to the man's head and face, were, as Bird had warned him, significant. It was difficult to recognise any features, as few remained. Glover found himself struggling to be objective. Given his job, and the number of dead bodies he'd seen over the years, it never ceased to amaze him that each one felt like the first – the assault to his senses being just as violent, and just as upsetting, each time that he had to force himself to look at what remained of a human being. He had no idea how Bert did what he did. He couldn't have stomached it, he knew that.

The facial injuries aside, Glover quickly assessed the body and noted the lightweight red jacket, from the inside pocket of which he extricated the man's telephone, the plaid shirt and khaki, brown-belted trousers, all torn by the sharp rocks and soaked by the sea. They clung to the body, wrinkled and gaping, revealing jagged puncture wounds. It was a sorry sight.

Re-zipping the bag, the orderlies followed Bird's instructions and took the remains off towards the waiting ambulance.

"Let me show you fellows where I think he might have gone over," said Bird, as Glover motioned to Stanley to follow, "then I'll get back as quick as I can and get going with a formal identification."

"Hmmm," mused Glover, lost in thought, as the threesome walked across the headland, their eyes narrowing against the descending sun and the stiff breeze, "we'd better proceed as though it *is* him. But let's see what we can find here first....."

'Here' turned out to be a grassy dell, below the highest point of the cliff-top and shielded from the wind by high rocks on all sides except that facing straight out to sea. The grass was badly trampled about and Glover could see quite clearly where the pointed end of a shooting stick had been stuck deep into the ground, then dragged out by a no doubt distressed little dog, probably wondering what had happened to its master.

"Hmmmm.......no obvious sign of a suicide note, or any other sorts of clues or items. Stanley - cordon off this whole area, and get those uniforms to do a proper search," said Glover, nodding his instructions to his DS. "If the dog's been running around, doubtless followed about by some pretty heavy-footed RSPCA types, there might not be anything here that's of much use for us. But we'd better treat the scene with all due diligence, Stanley. We'll hold off on the door-to-door for the farms and what-not in the area until we know more, and until we know it's GGR. Right?"

Stanley nodded his understanding, and started back towards the two Constables who were still kicking their heels beside their car.

"Anything for us down there?" asked Glover, peering downwards, but remaining at least ten feet back from the precipitous cliff-edge.

"To be honest, it would be hard to say," replied Bird. "When the surfers spotted him, down there on the sea-side of the cliffs, he was, apparently, upside down, lodged between two outcrops. It was the red of his jacket that caught their attention. By the time the Coastguard got here in their boat, the tide was coming in, and they couldn't get close enough to him to effect a retrieval: they'd have been pushed into the rocks themselves. In any case, it was clear to them, from the injuries they could see, that he was dead. I was in the office when the call came in and, frankly, I thought a run to the seaside might be more pleasant than ploughing through paperwork for more bloody inquests! And by the time *I* got down to him, the sea was already washing over the body. By now the sea's at least ten feet above where we found him – so I suspect that anything that *might* have been down there would have been washed away anyway. I had a good look up at the cliff face with my binoculars when I was down there, but I couldn't see any evidence of exactly where he might have struck as he fell."

Glover grimaced. How could Bird be so objective?

"Sorry Evan," added Bert Bird, noticing the effect his words were having on his colleague and friend of a decade, "I suppose I see it all a bit more scientifically than you…"

"You're not kidding!" was Glover's wry reply. "So…..not much chance of anything useful down there," he added as he nodded towards the bottom of the cliff, "and we're not likely to find much that's undisturbed up here, either. So it's over to you for a formal ID. But you know what I *really* need, Bert……"

"Let me guess!" was Bird's sarcastic reply. "Was the fall the actual cause of death? Any clues as to the manner of death – natural, accidental, suicidal or homicidal? Bluntly put, is there any reason to expect foul play?"

"Exactly. Pronto."

"Right-o, I'm off then," said Bird as he slapped Glover gently on the back, in a comforting way. "Sorry it's GGR," he said quietly. "It'll be big news this, I know – and I also know you're just the man for the job. I know how much you idolised him, and I know you'll deal with this case like you deal with all your cases – with intelligence, speed *and* respect for the dead. You'd better talk to the Super though – I know he was keen to hear from you after you'd seen the body: I'd told him about the wallet. No doubt he'll want to prepare for the media onslaught! Tell him I should have something formal by morning, if not before….but I'll get out of your hair for now and let you get on with your side of things. Cheerio!"

"Bye Bert, and good luck – keep me posted!" Glover called towards his departing colleague.

Glover turned his face to the cooling sun once more, and breathed deep. Such beauty marred by such a tragedy. No matter what the reason for GGR's demise, it was a sad day for Glover, and the seagulls cried above him as if mourning the passing of an extraordinary man, which GGR certainly had been.

Then Glover snapped his eyes open, and turned purposefully towards his car. Best get going!

# II

It was still only 4pm, according to Glover's watch. He thought it strange that it had taken such a short time for his little world to have shifted so much. But then, as he knew only too well, a lot could change very quickly in life. Maybe one missed step had ended the life of a man who had made pride swell in a nation's heart for a decade or more......or maybe there was an altogether more complicated, or dark, reason for the Great One's demise. It was up to him to find out. And he knew exactly where his next port of call would be: the Davies house, just up on the shoulder of the South Gower Road. Everyone knew that GGR had a small-holding from where his locally well-known wife, Gwladys, took their fruits, vegetables and eggs to the seasonal stall she had operated under the great glass roof of Swansea Market for at least the last forty years. The Glovers themselves had often benefitted from GGR's wife's green thumb, and he knew that many people shopped at her stall just to be able to say 'These are from GGR's place, you know' when they presented their family with an evening meal, or visitors with a hearty Sunday lunch. The cachet was not to be ignored, even after all these years.

Just minutes away by road, the squad car soon crunched to a halt on the gravelled hard-standing in front of the Davies' very typically white-painted stone Gower house, that was trimmed with shining black gloss paint details. The place looked spic and span – but deserted: all closed up and just a little melancholy. Knocking at the door brought no response.

"Probably still at the Market, if that's where she is today," commented Glover to Stanley, weighing whether they should set off for the City centre and try to catch Gwladys Davies before she left her stall for the day, but uncertain they'd make it by five o'clock, or if, indeed, she'd be there at all.

As if voicing Glover's own doubts, Stanley asked, "Do we know if she's at the Market at all at this time of year?" Even *he*, a relative newcomer to the area – five years wasn't *that* long – and an Englishman at that, knew about Gwladys Davies's stall. It was almost legendary! She was *always* the stallholder chosen by the local media when an interview about Swansea Market was required.

"I think with it being apple, blackberry, cauliflower and kale season, she's likely to be," replied Glover, listing some of his favourite foods. "They're the sort of things they grow here. But maybe you can phone the Market and find out, while I call in to the Super." It wasn't a question, and Stanley knew it.

The two men drew apart to allow for some privacy, and made their respective calls. Concluding their business almost simultaneously Stanley spoke first.

"Mrs Davies has been at the Market since she set up her stall at about eleven this morning, Sir, 'till about forty minutes ago: she'd sold out of everything so she left early, they said. In fact, if she was coming straight home, she should be here soon," concluded Stanley, looking at his watch.

Glover nodded. "The Super wants me to follow up with her as a first priority. Sounds like he's already pulling out his few remaining hairs with worry that, somehow, the presumptive identity will leak, and he wants us to break the news to the likely widow, before anyone else can. So we'd better hang about here. Not much else we can do right now." Glover felt full of impatience, like a wound spring: not because he was desperate to break the news to the woman he'd always known as a jolly, rotund person, smiling at customers across a well-stocked veg stall, but to *really* get going with the investigation. The trouble was, of course, as he had to acknowledge to himself, he didn't really know what he *was* investigating. He'd have to wait until Bert could give him some insight into how, and maybe even why, the man had ended up at the bottom of the cliffs.

Of course, there was always the chance he had jumped…..but the presence of the dog made that unlikely. Why would a man take his dog to the spot where he planned to throw himself off a cliff? Even Glover, not a dog owner himself, felt that would be an unkind thing to do, causing unnecessary distress to a, presumably, beloved creature. And that wouldn't be like GGR at all – not the man known for his support of youth rugby, and seen, almost weekly in the local newspapers, surrounded by beaming boys! No, it didn't look like a suicide. No note – though, of course, there might have been one tucked away inside the man's clothing. But, in any case, Glover found it hard to believe that GGR would choose to end his own life. The man was comparatively young, just sixty-five, which you couldn't call old in this day and age, and was still adored and respected by everyone who'd ever heard of him! He imagined that GGR's life was full of admiring fans and, conceding that he didn't really *know* the man, he couldn't come up with any ideas about why he wouldn't have been looking forward to a long and active retirement.

"There's a car coming, Sir. This might be her now." Stanley's comment pulled Glover back from his reverie.

Sure enough, a small vividly-metallic blue hatch-back with luminous yellow capitalised lettering announcing 'DAVIES FRUIT & VEG' pulled up alongside the police car, and a short, slightly greying woman, of significant girth, pushed herself out from behind the steering wheel. Glover recognised her as GGR's wife.

"Can I help you?" she asked cheerily enough, her bright blue eyes, which matched Glover's own, shining happily at the pair. She glanced at their car, then returned her gaze to the two men standing in her driveway. She froze. "You're the police!" it was like an accusation.

"Yes, Mrs Davies, we are," replied Glover, as comfortingly as possible, as he showed her his ID card.

Gwladys Davies's face was stony. "It's Geraint, isn't it? Something's happened to Geraint. What's the silly bugger been up to now?" Glover thought she seemed more angry than concerned.

"Well, maybe we could talk inside….." was Glover's hopeful response. But Mrs Davies wasn't budging.

"You can tell me *right* here, *right* now!" Definitely anger, thought Glover. "Drinking and driving again, is it? I'll give him what for, you see if I don't! *You* lot keep letting him off, and *he* keeps doing it. Where is he *this* time? Got him locked up somewhere safe till he sobers up, I hope! I suppose I'll have to come and get him again. Well, I'm emptying this lot out first – he can bloody well *wait*!"

Mrs Gwladys Davies opened the hatch-back of the car and started to pull out empty crates and boxes, throwing them across the little courtyard with strength and fury.

Glover could hear her muttering 'Bloody man!' under her breath, and felt sorry for her. This was probably the last time she'd ever be angry with her husband. It was hard to be angry with someone who was dead. Her anger would stop very soon…..as soon as he told her. But for now, she was happily cursing the man she'd soon be mourning, and Glover hardly had the heart to stop her. He grappled with how to break the news: it was *never* easy, but this time it really *would* be as hard for him to say the words as it would be for this woman to hear them. He knew that the couple had no children; he wondered about other relatives. Damn! He should have asked Stanley to call for a WPC.

"There's a WPC on the way, Sir," whispered Stanley into his ear, almost telepathically. "Coming in an unmarked car, Sir. We don't want any tongues wagging yet….though they will do soon enough I suspect, seeing us here. I called when we got here. Should be here in about fifteen minutes."

Glover smiled and winked his thanks. "Good man," was all he whispered in response.

Turning his attention to the rotund, angry woman in front of him, he knew he couldn't put it off any longer. He swallowed hard, and set about changing her life forever.

"Mrs Davies," he raised his voice to get her attention, and succeeded. "You're right, Mrs Davies, it *is* about your husband, but it's not what you think. I really *do* feel it would be better if we could speak to you indoors. Indeed, maybe there's a friend or a neighbour you'd like my colleague to fetch."

The woman tutted at Glover. "Why on earth would I want anyone with me? What are you going to tell me? That he's dead or something, is it?" Gwladys Davies smiled at her own silly, angry suggestion. For a split second. Then her face fell. She stopped in her tracks, a wooden slatted crate in one hand, a flattened cardboard box in the other. "Oh my God – he's *not*, is he?" Her eyes were wide with disbelief. Her mouth hanging open in a tragic 'O'.

"A man's body was found at the foot of Three Cliffs today, Mrs Davies, and we have good reason to believe it is that of your husband, Mister Geraint Gareth Richard Davies." It seemed strange, and almost heretical, to Glover to be speaking the man's full name like that. "We found Mister Davies's wallet and mobile phone on the body, and I believe you have a little dog….."

"Arthur….*where's* Arthur?" she cried looking around in horror.

"Arthur's fine – he's been taken away by the RSPCA," Glover reassured her.

"I want Arthur!" shouted the woman. "Tell them to bring him back to me! He doesn't like other dogs! He needs to be home with his Mum! Tell them to bring him home *now*!"

Glover was somewhat taken aback by the woman's fixation with her dog. He nodded to Stanley, and knew that his DS would understand that he meant him to call the RSPCA and arrange for the dog to be returned to its owner. But he also knew that he had to continue with his difficult task. It was far from over.

"Maybe if we could step inside?" he tried again.

Gwladys Davies held a bunch of keys towards Glover. "It's the little gold one," she whispered. She seemed to have shrunk, to have somehow deflated. She looked completely bewildered. Glover handed the keys to Stanley and moved to support the woman, who had dropped the boxes she had been holding with a clatter, and was hanging onto her open car door in an effort to support herself.

"Let's get you inside and organise a cup of tea, is it?" said Glover, gently, as he steered the woman, whose legs weren't working at all well.

"I can't believe it……I *don't* believe it……" she whispered, as Glover sat her down, carefully, on a wheel-backed wooden chair beside her large, well-scrubbed pine kitchen table. She looked up at Glover with dry eyes, silently beseeching him to tell her it was all a lie….but Glover couldn't.

"Look, Mrs Davies," he began, keen to spare the woman the ugly details of her husband's condition, "our people are working on a formal identification as we speak, but we're in little doubt about it being your husband. But I wonder….do you happen to know what he was wearing when he went out with Arthur this morning?"

Maybe the clothes would clinch it.

"I know *exactly* what he was wearing this morning – I lay out his clothes for him every morning," was the woman's proud, and somewhat more confident reply. "He had on his nice new beige trousers that I got him for his retirement do, they're that good old-fashioned twill material, they'll last for years they will….and he wore his yellow and green checked shirt. *And* he probably wore that horrible red wind-cheater thing they gave him from the brewery, knowing him, though why he *will* insist upon wearing it when he's got so many other, *nice* jackets, I'll never know! That waxed cotton coat I got for him – never wears *that*, does he?"

Maybe you *could* be angry with the dead, after all, thought Glover, or maybe Gwladys Davies was in denial. But her description did it for Glover – there was no doubt in his mind: it was GGR's body alright.

"I know this must be very difficult for you, Mrs Davies, a sudden death is very upsetting. So *is* there someone you'd like my Sergeant to get hold of for you? Maybe even your family doctor?" he was almost begging her to say yes. The presence of a friend or a relative, and the use of some heavy sedatives, usually meant that the burden of comforting a bereaved one could reasonably be passed along – and he could get on with his job.

Gwladys Davies thought for a moment, then said, quite sharply, "Get Ann from the farm across the road. Geraint's sister lives in Cardiff now – she's gone very posh has Janice – and she'll take forever to get here: drives like a snail, she does. I suppose I'd better ring her to tell her, though. Mind you........what *do* I tell her?" Gwladys Davies seemed to suddenly realise she had no idea what had actually happened to her husband. "What happened *exactly*? Are you *sure* it's him?"

Glover knew how long it had taken *him* to face the facts, so he wasn't surprised that the man's wife wasn't prepared to take it all in. He explained again about the dog, the wallet and the phone, then added the confirmation of the clothing. The woman looked pale as she took a cup of hot tea off Stanley, her hands shaking.

"Did Mister Davies seem quite his usual self when you left him this morning?" ventured Glover. The possibility of suicide had to be explored, however unlikely it might seem.

Gwladys Davies was quick to respond. "If you mean was he grumbling about anything and everything, shouting at me for no reason *and* hung over, then yes, he was. Didn't get home till after midnight – a taxi brought him. So of *course* he didn't feel like getting out of bed at six this morning – not like some of us have to!" She was *still* angry with the man! Glover wondered at just how much resentment had simmered, and maybe boiled, between the two of them when he was still alive. "Supposed to be walking Arthur then sorting out picking up the car this morning, he was."

"So there was nothing out of the ordinary then?" pressed Glover. "Nothing preying on his mind – worrying him?"

Gwladys Davies put down her mug and narrowed her now steely-blue eyes at Glover.

"You mean, do I think he flung himself over the cliff, don't you?" her mouth was pursed into a narrow, white line. The jolly woman Glover remembered from the fruit and veg stall in the Market seemed to have evaporated – maybe she was just a concoction for the customers, and *this* was the Gwladys Davies that GGR had lived with: the wrinkles around her lips seemed to sit very comfortably around her angry little mouth, indeed, they seemed to have been formed as the result of many years of forming this exact angry, judgmental expression.

"Yes, that's what I mean, Mrs Davies." Glover didn't mean to be unkind, but he thought that her direct approach should be met with an equal response.

"Don't be so bloody ridiculous!" was her venomous reply. "Geraint was many things, but he wasn't a man who would hurt himself. He'd no more jump off Three Cliffs than I would! Besides – he'd never do anything to mess up that face of his. I suppose he *is* a mess? They always *are* when they go off the cliffs."

Glover found her remarks curious, given the circumstances.

"Well, as you have already clearly deduced, your husband's remains bear the marks of a substantial fall. But I appreciate your insights, Mrs Davies. So you don't think it likely that your husband took his own life. Do you know of anyone who might have wanted to do him harm, then?"

"So, if he didn't jump, then he must have been pushed?" was her disdainful retort. Glover was beginning to hate that phrase.

"Well, we have to explore every possibility, Mrs Davies – I'm sure you wouldn't want us to leave any stone unturned." Glover was using his 'pacifying' voice. It wasn't working.

"Look *Inspector*," she made Glover's title sound like an insult, "there's no way Geraint would have jumped, and no, there's no-one I know of who would hate him enough to push him off. If you don't *know* how he ended up at the bottom of the cliff, and it's quite clear you don't," she was cruelly mocking Glover by now, "then might I suggest you go away and find out! The chances are that he was still half-drunk from last night and he slipped and fell. Always boasting about how he was still so nimble on his feet, he was. Well maybe he wasn't quite so nimble this morning!"

Glover was disappointed that this interview wasn't going the way he'd hoped: he was disappointed to hear about GGR's supposed drinking habits, and even more disappointed to find that his wife wasn't the cheery woman he'd expected, but a bitter and angry woman, who, even now, wouldn't stop making spiteful comments about Glover's hero!

"Um, excuse me Mrs Davies," Stanley seemed unhappy about interrupting, but felt it had to be done, "do you think it would be better for me to walk across the road to your friend's farm, or is there a telephone number where I could reach her?" Being a city boy himself, Stanley had learned the hard way, on the job, that in the countryside 'across the road' could well mean two miles away, so he felt this was a question worth asking.

"She's number three on the quick-dial thingy," replied Gwladys Davies in a businesslike manner, "the phone's in the hall out there – just ring star, 03, star and you'll get her. Ann Edwards. But don't tell her what's happened – I'll tell her when she gets here. Ta." Gwladys Davies looked at her watch. "She *should* be there....probably getting tea ready, I should think."

Suddenly, it appeared that the thought of her friend preparing an evening meal overwhelmed her, and it set Gwladys Davies off into floods of tears. Glover suspected that she was beginning to accept that her husband was, in fact, dead: that she'd never again prepare a meal for *him*. He could do nothing but wait, as she wailed and snuffled. Her sobbing gradually subsided into quieter tears. Glover couldn't help but feel relieved: relieved that she'd shown some sort of emotion other than anger, and relieved that she'd finally stopped.

Stanley re-entered the large farmhouse kitchen and announced, "Your friend will be right over, Mrs Davies."

"Thank you, dear," she managed to reply, her tone now much softer than before. "Maybe you *had* better get Doctor Morris – he's number four on the thingy. Thank you."

A knock at the front door drew Stanley's attention. "I'll get that, and ring the doctor," he offered. Glover nodded. Moments later Stanley returned with a young policewoman in tow, who busied herself around Mrs Davies: she offered more tea, enquired about the location of biscuits and asked if the poor woman fancied anything to eat.

Whilst Gwladys Davies was fending off the attentiveness of the policewoman, Glover whispered to Stanley, "Let's get the friend in, get the WPC to make sure the woman's taken care of by the doctor for the night, and we'll get out of here! 'Till we know a cause of death I don't know if this woman's just a widow to be pitied, or a suspect. Either way, we'd better make sure one of our lot is with her at all times – right?"

Again, it wasn't really a question, and Stanley knew it. He also knew that, as his boss took his leave of Mrs Gwladys Davies, he would have mentally noted every detail of how she was taking the news of her husband's death. Another knock at the front door announced the arrival of the neighbour.

Glover was only too well aware that most murders were committed by spouses. Of course, he didn't know if they were even dealing with a murder yet, but if it turned out to be that they were, he might already have witnessed something that would prove useful in their investigations. All that anger – it was quite something!

As he was leaving Glover turned once more towards the still-snuffling woman and said, as comfortingly as he could, "Be assured, Mrs Davies, that I'll be in touch if we get any more news, and a WPC will be here with you all night. We can't have you feeling lonely, now can we? But could you maybe just tell me the exact time you left your husband this morning? Was he due to meet with anyone up at Three Cliffs?"

"Ten to nine, I left," she answered confidently, some of the sharpness returning to her voice, "same as usual. Well, usual since he retired, anyway. I know it had only been a week, but he didn't know what to do with himself already – couldn't help but get under my feet, he couldn't, and he held me up something rotten. 'Helping' he said he was, but he wasn't helpful at all! Usually out by eight all those years, you see, him *and* me – him off to see his customers, me to the Market. But now, well, he'll *have* to find something to do with his time. I can't cope with his sort of help! And plans? No, no plans that I know of, other than getting the car back – that was his problem, see? *Never* any plans! I've been telling him and telling him to find something to do – he'll enjoy playing more golf I suppose, loves it he does, but you can't do that every day, can you? Well, I suppose *he* could, but he doesn't like the rain, see? Makes his arthritis play up, doesn't it? Those knees of his! Never give him any peace, they don't. He was just going out to walk Arthur when I left him this morning. Oh….poor Arthur!" And she was off again about the dog!

Glover found it all very interesting………..

# III

As Evan Glover was brushing his teeth the next morning, his mobile phone started to ring in the pocket of his jacket that was hanging on the banister downstairs. It was 6.45am. It had to be the Super!

"Shall I get it?" asked Betty, calling through from the kitchen.

"Yes please, Wife," came Evan's gurgled reply.

"Detective Inspector Evan Glover's telephone," said Betty, very professionally, after pushing the 'answer' button.

"That you Mrs Glover?" asked the Superintendant, formally.

"Hello Michael, how are you?" Betty made it a point to address all Evan's superiors as equals – they weren't *her* bosses, after all!

"Fine, thank you Mrs Glover – though this is a messy business....I expect your husband's told you all about it?" Detective Superintendant Michael Williams suspected that all his men talked about the job to their wives, if they still had wives, of course! The divorce rate in their profession was quite horrendous! And they weren't really supposed to share information with members of the public, which was what wives were, after all. But he was in no doubt that the sudden death of GGR Davies would have been the sole topic of conversation at the Glover household the previous night, knowing, as did everyone, of Evan Glover's great admiration for the man.

Betty Glover had been on the receiving end of several of her husband's rants about Williams over the years, and knew better than to tell the man that her husband had, indeed, given her all the facts. They'd spent hours the night before poring over Evan's old match-day programmes from Rugby Internationals and club games in the 1970's, and Evan had waxed lyrical about GGR's speed and efficiency on the field of play. Betty had enjoyed seeing him relive happy memories, but had been saddened by his sadness. She'd also been surprised at her husband's recounting of how GGR's wife had taken the news, but had reminded him that grief affects people in many different ways. She decided to tread carefully with Williams – he was a tricky man in many respects, but loved to have his ego stroked.

"Evan's the man for the job, you chose wisely there, Michael," said Betty, knowing she was right about Evan, but realising it had been their friend Bert who'd known he was the right man for the job. "He'll sort it all out – and you don't need to worry that Dave Richards is away right now – Evan will handle it all with kid gloves. He loved GGR, you know, and he'll get to the bottom of it, no worries."

DS Williams *was* concerned that Glover's immediate superior was on holiday, in fact, he was hating being that much closer to the 'front line' than when DCI Richards was around. He was bracing himself for all the media attention they were about to encounter, and not looking forward to it one bit!

"I intend being very 'hands-on' with this case, as you can imagine, Mrs Glover," replied Williams, silently impressed by Glover's wife's perceptiveness, as always. But he didn't have time for polite banter, he needed Glover. "Is your husband able to come to the phone?"

"Just a sec, here he is!" Betty handed the phone to her husband, and went off to pour his coffee from a china mug into a thermal one that he could take with him when he left, which she suspected was just about to happen.

She was right. Evan kissed her, grabbed the coffee and something she'd wrapped in a piece of paper towel, and shouted, "Bert's got something – I'm off to Swansea Hospital to see him....I might be late, Wife!"

"Don't worry, Husband......I'll keep the soup going!" came Betty's less than welcome reply, as Glover pulled the front door closed behind him and jumped into his car. It was just before 7am. Obviously Bert had been at it all night! Glover wondered what he'd found. As he negotiated the blessedly light traffic he slurped at his coffee – he hated those mugs...you could *always* taste the plastic - and he opened the little package Betty had thrust into his hand. Two peeled, hard-boiled eggs rolled around on the passenger seat next to him – good grief they stank! He assumed that they must be the prescribed breakfast for the day so, without even the benefit of salt, he decided to eat them as quickly as he could, and opened the car window to get rid of the dreadful smell!

# IV

"So, what's up with everything going through the Super then, Bert?" asked Evan Glover as he walked into Dr Albert Bird's office at 7.20am.

"Hmmmm," muttered Bert through a fast-food breakfast sandwich. "He's taking a very 'hand's on' approach with this one – his phrase - so he wants everything, and I mean *everything*, to go through him. He's been phoning me almost every hour, on the hour, through the night. Through the *night*! The man's driven me nearly insane! Frankly, I don't know how I've kept my cool!" Glover could tell that Bert was very close to losing his 'cool' right at that minute, just by recounting the pressure Williams had been putting on him.

"Poor Bert," was Glover's wry comment, understanding how infuriating the Super could be, quickly followed by, "so what did you find? I know we're all grateful that you've been at it all night, but the Super, for all his involvement in the details, didn't tell me a damn thing!"

"That's because I told him I wanted you to *see* something, not just be *told* something....come with me to the dirty rooms." Bird led the way from his office to the suite of 'dirty rooms' that comprised the majority of HM Coroner's Suite at the Hospital. Glover knew that 'dirty' signified the presence of corpses: the public were never allowed into 'dirty' areas – they only got to see the remains of their loved ones from a 'clean' room. None of this rolling out of corpses from chilled drawers, to be pawed over by anyone and everyone, like they always seemed to be doing on those American TV shows. The Swansea NHS Trust Health and Safety Regulations wouldn't allow for that sort of thing! They got enough stick about not keeping the wards clean, let alone allowing members of the public to come into contact with goodness knew what in the mortuary!

Glover hated the Coroner's Suite, mainly because the place smelled......and 'sweet' certainly wasn't the word for it! Of course, it depended on what Bert and his team had on the go at any given time, but not even the chilly conditions and the use of various chemicals could mask the smell of human flesh putrefying on the stainless steel tables. He hoped he wouldn't have to be there for too long, and tried to prepare himself for the unpleasant task of viewing the corpse, this time possibly completely splayed open, the cavity where the internal organs had once resided in full, and inglorious, as far as he was concerned, colour.

As Glover pulled on the required gloves and paper coverall, and donned the ridiculous little hat that completed the outfit, Bird brought him up to date.

"It's definitely him, Evan. I got the man's medical and dental records last night, and there's no question about it."

Glover was disappointed: somewhere inside him there'd been a slim thread of hope that the body had somehow been set up to appear to be GGR, but wasn't, in fact, his hero.

"He's had a huge amount of dentistry done over the years," continued Bird, watching Glover fiddling with the paper cap with great amusement, "some of it involving quite a lot of metalwork, but I think that what's most amazing is that, throughout all those years of rugby, he never broke a single bone, except his nose, which it seems he broke eight times, necessitating some septorhinoplastic surgery because of the damage to his septum. An ACL rupture, a couple of concussions, several teeth lost, as I said, but nothing terribly serious, considering *some* rugby injuries."

"Well, Bert, despite the fact that he played well into his thirties, very few people could catch him on the field," was Glover's glum reply.

"True....but, although he looked not too bad on the outside, except for the terrible injuries from the fall of course, his innards were another story," added Bird seriously. "Definitely the observable early stages of hypertropic cirrhosis: he probably thought he was suffering from constant indigestion, but it was an enlarged liver that was doing it. There are some faint signs of jaundice, but he might not have noticed that, given his generally ruddy complexion, and he also had a touch of liver-palm, but again, if he was out helping on the small-holding I dare say he would have put the characteristic reddening at the ball of his thumbs down to general wear and tear of the hands. I suppose that working for a brewery for forty-odd years has its damaging side-effects, after all," he concluded.

"Alcohol induced then?" asked Glover.

"Most likely – booze is by far the most common cause of cirrhosis here: lots of it, for a good number of years, I'd say. But I'm getting some other tests done too – liver, kidneys, heart, body and blood chemistry of course, toxicology reports and so on. I can't say too much right now, but there are a few other physical issues I'm concerned about." Glover looked quizzical. "Don't ask, Evan, because you know I won't *guess*! What do I *know*? Well, he was clearly a pretty heavy smoker; his arteries don't suggest that he was overly familiar with the words 'low fat'; he had surprisingly good muscle tone for a man of sixty-five who was obviously otherwise generally unfit, and he has very small testicles. As I say, internally he was a bit of a mess! He might have had a few years left in him, but only with a significant change in lifestyle, I'd have said." Bird was looking serious as he pushed open the swing doors that led from the 'clean' offices.

Glover was still grappling with the comment about the man's testicles! He felt compelled to speak! "Now, you know me, Bert, a man who likes plain language when it comes to your area – why the comment about the testicles? What does that mean?"

"Well," replied Bird, continuing to walk slowly towards the area where the post-mortems were conducted, "nothing, necessarily, by itself, and that's why I hesitate to make any assumptions....." Bird was obviously being cautious, "but what I can tell you is that the testicular atrophy, the relatively lean muscle mass for his age, the liver and kidney condition.....all taken together....and, well, I'll admit that the biggest clue is the number of hypodermic wounds in the man's thighs, lead me to suspect that GGR Davies was a long-term user of anabolic steroids."

Evan Glover took a moment to consider Bert Bird's comments. He was stunned. GGR on steroids? It made no sense!

"But he hasn't played rugby in nearly thirty years, Bert, why on earth would he be taking steroids?" asked Glover, somewhat confused.

"Don't go jumping the gun, Evan – I am telling you what I have found, and how I interpret those findings, without the benefit of any conclusive test results – so *please* bear that in mind?" Glover nodded his agreement. "So," continued Bird, "what we have here is the possibility of a man who might have become a steroid user at an early point in his career and continued to use them thereafter."

The thought horrified Glover: what would all those records, caps and cups *mean* if GGR had achieved it all because of steroid use?

"Or," continued Bird, noting his friend's horrified expression, "we have a man who began to use steroids as he aged and felt the effects of a life of taking knock after knock on the field: steroids aren't able to actually build muscle, you see Evan, they're used to allow for a quicker recovery time after exercise and to increase tolerance to pain, which allows the user to push their body further and faster so they can build more muscle and stamina. Maybe GGR used them to allow him to manage his aches and pains and to allow him to still mess about on the field, or play round after round of golf, which I understand he did."

Glover preferred that idea: if his hero *was* using steroids, then, so long as he hadn't used them during his career, and so long as they were for medicinal reasons only, well.....Betty's cousin had just had a steroid injection in her hip – not all uses of steroids were bad, after all, he reasoned.

"Is there any way to tell.....well, how long he'd been using them?" Glover dared to ask. Did he really want to know, was what he was asking himself.

"No, other than for years," replied Bird. "He's obviously been what you might call a 'responsible user', but there are some suggestions of cumulative liver and kidney damage, which would be normal, and some effect on the heart. Pretty well observed side effects of long term usage – meaning years, not months. But as for when he was playing – which I'm sure is what you mean Evan – there's no way of knowing. Of course, you have to bear in mind that anabolic steroids weren't banned substances in sports in those days – not like they are now. They're Schedule 4 drugs now, as I'm sure you know, and banned throughout sport. Now, GGR wasn't involved in the sport anymore, so no-one would be testing him or anything. But they are tricky to get hold of – though, not if you're determined, I'm sure. Many people have uninterrupted access to them for decades. Looks like GGR was one of them. But the steroids, if they are confirmed, aren't what killed him. At least – I don't have any test results yet that suggest they did. No....*this* is what I wanted you to see, Evan," shouted Bird above the fans that droned constantly inside the, ironically, spotlessly clean 'dirty' white-tiled room, and he moved purposefully towards the cadaver on the bench.

Glover was thankful that GGR's body had been stitched closed: giant 'scarecrow' stitches marked a large 'Y' shape across the whole torso. He was struck, once again, by the amount of damage sustained by the man in his fall.

"Let's have it then," said Glover, somewhat abruptly, wanting to get out of the place as soon as possible.

"Can you see this?" asked Bird, lifting the body to show the back of the man's skull.

"I can see lots of things," answered Glover bleakly, referring to the jagged cuts that had almost raked the man's scalp entirely from his head. It was difficult to work out which injuries had been sustained in his descent, and which had been inflicted when Bird had removed the top of the skull as part of his investigations.

"Here!" said Bird, and he pointed to a depression just at the base of the pitifully battered skull.

Glover drew nearer to the pathetic figure on the slab – he didn't want to, but he had to. He fumbled under his gown to find his reading glasses and pushed them onto his nose, conceding to the reality that it wasn't that his arms were getting shorter when he held a book these days, but that he really *did* need help when it came to focussing close-up.

Better able to see the dent to which Bird was referring, Glover's next question was obvious.

"How do you know that wasn't just something that happened to him as he fell?"

"I knew you'd ask that," smiled Bird, and flicked a switch on a light-box that was suspended on the wall beside them. "Because of this!" he exclaimed triumphantly, pointing to the illuminated, yet still somewhat indistinct, film in front of them.

Again, Glover had to squint to make out the detail. But this time, even when he managed to focus, he still didn't know what he was meant to see. Damned X-rays – how was anyone supposed to make any sense of them? They just looked like the side and front, or back – he couldn't tell which - views of a skull and spine to him. He assumed they were of the once-wonderful GGR. As Bird had mentioned, the man had a *lot* of metal implanted into his teeth and jaws: it looked like most of his teeth were actually screwed in!

"OK Bert – I'm sorry – *what* am I supposed to be looking at? All those screws?" Glover was puzzled and a little frustrated. Bird, on the other hand, seemed to be quite excited.

"See this here?" he pointed to a series of lines amongst many darker ones at the base of the skull area on the screen. "That wasn't made by craggy rocks – but by a blunt instrument!" Bird sounded as delighted as he might have done if he'd just discovered the usefulness of the Rosetta Stone. "It didn't kill him, but it would have probably disorientated him, or even made him semi-conscious. Yes, it *was* the fall that killed him – massive head and neck trauma as we saw, and the spinal shock he suffered as a result killed him almost instantaneously - but this initial injury was what might have caused him to fall in the first place, or might have made it easy for someone to steer him towards, or even over, the cliff edge."

Glover took a moment. He was trying to make sense of what Bird had said. It sounded a lot like murder.

"So...let me get this straight," responded Glover, keen to understand the full implications of what Bird was telling him, "GGR was hit on the back of the head *just* before he went over the cliff? The two are definitely related?"

"Yes."

"And do we have anything other than 'blunt instrument' at this point?"

"Ah ha!" was Bert Bird's delighted response. "I knew you'd ask me that too – and I am pleased to be able to oblige. Come with me, Evan. I've spent hours on just that question – and I'm pretty much 100% sure of my information." Bert Bird directed him towards a computer screen where he pushed a couple of keys and a golf club appeared. "Massive Martha III – the largest driver there is. Only been available for about six months. And it's the only face-pattern and size that fits what we see on GGR's head. *And* I can tell you that it was a left-handed club."

"They have left-handed golf clubs?" Glover was a keen non-golfer: he hated private golf clubs and all they stood for, and that had poisoned his mind against the game itself. For some years he had felt that he lived in a world where the ability to wear vividly coloured, ill-fitting clothing, waggle a few expensive bits of metal in the air and drive a Jaguar seemed to be the only requirements, along with piles of money, to achieve some sort of dubious social standing by belonging to an exclusive, in every sense of the word, golf club. It didn't surprise him at all that it might have been a golfer who'd done for the Great One! Putting his enmity towards golfers to one side, he listened to Bert Bird's explanation.

"Yes, Evan, they have left-handed golf clubs, for left-handed players, like me. But, no, it wasn't me! By the way, I suppose I am officially confirming that, unless anyone can come up with a way for a man to bash in the bottom of his own skull with a golf club, then we're looking at a murderous assault. Whether he was pushed, or whether he fell, it would be this that was the root of it. So you can tell the Super it's official – it's a murder investigation, which I'm sure will cheer you up no end, because now you'll get all the people, and all the resources you need!"

"Well, you're not wrong, Bert. But I still wish it wasn't *him*!"

"I know, Evan.....even if he might not have been *quite* the man you thought he was, it's *still* GGR."

Glover looked thoughtful. "Tell, me, Bert, would the blow have taken great strength?"

"On balance, and considering the physics involved, not really. And the angle of the injury doesn't help us with height – the ground where I suspect GGR was struck, in other words, where the dog had been tied up in that little dell, was quite uneven: so a short person could have been standing on higher ground, or a taller person on lower ground than GGR himself – so I can't help you there, I'm afraid."

Glover realised that Bird's comments allowed for just about anyone at all to have been the assailant, but decided to continue with his confirmation of the details, "So, a tall or short, strong or weak man....or a woman...." his eyebrows arched in query and Bird nodded, "could have inflicted the blow, right?"

"Right."

"And, to broaden the field further, should I assume that they would *not* necessarily have to be a left-handed person to be able to swing a left-handed golf-club?" Glover sounded despondent.

"It's a correct *general* assumption, but I'd think, then, that we'd see the other part of the club presenting on the skull." Bird drew back from Glover and adopted a teeing-off stance. "You see, if you're right-handed, you'll automatically swing through with the right arm directing from the back," he demonstrated, and encouraged Glover to work through the motions with him. "It's your strongest arm and you'll need it to control the club through the swing, but if you're left-handed, you'd swing through with the left arm," again, both men tried the motion, "so it would be very awkward for a right-handed person to swing a left-handed club the wrong way *and* achieve sufficient force at impact to produce what we see at the base of GGR's skull. It would be a very difficult job of co-ordination."

"Good work, Bert," said Glover. "Now all I have to do is find a left-handed golfer who wanted to kill GGR!"

"A left-handed golfer who's serious enough about their game to want to spend a few hundred pounds on just one club....let alone the rest of the stuff in their bag! But don't forget, the person wielding the club at GGR's head, might not have actually owned the club, or might not even have been a golfer at all. Frankly, these drivers are designed to be pretty fool-proof, so anyone making even a first attempt at a swing could have connected in the way the evidence suggests. Sorry!" Bird seemed to be apologising for the fact that he really wasn't making Glover's life any easier.

"Well, I can always start with the golfers, and go from there – this has been a great help, Bert, really. And I'll make sure the Super knows it."

"Ah yes, the Super," replied Bird. "I suppose I should warn you that he's a bit a of golfer himself – plays off a seven handicap at his Club, I hear."

"That fits," tutted Glover, rolling his eyes. "Maybe it was the Super, out there on Monday morning taking a swing at GGR....but then, that's too much to hope for I suppose...." he smiled at Bird, who knew that he'd soon be on his way. "Anything else I should know right now?" asked Glover, obviously keen to get away.

"Not until I have those results back, Evan. I can put in the hours, as can my team, but you can't rush science, and that's that! As soon as I know anything I'll phone you....well, alright then, I'll phone the Super, *then* I'll phone you, because that's how we're playing this time – the Super's 'hands-on'!"

"You, me *and* the Super, all with our hands *all* over it! Thanks Bert, talk soon," called Glover as he left Bird's insufficiently deodorized surroundings.

Tearing off his protective paper clothing with delight, Glover checked his watch – almost 8am. He'd ring the Super, then get to the office to connect with Stanley: he'd left a list of things for Stanley to take care of that morning, and had no doubt that he'd be well on the way to completing his tasks. Now he had a few other things to add to the list.

Glover knew that Stanley was good, but suspected it would take him longer to find the answers to all Glover's questions than it would take Glover to drive from Swansea Hospital to HQ, so he took a few minutes to sit in the car park and get the facts straight in his mind. He sent a comprehensive text-message to Stanley, *then* he called the Super – who warned him that the word was out about GGR, and that he'd better watch it when he arrived at the station.....the newshounds were already sniffing around!

As Glover finally eased out to join the rush hour traffic, he was glad it was moving slowly enough to give him time to think: that day the whole of Wales would begin to mourn its hero. GGR, gone; The Great One, dead. A national tragedy. How had he died? That would be the first thing on everyone's lips, of course. Murder? It was a scandal! A national scandal!! Who did it? And, without an immediate answer to *that* question, the next thing would doubtless be the comment that the police didn't know what they were doing! The importance of the task at hand began to weigh even more heavily on Glover.

He knew it wouldn't be easy: even with the extra manpower that a murder investigation allowed for, he and Stanley were going to feel the strain. Suddenly, Glover remembered that he'd be losing Stanley in a few days. He cursed aloud. Here he was, working on a case that might well splatter his name all over the local papers (which he always hated), a case that involved a man he'd idolised for as long as he could remember, a national hero no less - and he'd be stuck without Stanley! Wonderful! He didn't like the idea of telling Stanley he couldn't go off to Scoutmasters' camp, but he didn't *want* to work with anyone else! Of course, he could always talk things through with Betty: that always seemed to help. Indeed, often it helped a lot! But, however much she might be able to help him understand aspects of the case in a different way, however much insight she might be able to bring about the people he encountered and their actions and reactions, not even *she* could replace Stanley!

# V

Having managed to sneak around the back of police HQ, to avoid the mass of media vehicles that were beginning to clog the High Street, Glover clattered up the old stone staircase towards his office, and stuck his head into Stanley's pokey little shared room as he passed.

"Stanley!" he called, without looking inside.

"Sir!" came Stanley's reply from inside Glover's own office, further along the corridor.

When Glover entered what he often referred to as his 'cell', it was clear why Stanley was there – he was 'entertaining' Detective Superintendant Michael Williams, who wasn't exactly smiling.

"What the *Hell* are we going to tell them all, Glover? The Chief's all over me!" were the first words out of the Super's mouth. Glover stopped in his tracks. It was clear from Stanley's face that panic was beginning to get the better of him – the Super could be a bit of a bear when he wanted. But he was right, thought Glover, what *were* they going to tell the media? How much – or how little?

Of course, Glover reflected, there was always the safe fall back of 'ongoing investigations', but he felt that, without the guiding hand of DCI David Richards, the media coverage of the case might all spin horribly out of control. Dave was good at handling the media, and everyone knew it. He was charismatic, had a good face for TV and always seemed to say just the right thing – without it sounding trite. That's why the Super had always let Dave run with it, even though it really should have been *him* taking centre stage. All this had resulted in the Super never really getting the hang of it all: on the rare occasions when he'd *had* to face the media, he'd clearly felt uncomfortable in the hot lights, with cameras flashing all around him and embattled by questions. 'Region' had sent him off for 'media training', but it didn't seem to have taken – sweating to the point that the camera can see it running down your neck is not a good way to try to appear cool and confident to the public eye! Glover's stomach started to tighten – what if the Super made *him* do it! Glover hated the media: it didn't matter what you said, or how helpful you were trying to be, there was always one smarmy type who'd twist everything to make a good headline, or quote you out of context, and you'd end up looking like the stupidest Plod ever! He decided that the best way to protect himself from being flayed alive, and to allow him to get on with his investigation, was to come up with a plan of action that the Super could live with – and one that didn't involve Glover!

"Well, Sir," Glover began cautiously, thinking on his feet.....Stanley wondered what sort of a performance he was about to witness... "....our Detective Chief Superintendant from Region is very good with the media, Sir. And this *is* a very high profile case, Sir. National importance, not just local or regional. Maybe you could work with him, Sir? But, you see, we really *can't* say much right now – so how about you work with the Public Relations people at Regional HQ and get a statement prepared for the Chief Super to deliver - confirming identity, expressing regret, promising investigation of all possibilities and so forth – and you could offer to face them with him? He could just read the statement, put out an appeal for anyone who saw GGR out at Three Cliffs yesterday morning, and apologise for not being able to take questions because of the ongoing investigation. It would keep it short and sweet Sir, and they're a bit less frantic if you throw them a bit of something every so often, aren't they? Even announcing you're going to tell them something at a certain time seems to shut them up for a while........"

The Super seemed somewhat mollified at the thought of dragging *his* superior into the melee, rather than having to face it alone, and he wandered out of Glover's office muttering something about getting the top brass at Region involved with doing some *actual* work, so Glover assumed he was in the clear to get on with his job...at least for a little while. He was relieved. Time was pressing, and he didn't want anyone to think he was dawdling! He had a team to get together, brief and get working!

But first, Stanley. Bring him up to date with Bird's findings, then pump him for information as they set out to.......well, Glover wasn't sure quite *where* they'd be going, yet, but he knew he had to get out of the office as quick as he could – that way, the Super wouldn't be able to collar him and stand *him* up in front of the hyenas! Glover shut his office door, and rapidly gave Stanley the facts.

Stanley, it seemed, was much better versed in golfing than Glover might have expected. "We have golfing weekends with the Scouts, Sir," was Stanley's explanation for understanding all about golf clubs. Glover was beginning to wonder what other aspects of Stanley's Scouting involvement might come in useful. He had no idea that Scouts even *played* golf!

"So, it's going to be a murder investigation, then, is it, Sir? I'll get the team together next then, alright?" were Stanley's follow-up observations. Glover noted that he was finally beginning to adopt the Welsh habit of asking non-questions. Glover smiled. He liked this man! He didn't want to stop him from going on his well-deserved holiday. Maybe they'd be able to come up with a quick solution to this case, after all. He hoped so.

Stanley continued. "And, if we're looking for a certain sort of golf club, Sir, that inflicted his original injury, then I'm sure it's going to interest you to know that GGR Davies spent the whole of Sunday at a golf and rugby tournament. Sir."

Glover's face fell. Then he rubbed it hard, with both hands. A golf tournament. Dozens of golfers. Hundreds of golf clubs. Marvellous! So much for the possibility of a quick solution! Glover began to see his own holiday plans being put on hold, let alone Stanley's!

Stanley continued. "He was at the Brynfield Golf and Rugby Club, Sir. Annual tournament it seems. They play golf against each other in the morning, and then have a sevens rugby match in the afternoon. GGR was there to present the awards at the end of the day – guest of honour, Sir."

"So," said Glover, starting to burrow his fingers through his hair in what Stanley knew to be a habit that displayed distressed concentration, "maybe something happened that set someone off.....and they took it out on GGR the next morning on Three Cliffs?" It didn't even sound probable to Glover, let alone to Stanley.

"Could be, Sir," was Stanley's guarded reply: he knew that Glover liked to work this way....throwing out what might seem like bizarre scenarios, hoping something would fall into place, or set off a thread of an enquiry.

"Do we know anything about how GGR was involved in the event?" Glover asked.

"Yes, Sir. In fact – you can talk to Jerry about it – you know, Sir, DS Hill? We share an office. He was there Sir, and I've asked him to hang about 'till I knew if you wanted to talk to him."

Glover's face brightened a little. "Good man – let's have him in right away!" As Stanley left his boss to fetch his office-mate, Glover leaned back in his chair, and popped a peppermint into his mouth. He was crunching into it with vigour when Stanley reappeared.

"DS Hill, Sir," announced Stanley as a tall, thin, dark-haired young man, with a pallid complexion and deep-set brown eyes, walked apprehensively into Glover's office. Glover had spotted him about the place, of course, and had seen him in action when they pulled large teams together....but he'd never formed much of a real opinion about the chap. Not as a person. Not as a policemen. Now was the time.

"So, Hill, Stanley tells me you were at the Brynfield Club on Sunday when GGR was there?"

"Yes, Sir. I was, Sir." Polite, at least.

"And what can you tell me about the man, and the day, that might help with our investigations?"

DS Hill looked puzzled. "Well, nothing, Sir, I don't think, Sir." He half looked around at Stanley, awkwardly squirming in his chair. "I mean, if GGR died at Three Cliffs yesterday, I don't see how......"

Clearly the internal gossip mill hadn't got hold of the key facts yet. Glover was relieved: he was anxious that the details about GGR's manner of death didn't leak out, yet!

"Don't worry about *how* it might help me, man....just tell me!" shouted Glover. Hill jumped. Glover was beginning to wonder if the man was sound – he certainly didn't seem to have much backbone!

"Well – it's an annual match, Sir. I belong to the Brynfield Golf Club, and we share a Clubhouse with the Brynfield Rugby Club, as I'm sure you know, Sir. Every year we have a tournament – club against club, one set of twelve men per club, playing both golf and then rugby against each other. Usually the Golf Club wins the golf, and vice versa, but the big deal is to try to get the double – that's when you win the Howells' Cup, Sir."

"And GGR?"

"He was giving the after dinner speech and the prizes this year, Sir. Did a very good job of both, too – very entertaining."

Glover wondered if Hill was this poor at answering questions when his own DI asked them!

"So, tell me, Hill, did GGR arrive before dinner – after dinner, what? Tell me *everything* about GGR and the tournament." Glover knew he sounded terse. Maybe *that* would work!

Hill looked cowed. His tone suggested he was sulking. "Well, I was out following the golfers all morning, you know, supporting the team and all that, then we came in for lunch, and I saw GGR at the bar just as we were off to the rugger, Sir. Then he was with us for pre-dinner drinks at about six, sat at the top table for the dinner itself, made a speech and gave all the prizes, including the Howells Cup which *we* won, Sir, first time ever!" Hill seemed pleased with himself. Stanley could tell that Glover wasn't at all impressed and thought he'd better throw a life-line to his office-mate.

"What were you telling me about GGR at the end of lunch, Jerry – you know....." he nodded encouragingly.

"Oh yes, that," said Hill vaguely, "It's just that I saw GGR arguing with one of the rugby lot just as we were all off after lunch. It didn't seem like much – just a couple of raised voices and some finger wagging in my opinion." Glover didn't feel inclined to value this man's opinion very highly.

"Any bad blood between the teams? Anything on or off the field of competition?" asked Glover sharply.

"Well, you know Sir, boys will be boys..........but it's mainly good-humoured rivalry. Usually. But on Sunday night, well, there was the usual banter between tables over dinner, as I'm sure you can imagine, Sir, and GGR did his speech, which was very entertaining as I said.....something about knocking over a sheep on a country lane and shouting 'mint-sauce' as he drove off," Hill half smiled as he remembered the tale, looked up, saw Glover's stern look and hurriedly added, "well, it was funny at the time, Sir, and then, after all that, and the presentations and so forth, someone mentioned cockles and whores and it all seemed to go off for no reason!"

"Cockles? Whores?" Glover queried. "What do you mean, 'Go off?' Explain yourself, man!" he was quickly losing patience with this young officer.

"Yes, Sir, cockles, Sir, and, I think, whores, Sir. I have *no* idea what happened next, honestly I don't Sir, but within seconds it seemed like there were bodies all over the place!"

"Anyone hurt?" asked Glover.

"Not so you'd notice, Sir," was Hill's response.

"What about GGR?" Glover shot back. "Was he involved at all?" Hill looked thoughtful.

"Well, he did go down at one point – he was over by the bar, I recall, and just, well, disappeared. He, literally, went down. Then I saw someone picking him up and sort of dusting him off. But it was difficult to tell exactly what was going on where. I mean, it could only have lasted about two minutes, Sir, and then it was all over and done with."

"So I'm assuming it was you who stepped in to restore the peace?" asked Glover pointedly.

"Well...." DS Hill scratched his forehead in place of an answer.

"You're a policeman, Hill – you're *bound* to uphold the law and maintain the peace. So what did you *do*?" Glover was now standing up and leaning over his desk towards the young man. Hill looked apprehensive. When he finally replied, he did so in a voice that suggested he wasn't sure what to say.

"Like I said, Sir, it seemed to me that initially it was all pretty much par for the course, as far as the chatter and name calling was concerned, then one of our lot mentioned cockles, and before I really knew what was happening, one of the front row players from the rugby club, huge bloke, Sir, and I mean *really* huge, was sort of over the table and at someone else's throat! There was pushing and shoving, and chairs being punted around the place, and even a couple of tables went over, so there was glass and beer everywhere, then some of the older ones started pulling people apart, and it all seemed to stop. I mean, within *just* two minutes, it had started from nothing, blown up *and* calmed down and they were all shaking hands and buying each other pints. I didn't really have *time* to get involved, Sir."

"And all because someone mentioned cockles and whores, eh?"

"Well, it *seemed* so Sir, or could it have been 'cockle wars'?"

Ah, *that* made more sense......the Cockle Wars......that took Glover back! Back to the 1980's, just after GGR had retired, he recalled. Back before the donkeys and carts that were used by the women who back-breakingly hand-gathered the tiny little shellfish that were a local delicacy from the sands of the Burry Estuary were replaced by men driving Land Rovers. There'd been a few bad years back then: cockle harvests were down, and the families with the licences to gather them began in-fighting....which was a pretty complicated business, given that most of them had intermarried. One family member was set against another, sometimes splitting marriages, sometimes pitting children against their parents: there'd been a spate of nasty pub fights in the Penclawdd area right throughout one summer, Glover remembered, and the problems had simmered on for years. But he'd thought it had all finally been settled in the mid-'90's, when a co-operative had been formed between all the licence-holders, and they'd invested in a jointly-owned modern processing facility for the lucrative, and by now, internationally famous cockle-crop.

If the Cockle Wars were still causing fist fights, might they have had something to do with GGR's death? Glover had some vague recollection that GGR's wife had at one time sold cockles on her stall at Swansea Market. Could she be connected to the Penclawdd cockle business somehow? You only got to sell what you gathered, he knew that much. He'd get Stanley to check, but it might be nothing.

He looked at the young man in front of him: no comparison between him and Stanley, he thought. He'd trade five Hill's for one Stanley any day!

"Right-o – get out of here and get this all down on paper, Hill," he barked, annoyed at the man's lack of insight and action, "and fill in *every* detail – names, times, actions, who said what, who did what, and so on. *Everything* you can remember! And get it onto Stanley's desk before you even think about leaving the station!"

"I won't be much good with names, Sir," replied Hill sheepishly. "I don't know a lot of the people who were there...." he seemed to be terrified. Then he brightened, "But I know who would! Stan Waters, our Club General Manager....he'd have lists of names and everything. I've got his phone number in my office, Sir."

Glover looked up at Stanley. Stanley nodded. "I have Mister Waters' number here, Sir," he replied efficiently – even *he* was getting fed up with Hill. "Shall I bring the car around, Sir?" he asked, almost reading Glover's mind.

"Give me five and I'll be at the front door," replied Glover to Stanley, then he looked disdainfully at Hill and barked, "And what are *you* waiting for?" It was finally clear to Hill that he was dismissed, so he slunk out of Glover's office and back to his own little cubby-hole, to start typing up his statement.

Glover grabbed his peppermints, jacket and keys and walked with Stanley towards the stairs, "I just want to say hello to the team, though I expect they'll still be getting themselves sorted out, then I'll be with you. Call the club and tell the GM that we're on our way – I need to see him, with names etc – you know the drill. I want to see that bar where GGR 'disappeared from sight'!" he instructed Stanley. Soon he'd escape from HQ, and any chance of being accosted by the media, and be on the road to the Brynfield Golf and Rugby Club, which Glover expected to be populated by annoying little men with huge egos, wearing plaid trousers and unbecoming sweater-vests. In this, at least, he wasn't disappointed.

# VI

As they made their way through the City centre's early morning traffic, Glover asked Stanley to bring him up to date with his investigations. Stanley obliged as he drove steadily towards their destination.

Mrs Gwladys Davies, the victim's wife, had spent a fitful night, according to the WPC who had stayed with her. Having been attended to by her doctor in the early hours of the morning, she was now quite heavily sedated. It was unlikely that she would be fit for more questions before noon, the doctor had estimated. Upon Stanley's second set of enquiries, the WPC had confirmed the presence of a set of golf clubs at the Davies house. She had told Stanley that it was pretty clear that GGR had been a keen amateur player, and that it appeared that he belonged to several golf clubs in the Gower, Swansea and Swansea Vale areas – something she had deduced from a pile of membership cards and parking passes she had found piled on GGR's desk. Stanley passed this information on to Glover.

"I expect that simply being GGR was enough to get him into most places, without the membership cards," was Glover's observation, but he noted the WPC's endeavours in any case.

The enterprising WPC had also discovered, upon being encouraged to 'check' rather than 'search' the house by Stanley, that, other than the usual array of home medicines, GGR had no phials of any sort, anywhere. She had spotted that there was a small, padlocked fridge in the cellar, however. She thought this strange. So did Glover. He wanted that fridge opened – if GGR had any steroids in his house they'd need to be kept cool at least – a locked refrigerator sounded ideal. He asked Stanley to arrange for the appropriate paperwork. Stanley replied that it was already in hand, and that DC Hughes was following that through at the office.

Stanley told Glover that, so far, he hadn't been able to discover that GGR had any enemies and he seemed to have no financial problems – though he was a lot less well-off than Stanley had expected. In fact, even Glover was shocked at the figures that Stanley quoted as they sat in the stop-start traffic jam that was the Mumbles Road, especially when he considered how well-rewarded the young international rugby players were in an age of endorsements and sponsorships. GGR would, no doubt, have been a multi-millionaire if he'd been playing in the twenty-first century, thought Glover – but, as it was, most of the family's income seemed to come from the small-holding. Stanley and Glover agreed that GGR probably had quite a good source of undeclared income – the Brynfield tournament being one example: Stanley had managed to discover from DS Hill that GGR had been paid five hundred pounds by the club to be their 'guest of honour', a fee that was the norm for one of his appearances, it seemed. It was clear to both men that if GGR could manage just one such payment a week, he would have a nice little income that they suspected the taxman probably wouldn't know about – most of the organisations that would hire him probably being happy to cover his payment under some sort of 'miscellaneous' heading in their event costs.

Even so, GGR and his wife weren't living the high life: he'd stayed on at his job with the Fire Dragon Brewery until his 65th birthday, and they'd leveraged his role as their 'super-salesman' as far as they could. He earned a fair salary for what didn't sound like an onerous job. Indeed, Stanley had got the impression from GGR's boss at the brewery that he hadn't been so much a 'salesman' proper, but, rather, more of a 'relationship builder' – popping in to visit valued customers on a regular basis, likely as not hanging around for a couple of pints of Fire Dragon Dark, his favourite tipple, so the that the pub, restaurant or club in question could boast to its clientele that GGR was a 'regular'.

For Glover, this, worryingly, fitted with GGR's wife's assertion that her husband was known to drink and drive. On that topic Stanley was full of information: GGR had no police record – not for drinking and driving, not even a parking ticket. But Stanley had gone further: he'd carried out his own informal investigation across several local police stations throughout the Gower, Swansea City itself and up into the Swansea Valley, and had discovered that GGR was pretty well known to a lot of the local uniforms. Stanley recounted how GGR had spent quite a few afternoons, evenings and even nights at several stations, having been stopped for erratic driving. 'What were they to *do*?' Was the usual comment or question from the policemen that Stanley had spoken to....it *was* GGR, after all! They weren't going to do *him* for drinking and driving.....either they couldn't bring themselves to do it, or else they'd never have been forgiven for it by their brother, father, uncle, or even mother! He was usually pretty much in control, apparently, and none of them had even bothered to breathalyse him. His wife tended to collect him after a few hours, and, when he came back to the area the next day to collect his car....he'd sign autographs and pose for photographs and so forth.

Glover saw a pattern emerging....but didn't want to believe it. It looked like GGR's job led him to drink, and that the Regional police force couldn't overcome its admiration of the man to the point where they'd take him off the roads for good. Glover wondered what *he'd* have done if he'd seen his idol endangering others by driving what was, after all, a lethal weapon, when he'd been drinking: Glover hoped he'd have done the right thing. But had to admit he wasn't sure....maybe even *he* would have given the Great One just one more chance.......and what then....another? And another?

Stanley called Glover from his unhappy thoughts as he announced, "Almost there, Sir," and added, "any particular way you want to play this, Sir?"

Glover replied sullenly, "Follow my lead, as per, Stanley," and stepped from the car almost before it had stopped moving.

It was a beautiful morning: the sun was shining, the air was clear, the birds were busy and the clouds were bubbling on the horizon as Glover looked out across the sparkling sea. The Brynfield Golf and Rugby Club was one of the most prestigious in Swansea, and made no bones about being one of the most picturesque in all of South Wales: it sat atop a hill that ran right down to the seashore.  The rugby pitch was on level ground at the club's highest elevation and was surrounded on three sides by small stands, the fourth side being open to the sea. The golf course was largely 'below' the rugby field - an undulating little nine holes links course, generally acknowledged to be amongst the most beautiful and challenging in Wales – the wind and the weather coming in from from the sea meaning that conditions could change from minute to minute, let alone from day to day.  Below the golf course was the stunning Brynfield Beach itself, from which the club took its name. The Promenade was almost an anachronism in the new century, sporting, as it did, a row of dozens of identical little Victorian beach-huts, each with its own little glazed front door and an appealingly raked and ginger-breaded roof, and each being the rental property of a very lucky and much envied family, in perpetuity.  Whenever someone new moved to the area they did their damndest to get their hands on one of the huts, but were always beaten back by the archaic rental agreements with the local authority, and the ever-lengthening waiting list. There were local jokes aplenty about who you'd have to kill, or sleep with, to get your hands on a Brynfield Beach Hut.  To Glover's knowledge, no-one had tried the murder route at least!

    Turning his attention from the sea and the shore Glover was struck by two features of the clubhouse complex itself: the three smugly-gleaming Jaguar's that were parked in the car park – which was pretty much par for the course, quite literally; and the ugliness of the modern redbrick-built extension that had been stuck onto what had once been a pleasantly proportioned, and delightfully symmetrical, Edwardian yellow brick clubhouse building.  Glover wondered how on earth  the club had managed to get planning permission for the eyesore, then told himself that probably a couple of club members were on the local authority planning committee, and that maybe they'd been able to influence their peers...or something along those lines.  Glover wasn't a politician – he had no stomach for it.  However they'd come to be there, the aggressively red bricks of the extension, which was twice the size of the original building and which formed the middle and bottom sections of what was now a square 'C', the top section being the delightful centuagenarian structure that looked out towards the sea, were not being mellowed by the morning sun, indeed, they seemed to glow all the more incongruously for it, and Glover began to steel himself for what lay ahead.  Bloody golf clubs!

    Glover was not only a man who had little time for politicians, he was also a man who cared not at all for institutions he judged to be rife with either politics or social climbing.  Golf clubs came squarely under both headings in his mind.  True, he'd belonged to a few rugby clubs in his time, but only when he was actually playing: he hadn't hung onto them as the centre of his social life once his knees had given out and his playing days were over – he saw them as organisationally necessary to allow a team game to take place, and often a good facility for team members, and their friends, to socialise outside the boundaries of the games themselves.  But as for the 'golf club' and the 'rugby club' network

– the committees, the titles, the vice-this and the immediately-past-that - he couldn't bear it! Glover told himself to put his negative expectations to one side as he strode towards the main entrance to the clubhouse, but, for all his good intentions, it only took a matter of moments before he was quite happily considering throttling a very annoying, short, balding man, who accosted him while he was still outside the building and demanded to see his membership card.

Glover held up his Warrant Card instead, smiling inwardly, and introduced himself and Stanley very formally. Within moments the pompous little man was directing Glover to his Club Captain, and the General Manager, both of whom were sitting in the restaurant, nursing coffee mugs and looking at a large selection of photographs that were spread on the table before them.

"Good morning, gentlemen!" Glover spoke loudly and pushed ahead of the scampering man showing his credentials once again. "I am Detective Inspector Glover and this is Detective Sergeant Stanley. Following our enquiries surrounding the death of GGR Davies, we have discovered that he spent the majority of Sunday here, at the Brynfield Club. We have some routine questions we'd like to ask. I take it all three of you gentlemen were here for the tournament?"

Although clearly taken aback by Glover's appearance, it was the Golf Club Captain who pulled himself together first, and spoke with an over-jovial tone, that matched his over-jovial attire. Personally, Glover couldn't imagine how a man in his fifties, and measuring somewhere in the fifty-inch range around his middle, could possibly think that a canary yellow V necked sweater would be becoming under *any* circumstances, except if the clothing was designed to serve as a safety garment, allowing the wearer to be spotted at a great distance, presumably when in peril. Glover was saddened that people so often managed to live down to his expectations.

"Ah, Detective Inspector – yes, what a *tragedy*!" the Club Captain cooed unctuously, "The Great One, indeed, graced us with his presence on Sunday – I believe I am correct in saying that it was his last public appearance. Indeed, the local TV people have already been in touch with me about any photographs we might be able to make available from our tournament......something that our wonderful General Manager is helping me to discern at this very moment."

Glover controlled the gag reaction that was pricking at the back of his throat. 'More likely *you* couldn't get onto the phone quick enough when you heard the news!' was running through his mind, as he eyed up all three of the men now clustered around the circular table.

"And you are?" was what he actually said aloud to the obsequious man in yellow. It was the only way he could get away with appearing to be polite to a member of the public, yet still showing his total lack of acceptance of the golf club pecking order.

"Oh, this is our Club Captain, Mister Mark Edwards," piped up the annoying little man who had 'greeted' Glover at the front entrance, as though the man in yellow couldn't possibly be expected to account for himself – it would clearly be too much trouble.

"And you?" barked Glover at the little man.

"Why I'm the Assistant Club Captain, Frank Cuthbert." He seemed taken aback that Glover wouldn't know. "And this," he continued, clearly intending to do a complete job, "is our General Manager, Mister Stan Waters."

Stanley wrote down the names whilst Glover labelled the men in his mind – he couldn't help himself! The Canary Captain, the Argyle Assistant, and finally, the man who was presumably the only one actually employed by the club and about whom there was one very obvious feature - the network of mottled veins that stood out on his enlarged nose, marking him as a heavy drinker of some years' standing....his name might be 'Waters', but Glover suspected he only drank the stuff when it was mixed with something much stronger!

Having thus mentally labelled the group, Glover set about pumping them for all the information they could give him about GGR's movements on the Sunday.

With the Canary Captain leading, supported by the Argyle Assistant, and with Very Little Water nodding in silent agreement, Glover pieced together what GGR had done for most of the day: he'd arrived at about 10am, had eaten a hearty cooked breakfast in the restaurant, then had played a 'courtesy round' behind the tournament competitors: he'd paired with the Captain of the Rugby Team, and the Canary Captain had been joined by the Club's resident medic, Dr Bill Williams. They'd been last in off the course for lunch, by which time some people were beginning to drift out to get good seats for the rugby. GGR had partaken of a bar lunch, which seemed to have miffed the Canary Captain, then had a few drinks whilst chatting to various members, and had, presumably, finally taken himself off to watch the game, though none of the three men present had actually seen him there. No-one could recall seeing GGR until the pre-dinner drinks at 6pm. After mingling over drinks, GGR had provided entertaining company at the top table, at which, Glover noted with a wry smile, the Canary Captain had sat, but it was something to which the Argyle Assistant could only aspire! GGR had made a very well-received after-dinner speech, presented the awards and, finally, the much prized Howells' Cup, and had enjoyed a few more drinks before being taken home in a taxi at about midnight. It seemed that GGR had been entertained, entertaining and the life and soul of the party. The word 'tragedy' was repeated until it almost lost all meaning for Glover, and he was glad when the Canary Captain finally shut up.

No mention was made of the post-prandial pugilism. Glover wasn't surprised. In fact he rather looked forward to winkling the information out of the men.

"So, you had a pretty unremarkable tournament, gentlemen?" was Glover's sardonic question, at which all three heads nodded rapidly – and a little too violently.

"Everything pretty much as you'd expected?" Again there was nodding. Glover pounced. "So, just a bit of polite banter over the rubber chicken, and no fisticuffs at all, eh?"

All three men seemed suddenly very interested in their shoes, and Glover knew he had them. He suspected that the Argyle Assistant would cave first: he did, and gushingly at that.

"Oh Detective Inspector it was dreadful – honestly, we had no idea it would end up the way it did.......we've had a few harsh words over the years and even a bit of pushing and shoving....but this year – oh my word, it was quite frightening!" Glover added "old woman" to his mental note about the Assistant Captain.

"So there *was* a fight?' asked Glover, almost innocently.

The Canary Captain glared at his Argyle Assistant, but he recovered quickly, and tried to take control of the interview, employing his most slithering tones.

"You have to understand, Inspector, that *our* members abide by the normal rules of public, and of course golfing, etiquette when they are on the premises: unfortunately, some of the Rugby Club members are clearly used to a different set of guiding principles – and things rather got out of hand. Luckily, some of our more responsible members were able to restore peace." The man had no idea that blaming the fight on the rugby club was likely to rub Glover up the wrong way.

Glover waged a brief internal war with himself – and the publicly acceptable persona won. Stanley was not insensitive to Glover's inner turmoil, and was ready to step in should Glover have to leave the room to check on other areas of the club buildings. Glover sensed this, and decided to take advantage.

"I'm sure it was all *very* unexpected, gentlemen, and I also understand, from the member of our Force who was present, that the matter was quickly contained. Now, while I ask my Sergeant here to take a look through those photographs you were studying, and make sure he gets a complete record of all those who were here on Sunday, I'm going to take a look around, if you don't mind." It wasn't a question, and everyone in the room knew it.

"I could show you around, if you like," offered the, until then silent, Very Little Water. Glover thought he seemed keen to leave the others, and wondered if the man had something he wanted to tell him that he couldn't speak about in the presence of two of the men who probably signed his pay cheques - *and* made him jump through hoops for them.

"Thanks," replied Glover, "that would be most kind of you." But, before they could leave, they were joined by a small man with thinning fair hair and a worried expression. He walked towards the group, still beside the photograph strewn table, with quick steps. He smiled, but his mouth twitched nervously.

"Ah, some new members for us?" was the man's initial question. Glover felt himself cringe.

Waters looked at Glover and smiled, then returned his steady gaze to the worried looking man. "Members? Good Lord, no, Bill, this is Detective Inspector Glover, and this is his Sergeant – Stanley....same name as me!" The man looked pleased – DS Stanley less so. "They're looking into GGR's whereabouts on Sunday. This is Doctor Bill Williams, Inspector, our resident sports injury specialist. Both he and I live here, at the club, don't we Bill? We really are 'residents' in the true sense of the word."

"Ah, yes.......terrible news, terrible news. Heard it on the radio this morning," said the little man in a quiet voice. "Such a strapping chap! And such a hero! A terrible tragedy."

Glover got the impression he was simply saying what everyone would expect him to say: there didn't appear to be any real emotion in the man's voice at all.

"I understand from Mister Waters here that you played golf with GGR on Sunday, Doctor Williams. Is that correct?" Glover always thought it best to check 'facts': they often turned out to be nothing of the kind.

"Please call me Bill, everyone does," responded the nervous man in his quiet voice. "GGR arrived early – we weren't expecting him until about eleven, but he was here by ten, so we chatted over breakfast, you know the sort of thing. I hadn't actually met the man before, so it was a great opportunity for me. Luckily I wasn't called upon to really examine anyone on Sunday, so I was able to agree to make up a four with the Great One himself, and I was honoured to play with him."

Glover found the Doctor's manner odd: the words were all alright, but his manner of delivery was stilted. He couldn't help thinking of a poorly acted amateur dramatic production.

As Glover strained to catch every word, the doctor continued, "They can always reach me from the clubhouse on my mobile phone if there's a problem, but there wasn't, so we enjoyed a good – what, two, or two and a half hours, I'd say – just strolling and chatting and hitting the odd ball. Him and me, and the two Captains, of course. It was lovely weather: clear, a little light breeze off the sea, but nothing too chilly. The course is almost like a nature trail – so much to see as you play."

Put like that, golf sounded almost civilised, thought Glover. "What sort of things did you and GGR talk about?" asked Glover, hoping for something.....anything......

"Well, as I said, we walked, and talked. We talked about this and that. Nothing I can remember, to be honest."

The Canary Captain butted in. "I overheard you two talking about people you had in common in Clydach, didn't I?" he asked Williams.

"Maybe – yes, I think you're right," responded the doctor. "And I recall now that we talked about beer too: I used to live not far away from the Fire Dragon Brewery in Clydach, you see. We discussed the smell of yeast and malt on the morning air, and how it can affect your entire digestive system! Of course, GGR was the most famous man at the brewery and he often attended local functions, so we both knew some of the same people."

"And did you spend time with GGR after you'd finished the golf?"

"Let me think........." was Bill Williams' response, and he did, while everyone waited. After about thirty seconds of silence he added, "I saw him around and about through the lunch period, but then I was back in my clinic by 2pm – I didn't see the rugby myself, and I wasn't involved in the drinks or dinner at all: being an employee of the club I was merely required to come out after dinner so that I could be thanked by the Club Captains. I hung around at the back of the restaurant until they called my name, I got a round of applause and then I went back to my office. I'm not one much for speeches myself. I saw GGR at the head table at that time, but that was it."

"Well, thank you Doctor Williams, just one more thing – were you here all day Monday?" asked Glover.

"I was working from 2pm until 9pm, when I went for an early night, but before that it was my morning off: I ran into town for a few bits and pieces, and was back here by eleven and played a few holes before I had lunch and took my first appointment," replied Williams almost cheerily, adding, "it was a lovely day for it."

"As you say," said Glover, pretty sure he had got all he was likely to out of the man. "Now - Mister Waters was just about to show me around, so, if you'll excuse me, I'll let Stanley here just take a note of times and places and I'll be back shortly." Glover was still hoping that Waters was wanting to have a private word with him, so he allowed the man to lead him towards the new extension of the building, away from the little group and the golfers who seemed to be wandering about all over the place.

Once they were out of earshot of anyone else, Glover decided to take his chance.

"Am I right in thinking that there's something you'd like to tell me, privately, Mister Waters?" Glover thought it best to be direct – it usually was.

Waters looked around and said quietly, "It's Stan, and yes, I do. Let's go outside – I'll feel more comfortable in the open air," so the men pushed open the wide swinging doors and stepped out into the bright and surprisingly warm sunshine. They walked away from the clubhouse and Waters led Glover to what looked like a path leading down towards the beach below them.

Waters was obviously considering how to say what he wanted to say. He looked around before he spoke, and dropped his voice.

"Look, Inspector, I admired GGR a great deal: and I want you to remember that when I tell you what I have to tell you. I also don't like to speak ill of the dead, but I have grappled with all this since Sunday. You see, my whole life I've been involved in rugby: I've watched it, I've played it, I've loved it - I was even the Steward at two rugby clubs before I took this job here. And GGR was *the* greatest, bar none....but the truth is, well I saw some things I didn't like at all on Sunday. And I think you should know about them. But – well, frankly I don't want you to think badly of me Inspector. I'm not a nosey man, and I don't want you to think that I was.....well, snooping........but it's just that I sometimes see things other people don't. These functions, they all have a drink or two – and I don't touch the stuff. I had a few problems a few years back and, well, I just don't drink at all now."

That explained the nose, thought Glover. "I won't think badly of you, Stan – just tell me – you'll be glad you did," Glover was used to this – someone seeing something they shouldn't have seen, or wishing they hadn't seen, and then not wanting to reveal it because of what it might also reveal about their character: he was just glad that this man was coming forward so quickly – often people held information back for hours, days or even longer, and *that* could really hinder a case.

"Well, GGR was a pretty miserable drunk, Inspector, and I think he was getting worse. He doesn't come here often – maybe once a month or so, and, of course, he's always been the Fire Dragon rep for the club, so he's usually here on 'business'. But how downing five pints then insisting upon driving away from here can be called 'business' I don't know. I don't like that sort of thing, and if he'd been a member I'd have taken his keys off him and put him into a taxi – but he was GGR, so they wouldn't let me say a dicky bird to him."

It was a pattern that was beginning to annoy Glover.

"Anyway, recently, his temper seemed to get shorter with each pint he drank. On Sunday night, long before I knew he was dead, I'd been thinking about how many pints he'd tucked away through the day. I reckon he must have had about fifteen – and that's just what I *saw* him have."

Glover nodded sadly. "Well I'm glad then that he went home in a taxi that night, at least," was his sighing response.

"Yes, well, even then I had to dress it up like it was a treat for him because he was the guest of honour – it was the only way he'd let me get away with it. But that's not the main problem.............."

Waters hesitated and looked around again. He continued in a low voice. "Look, I'd noticed how much GGR was drinking, and I'd also noticed that he got fired up pretty quickly when the argy-bargy went off....he was in there swinging as quick as he could be, and someone decked him pretty quick too – and though I don't *know* who did it, or why, I do have my suspicions. You see......oh dear, it's all a terrible mess.......I knew we were going to be busy on Sunday so I had the daughter of one of the golfers come in to give us a hand with the serving. She's only sixteen – she wasn't serving drinks, just the food – and she's a sweet girl. But she'd come screaming in to me at about 4pm in tears, saying that GGR had touched her!" Waters noted Glover's expression and added, "Exactly – I couldn't believe it, but she said she'd gone to one of our locker rooms with him so he could sign a rugby club shirt for her Gran, and he'd put his arms around her and tried to kiss her. Very upset she was. So I told her to go home. Now, *I* think it was her father who hit GGR – though I have to admit I couldn't see who did it.....but I know that Dave – that's the girl's father – was standing by GGR over at the bar when the fight broke out, and they'd been having words."

Glover took the information on board - a drunk, and a lecherous one at that. He didn't like this picture of GGR – not one bit. It also opened up another avenue of enquiry for Glover – the girl's father might have been angry enough to have another go at GGR – maybe on a clifftop – with a golf club.

"That's something we should follow up on, Stan – I'll need the father's name, and their address if you have it, please?" asked Glover. Waters nodded.

"Anything else?" he added.

"Well, yes, there was......." Waters hesitated: Glover wondered how much worse it could get. "Well, you know I said he was drinking a lot?" Glover nodded. "Well, he was also going to the toilet a lot." Waters half-smiled. "Now I realise that the two are usually inextricably linked, but what struck me as odd was how long he was gone every time. I began to wonder if there was something wrong with the man.......so I thought I'd better check up and see....so I followed him in........" Stan Waters was struggling with his embarrassment, but managed to continue. It seemed the die was cast. "When I got in there, well he wasn't at a urinal, he'd gone into a stall, which is, you know, I mean, fine.....but one of the rugby lads was in the stall next to him, and I saw GGR pass him something under the stall partition."

Glover could imagine the scene – Waters following GGR into the toilets, not seeing him at a urinal, and bending down to check if he was in a stall and, if so, which one. But Glover thought it unlikely that Waters would admit as much.

"Did you happen to be able to see what it was that was being passed?" asked Glover – hoping for something that might be useful.

"Well there's the thing, see, I'm pretty sure I *do* know what it was....and that was the problem. A few years back I was Steward at the Glan-y-Mor club, and there was a big hoo-ha about a couple of the players who were on steroids – and they'd been storing them in their lockers at the club, so I saw a lot of the stuff then. And I'm pretty sure that's what GGR was passing to the chap in the next stall – three glass bottles. Steroids. Like I say.........I don't like to speak ill of the dead – but it's what I saw, really....and I thought you should know. I mean, I'm sure it's got nothing to do with him dying, but.....well.....what do you think?"

Glover knew exactly what he thought: it sounded like his hero hadn't just been injecting the stuff into himself, but that he was supplying it too. Glover could have cried. A doper, a drunk, a groper and now a dealer.....what else would he find out about his beloved GGR before the day was over? He felt sick. He steeled himself.

"Thanks Waters – I appreciate your openness. Do you know who it was he was passing the drugs to?"

"Yes, I know him – one of our front row – funnily enough, the one who seemed to kick off the fight that night. I've been thinking 'Roid Rage' ever since I saw it. And I've been having a think about a few other things too......"

Glover held up his hand to warn Waters that they were being approached by some golfers. Waters nodded and bowed his head, kicking at the dirt with his toe. He looked as deflated as Glover felt. Both men were seeing their hero in a different light: Glover was beginning to think that, quite soon, the rest of the world might see him that way too. After the golfers had walked past, Glover again drew close to Waters and said,

"Yes, Stan – you said you'd been thinking about some other things?" he dreaded what the man might say next.

"Well, yes, I was thinking – you know how GGR would come here on behalf of the Fire Dragon Brewery?" Glover nodded. "Well he used to come to Glan-y-Mor when I was there, and my other club too, and I know he goes to loads of rugby clubs all round....and I began to worry that maybe...well, you know...." Waters started to bob his head about like a character in a Monty Python sketch, "you know....." he said again, twitching.

"Spit it out, man," was Glover's exasperated response.

"Well....what if he was supplying other players with the same stuff....as he went around for the Brewery...........?" the thought hung in the warm air, and it made Glover's mouth taste bad. Dear God! Why hadn't *he* thought of it? Anyone else, and he'd have been right onto that! He could have kicked himself. He was annoyed that he wasn't seeing this case as clearly as he should. Could GGR really have been using his Brewery job to take supplies of anabolic steroids to dozens of rugby clubs in the area? And maybe for many years? Glover kept himself in check, and prayed that none of his thoughts had shown on his face.

"It's something we'll look into, of course, Stan – but I wouldn't trouble yourself about it for now," was about all he could muster. Luckily the sound of his mobile phone rescued him from having to say anything else. He checked the number – it was the Super. For once, he wanted to take the call.

"I really should take this Stan, it's my boss – is there anything else?"

"That's enough, isn't it?" asked Stan Waters.

"It's enough if it's all there is," replied Glover carefully.

"That's all, Inspector," was the man's reply and he waved as he took his leave of Glover.

"Sir?" was Glover's somewhat terse reply to the Superintendent's call.

"How's it going there, Glover? Come up with anything yet?"

Glover considered his reply carefully, "There are some interesting lines opening up for enquiry, Sir, and I'll be getting the team to do some checking up on various things for me just as soon as I can phone them, Sir." He hoped the Super would take the hint. He didn't.

"Anything you feel you can talk about right now?" the man was obviously desperate to know what was going on.

"All due respect Sir, I don't think I should go into any detail until I am sure of my facts, Sir. But, as I said, we do have some areas that need some pretty detailed enquiries made. So if I might, I'll hang up now, Sir, so I can speak to my team."

Superintendent Williams seemed taken aback, and agreed, which was what Glover had counted on. He walked back to the clubhouse as fast as he could, pushed open the swing doors and called for Stanley. Heads turned at his voice as it rang out in the relative quiet of the club, and within moments Stanley appeared at the front entrance. He had a video cassette and a large envelope in his hands.

"I've told them they can't release any photos till we say so Sir, I've got all the names and addresses you were after, and I've got this," he held up the video cassette with pride.

"And that is?" asked Glover, curious.

"They had a video camera on the premises, so they recorded GGR's speeches and presentations. This is the tape. I thought it might be useful."

"Good job, Stanley," Glover was pleased. "Bring it with you – we're going back to the team, I'll fill you in as we go."

"Get anything, Sir?" was Stanley's enquiry as they made their way back to the car, and Glover gave him the bare facts. Stanley's face was a picture.

"That's quite a lot of options, Sir: possibly an angry father, maybe some very angry drug users and the general chance of someone he might have annoyed when he was several sheets to the wind, Sir."

"Very politely put, Stanley," replied Glover as they pulled out of the car park. "You drive – I'm on the phone," he added redundantly, as Stanley was already behind the wheel and Glover was already dialling.

# VII

Glover had phoned in his requirements to the team back at HQ and had gathered that a very heavy sea mist on the Monday morning had completely obscured the entire Three Cliffs area, so no-one would have been able to see anything until about 11am, even if they'd been staring right at the spot where GGR was attacked, with binoculars. But it also raised the issue that maybe GGR hadn't seen his assailant until whoever it was had been quite close to him, making it easier for someone to approach him.

A call to Bird told Glover that the test results were back: Bird confirmed the man's use of anabolic steroids; at the time of death he'd had a blood alcohol level above the legal driving limit; his stomach contents showed whiskey, bacon, eggs and banana, but there was nothing else out of the ordinary – if those results could be called ordinary.

By the time Glover got off the phone the car was no more than five minutes away from HQ.

"What should I know about what *you* found out, Stanley – anything?"

"There are about forty Brynfield Club members who are lefties, and only about half a dozen of them have the golf club in question: the golf pro was pretty helpful with that, Sir – he knows the players and their clubs. I have their details. Oddly enough, the Captain, Assistant Captain, Waters *and* the Doctor are all lefties, as was GGR. Only the Captain and GGR had the Massive Martha III club though, Sir. I also observed that the Assistant Captain is a nit-wit, and that the Captain is a tosser, Sir. If you don't mind me saying so, Sir. If he'd called me 'laddie' one more time....well, I don't know what I'd have done. I feel better for telling you though, Sir."

Glover laughed out loud. "You're a sound man, Stanley, and I concur with your assessments," was all he managed before they peeled into the courtyard at the back of HQ, and Glover leapt from the vehicle, leaving Stanley to park the car.

Facing his team in the squad room, moments later, Glover had their undivided attention. "Right – waggle a limb as I call out," he shouted. "Door to door?" A hand shot up at the back of the room.

"Just one thing, Sir. The couple who found the little dog and called it in to the RSPCA: they're on holiday from the north of England and they confirmed that they first saw the dog, abandoned and running with its' lead attached to the shooting stick, at about 10.30am, Sir. They'd gone for a walk, hoping the mists would clear, which they didn't until about 11.00am, and they encountered the dog up on the top path, above Three Cliffs, Sir. They tried to catch it but it kept slipping away and then disappeared into the mists towards the top of the cliffs. Not knowing the area they didn't follow, but called the RSPCA. Might help with the time he went over, Sir?"

"Good point, West, thank you. Anything else?"

"Nothing more, Sir – the mist problem. No-one saw GGR himself that morning at all, Sir."

"Public tips?"

"Here, Sir, Bidder, Sir – not a thing Sir. Lines have been very quiet – except for the crack-pots."

"Who's on the Cockle Wars? It's Hughes, isn't it?"

"Yes, Sir. I pulled all the files, and there are a lot of them, Sir! I discovered that GGR's wife was a Davies even before she married him, one of three families in Penclawdd with the Davies name who each had one of the original cockle gathering licenses: Gwladys Davies's mother was a gatherer, and Gwladys herself was granted the stall in Swansea Market mainly because of the cockle license. She sold her family's cockles there until the co-operative was formed in the 1990's, but thereafter, what with the new health and safety requirements for selling foodstuffs, she decided not to move to a stall with chilling equipment, but her family gave their cockles to the co-op and she kept going with just the fruit, veg and eggs. Her father got into a bit of trouble in the 1970's and 1980's, but mainly pub brawls and public peace issues over the cockles. No mention of GGR in any of the files, Sir. Updates in the files suggest that everything's quiet on the cockle front, but that, if ever it does go off, it always seems to involve two particular families – the Dewi Davies family – which isn't connected to GGR or his wife at all - and the Hugh Price family: it seems that the Dewi Davies family lost their licence and the Price family got it instead, Sir. No love lost, Sir."

Glover suspected that the cockle war issue might be a dead end, but he'd follow it for a while yet.

"Stanley – what was name of the rugby player who started the fight at the Brynfield Club on Sunday night?"

Stanley looked through his notes. "It was a Bob Price, Sir, front row player for the Brynfield Rugby Club, Sir."

Glover gave it some thought.

"Hughes – liaise with Stanley and try to find out if the Price in the fight is related to the Penclawdd Prices, right? And, whether he is or not, I want him in here this afternoon for questioning."

Two voices shouted "Sir!", and Glover continued.

"Steroid abuse? Who's on steroid abuse? Any facts for me?"

"Evans, Sir! Here, Sir! The Welsh Rugby Union have what they call a 'rigorous anti-doping stance'. But there are 42,000 registered WRU players, and they only carried out 221 actual tests last year, Sir. Word on the street is it's not rife, but it is present. Dopers are risking it that they won't get tested. Seems especially prevalent at the lower club level, Sir. No incoming info about GGR being involved at all. I've printed up all the stats for you, Sir, including info about two blokes from the Valleys done for it a few years back – they're off suspension now, but aren't playing again."

"Thank you Evans: get hold of the two blokes done for doping and get them in here to see me this afternoon, please. Right-o, GGR's client list for the brewery – who's on brewery duty?"

"Me, Sir – I've got the list: 22 rugby clubs, 35 pubs, 10 restaurants, 5 golf clubs. Seems he went to each rugby club about once a month, then bi-monthly for the rest."

"Stanley – movement on the home front?"

"Yes Sir – the fridge in the cellar revealed three hundred phials of anabolic steroids, all on their way in now Sir; they've also confirmed that GGR's own golf clubs *are* a left-handed set, but there's no Massive Martha III there, but they've taken the rest of them anyway. The Missus is still out of it – WPC still on the scene. The sister's due to arrive from Cardiff this afternoon Sir, and plans on staying over. No luck finding any hidden bank accounts etcetera so far, Sir."

"Right-o – thank you for all your work people – now don't let me keep you from anything! Back to it – I know I've just given you a lot more you can be getting on with."

Glover turned to leave the room.

"Sir?" it was the DC handling the incoming public calls.

"Yes, Bidder, what is it?"

"I know I said there was nothing on the tips, Sir, but there *was* a call from a Mister Everett – said he needed to speak to you urgently, Sir. He said he'd hit GGR on Sunday and needed to explain it to you. He seemed a bit distressed, Sir."

"And what did you tell this distressed Mister Everett, Bidder?"

"I thought you'd like to see him, so I asked him if would be convenient for him to come in to talk to you. He got here about twenty minutes ago Sir. He's in Interview Room One."

Glover beamed. "Your quick thinking has just saved me a drive out to Rhossilli - and I thank you for it, Bidder." Bidder glowed, inwardly, and stood more erect. Glover was known to be generous in his praise and thanks for a job well done, but it made all the difference to hear the words.

"Go and tell the man I'll be with him in five, Bidder," Bidder nodded and left, "and you come with me for a second, Stanley."

The two men left the team room and stood in the corridor. "Stanley, what do you think of the mood in the room, eh?"

"Grim, Sir," was Stanley's considered opinion.

"I agree, Stanley – I know they all want to find out what's happened, but there's a pall hanging over everyone – it's like they've all lost a family member. I'm sure they'll work hard, but I need them firing on all cylinders......I tell you what – get the video equipment set up in the squad room, and we can all have a look at GGR's speech from Sunday night *together* when I've seen this Everett chap. It'll give me a more appropriate chance to focus them on the nature of our job. So sort that, then meet me downstairs - I want you to come with me to see Everett – he's the girl's father that Waters told me about. Watch him like a hawk, Stanley. Right? And I need *you* to be the one pushing his buttons about his daughter's possible promiscuity, right?"

Stanley nodded, unhappily, and muttered, "Sir," glumly. He didn't like *everything* about his job.

Glover popped to the loo – it might be his best chance for ages - then he bumped into Stanley at the end of the corridor, and they clattered down the stone staircase together.

As they walked to the interview room, Glover said, "Looks like GGR was planning on carrying on with his supply system, even if he *had* retired from the brewery: I don't suppose anyone would bat an eyelid if GGR showed up at their rugby club for a few pints once a month....they'd probably let him have it on the house! And it seems that we have more proof of his love of booze – whiskey that early in the day, and considering he would have been off to collect his car from the golf club if he hadn't died....well, there you go. The car's being checked too, right?"

"Yes Sir," was what Dave Everett heard the younger police officer say as the older one opened the door.

"Detective Inspector Glover, Detective Sergeant Stanley," said Glover by way of introduction. "And you are....?"

"I am Dave Everett, Inspector, thank you for seeing me." The man was tall, slim and red-headed. Glover wondered if that indicated a temper. It didn't look as though he'd slept much – there were blue marks beneath his watery grey-green eyes.

"Thank *you* for coming in, Sir, I understand you have something you wanted to tell me?" Straight to the point. Always the best way, thought Glover.

"I struck GGR Davies a hefty blow on the chin at a golf and rugby tournament on Sunday evening. The man had acted inappropriately towards my young daughter and I struck him. He fell to the floor with the force of my blow. I am not apologising, he deserved it. But I thought you should know."

Glover suspected that the man had been rehearsing that little speech for some time. It sounded very theatrical.

"How do you mean 'inappropriately', Mister Everett?" asked Stanley.

Everett looked at Glover in query, and Glover nodded. Everett nodded back and looked at Stanley. He'd been given permission to answer.

"My daughter had never met GGR before – though, of course, she knew all about him. Her grandmother, my wife's mother, has always been a big GGR fan, so Heather, that's my daughter....she's only sixteen.....asked GGR if he would sign a Brynfield Rugby Club shirt for her grandmother. She was going to be paid twenty pounds for working there on Sunday, and the shirt was nineteen pounds and ninety five pence – she bought it with the money she'd have been paid. *That's* the sort of girl she is. Thoughtful. Selfless." He looked at Glover pointedly, then continued. "GGR asked her to bring the rugby shirt to the women's locker room so he could sign it – the men's locker room was busy with the men who'd been playing in the rugby competition. She took the shirt along at the time he'd said - 4pm." The man was shaking. "When she got there he said she'd have to pay him with a kiss, so she pecked him on the cheek – but he grabbed her.....bottom and her....." he swallowed hard, "he grabbed my little girl's breasts, the bastard!" It was clear to both officers that Everett was overwhelmed.

"Try to stay calm, Mister Everett," cooed Glover.

"Do you think your daughter led him on?" asked Stanley.

Everett looked horrified. "Why would you say that? She's shy. She's not like that. You don't know her!" He was shouting. *There* was the temper Glover had been wondering about.

"We often find that parents don't really *know* their children at all, she might be a very....outgoing girl in reality," added Stanley, using his most unpleasant tones.

"I take offence at that!" Everett was on his feet. "Can't you tell him to stop?" he shouted at Glover. Was Glover seeing the reaction of a man who'd gone and bashed his daughter's groper over the head with a golf club? Or of a man torn apart by anger that a national hero, essentially untouchable, had stepped across a line that any father would draw?

"No need to get upset, Mister Everett – I'm sure my colleague means that, sometimes, we see our children as just that, children: even when they start to grow up and change....we just don't see it. But others do – outsiders see a beautiful young woman, where a father still sees a child. Maybe GGR misunderstood her childish enthusiasm for a bit of a come-on. He wasn't a father himself, you see, so he might have misinterpreted."

Everett resumed his seat, but still glared angrily at Stanley. "Don't make excuses for the man! Heather is *tiny*, I mean she's not, well.....*developed* at all if you know what I mean – I mean she *is* still a child. Anyone groping her must have had some sort of a *problem*. I mean she's a *kid!* Look!"

Everett handed Glover a photograph of what looked like a twelve year old in a school uniform. Glover passed it to Stanley. The girl was pretty, in a fresh faced way: she wore her hair short, in a boy's cut, and had a smile that was still toothy and unaffected.

"When was this taken, Sir?" asked Glover, politely.

"Two months ago – that's what I mean.....she looks like a kid still, doesn't she?"

"Oh, I don't know, Sir – a bit of make-up, lipstick, and her hair played around with and she could look quite different, I'd have thought," said Stanley, almost leering.

"Shut him up!" shouted Everett at Glover. "She never wears make-up, see! And I was there on Sunday – and I know she wasn't then.....she was wearing a golf shirt and track-suit bottoms – it's what all the bar and serving staff were wearing. Not dressed up at all, she wasn't!"

"So what happened exactly, Mister Everett?" asked Glover patiently - they weren't going to get any further with that line of questions.

"You mean, about hitting him?" replied Everett.

Glover nodded.

"Well, Heather didn't come to me about it at all – she'd gone to Stan, he's our GM and the one who asked her to come and work on Sunday, and he sent her home. I was at the rugby, see – or, at least, I hadn't got back to the clubhouse, and I don't suppose she knew where to find me. Fine father I turned out to be!" Glover had suspected guilt – and there it was at last....the man hadn't been there when his daughter needed him! "Anyway – I didn't even notice she wasn't around until about half way through dinner – I hadn't seen her serving, so I asked Stan about it – and he took me to one side and, eventually, told me what she'd said. I couldn't believe it!" Glover spotted the incredulity in the man's voice: it was to be expected. "So I went and phoned her at home, right then. She was in tears on the phone - she hadn't talked to her mother about it, it seemed, but it all came out when I asked her. And I have no reason to doubt her – she's a good girl, is Heather."

Glover suspected that Everett believed this to be the truth, even if it proved not to be the case. He'd have to meet the girl himself and decide. But that was for later.

"I am assuming you were *angry*, Mister Everett?" Stanley asked.

Everett glared at him. "Of course I was bloody angry! Any father would be!" He spoke to Stanley as though he was an idiot.

"So how did you happen to hit GGR?" asked Glover.

"Well, after phoning home I went up to the bar for a drink – a big one – and GGR was in that part of the room too. He'd finished all his speeches and all that – I'd missed it all when I was on the phone to Heather. Now I don't know what happened – I wasn't really taking any notice, but all of a sudden a fight broke out – people were taking swings all over the place and.....well,

Inspector Glover....something just snapped inside my head and I lashed out at GGR. I don't think anyone saw me, and I'm pretty sure not even he knew that it was me who hit him. I just whacked him one on the chin, and down he went. It was a sucker punch – cowardly and not my sort of thing at all. And when I'd hit him I felt normal again, and I just walked away. I don't know what happened afterwards. I went to the Gents and washed my face. By the time I went back into the bar area everything was back to normal – people patting each other on the back – someone was handing GGR a pint. It was as though none of it had ever happened. But it did. And.....well, now that he's dead, I thought I'd better tell you......." Everett seemed drained.

"So you didn't see GGR again that evening?" asked Stanley, abrasively.

"I didn't stay long after that, I couldn't face it. I just got in a taxi and went home to see Heather. I never saw him after that at all."

"So where were you on Monday morning, Mister Everett – between 8am and noon?" Stanley's tone was abrupt.

"At work – you can check with my office. So, no, I wasn't pushing GGR off a cliff in the Gower!" was Everett's equally sharp reply.

"If you could give us your work details we could check that quite easily, Mister Everett," said Glover in his most reasonable voice. "Maybe you'd like a coffee while we just follow up on that? You could tell Stanley here how you like your coffee and he could bring it for you."

The man looked delighted that the spiteful minion would be relegated to being his fetcher and carrier, which was what Glover wanted, and he instructed Stanley to follow up on the office alibi – which he suspected would hold. Glover thanked the man for coming and told him that, if everything checked out at his office, there'd be no need to bring the girl in, at that time.

As Stanley sorted out Everett, Glover dragged himself back upstairs and looked at his watch: 1pm. He was making progress, but it was slow. And his main emotion was of hopelessness – he was utterly dismayed at his findings so far about GGR. He decided he deserved a break – just five minutes.....he'd call Betty, and hear a sane voice just for a few minutes. But not right now – now he wanted to see that video of GGR, and he needed to do something to rally the troops a bit. He was pretty sure he'd have to face the Super soon, too, though he congratulated himself on having managed to avoid him for so long, then Glover kicked himself for even thinking of the man – as he heard his superior's voice behind him in the corridor. Inwardly, Glover rolled his eyes, but to his Super's face he said brightly,

"Sir – *just* the person! I was about to call you into the squad room: we're about to watch a videotape of the speeches GGR made at the Brynfield Club on Sunday night, and I thought you'd be interested in seeing it." Glover was a pretty good liar, all in all, and he knew the Super'd never pick up on the sarcasm in his tone.

Whatever the Super had been about to say, it was clear that the thought of actually seeing GGR's last speech before he died put it out of his mind, and the man beamed!

"Thank you, Glover – I think it will be an important event to witness." His serious tone almost made Glover smile.

By this time the two men had reached the squad room, where they were joined by Stanley, who whispered to Glover, "Everett's alibi checks out – I've sent him home, but asked him to remain available, Sir."

"Good man," replied Glover. One door had closed then, thought Glover to himself, as he asked everyone to take a seat so that they could see the TV monitor that had been set up in the corner of the room. Of course the Super got the best seat in the house.

Glover stood at the front of the room and told the team what they were about to see – adding that it would be a chance for them to see if anything had been said, or had happened during the speeches, that might have a bearing on what had happened to GGR the following morning. The mood in the room was one of apprehension: people seemed uneasy at the thought of watching GGR just before he died. Glover and Stanley took their positions at the rear, perching on the edge of a desk together.

Hughes was in charge of making the screen and the tape work, and, after a few hiccups, a rather dark and somewhat grainy picture appeared. It was clear that the microphone was nearer the camera than the speaker, so the voices from the top table echoed, whereas whispers at the back of the room could be heard more clearly. Still, thought Glover, it was better than nothing. Maybe there'd be something.........

The Golf Club Captain and the Rugby Club Captain made a few comments, then there was a vote of thanks for Doctor Bill Williams, who couldn't be seen in the shot, as well as one for Stan Waters and all the staff who'd helped make the day a success. Then GGR was introduced, with all the usual references to his stellar career, and a few comments about how he'd been a regular at the Brynfield Club for so many years. Glover watched with very mixed emotions: had he seen this tape before his day had begun he'd have been watching it as an avid fan – a chance to see a more intimate side of his boyhood hero. As it was, he was looking at the face of a man he was beginning to hate – a man who'd had it all, but had decided to abuse the trust put in him by young players, a young girl and, frankly, the whole community.....if only people had but known it.

The applause on the tape finally subsided to allow GGR to speak. Glover heard, once again, that familiar voice: gravelly, and jovial; warm and comforting. Not slurred at all, which made him wonder about how very used GGR must have been to drinking large quantities of beer, given that, by all accounts, he'd probably have sunk the best part of two gallons of beer by that point in the proceedings.

Glover felt the mood in the squad room become more intense as GGR began to speak – all ears and eyes were focussed on the Great One.

GGR opened with the expected acknowledgements to the club and all its officers and staff – he expressed surprise that the day had gone so well, given that both golfers and rugby players were involved, which earned him a good laugh, then he began his speech in earnest.

"Now I've thought long and hard about what to talk to you about tonight, gentlemen, trying to work out what it is that golfers and rugger buggers have in common – and then the answer came to me......of course....it's beer!" A round of applause and laughter followed. "About which – given my years with the brewery, I know quite a bit – you could say I know beer inside and out!" he shouted "Cheers!", raised his glass to the crowd and drank down a full pint in a matter of seconds. The roar from the room showed its appreciation of this feat. In the squad room there was a ripple of chuckles.

Glover wondered if the mood might lighten at all, as GGR continued. "I suppose I've had a blessed life – the *perfect* life some might say – playing rugby for Wales and working for a brewery....the only thing missing is being the lead tenor in a male voice choir......." Laughter. ".....but the truth is, I can't carry a tune. But there – the rugby and the beer make up for it, I suppose." The man knew his audience, there was no doubt about it. Glover wondered how many of the men in the room suspected just how well GGR really did know beer, from the drinker's perspective: he guessed that, even if they'd known, they wouldn't have cared.

"So – beer. It is what I think the writers of 'Bread of Heaven' had in mind when they wrote that hymn: I know that many a time it's been a meal in a glass for me! All that goodness in there gentlemen – hops, barley, water – it's almost a health food! But not all beers are created equal, it takes years and years to invent a good new beer. I'm sure many of you are aware that Fire Dragon Dark has been my tipple of choice for as long as I can remember, but I wonder if you knew that I was involved in the development of a beer that they actually wanted to name after me?" Clearly no-one knew. "But I said that I could think of a better name – and so they called it Fire Dragon Fireworks!" A ripple of understanding ran through the squad room, while on the tape a series of "ah's" and "oh's" flew about, and a round of applause broke out. Even Glover, not a frequenter of pubs, except when work required it, knew about Fire Dragon Fireworks: the brewery sold it for only two months each year and it was powerful stuff!

GGR seemed pleased at the reception he was getting, and carried on with enthusiasm.

"Believe me, gentlemen, there was a lot of tasting that had to be done to get it right!" Laughter. "And it took about a year, all in all. Then, to launch it we had a big party up at the brewery. All Top Secret it was – hiding the packaging, not letting anyone see the end result – then they allowed me to have the first pint pulled......and the second, and the third.....well, it's good stuff, isn't it!" A cheer went up. "Just as well they only sell it for two months....Fireworks is right, eh chaps?" Glover could hear comments close to the microphone about how strong the beer was, and how the hangover the next day was equally powerful. "I'm not too sure about this 'Seasonal Beer' thing myself, but if you're going to have one at all, it should be a good one. Not too keen on the

Christmas Ales – all messed around with and too fruity for my liking, but I have to admit that I thought that a beer to celebrate Guy Fawkes night was a good idea....all that standing around in chilly fields waiting for the dud Catherine Wheels to turn, you need a good beer to keep you warm....and speaking about Catherine Wheels, the launch party at the brewery had some of those girls there who wander around with the free beer, and I bet you can guess where their Catherine Wheels were! No duds there, gentlemen!" There was even a laugh in the squad room for that one.

"Yes, it was a delight to be able to develop a beer that people like – it'll be here in the bar at the beginning of November – the fifth year for the brewery to put it out, and I hope you all lap it up, I know I will! And I'm saying that even though I don't work for them anymore! Oh but that launch party – I have to say, and again, remember I don't work for them anymore, the Fire Dragon Brewery really does a good job with its beers and its parties. I had to leave before the fireworks display they were having though – the little woman had plans for the evening, and I didn't want to be late......or there'd have been fireworks of a whole different sort!" Big laugh for that one, on the tape and in the squad room. "No, no, seriously gentlemen, I don't want to speak ill of the wife – I'm sure many of you know my Gwladys....." spontaneous, if polite applause on the tape, "....she's put up with me nearly forty years now....." more applause, ".....and she's happy that I've finally retired.....not 'cos we'll get to spend more time together, but because she won't have to kick me out of bed in the morning to get me on the road. Encouraging me to play more golf right now, she is......but I'm sure that those of you who have already retired know what it's like......they have their funny little routines, don't they, our wives......." wry comments could be overheard on the tape.

"But, back to the launch of Fire Dragon Fireworks: like I said, good party, good beer, and strict instructions from the wife to not be late home. So there I am, wending my way through the lovely lanes of Clydach. It's pitch dark out there – I don't think they can afford street lights out that way – and I have to admit that I was putting my foot down a bit – when all of sudden what's in front of me but a bloody big sheep. *Huge* it was, and right on the side of a narrow bit of road. Well, gentlemen, there was no way I was going to miss it! Luckily I drive one of those Swedish cars that they say are safe because they do a 'moose test' – if the car can cope with hitting a moose, it's safe - well, in this part of the world I can now confirm we have developed the 'sheep test', and I can tell you I hardly felt a thing.....I was tempted to stop and stuff the sheep in the boot and take it home for a stew....but as it was, I just wound down the window and shouted 'mint sauce' at it and got off home." There were laughs and calls of 'mint sauce, mint sauce' around the room on the tape. In the squad room the joke didn't seem to go down so well, but there were a few chuckles. GGR was enjoying himself as much as his audience was – Glover could tell he was a man who knew that it wasn't just *what* you said to a crowd like that, but *how* you said it – and GGR was hamming it up a treat. "Now don't get me wrong," GGR continued, "......I'm not one for 'hunting and gathering' my own food, that's what the wife's for..........and who knows, maybe that poor sheep was somebody's darling........." laughter broke out, ".......see, now – there's a chap who knows what his wellies are for," cracked GGR pointing at someone in the crowd, there were hoots of laughter at that one, ".....but when I got home and the wife saw the mess on the front of the car, she laid into me good and proper......so I *did* get to see the fireworks after all!"

Hoots of laughter and applause. GGR quietened the crowd. "But enough about beer – I am well aware that you'd rather be drinking it than hearing me talking about it, so I'd better get on with these presentations and let you all get to the bar............"

For the next ten minutes GGR read out names, handed out plates and cheques and finally the Howells' Cup – which was accepted, to the accompaniment of much cheering, by the Golf Club Captain and the twelve members who'd played in the tournament. GGR had thanked everyone again, encouraged them all to visit the bar one last time, and not to forget the arrival of Fire Dragon Fireworks in about five weeks' time, and then the tape shut off. There was, disappointingly, no sign of the fight that had ensued what must have been a few minutes later.

Everyone in the squad room was quiet. Glover rose and addressed the room.

"Well, there we have it – GGR's last public appearance. Any questions? Observations?"

Before anyone had a chance to comment, Detective Superintendent Michael Williams rose to his feet and turned to face the room.

"Wonderful man – quite wonderful. Talented, entertaining and a real supporter of youth rugby. He'll be sorely missed. And it's us who have to find out who killed him. He might not have been playing any more – but he was a man in his prime, with a full and busy retirement ahead of him. Whoever killed him has robbed him of that – so come on, let's have some action. I want results! Glover – my office for an update, now!" and he was gone. He'd said all the things Glover *hadn't* wanted to say! The team had been on a little up-slope: now Williams had sent them down again! They needed a pep talk – they knew what their responsibilities were – they didn't need reminding of that! Glover could have happily strangled the man!

"Sir – I'll just be ten minutes Sir – have to make a couple of really important calls, Sir!" called Glover towards the Super's back.

"Quick as you can, Glover," was what he heard in reply, but was half way to choosing to ignore.

"Stanley, did you get anything from it?"

"Well, Sir.....I do have a question..........," Glover noted his hesitation.

"Ask away, Stanley."

"What did he mean about the wellies – everyone seemed to think it was hilarious – but I don't get it."

Glover smiled. "How long have you been here now, Stanley, five years is it?" Stanley nodded. "And you know what wellies are?"

Stanley looked bemused. "Yes, Sir, they are tall rubber, waterproof boots, Sir, named for the Duke of Wellington, I believe, Sir, and an essential for any camping trip to be undertaken by Boy Scouts, and their Scoutmasters, during a British summer."

Glover smiled again. "Exactly. And it's their length that is critical in this instance."

"Sir?" Stanley looked confused.

"It's all very Welsh, Stanley: we have a lot more in common with Australia and New Zealand than just rugby – we all live where there are more sheep than women, so in all our countries there are any number of 'sheep-shagging' jokes.....men who can only find themselves a sheep, when what they really want is a woman. And the wellies – well, the joke goes that you have to put the sheep's back legs in your wellies to stop them from running off as you have your way with them............"

Stanley looked surprised. Then he said, "So that's why they have inflatable sheep at stag parties then, Sir? I once saw a Best Man give a pair of wellies to the bridegroom – that makes more sense now, I suppose." Stanley looked serious. Glover smiled and nodded. Stanley continued. "And that's why the blokes back in Bristol call me a 'sheep-shagger' now, Sir?" Glover nodded again. "Ah......" observed Stanley. Glover smiled at his innocence, which was diminishing by the second. "So that's what GGR meant, Sir?"

"Yes, Stanley – he was making a very old joke about sheep, knowing it would get him a cheap laugh."

"And it did, Sir," observed Stanley, seriously. "So the Welsh don't mind that sort of thing?" He seemed genuinely puzzled.

"Well, I wouldn't go around making jokes about it *yourself*, Stanley – it's the sort of thing we take pretty well from one of our own....but from an Englishman? *You* clearly know how the English like to use the reference as an insult, Stanley – being on the receiving end yourself now that you live here – so I'd steer clear of the whole thing, if I were you."

"Yes, Sir, good advice, I'm sure, Sir." Stanley seemed to consider the matter closed, as did Glover, who headed off to his office, and a chance to call Betty. Now, maybe even more than earlier, he wanted to hear the voice of his wife: not 'her indoors', not 'the little woman', not 'the ball and chain', but his wife – his love, his comfort and his anchor. He didn't like it when people made fun of their wives just to get a cheap laugh – something else that rankled about GGR.

"Husband – is that you?" asked Betty as she answered the phone.

"Yes, Wife – it is. How are you?"

"How are *you* is more like it, are you alright?" replied Betty, sounding concerned. "I just saw the lunchtime news – God it's a mess, Evan!"

Glover was suddenly aware that he'd managed to not only miss the media people who might have been trying to talk to him, but that he was completely unaware of what the public was being fed by way of what he had no doubt was misinformation. He thought he'd better find out what the rest of the world *thought* was going on!

"So what's the news then, Wife?"

"Well, first of all I had to go down to town this morning – we're almost out of cabbage and I needed to make you some fresh soup for tonight....." Glover swallowed hard – bless her, he knew it was for all the right reasons but he hated that she was feeding him that soup! Betty continued, unaware of, or else choosing to ignore, her husband's silence on the matter of the soup. "So anyway – I popped into the market and you should see Gwladys Davies's stall: her name is draped in black, and where the fruit and veg should be there are dozens of photographs of GGR, all with their own little funereal attachments, and flowers and candles and all sorts of little notes. It's like a shrine! They've even set up a book of remembrance that people can sign: the queue was right around the middle of the market! And I tell you what, Evan – the mood all around town was like a funeral itself: we Welsh are good at this sort of thing. Lots of conversations in hushed tones – even the market itself sounded like a church!"

Glover wasn't surprised: Betty had hit the nail on the head – the Welsh had a talent for enjoying misery. Mind you, with the history that the nation had, it was hardly surprising: marginalise a people, take all their land off them, try to wipe out their culture and tell them they aren't allowed to speak their own language and see what you get! And that was one of the reasons why GGR had been such a hero – he'd always managed to stuff the rugby ball right down England's throat! It was a small compensation, but the nation had taken it, and had loved it. And had loved him for it. He'd been even more popular than Owain Glyndwr: indeed, Glover reflected, as Shakespeare had referred to Glyndwr as "not in the roll of common men", so ran the general opinion about GGR Davies.

His momentary lapse of concentration had been noted by Betty, who had stopped speaking: even on the phone she could tell when Evan was distracted.

"Sorry, Wife," added Evan Glover, "I was just thinking about what you'd said – and you're right, we're good at that sort of thing."

"So it seems," said Betty, confident she'd regained her husband's ear. "And on the news on TV today it seems that there's a fight breaking out about where and when his memorial should take place: they interviewed his sister in Cardiff and she was all for the WRU dedicating the next Wales/England International to him at the Millennium Stadium, but then there's a group that says there should be a special service at the Cardiff Arms Park, because he never actually played at the new stadium. Swansea's Lord Mayor was on saying it should be at St Helen's – where he played for the All Whites. *Wherever* it is there's going to be a lot of singing – it looks like every male voice choir in existence will be there; they had Bryn Terfel on the telephone from Milan saying he'd drop everything and come in from wherever he was in the world, *and* they had Max Boyce on camera saying he would write something especially for it!

They expect the biggest ever gathering of International players from the 1970's too. It'll be quite the event."

"Sounds lovely," was all Evan could manage. The thought of it all was like dust in his mouth: all that celebration for a man who was......well, not what people thought he was in any case.

"But enough about my day – how's it going with you, Husband? Need to talk?"

"Oh Betty, love, you have no idea how *much* I need to talk. Have you got five minutes? I can't let the team see how I'm feeling – but I've got to let it out somehow."

"Always got five minutes for my husband," replied Betty, warmly. Evan Glover could imagine her settling into the kitchen chair to listen, so he talked, and talked. Betty was quiet, except for the odd exclamation of disbelief. In just a few minutes she, too, was made aware that the man being lauded by everyone who'd ever worn a daffodil or eaten a leek on St David's Day was not what they had all thought. Her heart went out to her husband: she'd seen the sadness in his eyes the night before as he'd relived old memories of GGR, but now she knew he'd be mourning the man in an entirely different way. To try to distract him from the depths of his sadness a little, she picked up on one of the names he'd mentioned.

"Did you say there was a Doctor Bill Williams at the Brynfield Club?"

Betty Glover was right, her husband was distracted. His voice lifted a little.

"That's right. Know him?"

"Short man, fair hair – worried expression?" she asked.

Glover was always proud of his wife's perspicacity. "That's right – used to live in Clydach.

"It sounds like him – very sad. When I was grief counselling for that couple of years I spent a lot of time with him and his wife, Linda. In fact – they were a big part of the reason I gave up."

Glover was glad to talk about something other than GGR. "Why so, Wife?" He knew that Betty had gone through a tough time, but she'd never been very forthcoming about the details: he wondered what it had to do with the Doctor.

"Well, their little boy was killed, and they came to me because they wanted some help outside the NHS: Bill was the GP up there and he didn't want to work with anyone he knew. So *I* got them and they came in for sessions for about six months. But, obviously, I couldn't help them – or else I didn't help them enough, because she committed suicide and he had a complete breakdown. Like I said, it was all terribly tragic and that's why I lost confidence in myself. When I found out she was dead, I didn't feel I could do it anymore."

Evan Glover could feel his wife's sadness. "I'm sorry, love," he said gently. "What happened to their son?" He felt he should have remembered, but he was ashamed to admit that he didn't.

"Oh it was bad, Evan – a hit and run in the lane right outside their house. He was only four, and she thought she'd strapped him into the child seat in the back of the car, then she'd gone back to make sure their dog was safely inside the house and to lock the front door. She couldn't find the dog and thought it might have gone out onto the road. As she went to look she was passed by a car and she saw the car hit the dog, and it just kept going! Of course she ran to the dog, all upset, only to discover that her little boy had also been struck. She couldn't be sure what had happened – but it seemed that the dog had run out onto the road, and the little boy, Josh....Joshua Williams that was his name....well he'd somehow got out of the car and he ran after the dog."

Glover was beginning to remember something about it: it hadn't been a case in his area, but there'd been a lot of man-hours thrown into it, he seemed to recall.

Betty continued, "The car had hit them both. The dog was dead, and by the time the ambulance came, so was the little boy. They never got the driver. And she just couldn't come to terms with the guilt. Bill had been at work at the time, and had rushed home of course, but even *he* couldn't help his boy. Their sessions were always very fraught: she couldn't forgive *her*self, he couldn't forgive *him*self – he thought that if he could have got there sooner he might have been able to help the boy. She used to go on and on about the driver – how fast the car had been going, how it almost knocked her down too, and how the man – she was sure it was a man, a man in a silver car – was shouting and laughing as he ran into the dog. She always wondered if the man had done it on purpose. She often said that if only he'd hit *her* he might have missed her boy. She was a mess. I was always pretty sure their marriage wasn't going to survive it in the long-run – often that's the case – but I'd never seen her overdose coming. Looking back, I suspect the signs were there – but I'd missed them all – completely. I suppose his breakdown was the only way his psyche could cope with it all – complete shutdown. So it's nice to know that he's back on his feet. I'd never met him before the tragedy, but I suspected he'd have been a nice chap: probably *always* lived on his nerves, but a nice, steady sort."

Evan Glover's mind was racing – his thoughts weren't wandering though, he heard every word, and it got him thinking.

"Betty, love, what sort of dog did they have?"

Betty was puzzled. "Why on earth do you want to know that?"

"Humour me, Wife," was Evan Glover's gentle answer.

"Well I happen to know it was a white standard poodle, because she would show it at the Clydach fair every year – won some sort of prize up in London at some point."

Glover was silent, then he asked, "And do you know when the boy was killed?"

At least Betty thought *that* was a more sensible question. "I know exactly when it was: it was November 5$^{th}$ five years ago this coming November – it was Guy Fawkes night and they were off to a fireworks display....that's why she wanted the dog inside: it would have been frightened by all the fireworks going off that night. I don't know where the display was to be, though."

"I think I do," answered Evan Glover, cryptically. "Listen Wife, I have to go....I'll phone later, but I think it might be a late one tonight."

"I love you."

"And I love you too, Betty.....I don't think I tell you enough, but I hope you know it."

"I do, be safe," and Betty blew a kiss into the receiver.

Glover put down the telephone and was out of his chair in one movement. Sticking his head into the corridor he shouted "Stanley!" as loud as he could.

Stanley was there in seconds – he could tell from Glover's tone that there was urgency involved.

"Stanley – get me everything we've got on a hit and run – November 5th, five years ago – boy named Joshua Williams, Clydach....and make it fast!"

"Sir?" Stanley was puzzled.

"New line of enquiry – just get it done, and back to me pronto! GO!"

Even though Stanley had no idea why he was doing what he was doing, he could tell that his boss thought it was important, so he went! As he was going Glover called him back.

"Stanley – where was Doctor Bill Williams on Monday morning?"

"I'll have to check my notes, Sir, but I'm pretty sure he said it was his morning off and that he went to town."

"That's how I remember it too," replied Glover. Then he looked up and shouted, "Go on, scarper!" And Stanley scarpered....again.

Glover paced around his little office. If it wasn't the Cockle Wars, and it wasn't something to do with steroids, and if it wasn't the distressed father of a groped girl, maybe *this* was it. He pulled open his office door and marched back to the squad room. "Let me see that video again," he said to Hughes, who wound the tape back and got the machine working for Glover. Glover turned down the volume so that the team wasn't distracted, but so that he could still hear clearly, and he listened again to GGR's speech. That *must* be it!

"Sir," Stanley was back. "We don't have anything here on the Joshua Williams case, because all the paperwork is up at Valley HQ. But I know who led the case Sir: DI Treharne," said Stanley.

"Right-o, Stanley," replied Glover, and he reeled off a list of questions to which he wanted Stanley to discover the answers. "When you know all that, come into my office – if I'm on the phone, wait with me."

"Sir!" was Stanley's efficient reply.

Glover made his way back to his office: he was mindful of the fact that the Super was waiting for him, but, if he was right, then it was much more important for him to talk to DI Treharne at Valley than to bring the Super up to date. He suspected that the Super wouldn't see it that way, but, then, at the moment, that was tough luck!

# VIII

Glover put down the telephone: DI Treharne at Valley HQ had pretty much confirmed Betty's version of the Joshua Williams story, in all its tragic details: a family destroyed by a careless driver. They'd never had anything much to go on: the wife had only been able to tell them it was a silver car – no description beyond that. It had been dark and misty. She'd been distracted. They'd monitored car repair shops for six months with no luck, and there was no forensic evidence, no glass or paint transfer, for them to work with. There hadn't even been any skid-marks – the driver hadn't so much as slowed down or braked at all, it seemed. It had been a brick wall, and Glover believed Treharne when he said they'd all done the best they could – Doctor Williams was their area GP: everyone knew him and liked him.

Glover crunched into a peppermint; where the hell was Stanley! No point calling him – if he wasn't in Glover's office then he didn't have all the answers Glover needed, so he'd just be interrupting him needlessly, and, given the way the Super'd been acting the last couple of days, he knew only too well how unproductive that could be. Think – that was what he had to do. He needed to consider all the facts, yes, but then he had to work out the truth: Glover knew only too well that there could be a world of difference between the two.

"Sir!" It was Stanley.

"Sit – and speak," was Glover's reply. Stanley did both.

"Waters, Williams *and* the Golf Captain have all left the club, Sir."

"Times?" asked Glover, crunching a fresh peppermint.

"Waters almost immediately we left, the Captain decided against playing today and left shortly after we did and Williams left about half an hour ago."

"Thanks."

"GGR *did* use a left-handed Massive Martha III, Sir – I checked with the club pro, but it's definitely not at his home, and no one has reported finding a 'spare' lying about at the Brynfield Club. GGR's wife, who is now quite with-it by the way, has confirmed that he would often take 'a bloody big golf club' with him when he walked the dog: to 'play about with his swing' she said. I have to say, Sir, she's in no better a mood today than yesterday – and she rather flew off the handle with me about us 'allowing Geraint's sister to give all those TV interviews'. I did try to explain that we have no control over that sort of thing, but I think that one might come back to you, Sir."

"Thanks for the warning," was Glover's eye-rolling reply.

"Next – the car. GGR's car was at Brynfield, as we knew Sir, and there's no reason to think that it couldn't easily be identified as his: it had Fire Dragon Brewery and Welsh Rugby Union Youth stickers on the back window, and all sorts of things with his name on them strewn about inside it. It's a six year old silver Volvo. Otherwise, no distinguishing marks or features. No accidents reported for the VIN number, Sir."

"OK, next," crunched Glover.

"The Brynfield Rugby Club Captain, who was playing with GGR on Sunday, confirms that they had a lengthy conversation about how GGR liked to walk on Three Cliffs: he portrayed it as his 'morning ritual', though the Captain did comment that, since GGR had only been retired a week, he suspected that it was a good intention rather than a ritual. They even talked about the 'harvest mist' that comes in at this time of year, Sir, and GGR made it clear that he loved it – they talked a long time about how the mist changed sounds and smells: apparently he was quite taken with mist, Sir."

Glover raised his eyebrows. "I know, Sir," was Stanley's understanding reply, "It does seem a bit......poetic."

"And finally.......?" asked Glover, as he rose from his seat and looked out of his grubby little window.

"And finally Sir – the launch date *was* Guy Fawkes night five years ago, Sir."

"That nails it," said Stanley gravely. "So we have motive, means and opportunity, Stanley."

"It seems so, Sir."

"But a missing suspect."

"As you say, Sir."

"So what do you suggest, Stanley?"

Stanley looked taken aback: this was the sort of thing *Glover* was good at – why ask him! Glover was putting him on the spot: Glover often did that, and Stanley didn't like it very much. True, it made him try to think, but he wasn't sure he was very good at that.

"Well, we *are* looking for his car, Sir," he replied, hesitantly.

"Yes...."

"And they know at the Club that we want to interview him," he continued, painfully.

"Yes......"

"I suppose we could consider where he might go?"

"We could Stanley – and where do you think that might be?"

Stanley thought, with his eyes getting wilder by the second.

"Think like a Scoutmaster, Stanley: how would you track him? Where might a psychologically wounded assailant go?"

Stanley seemed to buck up a bit. "Well, Sir, a wounded animal often tries to return to its lair, to an area it has scented a good deal....so maybe he'd head for his old stamping ground?" Glover, his back still turned toward Stanley, nodded his encouragement. "Or....what about where he can visit his loved ones?" Stanley looked impressed with himself.

"Very good," replied Glover. He wasn't patronising Stanley, he was pushing him, and was pleased with the results. "So we could check his old home, wherever his family is – anywhere else?"

"Scene of the crime, Sir?"

"Less likely, I think – it's probably a zoo down on the South Gower Road today, Stanley, I can only imagine what Traffic Division is having to deal with down there."

Stanley looked rather less pleased with himself.

"Well, I'm not sure where else to suggest, Sir." Stanley seemed disappointed with himself.

"We could always try downstairs, I suppose."

"Downstairs, Sir?" Stanley looked confused.

Glover smiled. "Sorry Stanley, I've been leading you on a bit. While you've been talking, I've been looking out of the window – and I've been watching him walk along the road towards the station: he's not having an easy time of it – it's busy with the press and all that lot. And he's doing a sort of crab-like dance – he's not coming straight to us, he's wandering along the other side of the road, going back and forth, not forward, towards us." Stanley rose and joined his boss at the window.

"I see him, Sir. Shall I pop down and unofficially make sure he gets through the front door? Or do *you* want to do it officially?"

Glover thought for a moment. His quarry finally crossed the road towards the front entrance of the police station.

"Let's just get downstairs so he doesn't have time for any second thoughts, Stanley. I'm sure you're quicker than me – off you go!" Stanley shot out of Glover's office, with Glover himself in hot pursuit.

As Glover left his office he heard the unwelcome voice of the Super behind him. "Glover – where the hell have you been – I've been waiting in my office for you. I've promised the Chief an update – come with *me – now*!" The man was almost squeaking he was so angry.

Glover stopped in his tracks, sighed heavily and turned to face his boss. "Sir," he began politely enough, "I *cannot* talk to you now, Sir. But I promise you will be the first to know of any developments – which I am expecting imminently. Now, if you'll excuse me, Sir!" and Glover was off.

"No I will *not* excuse you, Glover.....come back here.....!" Glover suspected that, behind him, there was a certain amount of foot-stamping going on, but he didn't look back to see the expression on his superior's face....he could imagine it!

As Glover reached the bottom of the staircase he could see their man talking to Stanley just inside the front door. Glover tried to catch his breath, and he pushed open the security door that prevented anyone from just barging into the station.

He smiled, and extended his hand. Once their hands met, he tightened his grip and his face grew serious.

"Doctor Williams, I am arresting you on suspicion of murdering Mister Geraint Gareth Richard Davies. You do not have to say anything, but it may harm your defence if you fail to mention when questioned something which you later rely on in court. Anything you do say will be given in evidence. Do you understand that you have been cautioned?"

Doctor Bill Williams looked at Glover with dead eyes. "I understand. And I did it." He spoke simply, it was the voice of a man who was utterly defeated.

The Desk Sergeant dropped his pen and his mouth fell open. Good grief – Glover had done it! They'd actually got the man who killed GGR! And he'd walked right in and given himself up – just like that – to Glover! Glover could feel the uniformed officer's excitement – it was palpable. "If you mention this to anyone – I'll have your job and your pension," Glover said to the Sergeant. The Desk Sergeant's response was quick, and to the point.

"I understand, Sir. I'll open up and let you gentlemen get into Interview Room Two, then Sir. Right?"

"Thank you." Glover looked pointedly at the officer and said, "Not even a phone call home...if I get so much as a sniff......."

"You've been very clear, Sir," was the terse reply as the buzzer sounded and the heavy door was released.

"Would you like some coffee, Doctor Williams?" was Glover's question as they entered the interview room.

The doctor looked dazed: he peered at Glover with bloodshot eyes, then half smiled. "That's very kind of you, Inspector, but I don't really feel like a coffee. But I wonder – might I have a cup of tea.....out of a proper china pot, if that's at all possible. I don't want to be a bother – but that would be lovely."

Glover nodded at the PC who was standing inside the interview room door, then he took his seat, indicated that Williams should do likewise, and nodded to Stanley to start the recording devices. He stated the facts for the record: the names and ranks of those present, the date and time, and the nature of the interview. He repeated the words that Williams had spoken at the door, and asked him if it was true – had he really killed GGR Davies?

"Oh yes," was Williams' matter of fact reply. "I don't know that I meant to do it when I went there – but it seemed like the right thing to do when I was face to face with him. An eye for an eye. It seems fair."

Glover couldn't see any emotion in the eyes of the man in front of him. Bill Williams had shut down. An automaton was speaking for him. The nervous energy he'd seen in him earlier in the day had evaporated. Glover felt sorry for him: he tried to ease him through the interview.

"Can you tell me what happened, Bill? Was it the speech on Sunday night that set you off on this path? You didn't miss the speeches at all, did you – you heard GGR alright – right?"

Williams didn't lift his downcast eyes. He nodded. "You saw the tapes?"

Glover nodded.

"Then you know what he said. He was actually making a funny story out of it. It made me see that Josh's death meant nothing to him. The man was too drunk and too stupid to put two and two together – he didn't even know what I was talking about when I confronted him with it."

"So, it was when he said that he'd hit a sheep leaving the Fire Dragon Fireworks beer launch that you knew that he'd at least seen that he'd knocked down your dog – a big white standard poodle, wasn't it?"

"Yes – Milly. She was a lovely girl. Won a prize at Crufts one year, she did. But that wasn't why we loved her: she was such a gentle old girl. Linda and I had her before Josh: we couldn't get pregnant, and for four years she was our baby. Then Josh came along, and we had the complete family. He was such a happy little boy: he and Milly would play together, she looked after him like he was her own – she was still taller than him when they died."

"And when GGR joked about leaving the launch party with a fair few pints in him I suppose your next move was to look at his car in the car park."

"Oh no, I'd been with him earlier in the day when he was rooting around in the boot trying to find something. I knew he had a silver car. But until he told the story, that meant nothing. But I didn't sleep at all Sunday night – I just went through it all in my head and worked it out."

"I see," said Glover gently. "So why did you go to Three Cliffs yesterday morning, Bill? What was your intention?"

"Well, I hadn't even bothered going to bed, so I was out early – I just wanted to.....get away.....but you can't, can you? You can't get away from what's in your own head......and somehow I intended to confront him with it. I wanted to see something in him that showed that he understood what he'd done. He'd talked about his own little dog, which he didn't seem to care for a great deal I must say, and about where he liked to walk it, so I knew where he'd be. In fact, I was there long before him. I sat in the little dell at the top of the cliffs that he'd described for what seemed like hours before he arrived. It was a wonderful spot: everything was grey and shifting. I was completely enveloped in thick mist. And although the sea was a hundred feet below me, it sounded as though I could reach out my hand and touch it. I can't tell you how much I enjoyed that time there – I don't know how long it was, but I wanted it to go on forever. I felt very close to Linda and Josh there – as though I could hear them calling me. I felt safe. I could actually *feel* them there."

Glover nodded sympathetically. Williams kept on talking.

"Then he came blundering along. Just like he'd taken them from me before, he did it again. I couldn't feel them anymore. He was singing loudly and totally out of tune, puffing on a horrible cigar and he had his giant club with him: I don't even like those things at the golf club – they're so unnecessarily big! If it hadn't been for the 'harvest mist' he'd have seen me from some way off, and might even have avoided me. But, as it was, he was almost right next to me before he saw me at all. Anyway, he was surprised to see me, but greeted me jovially enough. He reeked of alcohol and he was swaying a little on his feet. Loud. Drunk. Insensitive. I didn't see GGR the way I'd thought of him for years. All I could see was a murderer. He asked me why I was there and I told him – 'because you killed my son'. He laughed and told me not to be stupid. *Me!* Stupid! I told him about Josh and how he and Milly were knocked down in the lane outside my house in Clydach, not far from the brewery, on the night he'd been at the beer launch. I described Milly and told him that my wife saw him. And do you know what he said, Inspector?"

Glover had to admit he keenly wanted to know.

"GGR Davies laughed. *Laughed!* He said I was talking rubbish. Then he said that, even if it was true, there would be no way to *prove* it. Besides, he was GGR and no-one would believe it of him."

Unfortunately, Glover could imagine the GGR he'd just begun to know saying that: he'd begun to understand the level of entitlement the man had felt....had been led to expect......in a society where he was all but a God. Glover sighed.

"I'm sorry to hear that, Bill," he whispered. And he was, in every way.

"And then – I don't really know what happened. Honestly....." Williams looked up at Glover with pleading eyes, "....I'm not trying to cover anything up – I just don't *know* what happened next. I know he'd tied up his dog and laid the golf club up against the rock face, and I seem to remember picking it up. I think he turned away and I just swung at him with his club. But then.....it's all a blank. I don't even know what I *did* with the golf club – did I throw it over the cliff – did you find it?" Glover didn't react. Williams didn't look up. "I don't remember getting back to my car and I don't remember driving. But I must have done because I do remember getting cash out of the wall at the bank – in fact, that's the next thing I remember, and I don't even know why I did it! As I put the cash in my wallet I could see I already had money in there. Then I realised what had happened, but I still didn't know the whole story. I went back to work on Monday afternoon and I just sort of got on with things. I didn't *feel* right, but no-one said anything, and I got out of there as soon as I could......but I still couldn't settle. I didn't sleep much Monday night – I woke in the chair at one point, all sweaty and aching, so I went out for a walk on the front, along the beach. Then I got ready for another day.....and I wondered if I'd actually gone to Three Cliffs and seen GGR or not: I was beginning to think I'd dreamed it all. Then I heard the news on the radio, and I knew I hadn't. Then you came....and I knew I couldn't do it....I couldn't keep on lying about it. I tried to carry on, but it's always been difficult without Josh and Linda, and I knew that I just couldn't do it anymore. Besides....with him gone, there's no *need* for me to carry on. It's over now."

Glover looked at Stanley – who pushed the tea the PC had brought towards Williams: he hadn't touched it so far. Williams took the mug and drank it down.

He looked up and smiled at Glover and Stanley over the mug. "That was the best cup of tea I've ever tasted," he said. It was the first emotion he'd displayed. "Strong, sweet, just the right amount of milk." His words slurred a little, but he looked happy.

Glover smiled back at the man. But then he stopped, abruptly. Something was wrong. Williams' eyes were out of focus....his pupils dilated. He'd kept his eyes firmly fixed on the desk during his confession, but now

Glover could see something was amiss. "*You* – get the paramedics now and bring the doctor from next door – *NOW!*" he shouted to the PC at the door.

"Bill – what have you done, Bill?" Glover shouted at Williams, who was beginning to slump in his chair.

Stanley and Glover were on their feet in a second. Stanley caught Williams before he slid out of his chair.

"Overdose?" asked Stanley of Glover.

"I suspect so....." was Glover's response.

"Have you taken something, Bill?" shouted Glover again.

"Nothing you can do.....over now......" replied Bill Williams dreamily.

"We've got to try to keep him moving, Sir," was Stanley's unusually assertive comment and Glover nodded. He patted Williams' cheeks and tried to keep him conscious.

The doctor who practiced as a GP in a building next door was with them in a matter of moments, the paramedics moments later. Glover and Stanley paced about as every revival technique was attempted. But it was too late.

"He probably walked about until he began to feel the effects," was Glover's observation, "then he came into us to tell us before he went."

Stanley nodded. "Do you think he might have got away with it, Sir? I mean he's had one nervous breakdown already – and it sounded to me like he snapped – another break with reality. They might not have locked him up at all – it might have just been treatment."

"I think you might be right, Stanley.....but there was nothing for him to 'get away' *with:* he was living in his own hell already. He lost everything when GGR killed his son."

"So you think it's what happened, Sir?"

"We'll never know for sure, but GGR's version of events that Guy Fawkes night, and the Josh Williams case, do rather line up. And GGR was probably right – we wouldn't have been able to prove anything, not after five years. Frankly, from what I've seen in the last twenty four hours you could have had photos of him doing it and people wouldn't have believed it of him, anyway!"

Stanley could tell that Glover was angry. Angry and sad. The fact that Williams was pronounced dead didn't help.

Back in his office, Glover was raking his hands through his hair, crunching a peppermint and slurping boiling hot coffee – three devices Stanley knew he used to try to calm himself: none of them were working. They sat facing each other across Glover's desk for a moment. Dr Albert Bird was on his way from Swansea Hospital: a death in custody was a nightmare, and they needed the best on the case. The Interview Room had been sealed off and Glover suspected that the Super would be after his blood. Word had got out about the fact that Williams was a suspect in the GGR case but, Glover thanked God, it hadn't left the station and reached the media yet – though they, of course, were beside themselves with glee when an ambulance came screaming up to the place and paramedics started running around. The clamour to know what was happening was clearly audible through Glover's window.

"Right, Stanley – I'm off to see the Super. He needs all the facts – and I intend to give them to him."

"Any requests for a last meal, Sir?" was Stanley's wanly smiling reply.

Glover smiled back. "I'll just take my peppermints - that should do it!" and he went off to face his fate.

Stanley sorted through paperwork and helped to begin to tidy everything away in the squad room. He couldn't tell the team what had happened, not until they got the all-clear from the Super, but they all seemed to know that it was over. Stanley didn't have long to wait.

Glover was calling him back into his office within ten minutes. As Stanley entered the room he could feel his boss's anger.

"Shut the door, Stanley, there's a good chap." It was Glover at his most dangerously polite.

Stanley didn't have to ask what the Super had said: he could sense that Glover was about to tell him.

"Sit down lovely boy," said Glover quietly. Stanley did as he was told. Glover rubbed his face hard with both hands, then looked at Stanley with a face that was a picture of tiredness.

"I've told the Super everything: about Joshua, Linda and Bill Williams; all about GGR taking steroids and our suspicion that he was supplying them around his Fire Dragon client list; about him groping that girl at the Brynfield Club; about GGR's drinking and driving, and how our lot have been letting him get away with it.............and do you know what he said?" Glover's voice made it clear that this didn't need a reply. "He said that we'd never be able to prove anything about GGR killing Josh Williams; that his own steroid use was his own business, and the dealing was something we'd never be able to get anyone to testify to; that no breath tests meant we'd never known, as a Force, that he'd ever been drinking and driving. He said that the man's reputation had to be protected, and that we would have to proceed as though Williams' statement was one made by a man in extremis, but which couldn't be used to damn GGR after his own death. He wants a cover up Stanley! The bloody man wants a cover up. So that there can be a national outpouring of grief for a pompous, drug-taking drunk who was enabled by everyone around him!"

Stanley thought it best to remain quiet. He didn't think Glover was finished. He was right. Glover stood up and started to pace.

"It's not *right*, Stanley. The *truth* should come out about that man! The Super says we can't undermine him – that he's more important as a dead hero. That his inspiration is important. More important than the truth." Glover was raking his hands through his hair so fiercely that Stanley wondered it didn't come out in clumps.

"I know he's got a point Stanley - that's the trouble! What good would it do to smear the Great One in death? We can clean up after him as far as the steroids are concerned, no-one except the Williams boy, and his mother and now his father, were affected by his drinking and driving and he did, and still does, inspire a great deal of good. But let me tell you this, Stanley – it feels all wrong! I feel sick to my stomach about it!"

Glover resumed his seat, and Stanley waited. Finally Stanley spoke.

"So.........?" his question hung in the air.

"So we'll do as the Super instructs," replied Glover bleakly. "Williams' confession to the killing will be made public, but not the reasons for it. Of course they'll come out at the inquest, but I have a feeling that someone – and I can tell you right now that it won't be *me* – will be there to undermine the 'suggestions' that Williams made in his statement. No mention will be made of the drinking, the groping or the steroids because they are not 'pertinent to the case', as the Super put it. And that's that. There's no-one left to jump up and down on Bill Williams' behalf, so it'll be GGR who wins and Bill Williams' name will always be mentioned with GGR's: he'll be known as the man who went mad and killed a hero. It's disgusting! Why the *hell* do we do this job, Stanley?" Again, Stanley knew that Glover was about to answer his own question.

"Why do we do it? Why do we not stop to eat or sleep or see our loved ones while we pursue the case, gather the facts, interview the endless, endless suspects......? Why? To bring the *bad* buggers to justice! That's why! To allow people to sleep soundly in their beds knowing they are safe. Bill Williams was a healer – a medical practitioner who apparently worked hard to ensure good health in his local community. GGR Davies habitually sat behind the wheel of a car drunk; he was the epitome of a dirty old man, groping a sixteen year old, indeed; he endangered the long term health of maybe hundreds with those steroids, and that's without considering the cheating aspect at all......and he *killed* a little boy. He *killed* him. I'm as certain of that as Bill Williams was. I cannot believe that we're going to have to live with this Stanley."

Glover squeezed his eyes shut and rubbed them hard. Then he looked at his watch. It was 6.30pm. It hadn't even been twelve hours since he'd taken that call from Bert Bird that morning: in twelve hours his life had changed forever. He resigned himself to a long night at the station: a death in custody entailed a huge amount of paperwork. He and Stanley would have to be interviewed by officers from another area: there'd be no veg soup for him that evening.

"Stanley – I'll be out in five – go and tell the team the Super's version, and let them go. They've had a long day."

"Sir," was Stanley's remark as he left the room. Already Stanley was breathing a sigh of relief: however much paperwork there was, at least he could, once again, look forward to a week of the simple life on his holiday, where people didn't care that he was a policeman. But he knew he'd keep it quiet about working on the GGR case: that was something he'd never want to answer questions about!

Glover picked up the phone and dialled Betty. She answered in her sing-song tones.....which always lifted his spirits.

"Wife – I'll be late, sorry, love, no dinner for me – you go ahead."

"You alright?"

"Fine."

"Get someone?" asked Betty, knowing just how her husband's voice sounded when a case was finished, and the administrative process was about to kick in.

"Yes. A confession. Then he died in front of me, poor bugger."

He could hear his wife's voice catch as she said, "Oh Evan, I'm so sorry my love. It must have been *awful* for you."

Had it been awful to see Bill Williams slip away, rather than be paraded about to be vilified by all? Actually, Glover thought it might not have been the worst thing that could have happened to the man. Williams had no-one left in the world that he loved; he felt that he had visited retribution upon the man who had killed his son and, eventually, taken his wife from him. For Bill Williams, it was all over.

"I think he was happy, Betty – happy that he'd done the right thing, in his own mind, and happy it was all over. Not that I'm saying that people should go around taking justice into their own hands, mind you......but I'll tell you *all* about it later, when I get home."

"Alright, Husband. I'll be up – whatever time it is. And we can talk as much as you like. Or as little as you like."

Glover had known she'd understand.

"Just one thing, Evan......"

"Yes.........?"

"Did you find out – did he fall, or was he pushed?"

Glover thought about it, and realised he still didn't know.

"I know he didn't jump – but as for the other questions, I don't think we'll ever get the answers. But there's one thing I *can* tell you, Betty.......he'd fallen so far before he even got to the top of Three Cliffs that morning.......so *very* far........I don't know how I'm going to stomach all the memorials......maybe we could postpone the trip to Scotland and fly off somewhere – somewhere warm, where they don't play rugby at all, and where GGR isn't known, or mourned.....where he doesn't mean *anything*."

"We'll talk about it, Husband, but I think you're hoping for a bit much.....wherever we go we're still *Welsh,* there's no hiding it, is there? And Wales *means* rugby, it's defined by rugby......and rugby *means* GGR. So, unless we change *ourselves* we'll never escape it.......not until the Welsh stop playing rugby........"

"And that'll never happen........" reflected Glover. "Like I'll never *not* be a copper..........."

By the same author............

# MURDER: Month by Month

## TWELVE TALES OF MURDER – EACH LINKED TO ONE MONTH ON THE CALENDAR!

From her prize-winning story 'Dear George', which begins her murderous year, to the hatred that drives a guilt-ridden woman's Christmastide memories, Ace never lets up!

A sociopath plots in an English teashop, a Florentine vendetta threatens a hapless Scottish tourist and a self-absorbed Shakespearian scholar protects his reputation in a most unusual manner! Add a Vancouver-based criminology professor and a Welsh Detective Inspector who finds his wife's insights invaluable, and you've got a book that will keep the reader turning the pages from month to murderous month!

'Dear George' first appeared in print in 'Murder and Company', published by Pandora Press in the UK. It was broadcast on the BBC's Radio 4 in 2007 with the actress Alex Kingston reading (Dr Elizabeth Corday in television's hit series 'ER') and was especially updated for this collection. It is joined by eleven other stories crafted by Ace.

Ace's style is easy to read – she engages the reader right away...you might never look at a cup of tea or a Yuletide Wreath the same way, but you're sure to enjoy reading this book.

The author lives in British Columbia, Canada, and is of Welsh origin. She likes to write about places she has visited….and people and situations she has never encountered! She hopes you have enjoyed this collection of stories. You can keep up to date with her news and publications by visiting her website.

*For further information about*
*Cathy Ace*
*please visit*

# cathyace.com